"Featuring a unique and unconventional ensemble cast of both faith-driven and morally-bankrupt characters ... this page-turner of a read features fully realized characters; an intricate, tension-filled storyline replete with political and religious intrigue; and more than a few bombshell plot twists."

—*Blue Ink Reviews*

"The narrative's momentum is so expertly handled, and the writing so sharp and natural, that ... Readers of Christian end-times fiction will be hard-pressed to find it done more intriguingly than this.

"An extremely readable and fast-paced religious thriller about a desperate struggle for world domination during the end-times Tribulation."

—*Kirkus Reviews*

PENANCE

THIS GENERATION SERIES: BOOK 3

PENANCE

THIS GENERATION SERIES: BOOK 3

TC JOSEPH

ARCHWAY
PUBLISHING

Joseph

Scripture references are taken from the New King James Version. Copyright
1982 by Thomas Nelson, Inc. All rights reserved. Scripture references
in this book fall within Thomas Nelson's Fair Use Guidelines.

Archway Publishing books may be ordered through booksellers or by contacting:

Archway Publishing
1663 Liberty Drive
Bloomington, IN 47403
www.archwaypublishing.com
1 (888) 242-5904

ISBN: 978-1-4808-3437-8 (sc)
ISBN: 978-1-4808-3439-2 (hc)
ISBN: 978-1-4808-3438-5 (e)

Library of Congress Control Number: 2016947823

Printed in the United States of America.

Archway Publishing rev. date: 10/5/2016

For Mimi, Sissy, Bagel, Pearl, and Dieter,
and for the readers who have enjoyed the journey so far.

ACKNOWLEDGMENTS

I value my privacy and have joyously written under a pseudonym to preserve it. All in all, I think it was a marvelous decision, but it troubles me when it comes to an acknowledgments page because it precludes me from thanking, by name, so many people who have been instrumental in the production of this book. The failure to mention individuals is no reflection of the gratitude I feel. So I would like to offer special thanks for the encouragement of a veritable cadre of family and friends who started with this series in draft form. Each word of encouragement is met with a grateful heart.

I also would like to thank the staff at Archway Publishing for taking time to make this the best book series it can be.

PREFACE: CATCHING UP

The This Generation Series is built on the premise that our generation has been the subject of prophetic writings from many traditions down through the ages. The series asks the following questions:

- What if these prophecies are right?
- What if these prophecies and visions view the same events from different perspectives?
- What would it look like in the lives of three families if the visionaries were right?

In *Precipice*, we joined our characters in 1969, 1979, and 1989. In *Pentecost*, we caught up with them in 1999, 2009, and the present. If you have not read these books, I encourage you to do so. But if you want to start the series with *Penance*, here is a summary of the storyline thus far.

The year 1969 introduces nineteen-year-old orphaned heiress Kimberly and her older, manipulative half-brother, Benny, a Catholic priest with unbridled ambition. Plagued by alien visitations, Kim is convinced that only her pregnancy will end the aliens' plans for her. Following an ill-considered visit to a backwater bar, Kimberly becomes pregnant. Not entirely thwarted, the aliens manipulate her son's DNA to enhance his intellect for their own purposes.

We also meet Fran and Sarah, seniors in a Texas Bible school. On the eve of her wedding to Mack, Sarah is visited by an angel who tells her she will have a son who is destined for greatness.

Throughout the year, there are periodic appearances of the

nefarious international financier Luciano Begliali and a mysterious alien presence, the Lady.

In 1979, we meet Fran's husband, Tom, a missionary in Uganda, and their daughter, Gloria. Tom befriends Father Chris, who is also ministering to the war-torn nation. Tom dies as he, his family, and Chris attempt to flee Uganda during the fall of Idi Amin's regime. Badly injured in their escape, Chris returns to Rome, where he is given the assignment of working for Kimberly's half-brother, Benny.

We also meet Kimberly's sons, Michael and Gabe. The intellectually enhanced Michael negotiates a twenty-year loan of $100 million to his uncle Benny. His intent is to protect his newfound half-brother, Gabe, from Benny's displeasure at the discovery of another heir to Kimberly's fortune. Benny puts the funds at the disposal of Luciano Begliali in exchange for a Vatican appointment.

Fran and Gloria move back to Texas to start a life without Tom. Fran's affiliation with a Catholic priest causes discomfort to Sarah and Mack, who are among the first televangelists. Their son, Zack, who is in contact with the Lady, convinces Mack that Fran may have had an affair with Father Chris. Fran lashes out against the accusation, and a feud ensues.

In 1989, Michael and Gabe enjoy a raucous semester abroad in West Germany. Their revelry is undermined as Gabe becomes addicted to drugs and as Michael has a horrific encounter with the Lady. Chris barely saves Michael and Gabe from Benny's attempt on their lives.

In college, Gloria falls in love with Zack, now a marketing major with dreams of turning his parents' televangelist ministry into a gold mine.

In 1999, the characters meet each other on a Caribbean cruise. Benny tries to discourage a budding romance between Gabe, now the cruise ship's activity director, and his future bride, Tina. Michael must decide if he will take vows to become a Roman Catholic priest. Things get complicated when he meets his soul mate—none other than Gloria. She senses it too, much to Zack's dismay, but neither of them acts on their instincts. Michael, Gloria, and Zack all have dreams wherein the Lady implants in Gloria a zygote created from their combined DNA.

Mack and Sarah decide to close their ministry. Infuriated, Zack, with Benny's help, throws them overboard. He tells everyone that his parents retired in Grand Cayman, leaving the ministry to him.

Later in the year, the newly ordained Michael gets an assignment he loves—working in the archeology department at the Vatican. Impressed with his abilities, his superiors take him into extreme confidence and show him an ancient gold disc unearthed in Iraq. The disc contains the cumulative knowledge of an advanced civilization predating modern history. Michael becomes consumed with unlocking the disc's secrets.

The year ends as Benny and Turkish President Kurtoglu preside over a candlelit Islamic ceremony. A small dancing image of light coalesces into a young boy. Gloria's fetus, harvested by the Lady, has matured rapidly and returned to Earth. He declares himself the adopted son of the Turkish president, naming himself Isa Kurtoglu.

By 2009, Michael has uncovered enough information from the disc to believe that history, specifically the Bible, needs some revision. He masterfully forges an ancient Gospel of John to refute claims of Christ's deity and then plants it in a Vatican archeological dig in Turkey. At the dig site, an unsophisticated threesome of would-be jihadists kidnap Michael. Chris and Gabe rush to Turkey with an agent from the Vatican's secret service. During Michael's rescue, the agent is shot and presumed dead, and Gabe is seriously wounded.

In the lab, Michael and his subordinate, Kurt, want to secure the information on the disc from a group of programmers who work on the project. Kurt relies on his prior experience with the intelligence community to create in each programmer an alternate personality designed to forget everything about his assignment when outside the Vatican's science labs. Michael reluctantly funds the project in the belief that the potential benefit to society outweighs the harm done to the five programmers.

While visiting Rome, Isa Kurtoglu takes the reins of an international cabal of businessmen when he kills Luciano Begliali in Benny's presence.

By the time *Pentecost* moves to the present day, Michael is estranged from Gabe, who now walks with a pronounced limp following his shooting in Turkey. He loves his brother but can't get past Michael's promotion of a savior-less Christianity. For his part, Michael harbors guilt that his forged manuscript led to Gabe's injury. Kimberly tries to bring them together by throwing herself a birthday party. She invites all of her family, as well as Fran's family. Zack attends to enlist Benny's help with a problem—his pregnant secretary. Benny, agreeing to help only if Zack becomes his paramour, suggests they begin the new arrangement in the family chapel. Chris finds them. In deference to Kimberly, Chris won't make a scene, but he promises to bring charges against Benny at an upcoming meeting of the cardinals. The likelihood is that Benny will be defrocked.

At dinner that night, Zack openly scoffs at end-times theology. Gabe, having penned several books on the subject, defends the concept. Gabe's teenage daughter, Michele, joins the conversation with an announcement that she doesn't believe in Jesus, referring to an earlier talk with Michael. Outraged, Gabe orders Michael to leave the estate. He asks Michael to consider his actions in light of a book that examines the similarities between demon contact and alien abduction. Michael leaves in tears, taking the book with him.

Gabe flies to Rome to make peace with Michael. Meanwhile, Michael reads Gabe's book and examines the negative effects the Lady and the disc have had on his life. He decides to analyze the most recent round of data from the disc with a view toward determining whether it is of demonic origin. If so, he will destroy the disc, announce his forgery, and give his life to Christ. Gabe urges him to get on with his life in Christ, but Michael, as a scientist, wants one last shot at the data.

A flash of lightning and a huge peal of thunder strike the entire world at once, leaving Kimberly's car in a heap of tangled wreckage along a road. Gloria and Zack witness the disappearance of Fran and David, and Michele finds herself alone at the family estate.

Benny has decided not to go down easily. He has received poison and its antidote from Isa. Early in the morning, he poisons the soup to be served to the cardinals. Later, as he rises to face his accusers, he informs them of the poison and tells them that he alone has the antidote. The lightning strike takes the pope. Benny claims the papal miter and announces to the remaining cardinals, "With your votes or with your deaths, I will leave this convocation as Pope Peter Romanus."

In distant Turkey, the lightning sends Isa into delighted laughter. He knows his time has come.

Michael hugs his brother just before he leaves to make his final visit to the lab. At that instant the lightning strikes, and Michael feels Gabe dissolve in his arms. He immediately understands it to be the rapture. He runs to the lab in a panic only to find the Lady. She thanks him for his work—it has opened a portal allowing her to come to Earth in the flesh.

He screams "No!" and runs off to an uncertain future.

Michael, Michele, and Gloria now have to deal with their losses and prepare for the onslaught of evil to befall the world. Each has regrets, but Michael's are the worst as he comes to terms with the damage he has done. In short, they experience true penance.

TIMES

ONE

Father Michael Martin ran in a fury from his laboratory and the wheezing laughter of the Lady. Tears gushed from his terror-wrenched face as he pounded the call button for the elevator to take him to the surface from the complex of hidden laboratories beneath the Vatican. As Michael waited, his thoughts raced through recent events.

It seemed like a lifetime since he had been in a local piazza with his brother, Gabe. There they had come to renew their friendship and had shared the first open, honest conversation with one another in more than a decade.

Michael's top secret work at the clandestine lab consisted of exploring the secrets of a vast depository of knowledge from an ancient advanced civilization. The data was stored on a huge CD, and the information was so densely encoded that it took Michael years to determine how it was arranged. More years were allotted to building supercomputer programs to decipher the data. Along the way there were hints at incredible scientific advancements that Michael farmed out to research laboratories under strict confidentiality agreements.

But there were some concessions made as well. The ancient history and its philosophic underpinnings stood in stark contrast to the most basic Christian beliefs: the need for a savior and the deity of Christ. To prepare the world for such a life-altering disclosure, Michael pulled off one of the greatest forgeries in history, an early version of the Gospel of John depicting Jesus as a great teacher but not someone claiming deity. He carefully salted the bogus document at a Vatican archeological dig in Turkey. Would-be jihadists kidnapped him there. Gabe was permanently disabled when he and an agent from the Vatican's secret service attempted to rescue Michael. Gabe's knowledge of the forgery was too much for him to endure in light of his career as a Baptist minister and author of books proclaiming Jesus's imminent return. As Michael's "revised" Christianity, devoid of a savior, took the world by storm, adherents to traditional ways, like Gabe, became societal anachronisms.

Opening doors followed the ding of the arriving elevator. Michael threw himself into the car, poked insanely at the button to send him to the surface, and fell to the cold marble floor in despair. His mind flashed to his first encounter with the Lady, an ethereal being from another planet. The beastly thing scared him to his core, so much so that she successfully herded him to the priesthood and away from any semblance of intimate human contact. He had all but convinced himself she was nothing more than his own psychotic break with reality, but the fullness of truth came crushing in on him when he met Isa Kurtoglu, the Lady's creation from Michael's stolen semen and the ovum of Gloria Jolean, a woman with whom he could easily have fallen in love.

"Michele!" The name of Gabe's daughter escaped Michael's lips in a moan. How he had hurt her! "Oh, Gabe, I'm so sorry!" he screamed as his fists pounded the floor of the elevator car. When the elevator whined to a stop, Michael half stood, half crawled into the hallway. As he straightened himself, he fell into a run, his mind still flooded with events of the past few days. Gabe had been irate when he learned of Michael's influence on Michele's beliefs. He tried to show Michael how the Lady and the information on the disc could, in fact, constitute contact with demons. At first Michael didn't believe him, but in the end he agreed with Gabe to run one last test of the disc's data. If there was any evidence of evil, he would destroy the disc and give his life to Christ. After Michael had reconciled with Gabe over lunch at an outdoor piazza, the two hugged before Michael headed off to his lab, sure in his heart that he would destroy the disc. Gabe disappeared in his arms as the brightest lightning surrounded them. In the deafening thunder that followed, Michael instinctively knew it to be the rapture. He ran to the lab to destroy the disc, knowing he would have to spend the tribulation trying to undo the evil he had perpetrated on the world. To his abject horror, the Lady greeted him. And he ran.

His feet pounded on the hard, worn marble floors of Casina Pio IV, the home of the Pontifical Academy of Sciences. Bursting through the door, he fell into a dead run amid the humid aroma of the roses, lavender, and moist soil of the Vatican gardens. He didn't slow until he came to St. Peter's Square, now writhing with a sea of people trying to find an explanation for what had just occurred. All were terrified, shell-shocked. Responding to his priest collar and cassock, person after person gravitated toward Michael as he pushed through the crowd.

"What happened, Father? Do you know?"

"It was the rapture," Michael said repeatedly. "The Lord has taken the faithful, and times of great trouble are upon us. But it's not too late to give your lives to Jesus."

"Why would I give my life to a God who left me here?" a businessman in a tailored gray suit yelled. Then the man spat at him.

"No!" Michael screamed in a frenzy as the spittle rolled down his cheek. "That attitude will only earn you hell."

The time is now. The time is now! His own words rang in his ears. He had to get to a quiet place where he could apologize to Jesus and invite Him into his heart. He pushed through the burgeoning crowd toward St. Peter's Basilica. Those around him seemed more inclined to follow the man who had spat at him. They jostled him and hurled angry insults. He squared his shoulders, bowed his head, and shoved through the crowd.

The hard popping of a gunshot was followed by a shove that nearly knocked Michael off his feet. He turned to see a man writhing in pain. While he assessed the man's condition, gunmen appeared throughout the crowd and around its periphery. Michael froze, staring into the screaming crowd, as his mind tried to make sense of the growing mayhem. As another bullet whizzed past him, strong arms grabbed him and pulled him to the ground.

"Better to stay low, Father," a stern voice said deliberately.

Michael looked at the severe face of the man lying on the ground next to him. Dressed in a nondescript black suit, white shirt, and thin dark tie, he looked like an FBI agent from a 1960s film, down to the crew cut and expressionless face. And yet the man looked vaguely familiar. "Thanks," Michael responded. "I've seen you before, but I can't place where."

"I rescued you from would-be terrorists years ago," the man said distractedly as he eyed the crowd. Michael's mind filled with memories of the time when Gabe and the agent found him in the foothills outside Antakya, Turkey, with his three young kidnappers.

"You were shot," Michael yelled above the rising screams of the maddened crowd.

"Not fatally," the agent said offhandedly. He moved to one knee to get a solid shot at the crazed man who was bearing down on them. With one quick pull of the trigger of the agent's Glock, the man fell, all the while screaming enraged epithets against the agent, Michael, and God Almighty.

"And so you're saving my life again today," Michael said as the agent helped him stand.

"Stay low and follow me," the agent commanded before he ducked and ran through a brief opening in the crowd. Michael stayed close behind as the agent pummeled and pushed at crazed men and women in their path.

At the edge of the square, they found cover among the pillars leading into St. Peter's. One of the large doors of the cathedral swung open to reveal an old priest with a maniacal grin and an AK-47 automatic rifle. He drilled into the crowd, laughing with horrific glee as row after row of innocents shrieked and fell to the cobblestoned ground. The humid air rapidly filled with the metallic odors of blood and gunpowder.

"Stay down!" the agent screamed. Michael took cover and watched as the agent studied his prey. The moment the old friar looked in another direction, the agent leaped from behind the pillar, aimed his Glock carefully, and pulled the trigger. In fractions of a second, the old priest's head exploded into a rain of blood and brains as he fell backward.

The agent grabbed Michael's cassock and yanked him to his feet. "Follow me." They ran into the basilica, stepping over the bleeding corpse of the onetime mass murderer and into the darkness of the church.

"What the heck is happening?" Michael demanded, his adrenalin-filled voice booming in the relative calm of the cathedral.

"No time to explain now, Father," the agent said quietly as he placed one finger to his mouth. He led Michael to a place under the great altar, descending to St. Peter's tomb. They exchanged a modern death scene for an ancient one as they ran through the Scavi, a dimly lit unearthed necropolis beneath the cathedral, to a darker, rarely trodden tunnel. There the agent used a key to open an iron gate guarding entrance to the old Roman catacombs. He pulled Michael in and locked the gate behind them. With a small flashlight, he led Michael into the bowels of the Eternal City.

"Where are we going?" Michael asked.

"To your apartment building," the agent answered mechanically.

"The thought of actually being home sounds like a miracle," Michael said.

"You can't go to your apartment, Father," the agent said, barely turning his head toward Michael, who followed behind him. "It's not safe. Go instead to Father Chris's apartment. His beliefs were well-known to the creators of this darkness. They won't suspect that anyone will be there."

"Just what is 'this darkness'?" Michael demanded.

The agent stopped with a huff. "Do you really think you and your friend Kurt cornered the market on alternate personalities, Father?" he asked with scorn.

Michael blanched in shame as he thought of the lives of his programmers ruined over his insane belief that preserving the secrecy of the disc should take precedence over human life. "That was a long time ago," Michael offered weakly. "I've changed since then."

"Which is the only reason I am saving you," the agent offered. "You have to get to Father Chris's apartment and learn all the information he has gathered about the tribulation. First, though, you have to renounce all of your past works and give your life irretrievably to Jesus."

"I'm with you there," Michael said wholeheartedly. "If only I had done it an hour ago, I wouldn't be in this mess."

"You are in good company, Father," the agent said, pointing a finger to his own chest. "I believe some of us were meant to delay our acceptance of Him because He has specific roles for us to play in this day. Ours is not an easy lot, my friend." He motioned forward with his light and led Michael deeper into the catacombs.

Michael followed. "But you didn't answer my question," he said to the agent. "What's happening right now?"

"They call it the 'Dark Awakening,' Father." The agent slowed his pace, shaking his head at the gravity of the words. "The end of World War II brought with it a scattering of Nazi scientists throughout the world. In your country, many were integrated into your government's nuclear, space, and population-control programs under the name of Operation Paper Clip. Millions of unsuspecting people were abducted and abused, forming hidden alternate personalities.

"That's not the least of it, Father," the agent continued with shallow breaths in the thick air. He stopped abruptly, overwhelmed by what he felt. "Once the alternate personalities were born, they were attached to specific demons in horrific rituals."

Michael gasped. He could barely believe what he'd heard.

"They lived their lives never knowing that a deep hatred had been secreted away in them, awaiting a sign to come to the foreground."

"The sign was the rapture," Michael said, as much to himself as to the agent.

"Exactly, Father. These demon-controlled alternate personalities have been programmed to wait for the rapture to commit mass murder. Others have lists of specific targets in the governments of the world. In the end, their objective is a complete collapse of society."

"That can only be healed by alien intervention," Michael said, continuing the thought.

"Or a carefully crafted hybrid entity bred to rule the world."

"Isa!" Michael winced at the thought of this horrific half human that shared his own DNA.

"Exactly," the agent said gravely.

Michael let out a guttural scream of aggravation that echoed throughout the tunnels, and then he fell to the damp stone floor. "How much evil has come to the world through me? What have I done?" He pounded the ancient stones beneath him.

The agent sat beside him in the musty darkness. "This is not the time for self-recrimination, Father. We have made choices, to be sure, but some things were prophesied of old and were simply meant to be. If not through you, then Isa Kurtoglu would have come into the world through other means. His time is at hand, Father, a time set forth from the beginning of creation. You can lament your participation, but don't fool yourself into believing you could have stopped it."

The words calmed Michael a bit. The agent was right. And yet his heart broke with every remembrance of how smugly he had criticized Gabe's beliefs. Hot, silent tears coursed down his face.

"You'll be okay, Father," the agent said with as much comfort as he could muster after years of practiced nonchalance. "Let's take a few moments for you to seal yourself in Christ. Father, do you reject the works of Satan? Do you believe that Jesus is the only Son of God?"

"I do," Michael croaked.

"Do you believe He was born of a virgin and became man to die for our sins?"

"I do."

"Even your sins, Father? Do you believe it in a personal way?"

"I do," Michael said as a flood of warmth overwhelmed him.

"Do you believe He rose from the dead and ascended into heaven to sit at the right hand of God the Father?" the agent continued.

"I do," Michael said through tears of sudden joy.

"Do you believe He will come again in glory to judge the living and the dead?"

"Yes," Michael said softly.

"And do you believe He loves you more than life itself, Father?"

"I do." Michael grinned in the dim light of the flashlight.

"Do you believe in the Holy Spirit, who is one with the Father and the Son?"

"Absolutely," Michael said to the spreading warmth within.

"Do you believe He spoke through the prophets and wishes to live in you?"

"I do," Michael answered.

"Take a few moments to place yourself in His arms, Father," the agent said as he patted Michael's shoulder.

Michael spoke softly. "Father, I'm so sorry for all my sins—for my participation in the horror that has come upon the world. I accept the forgiveness that can come only through the blood of Jesus. Change me. Renew me with the strength I need to play the role You have for me in these final hours. Thank You so much for not giving up on me. In Jesus's name, amen."

"Amen," the agent agreed as a new flood of warmth overwhelmed Michael. It was an absolutely insane notion to his analytical mind, but here he was in the presence of the living God. He had missed the last train out before worldwide disaster. He had lost the people he loved most and had been left to witness the horror he had helped to bring upon the world. And yet … and yet, he had never known such peace. Now the living God was alive in his heart. He had heard the phrase *born again* all his life, but now he was experiencing it. He really was becoming a new creature in Christ. If only Gabe and Chris were here to witness it!

"Congratulations, Father," the agent said, rising from the floor and pointing his flashlight to the way ahead of them. "Your eternal destiny is sealed, but now I have to get you to Father Chris's apartment to keep you safe from the Dark Awakening."

"How long will this pandemonium continue?" Michael asked as he got to his feet to join the agent. They continued their trek through the stifling underbelly of the city.

"Until they achieve their objectives. Each multiple personality has been programmed to complete a certain task. When they complete their respective tasks, most will take their own lives."

"That sounds pretty ugly," Michael muttered as he followed close behind the only light in the pitch-black tunnel. "I can't very well spend the entire tribulation in Chris's apartment."

The agent offered a sad chuckle. "You won't have to. This is a shock-and-awe program. Estimates I've read indicate that society will collapse in three days to one week."

Michael whistled in awe and then caught himself when he heard the whistle reverberate down the dark passages.

"Remember, Father, this program has been going on since the end of World War II. They have created second-, third-, and fourth-generation multiples by now. Some of my people estimate there are as many as thirty to forty million in the world."

"Thirty to forty million?" Michael asked in disbelief.

"Imagine the damage they can do," the agent answered. "Of course, the United States probably has the highest concentration. It's the country that sets the tone for the rest. As goes the United States, so goes the world."

Michael said nothing, hoping against hope that Michele had come around to Tina and accepted Jesus before the rapture. He followed in silence, praying—begging—not to live with the guilt of setting up his namesake and niece to go through the Dark Awakening alone. In a few moments, there was light ahead. It grew steadily as they approached another gate. Unlocking it, the agent led Michael through a short tunnel to the basement of the apartment building.

"This is where I leave you, Father," the agent said with an air of finality.

"Will I see you again?" Michael asked.

"I don't know. If the Lord leads me to you again, then yes. If not, then I will see you in about seven years." He offered Michael his hand. Michael took it. "There is much for you to do. But for now, hide in Father Chris's apartment and study until it is safe." He locked the gate and then disappeared into the darkness of the tunnels.

Michael walked up the stairs to the lobby of the building. Its locked doors protected him from the violence outside. As he waited for the elevator, he heard repeated shots and screams from the street. It sounded like all-out war. He cringed at the horror of the situation and fairly ran into the elevator car as the door opened. Once inside, he saw the dead body of a priest who had lived on the fifth floor. He had been beaten to a pulp. Michael prayed a blessing over the body as the elevator took him to Chris's floor.

After fumbling through the keys on his key ring, he entered the apartment. Then it all hit him—hard. Smelling Chris's cologne, he remembered all the times he had taken comfort in that scent as he grew up. He would do anything to be able to hug him one more time, to offer him his deepest apology for never listening when Chris told him about a relationship with Jesus. Through eyes clouded with tears, he found his way to the brown tweed couch in the little sitting room off the kitchen. As he sat, everything gave way to wrenching moans, sobs, and tears.

"Chris, you'll never know how sorry I am," he blurted out. The tears came with no end. There was no relief until sleep mercifully overtook him.

The air was crisp as Michael found himself seated on deck behind a white table at the bar of a cruise ship. The crisp smell of the sea enveloped him. Brilliant crimson shards of light from the setting sun were mirrored in the smooth seas ahead of the ship. Gabe came to the table with their drinks while Chris joined them from the other direction. Michael's eyes filled with tears at the joy of seeing them. He knew it was a dream, but it felt so real!

"It's not exactly a dream." Chris grinned as he hugged the younger priest.

"He's right," Gabe said, handing Michael his drink, a cold root beer. The foam tickled at Michael's lips as if he were enjoying it in real life. "The prophet Joel said, 'And it shall come to pass that I will pour out My Spirit on all flesh; your sons and daughters will prophesy, your old men shall dream dreams, your young men shall see visions.' Let's face it, bro, you're a little long in the tooth to be on the visions side of the equation."

Michael chuckled. Gabe ruffled his hair as he had done in their youth. Then it dawned on him that Chris and Gabe each looked to be about thirty years old.

"You two look great!"

Chris grinned.

Gabe stood to do a little shuffle, something he never could have done following the injury to his leg. "Michael, it's so wonderful here. Whatever you do, don't turn your back on your decision to follow Jesus."

"You know about that?" Michael asked.

"The expanded consciousness of the resurrection body is like nothing you could imagine," Gabe explained. "In fact, for the next seven years, I'm going to be the smart brother, dude."

"Considering our relative positions, I'd say you were the smart one all along," Michael mused glumly.

"You can't waste time wallowing in the past, Michael," Chris challenged. "There's too much to do. The Lord doesn't permit these visits for the fun of it. He allows us to encourage you to take your stand in these last days."

"What does He want me to do?" Michael asked.

"First of all, you have to protect my kids," Gabe said with a stern gaze.

"Oh no!" Michael exclaimed. "Both of them?"

Chris interrupted. "Eventually there will be no safe place in this world for Christians, Michael, except maybe one." He stared at Michael gravely before continuing. "You have to seek the protection of your uncle Benny."

Michael spit a little bit of his soda as he laughed at the suggestion. Chris turned into a being of brilliant light as Michael looked at him. It was at once thrilling and terrifying to be in the presence of the sheer power radiating from Chris.

Chris's voice poured forth from the brilliance. "The resurrection bodies are really amazing, Michael. The Lord has honored a lifetime of your mother's prayers. She will visit Benny, much as we're visiting you. Between his love for your mother and his fear of what she has become, he will keep you and the kids away from Isa's outrageous demands."

"What does Benny get out of it?" Michael asked skeptically, knowing his uncle's personality.

"He'll need a camerlengo he can trust," Chris said as his body resumed its more familiar form.

"Benny's the pope?" Michael screamed.

"He took the pope's miter when the rapture happened," Chris said with a shake of his head.

"So the grand usurper has usurped the papacy," Michael said in awe. "I can't believe I share genes with that man."

"He was always evil," Gabe said gravely, "but he'll now have the full support of Isa Kurtoglu. He's the False Prophet spoken of in the book of Revelation."

"And now I'm his camerlengo," Michael said morosely. "And I thought this day was bad when I just barely missed the rapture."

"Michael," Chris said in the fatherly tone of Michael's youth, "you're saved now and have a place in heaven, but you did some real damage to the body of Christ with the forged manuscript."

Michael immediately burst into tears. "I know, Chris. I want you to know how incredibly sorry I am for my actions."

Chris moved his seat closer to Michael's and placed his arm around the younger man's shoulder. "I know you are, son, but there is something you have to realize. Even though you are saved, the consequences of your actions live on in the lives of those around you."

11

Gabe joined them. "Michael, God is allowing you to repair some of the damage. It's a blessing, but it will come at great hardship. You'll be able to help others see what has come upon the world. That's the good part. The bad part is that there will be a lot of pain. St. Paul referred to it as 'working out your salvation' in his letter to the Philippians."

"In your training as a priest, you learned another word for it, Michael," Chris said as he tightened his hug.

"Penance," Michael said deliberately.

"Penance," Chris agreed somberly.

When he awoke, Michael felt refreshed. His visit with Gabe and Chris had been so lifelike that it affirmed his faith and his belief that he would see them again in as short a period as seven years. Seven years, the tribulation, the last week of Daniel. He had so much to learn. With only a few more hours of daylight, he took four books from Chris's bookcase. Thankfully, he was a quick reader. He wanted to finish them before sunset, fearing that lighted windows would be an invitation to the violence in the streets below.

He learned that the ninth chapter of Daniel included a time line of prophetic events affecting the Jewish people until the appearance of the Messiah as their ruler. The prophet foretold seventy weeks of years left to the Jewish people "to finish the transgression, to make an end of sins, to make reconciliation for iniquity, to bring in everlasting righteousness, to seal up the vision and prophecy, and to anoint the Most Holy."

"Quite an agenda, Lord," Michael whispered. He learned that sixty-nine weeks had passed to the death of Jesus, leaving one week of years hanging. It was as if Jesus's death and resurrection pushed the button on a stopwatch. Israel was destroyed shortly thereafter, and all the remaining prophecies were suspended. But suspended for how long?

Chris's books answered that question in an odd quote from Jesus in Matthew's Gospel. He told the disciples to take a lesson from the fig tree, long understood to be a symbol of Israel. Jesus told the disciples that buds on the fig tree would signify the nearness of the kingdom of

God. Michael remembered the text from Matthew where Jesus said, "Assuredly I say to you, this generation will by no means pass away till all these things take place." It was what Gabe had tried to tell him all those years ago—the generation to see Israel reborn was the generation to see all the prophecies fulfilled. Israel became a nation in 1948.

"As usual, You're right on time, Lord," Michael muttered. Then he chuckled to himself. He had never in his life had this type of familiarity with God, speaking to Him throughout the day.

Something had to start the stopwatch again in order to initiate the final seven years. Was it the rapture itself? Michael wasn't sure. Daniel's prophecy was specifically directed to the Jewish people. Why would the distinctly Christian rapture herald the tribulation?

Michael soon found his answer. The tribulation wouldn't officially start until a profane world leader made a peace agreement with the new nation of Israel. Well, Michael had firsthand knowledge of the profane leader. The thing culled from his, Gloria's, and Zack's DNA had then merged with a strand of alien design. At some point Isa would offer a peace deal to Israel, and the seven years called Jacob's Trouble would begin. Given that a year in biblical times was calculated as 360 days, Michael reasoned that the seven-year period would likely be 2,520 days, or about a month shy of a modern seven-year period. He wondered if the peace accord would come within the next month so that the modern period of seven years from the rapture would coincide with the biblical reckoning of seven years from the peace agreement.

"It would be like You to be so precise, Lord. And it would be like the world to miss it. I can't believe I was so blind to this less than a day ago!" Long rays of the sun from the horizon flooded the apartment with auburn light. It would soon be dark. Curiosity drove him to turn on Chris's small television to see what the world was making of these events.

The anarchy of the Dark Awakening played out in the streets of every city and town in the world. People had gone on insane killing sprees across the globe. The violence was extreme and pervasive. The news covered nothing else. The Lord of the Universe had visited planet Earth and had taken His own, but the news was eclipsed by Satan's demented rage. It was as if nobody in the world even knew the rapture had occurred. Michael mused, *When the blood stops flowing, the world will assume the raptured Christians are just missing victims of the violence.*

Michael turned off the television and lay on Chris's bed as the sun set. No more crimson and ginger. The sky had filled with smoke as the rioters set aflame buildings near and far. Endless car alarms sounded, and nonstop horrified shrieks filled the air. He went to the window to peer out. By the light of several cars set ablaze, he saw a man strike an old lady so violently that she fell dead in the street.

"Oh, Lord, I don't think I have the strength to live in such a fractured world for seven years." He covered his head with his arms, buried his face into a pillow carrying the scent of his earthly father, and prayed for his heavenly Father to keep him close. He slept fitfully, stirring every time he heard an explosion in the street below. The implications of what he had learned passed through his thoughts in scattered dreams and glimpses of situations, faces, and names. When he awoke, he couldn't remember much more than an image of Gabe dressed in some sort of medieval garb and shooting a crossbow. It would have been laughable had it not been part of a stream of uncomfortable sights that now lurked just beyond his ability to remember. He lay still on the bed, listening to the unabated pandemonium below, hoping against hope for the return of sleep.

When morning finally came, Michael grabbed some orange juice from Chris's fridge, tuned out the world, and forged on with his study. According to scripture, Isa would need a henchman, someone to force the world to worship him. The False Prophet of Revelation. "Wait a minute. Didn't Gabe say that would be Benny's role?" Michael asked the empty room.

"So I'm supposed to be his camerlengo and not go crazy over the next seven years?" He paced the apartment. Part of him preferred to just go into the street and let himself be mowed down by the prowling lunatics there. It would be so much nicer than hanging out with Benny. But then his mind wandered to the kids. He *had* to protect Gabe's kids. If staying close to Benny was the way to keep them out of Isa's radar, then he would do it.

He sat on the couch and picked up another book expositing Daniel. At some point, Isa would violate his pact with Israel and commit the abomination of desolation. The book said this would entail enthroning himself as God in a rebuilt Jewish temple in Jerusalem. Maybe that's what the peace agreement would be all about. Isa would seem to be a benefactor to the Jews by allowing them to build the temple, only to declare it as his own once it was built.

More than anything, Michael wished he could look at the texts in their original languages. So much could be gained by studying the author's syntax and specific choice of words. He had seen enough over the years to know that any translation was inadvertently affected by the worldview of the translator. If Michael wanted to get the best possible understanding of the prophecies, he would have to see them in the original Hebrew and Greek.

He went to Chris's computer and smiled upon seeing that Chris had used a family photo as his screen saver. He took a few moments to stare at the lines of his mother's face. He would miss her most of all. From the very beginning of his life, they had instinctively had each other's backs. She had to be very disappointed at how badly he had messed up. Wiping quickly at the stream of tears on his face, he forced the emotion away and set about finding the ancient texts online.

To Michael's dismay, Chris's computer was password protected. But then again, Chris worked for Benny. Of course he would play everything close to the vest. For the better part of an hour, Michael tried every possible combination of words and phrases he could imagine. None of them unlocked the computer. He paced the floor in frustration, knowing he had the applicable texts just two floors below in his own apartment.

By the afternoon, the street sounds seemed quieter—or was it just his imagination as he began to rationalize a trip downstairs? After all, how long could it take to move quietly down the stairs to grab a couple of books and his laptop? Five minutes, tops. He could think of nothing else.

He slowly poked his head out of Chris's apartment. The hallway was dead. There was no movement other than a curtain fluttering in the breeze through an open window at the opposite end of the hallway. So far, so good. He moved quickly but silently down the hallway to the stairwell. He gingerly turned the doorknob to the right and slowly pushed the old door open just a bit. The door made a moaning screech. He froze with his body halfway in the stairwell, listening. Silence.

Hopefully nobody had heard the door. He slid through the doorway into the stairwell and closed the door a millimeter at a time to avoid the protracted screech.

Only after the door was closed did he get a good look at the stairwell. Rorschach patterns of bloodstains covered the walls. Several of the building's residents lay on the stairs, literally hacked to pieces. Michael jumped at the sight and put his hand to his mouth to cut off a scream building there. The bitter iron smell of the blood mingled with the scent of early decay. Michael swallowed hard to avoid vomiting.

What if the guy who had done this was still around? He moved cautiously among the bodies and the blood in a soundless descent to his floor. He pulled his apartment key from his pocket, shut the stairwell door behind him slowly and quietly, and took the few steps to his apartment.

The door to his apartment was ajar. Cautiously, he pushed it open to reveal an unmitigated mess. Someone had ransacked the place. Nothing was where it once stood. All his books had been thrown in a heap on the floor. He scrambled quickly through the pile to find the two texts he needed. Footsteps in his bedroom! He slowly stood, eyes focused on his bedroom doorway, and deliberately backed toward the apartment's exit. One step. Two steps. Three.

"Going somewhere, Father?" a thick Italian accent asked from behind him.

He turned to see a blood-covered Swiss guardsman with a menacing expression.

TWO

The US president sat in the anteroom, waiting for his triumphal entry to "Hail to the Chief." But first, the vice president had to call to order the joint session of Congress. The rioting, looting, and murders of the past twenty-four hours had turned America's streets into rivers of blood. There was no telling the dollar value of the property damage or the loss of life. Conservative estimates put the death count at ten million, but negative assessments touted nearly ten times that number. Hospitals around the nation were flooded with the worst of the victims. Others remained in triage tents in parking lots and fields adjoining the hospitals.

The National Guard had been called to action, but the crisis was simply too large for them. In fact, there were disturbing reports of National Guard troops firing at each other instead of containing the crowds. Congress was meeting to approve a series of measures to suspend the Constitution and enable the establishment of martial law. Power would cede to a quorum of individuals: the president and vice president to represent the executive branch, the Speaker of the House and the Senate majority leader to represent the legislative branch, and the chief justice of the Supreme Court to represent the judicial branch. Until the quorum determined the country to be secure and at peace, these five individuals would mandate by fiat all rules necessary to stabilize the nation. Once control was reestablished, they would reconstitute the government in full. The remaining members of Congress and the Supreme Court would serve as advisors to the quorum.

The vice president banged his gavel and called the meeting to order. Congress had never looked worse. Nobody had slept the previous night. Most had loved ones in jeopardy in their home districts, and unsafe conditions in the streets confined them to the Capitol Building under constant military surveillance. After an excruciatingly long speech detailing the plan, the vice president turned the podium over to the chief justice. The chief justice explained that the proposed plan satisfied the basic precepts of the Constitution in that it enabled the three branches to function, but in a streamlined manner to meet the immediacy of the crisis. Where the spirit of the Constitution would not be maintained, however, was in the rights held by citizens. The recent events indicated some sort of social madness, and the US populace could not be trusted to act responsibly. Until Congress and the Supreme Court were reconstituted, the Bill of Rights would be suspended in its entirety.

The president waited patiently for the perfunctory vote. Behind the scenes, the majority leaders of both the Senate and the House of Representatives had guaranteed passage of the bill. What else could they do? The country was falling down around them and nobody had a clue about how to save it. It was the pleasure of congressional members to shift the responsibility and resultant blame to the quorum. When the vote was completed and tallied, the president would enter the room to be granted his new authority as head of the quorum. Immediately thereafter, he would address the nation, or at least those who had the presence of mind to watch the televised message. The president's media experts believed that fewer than 5 percent of the citizens would actually tune in.

As expected, Congress passed the bill by a huge majority. The vice president was about to pound his gavel, bringing the bill to life, when a commotion arose at the back of the chamber. A senior senator from Arizona began to rant about the end of the world. Brandishing a pistol, he shot indiscriminately at the men and women around him. At the sound of gunshots, military security entered the room. Ten men with automatic weapons mowed down the remaining legislators and justices as they surged in a panicked run to the doors. None of them escaped the gunfire, save the vice president. Those who were not yet dead lay on the cold floor emitting labored death rattles. The soldiers walked calmly to the dais.

Seeing it all on the monitor in the anteroom, the president could barely contain a smile. Could the coup of a nation as powerful as the United States be this simple? He moved into the chamber.

"Mr. Vice President, are you all right, sir?" one of the soldiers called.

"I think so," the normally befuddled man called out with stunning clarity.

"What a shame," the president said sarcastically from behind the soldiers.

"You caused this?" the vice president muttered in shocked disbelief. "Why, Barry?"

"Why not?"

"America trusted you. I trusted you," the vice president screamed.

"You know, Dan," the president began in the same condescending monotone he often used to address the nation. "You were never a part of my team. You were a prop—the slightly off-color old grandpa who amused voters. Your constant misplaced remarks and faux pas were cute, Dan. Hell, Fallon had a heyday with you every night."

"I love America, and America loves me," the vice president challenged.

The president shrugged his shoulders and held out his hands, palms up. "Like a beloved pet, Dan. You brought the missing trust factor when voters started to question my background."

The secretary of state moaned on the floor, attempting to sit up. The president cast a sidelong glance to the nearest soldier, who in turn shot the man in order to silence him.

"Now I suppose you'll have them shoot me too," the vice president said with sad resignation.

"You know, *Dan*," the president said, taking a pregnant pause as if it were written on some unseen teleprompter, "if these soldiers shot you, it just wouldn't be right. I was the one who had to endure your sophomoric sense of humor and mind-numbingly slow linear thought. In fact, *Dan*," he continued as he spat the man's name in hatred, "it's not just that you are a linear thinker. It's that all those linear thoughts are tangential—one line of thought on a constant train away from the center of the conversation. Year after year I had to endure that vapid, empty smile of yours. I can't take it anymore, *Dan*. And I can't let a soldier deprive me of what I've wanted to do from the moment it became apparent I needed you on my ticket."

The president held out his hands for the nearest soldier's automatic weapon. The soldier gave it up with military precision as if presenting it for inspection. The president pointed the weapon at the vice president and pulled the trigger. Nothing happened. The soldier leaned over to release the safety. The vice president made a run for the door, but the president pulled the trigger a second time, sending a relentless round of bullets into the man until his corpse was unrecognizable. Handing the rifle back to the soldier, the president said calmly, "Bring in the television crew."

As the crew rapidly set up, the president worked to create a face tormented by tragedy.

"Ready, Mr. President? Three ... two ... one."

"My fellow Americans, the tragedy befalling the world has struck the very heart of our nation. As a joint session of Congress met with the Supreme Court justices to determine a solution to the insanity in our streets, a group of gunmen with automatic rifles fought their way into the Capitol Building and massacred our legislative and judicial branches. I stand in the midst of this carnage with a broken heart, trying to deal with my rage that someone would try to deprive the American people of their government. Well, ladies and gentlemen, as your only remaining elected official, I am determined that this government of the people, by the people, and for the people shall *not* perish from this earth." A catch in his voice during the Lincoln quote gave him pause to wipe at the tear he had struggled so valiantly to produce.

"Immediately before the massacre in this room, your representatives voted overwhelmingly to a plan to right America and put an end to the pandemonium engulfing us. They agreed to a quorum of individuals to rule until order is reestablished. At this unfortunate hour, however, I am the only remaining member of that quorum. My path is clear and my mind is resolute. I will use all governmental authority to quell the rebellion in our streets and put America at rest. When stability has returned, I will call for congressional elections. At this critical juncture, I am the only person standing between the United States and anarchy. I will not let you down, my fellow Americans."

The president's voice crescendoed as he presented the image of a strong leader. "Effective immediately, the Bill of Rights is suspended until the reemergence of Congress. As commander in chief, I will deploy all branches of the United States military to police our streets so that order may ensue."

He paused and put his hand to his mouth as if to stifle a sob. "God willing, and with your help, I will restore our country to the beacon of freedom it was before this worldwide attack of dementia. But to do that, we need to acknowledge a few things. First, we don't know the origin of this disease. Second, the afflicted people are extremely dangerous. Third, we don't have the time or infrastructure to develop a medical cure. Fourth, we don't have sufficient infrastructure to incarcerate them. With that in mind, I am directing the military to use extreme force to stop all rioters and those who seek specifically to harm the people and property of the United States.

"Finally, ladies and gentlemen, I am placing our nation on high alert. We have seen enough to know that our situation is not unique. We cannot allow our vigilance to fail at this hour. We have no way of knowing whether a rogue regime, an unfriendly nation, or even an ally could join the insanity and launch an attack. As part of this alert status, I am imposing a nationwide curfew. Any individual on the streets between nightfall and daybreak will be considered a threat to our national security."

With a final reassuring smile, he ended. "We can rebuild. To quote the prophet Isaiah from millennia ago, 'The bricks have fallen down, but we will rebuild with hewn stones. The sycamores are cut down, but we will replace them with cedars.' Tonight we begin to rebuild. Thank you."

When the red light of the camera dimmed, the president left the dais and strode to the door. To one of the soldiers, he said derisively, "Clean up this mess," as his arm swept about the room to indicate the carnage. To two more of his guards, he ordered, "Take me to the White House."

The soldiers turned the president over to the secret servicemen, who then escorted him to the Oval Office. He had much to do. The military was about to hit the streets. Tomorrow he needed them to round up the heads of the six large media companies to ensure they portrayed him as a hero.

As the door to the Oval Office closed, he heard a clapping sound. A man sitting behind the desk slowly turned around.

"Bravo. Quite the performance," Isa Kurtoglu said with a sparkle in his eye.

That smart-assed young Turk! "How did you get in here?" the president demanded. Throwing the door open, he yelled for the secret servicemen in the hallway. They came running.

"Throw him out!" the president demanded.

Isa raised his hand in a calming gesture to the servicemen, who nodded slightly, backed out of the room, and closed the door.

In total shock, the president yelled, "What's the meaning of this?"

"The meaning of this, Mr. President, is that I will allow you to stay in power for one week."

"Get the hell out of my chair," the president said derisively. "I could blow your country to hell and nobody would care."

Isa smiled. A sharp pain overtook the president's head. He could no longer stand as Isa's mind probed deeply into his. The pain was excruciating.

"Are you listening now?" Isa demanded.

"Yes," the president screamed. "Make it stop."

"As you wish." Isa grinned. The pain now subsided, the president stood slowly to his feet before Isa continued. "As I was saying, in one week you will join other leaders of the world, who by the way are in the same position as you, at a meeting of the United Nations. There you will declare your allegiance to me."

"Like the American people would ever go for it," the president huffed.

"They will when they realize that only I can bring peace to the world, Mr. President."

The president spoke with unmitigated disdain. "As if you're the One we've waited for. Please. Why would some punk Turk be the One? Clearly the person controlling the world's largest arsenal fits the bill."

"Or the one who controls the man with the largest arsenal," Isa said with a casual flip of his hand. The pain in the president's head resumed with much more intensity. He clutched at his head and fell to the floor again in a seizure. As the president thrashed, Isa nonchalantly picked up his briefcase and strode to the door, stepping over the incapacitated leader of the free world.

Through the anguish, the president spoke in stuttering fits and starts, saying, "But I'm the One. Even Oprah said so."

Isa let go of a belly laugh. "That Oprah. What a minx!" To the secret servicemen he said, "Get him to bed."

THREE

Tears streamed down Michele Martin's face as she watched the president's address. She would have thought she'd be cried out by now. Immediately following the rapture, she had run around the family's old Georgian mansion, hoping against hope that Jesus hadn't really come to take His own. At every corner and at the entrance to every room, she was sure she would hear the voice of her mother asking, "What's up, sweetie?"

She dialed the cell phones of everyone in her family, even Uncle Michael in Rome, but got a message saying that the system had crashed. Surely everyone left behind must be trying to call their loved ones too.

Loved ones. The very thought threw her into near convulsive anguish. All of her family had been taken. How could she have been so stupid? She saw in her mind's eye how arrogantly she had interrupted her grandmother's birthday party with a proclamation that she didn't follow her father's old-fashioned beliefs. *Oh, Daddy, I'm so sorry.* She remembered her mother's stern look of disapproval. What she wouldn't give to see those beautiful hazel eyes just one more time.

Her tears streaming in an unending flow, she watched television coverage to see how the rest of the world was faring. To her horror, she saw news reports of endless riots, looting, and murder. City after city in the United States was being torn down. Citizens were dying in the streets. The images terrified her and accentuated the fact that she was alone now. Her only saving grace was the remote location of the estate. Although violence had erupted throughout the urban communities, there was little chance it would find her. At least that's what she told herself—and she'd believed it until she heard the president speak. His

24

curfew and retraction of civil rights could drive people out of the cities. Would some freedom-loving patriot find the mansion after fleeing the city? She ran to the alarm system and put the property on high-alert status. Thankfully, Mimi had been a decisive woman who knew the value of protecting what was hers.

Oh, Mimi. Did I tell you enough how much I love you?

In her heart, she knew her grandmother's strong personality was the answer she needed. When Mimi was her age, she had been in charge of Great-Grandpa's entire fortune. Michele had the good fortune to spend time with the woman every day. Surely some of Mimi's character had leeched into her own. So what would Mimi do given this set of circumstances? Well, first she would assess her losses. Michele had done that—she had lost the entire family. Second, Mimi would triage the situation by looking for immediate vulnerabilities and taking measures to mitigate them. To a large extent, Michele had done that by activating one of the most advanced security systems money could buy. Next Mimi would set up a long-term survival plan.

That was the hardest thing to imagine. How could Michele endure without her family? She started to breathe heavily but then checked her emotions. *Think about this rationally, Michele. There will be plenty of time for pain later.* Here were the facts: The family was well-heeled. There was money. She wouldn't go hungry, and she'd have a considerable amount of influence if she could muster the will to take control of the family businesses.

But she felt a check in her spirit. True long-term security could only be gained by a relationship with Jesus. She had been such a fool before the rapture, and now the entire world was turning upside down before her eyes. Her only real security would come from committing her life to Him. She knew she could commit to Him anywhere, but her heart wanted to be away from the house where she had embarrassed her family just a few days before. All of the really important spiritual and religious events of this family took place in their chapel—her chapel now.

"Well, it's time for me to do the smart thing," she said. Turning off the security system, she snatched up the key from the mudroom key hooks and ran to the chapel along the manicured paths of the estate's garden.

She inhaled deeply of the polished wood, wax candles, and faint traces of incense as she entered the chapel. The late afternoon sunlight danced through the deep reds, blues, and greens of the stained glass windows, forming swirling patterns of reflected color on the highly polished mahogany floor. There was a constant feeling of peace in here. The cares of the world never entered this serene environment. The chapel had been such a part of her family history. It was as if sitting here could bring her closer to her grandparents, mother, father, brother, and uncle. The thought of them brought a choking sob of loneliness, anguish for people and opportunities lost, and self-recrimination. How could she have rejected the faith of her family? How could she have turned her back on Jesus? He had died for her. It was His presence in the chapel that made her feel loved, warm, comfortable, and at peace.

She cried for a long time in the last pew, calling out to Jesus. He met her needs, offering salvation, comfort, and an unshakable knowledge of His love. Whatever was to come, she knew He would be with her. That made all the difference. She remembered every word of her father's books. There would be a world ruler who would hate Christ and anything Christian. Soon events would transpire to start the seven-year tribulation period. There was every likelihood that she would be among the countless millions slaughtered for her faith. Well, she was ready for it. She would do whatever it took to survive, thrive, and help others during this period. But when the time came to join her Savior and her family in a much better place, she would gladly jump at the opportunity.

She was getting ahead of herself. She had to take each day at a time, living in the moment, and right now was a time of restful celebration that she had found her true Love. She watched the patterns of light from the windows and slowly fell asleep telling Him how much she loved Him.

***

Michele awoke to a gentle tugging on her sleeve.

"Wake up, sweetheart. We have to talk."

She opened her eyes groggily to the warm smiles of her parents.

They looked so good! Every trace of anguish and pain was gone from their faces. They looked to be in their thirties and full of life. A faint glow surrounded them as if the atmosphere reflected energy from their bodies. She wiped the sleep from her eyes and hugged them. She knew it was a dream, but it felt real. She smelled her father's soft citrus cologne and her mother's Prada perfume.

Hard tears cascaded down her face. "I'm so sorry," she cried desperately as her mother held her close and her father stroked her hair.

"Sweetheart," Gabe said softly, "the important thing is that you've made the right decision. Jesus let us visit here to encourage you, but times will be tough. You're going to need to be tough too."

"And smart," Tina added.

"I know," Michele agreed. "I was thinking I'd have to go through Mimi's stuff to figure out what to do with the businesses."

Tina laughed. "You've spent too much time with Mimi!" she exclaimed with a tease.

Michele and Gabe laughed too. It was as if they had never been separated, as if her parents weren't now entirely new beings.

Gabe said, "We're the same people, Michele. Only now we can see and move through more dimensions. These glorified bodies are awesome, but they house the same old Mom and Dad."

He continued, his green eyes dancing like emeralds. "There was a time in the late 1990s when Mimi redecorated the entire mansion and did a lot of work on the grounds. She was always forward-thinking and a little secretive. During the renovation she built a bunker to use when times got tough." He walked to the far wall of the chapel and motioned for Michele to follow. Pressing on several stones in a specific pattern set about a chain reaction, eventually opening a portion of the hardwood floor. Underneath, lights came on to flood a stairwell. "Shall we?" He motioned to the stairs.

As they descended, Gabe sniggered. "Now I know where Michael got his penchant for high-tech cloak-and-dagger stuff. I can't believe two people in my family had secret lairs!"

"Me neither," Michele said in awe. The space was large, taking up the entire underbelly of the estate's sculpted gardens. There were several bedrooms, a number of bathrooms, and a kitchen. "Who else knows about this?"

"Mimi didn't tell anyone," Tina said. "That's one of the reasons the Lord allowed us to come to you now."

Gabe continued the tour. "The place is set up with sophisticated water and air filtration. Somehow, Mimi managed to hide solar panels in the roof of the estate. She also diverted the gas lines going into the house. They all feed to this room." He opened a door to the roar of an electric generator, which was surrounded by huge boxes of lithium batteries. "Together, these should keep you powered up. This room is superinsulated, so the generator noise can't be heard above." He shut the door and smiled at the resultant silence.

"There are a few things that need to start up, honey," Tina said, leading them to another room. She opened the door to a large room filled with hydroponic tables. Sunlamps hung over each table, and over a large tank at the end of the room. "This will be your garden, and the tank over there is for fish. Basically, the water gets recycled throughout and the fish waste fertilizes the plants."

"Looks like I'll be a farmer," Michele said with a shrug.

"It's designed to be pretty automatic," Gabe said, "but you'll have to get it established. On the table over there, you'll see the seeds as well as a list of the number and types of fish to order. Once they're in and the seeds are planted, go to the computer at the desk over there and start the program called Envirolab. There are sensors to measure everything. The program will control sunlight and water for the plants and will feed the fish."

"Beyond cool," Michele said wondrously.

"There's something else," Gabe said, leading her to another room decorated as an office. "Mimi had quietly been buying up small businesses she assumed would become large amid the New World Order. Mostly they involve graphene, which is a superconductive form of carbon, and there is one company that edged out others in quantum computing. Stocks of these companies are already going through the roof, but nobody knows the mysterious largest shareholder of each."

"Mimi," Michele said with an air of pride.

"You and Uncle Michael now." Gabe smiled as he pulled up a file on the computer merely by pointing at it. "Mimi found a few back doors around SEC disclosure rules. She did a *very* good job covering her tracks. Also, she bought precious metals. There's a storeroom over there with gold, silver, and platinum to use in transactions that you want to keep under the radar of the government."

Tina's face grew stern as she pointed to a closed metal door. "That room is an arms cache. Don't take the weapons out of here. Promise me. Use them only to protect this space, okay?"

"I promise, Mom. Besides, I don't want to even pick up a gun."

"You may need to at some point," Gabe said. "But only as a last resort, sweetheart. If I had my way, you would hide out here for seven years eating fresh vegetables and fish. But that's not what the Lord has planned for you. This is a refuge when things get too tough."

The gravity of it all filled the room. At least now she had a fighting chance, thanks to Mimi. But now the terrible time had come. Her parents hugged her good-bye. She wished she could spend the next seven years locked in their embrace. Their forms disappeared as they held her.

She awoke on the pew where she had fallen asleep. The dream had been too vivid not to be real. Walking to the other end of the chapel, she tapped the stones with the pattern her father had used. The stairwell opened to her, and she went down to inventory the bunker.

She found everything as her parents had shown her. In the office space, she looked carefully through Mimi's files. Mimi had left a detailed notebook for each of her businesses—secretly owned and otherwise—including an analysis of the strengths and weaknesses of each business and each member of top management.

"I have so much to thank you for someday, Mimi." She grinned at the thought of finally being together again with her family. Looking at her watch, she realized the late hour, quickly gathered up the notebooks for two of the nonsecret businesses, and left the bunker.

Only when she ascended the stairs into the chapel did she realize how dark it had gotten. No sunlight played on the floors now. The chapel was dim in the light of only one candle at the altar. Shadows played eerily on the floor, and the darkness felt palpable.

Pulling the door shut, she shuddered and locked it behind her. The full moon darted from behind clouds to cast occasional soft light. She had turned off the external lighting when she turned off the alarms. The alarms! She had turned them off to go to the chapel.

"It's been a long day, Michele. Don't let your nerves get the better of you," she said softly as she hurried down the path to the house, lighted only by an occasional touch of moonlight peeking through the clouds.

A loud scream in the distance startled her. As she had feared, the insanity had spilled into the countryside. She couldn't wait to get in the house, set the alarm, and curl up on the family room couch.

Another scream. This one seemed closer. Just a few more steps and she would be home free. She could feel the fear boiling up inside. She clamped her hand over her mouth to stifle a scream. The glass doors to the informal part of the house looked very inviting. The television glowed warmly through the wall of windows in the family room. Abandoning all stealth and pretense of calm, she ran headlong to the house as another scream erupted. She thought it was more of a howl— definitely human, but primal and filled with wild rage.

Her hand found the door handle and yanked it open. She flew into the house and ran to the alarm control panel. She armed every protective device: window sensors, door sensors, pressure sensors in the formal part of the house, and laser trip switches in the driveway and along the pathways. She pushed a button to close and lock the large iron gates at the front of the estate. She even turned on the electric shielding. A smile passed across her face. Her brother used to call it "putting up the shields," like in *Star Trek*. Basically, the large gates and iron railings atop the fieldstone walls surrounding the estate conducted a small electric charge. It would cause some discomfort, but it really wouldn't stop a crazed individual. Apparently, Mimi had installed a formidable charge in the 1990s, but when Michele and her brother came along, her father pulled back the voltage.

"You should have listened to your mom, Dad." Michele would have preferred the bigger bang right now, but she was happy to have the low-voltage version. The alarm system was elaborate. In the event of an invasion, it would give her enough time to take cover in the chapel bunker.

"I wish I had just stayed down there tonight," she said to nobody in particular, but she knew she wouldn't have. The bunker was a last resort, not the place from which she intended to start this new phase of her life. Besides, the sterility of the bunker couldn't compare to the comfort of this big old home. Years of laughs, hugs, kisses, and good times with her family ran through her mind in a single download.

"Thanks, Lord," she said with a smile as she closed the heavy floor-to-ceiling drapes in the family room and nestled into the big old afghan on the overstuffed couch. The memories comforted her and made her feel less alone. The very real experience of being with her parents today made her feel as if this next bit of time would be doable. Tough, no doubt, but doable. She had to stay in God's Word and in His presence, but that would be a joy anyway.

She turned off the television, turned on her father's MP3 Bible readings, and set the sleep timer. The readings picked up where he had left off, in the book of Ruth. She drifted off to the beautiful story of a widow who followed her mother-in-law to Israel. "Wherever you go, I will go. Your people will be my people, and your God will be my God." Her last thought was, *Yes, Lord, I'll go wherever You go.*

Michele awoke with a start upon hearing a noise coming from the formal area at the front of the house. The pressure sensors near the doors and windows hadn't triggered the alarm. She had set the alarm without first checking to see if anyone was in the house! Her delusion of security fell away as she heard another footfall.

Praying in her mind, she slid silently off the couch. Intimate knowledge of the house's layout wasn't an advantage. The mansion was never really dark. Carefully placed dim lighting accentuated the highly polished staircases and other architectural features of the place. She decided to stay low, hopefully remaining out of the intruder's line of sight long enough to sneak out the back door and then run like the wind to the chapel.

The alarm. The flaw in her plan. If she opened the door to leave the house, the alarm would go off, alerting the intruder to her presence. The house would light up like a beacon, and the alarm would sound like a siren, calling any number of the crazed miscreants to her location.

On her hands and knees, she crawled quietly to the alarm panel in the mudroom off the kitchen, being sure to stay in the shadows. There was a specific code to turn off the system silently, but she couldn't remember it. Who was she kidding? She never even knew it. Until a few hours ago, she had been a carefree teenager, not the master of the estate. Sitting in the shadows under the alarm panel, she gathered her thoughts. Once she turned off the alarm, there would be a deactivation tone that would no doubt alert the intruder. If he was someone who hadn't caught the madness, the tone would probably cause him to flee rather than risk detection. If, however, he was one of the crazed ones, he would be alerted to her presence.

She had a few advantages. First, she was fast. Second, only she knew about the bunker. Third, she knew the property intimately, and the alarm panel was only a few quick steps from the door.

She took a deep breath and then moved like a machine. She quickly deadened the exterior lighting, disabled the alarm, and sprang through the door after fumbling briefly with its lock. Then she threw caution to the wind and ran into the night. The moon had lost the fight. Clouds had overtaken it. She focused on the shadowy silhouette of the chapel's roof against the dark sky. As she stared at her objective, the altar candle's soft glow made nearly imperceptible flickers in the chapel's stained glass windows.

For a few seconds she was alone, but then she heard footsteps behind her. She ran faster, panting. Her pursuer picked up the pace. The footfalls were heavy and athletic—a man. She thought he would have more difficulty in the darkness. He ran quickly as if he knew where he was headed.

Just then she heard a bloodcurdling scream. She looked over her shoulder to see the flash of a gunshot. In the brief seconds of light, she saw that her pursuer was Jimmy Sheradon, the oldest at an orphanage run by her parents. In fact, when he had turned nineteen, he took a job there as a sort of dorm parent. It had been a constant source of frustration for Tina and Gabe that they couldn't convince this young man to give his heart to Jesus.

Totally disarmed by the sight of a familiar face, Michele stopped to see his expression of terror and pain. "Jimmy!" she screamed.

"Run!" he yelled back to her.

The sound of another shot rang out, and he fell.

FOUR

I t was such a bright, beautiful day in Rome. Well, to be honest, the sounds of screaming, gunshots, and explosions coming from street level could be a bit annoying. But Benny wasn't about to let any thing ruin his first full day as pope. This was his day, damn it, and he was going to enjoy it. Sunlight and shadow played tricks through the large windows overlooking the papal gardens as he inventoried the papal closet. The quality of material and workmanship in each cassock and robe were beyond compare. Unfortunately most of his predecessors didn't have much sense of style, so there was bound to be some updating.

First things first, though. In all the tumult of becoming pope, he had barely eaten. The staff seemed to be in disarray, but maybe they could scrounge something up for him. He pressed the buzzer and then continued his inventory. There was a wealth of gemstones. Sadly, most were bound to religious-themed settings. Benny made a mental note to appoint a papal jeweler as soon as possible. Surely the stones could find more fashionable homes.

Where is the staff? He pushed the buzzer again and then a third time. Finally, he just lay into it until a member of the Swiss guard appeared at the door.

"Holiness. My apologies. Most of the staff is gone, sir. The insurrection has come close to breaching our location, but we have maintained control." His festooned uniform was spattered with dried blood, a sign that hand-to-hand combat had been the order of the day at street level.

Benny said nothing and showed no emotion, despite the thrill of being referred to as "Holiness." He looked into the young soldier's

33

frightened eyes as they pleaded for a word to make sense of the mania descending upon the world. The two stood like that for a few seconds.

Finally Benny spoke. "*Ho fama*," he said with an imperial air. "I'm hungry."

The soldier jumped for a second at the impropriety of the comment, but then his puzzled expression broke into a slight grin, which grew broader as the seconds passed. In a string of Italian, he thanked the new pope for having the insight to bring him back to his senses, as if Benny had issued some sublime message to look only at the things we can control and place the rest in the hands of God.

Benny smiled graciously. It was great to have this man's undying gratitude. And it was awesome that he could say just about anything and this guy would think it to be a word from God Himself ... but he was looking for a menu. "And yet I'm still hungry," Benny said to the young man.

The soldier winced. "There is no staff in the kitchen, Holiness ... some unfortunate murders. The kitchen must be sterilized before cooking resumes. Perhaps there are some leftovers ..."

"Fine, fine," Benny said with an exasperated wave of his hand, turning his back on the man to indicate an end of the papal audience. This was getting tiresome. He was the new pope, for crying out loud! There should be white smoke, cheering, mesmerizing addresses to adoring crowds, worldwide media coverage, fittings for a new wardrobe, and above all a series of fine dinners in his honor. Now he had to eat leftover crap from the previous dynasty. The last pope was German, and Benny was no fan of German food. They would probably bring him an old salty pretzel and ghastly dark beer.

"Well, I understand the world is in a bit of a state right now, but changes will be made. I won't live like this for long!" His imperious rant became full-blown rage as he strutted around the room like Julie Andrews in a musical number. "Chris!" he yelled, as was his custom for years. Catching his mistake, he sat silently on one of the facing white sofas before the wall of windows overlooking the garden.

For so many years he had placed matters into Chris's hands with full confidence that they would be handled as well as if he had done them himself. In a painful second of self-awareness, he muttered, "Let's be honest, Benny, you knew he would do them better." So there it was. For years he had considered Chris to be the bane of his existence, and yet Chris was the first person he missed.

Looking into the air as if Chris could hear, he said, "Well, don't flatter yourself, Chris. Everyone was upset when our butler Joseph was gone too. Do you know what they missed? His punctuality and his pancakes! I miss your dull-witted acceptance of tasks." As he sat there, Benny realized he would miss more than that. Chris had beautiful eyes that, despite every reason not to be, were often kind toward him. Chris had the hearts of Kim and the boys, and provided a way for Benny to know them. He remembered in detail Chris's stories about the boys when they were growing up and the stories about Gabe's kids. Benny would make light of it, but now in this silence, he realized Chris had become his connection to the family.

"Well, now you've let me down, Chris," Benny said to the air. "Just when I need my family to share in this greatest day of my life, you are nowhere to be found."

His rant gave him no solace. There was a slight buzz, indicating someone in the service entrance. The festooned guard placed on his desk a dish of chicken soup and a roll. "This is all I could find, Holiness. *Buon appetito.*" The soldier backed out of the room with a slight bow.

Benny gingerly tasted the concoction before him. He was so hungry. Even something as mundane as this watered-down soup tasted great to him. He ate ferociously for a second and then moved to a box of personal items from his old quarters. He rummaged for a second and then said, "Ah. Come to Papa," as he pulled out a bottle of chardonnay. Pouring himself a glass, he sniffed its bouquet and then swallowed a huge gulp. Filling the glass to the full again, he returned to his desk and the bowl of soup.

"Well, this is better," he said with a grin of satisfaction. There would be time for pomp and circumstance, but for now the Vicar of Christ would content himself with a simple meal. It would look good in the press reports someday. Over the years he had conjured every detail of the image he wanted to present as pope. Years of watching Luciano Begliali in action had been a marvelous training ground in how to wield power subtly and in a manner that draws people in.

Polishing off the soup, he looked around the office. It was beautiful and very stately, but it needed just a bit of a whimsy—maybe a well-placed vase of red roses or something with a zebra pattern. Taking a step toward the facing white couches, he stumbled a bit. "Maybe a little too much wine," he said offhandedly.

He lay back on one of the couches and began to nod off, thinking of recent events. What a ploy it had been to poison the cardinals' soup. The soup! He tried to rouse himself. That stupid guardsman must have found some of the poisoned soup! The thought crossed his mind that the guardsman may not be as stupid and unassuming as he looked. The remaining cardinals hated Benny. Could they have decided literally to give him a dose of his own medicine? If so, then he had proven to be even a bigger putz than that priest from Hoboken who had died at Benny's hand years before. Chicken noodle soup did in that old buzzard too.

"Stay conscious, Benny," he said to himself. "Think. Think! Where's the antidote?" He felt as if he were screaming, but only a mumble came from his lips.

He fought sleep long enough to remember the antidote in the box of personal belongings from his apartment. He distinctly remembered deciding whether to throw it away so there'd be no evidence. In the end, he had decided he would rather keep it as a trophy to celebrate his victory.

"Some victory! The shortest papal reign in history," he muttered. With extreme concentration, he managed to roll his unwilling body off the couch, falling with an uncontrolled thud to the floor. Pushing for all he was worth with his legs, he barely moved his huge frame a few inches along the highly polished marble floor. He forced his eyes open to see that he was still several feet away from the box containing the antidote.

Agh! he screamed in his head as he tried to engage his arms. It seemed to him like a massive exertion, but his limp body only moved another six inches. He was going to die. He was going to die! His breath became shallow. He had to try again, but he was so tired. "Come on, Benny!" he said to himself.

"Come on, Benny," he heard in reply. Picking up his head was a massive effort, but he managed at least to turn it in the direction of the voice. With all his might he willed his eyes to open. They were accosted by dazzling brilliance. Whoever was in the room was not of this world.

He pushed and pushed again until finally his unwilling arm came to rest above his eyes. Shielding them from the radiance, he slowly looked up the length of a dazzling white tunic to see the eyes of his sister, Kim, who held the antidote. His heart jumped at the familiar lines of her face. She was the only person he had ever really loved. And yet his mind cowered at the sheer power emanating from that face. That face!

"We have to talk, Benny," she said sternly.

"Kim," he muttered. "Help me."

"I will, Benny, but there's a price."

"Whatever it is, I'll pay," he tried to say.

"Swear to me, Benny," she said, much as she had done many years before when they were children.

"Swear what?" he managed to mumble.

"Swear that you'll do everything in your power to protect Michael and my grandchildren." Her face looked totally serene, but every word she spoke carried unbridled power to unnerve him. Suddenly, he was catapulted into the past, seeing events through Kim's eyes: the pain she felt for him when her father carried his nearly catatonic body home from one of their "excursions," her fear when he threatened to bring the boys' father into their lives, her exasperation at his constant con niving to get her fortune, and something else. Despite it all, she loved him, constantly trying to undo the harm caused by her father. He loved her as well, but he had been consumed with hurting her father through her. He sensed the slowing of his heart, each beat sounding as if it were further away down a dark cave.

Her brilliance faded, leaving the beautiful thirty-something Kim. He pulled his hand away from his face, looked into her lovely green eyes, and found there clarity of understanding that had eluded him all his life. "Kim, I'm so sorry," he mumbled.

"I forgave you a long time ago, Benny," she said with a wistful smile. "But you've made decisions and choices that have ruined you for eternity. And it breaks my heart."

"I know my choices, Kim. I worked so hard to get where I am today, and it's all slipping through my fingers." His tired eyes welled in a burst of self-pity.

"It doesn't have to, Benny," she said sternly. "Swear it, and I'll give you the antidote."

Pulling at the last bit of remaining strength, he uttered a guttural primal scream. "I swear!"

She bent to him and kissed him lightly on the forehead. He felt a jolt of power surge through him as she cradled his head and poured the antidote into his mouth.

"There's something you should know," she said as she gently lowered his head to the floor.

"What's that?" he asked as the paralytic effects of the drug began to wane.

"I'm only here because Jesus wills it. I only gave you the antidote because prophecy has a lot to say about what you will do. From the timeless perspective of eternity, you've already done it. I wish so much you had made different choices, Benny. I love you and wish you could know the joy we're experiencing now."

The antidote was reviving more than Benny's body. He was instantly put off that she could look askance at his lifetime of achievement. "There's plenty for me in the future, Kim," he said pettily.

"Yes," she said sadly. "In the meantime, know this, Benny. I'll be watching, and I expect you to live up to your end of the bargain." At that her brilliance returned to bathe the room in light. Benny cowered in fear before it.

Benny awoke to the ringing of his satellite phone. Lifting himself from the floor, he held his pounding head. The caller ID indicated a call from Turkey. Isa no doubt.

"*Pronto,*" Benny managed to squeak. His throat was dry and his mouth felt pasty. There was no telling how long he had been out.

"And how is your first full day as pontiff?" Isa asked in a happy voice.

"Well, it's had none of the pomp and regalia I had imagined," Benny said pertly.

"Now, now, Holiness." Isa chuckled. "All in due time, my friend. As they say, 'Rome wasn't built in a day.'"

"Built, my butt," Benny said sourly. "It looks like everything is coming down around us. Have you seen any news reports? There is mass pandemonium."

"You have to break a few eggs to make an omelet. 'Order out of chaos' is our motto, you know. Let me set your mind at ease, old friend," Isa said as Benny took the phone to one of the couches, lay back, and rubbed his throbbing head. "This is a necessary step. It's known as the Dark Awakening. In about a week, the reign of terror will end. But by that time, the world will have seen more casualties than World War I and World War II combined. Hand-to-hand combat in every street."

Benny moaned. He had longed for the day when Isa would be in charge, but he hadn't really considered the bloodstained road he would take to get there. Isa continued. "Western civilization is in meltdown. Law and order have given way to chaos. In the Muslim world, Sunnis and Shiites are uniting as never before, marching in the streets and demanding a restoration of the caliphate. Russia and China are outliers, but they will be brought quickly to their knees with the USA."

"All of this in one week?" Benny asked weakly.

"A week is enough. Trust me, my friend. Next week, I will present myself at the United Nations with a plan to restore order. The world will jump to support me. That's why I'm calling. I will require your presence in New York next week. My unveiling will be yours as well."

"I see," Benny said with renewed interest. "Exactly what will occur there?"

"Well, you'll be happy to know that your nephew completed his work. The Lady has successfully entered our world in physical form, and I have transported her to a secret location. She will join me at the United Nations. Together we will explain that this pandemonium is the vanguard of an infiltration by a malevolent alien race. The Lady will present herself as an emissary from a friendly race, sent here to help us defend ourselves. She will then extol my unique heritage to declare me the only person on the planet qualified to manage this challenge."

"Intriguing," Benny said, noting that Isa's once grand ego had grown even larger since they had last spoken. He was at once in awe of the ease with which Isa would successfully manipulate the world's population and concerned that Isa would allow him no real role to play in the new order.

"Now, now, Benito," Isa cautioned. "There will be plenty for you. At that same meeting, I will call for unity and demand that political and religious differences be subjugated to the more immediate existential threat at hand. I will introduce you as the new Holy Father, not just of Catholicism but of the people of the entire world. You will then lay out your plans to bring together the world's religions. You will speak of finding light in this present darkness and say how the human race can use this danger as a defining, unifying event."

"I like it," Benny said admiringly. "Pope to everyone is better than just being pope to the Catholics. I hope I can pull this off for you, Isa."

"Never doubt my abilities," Isa said with slight annoyance. "Before you speak, I will meet with you privately to anoint you with power you can't even imagine."

"Oh, do tell," Benny said like a vixen from a 1940s movie.

"First, you will gain the ability to draw people to you. This anointing will enable you to elicit instant devotion. You will come across as a bold leader of immense spiritual power."

Benny's mind moved to the dream conversation he'd had with Kim. She said he had a role to play. The thought of Kim brought an instant stabbing pain to his already sore head. "Protect Michael and the kids," he heard her say.

He rejoined the conversation with Isa, who was saying, "Europe will be totally decimated in the Dark Awakening. For decades, Turkey has been refused membership in the European Union; but trust me, Benny, within a week the EU will be begging for admission to my new caliphate. I'll dangle it in front of their smug faces a bit, but in the end I'll grant them entrance to the New World Order. America will fare much better. Without its superior military strength, I would be nothing but a paper tiger. Thankfully, the Dark Awakening has incapacitated the United States' government, and the president has agreed to endorse me fully in return for his new status as my vassal king."

Benny heard it with less awe than at first. He couldn't get his mind off the experience with Kim. It was just a dream, right? He sat up on the couch and his eye caught it, the empty vial of antidote. It was more than a dream. Certainly he had eaten the poisoned soup and drunk the antidote. The question was whether Kim really had been there or if it had been some sort of delusion brought on by the poison. In the periphery of his vision, he saw a flash of light. Kim appeared in full radiance for a brief second and then disappeared. His body convulsed with the power she exuded. He knew what he had to do.

"Isa, there is one small matter that I'd like to bring to your attention," Benny began. "I know the world is going to change, and changing times demand sacrifices. Yet I worry about my family, specifically Michael and my sister's grandchildren. I haven't been in touch with them, but I'm given to understand they weren't taken in the rapture."

Isa's voice erupted with anger. "First things first, Benny. There was no rapture; do you understand me? There was only the Dark Awakening!"

Benny recoiled. "Isa, I'm sorry. I didn't mean to upset you."

"I'm not upset, Benny," Isa said in a much more measured tone. "But it is important that we not give credence to Christian thought of the past. It is a new day, Holiness. You must *never* mention that word again."

"I promise," Benny said, thinking of the vision of Kim. Whether Isa wanted to admit it or not, and clearly he did not, something other than the Dark Awakening had happened to Benny's family.

"Not to worry," Isa said in a much kinder voice. "Once you share my power, you will not be so prone to slips of the tongue."

"But, if I may, Isa, back to Michael and the kids."

"Yes, yes," Isa said dismissively. "The new rules will be for the masses, Benny, not for us. If you want to indulge your family a bit, it's fine with me. In fact, I have an unspoken familial relationship to Father Michael as well. And he has done a marvelous job of giving birth to the most sophisticated computer program on the planet. I have plans for that system. Unfortunately, those plans require that Michael never again interface with it. You may offer him the full benefit of my protection as a consolation prize."

"A small price to pay for his life," Benny said in tacit approval. "And the children?" he asked cautiously.

"Absolutely. I know your loyalties are to me. You have proven yourself to be a true servant of the New World Order. It is a small price for me to grant your family safety."

"Thank you, Isa," Benny said with true gratitude.

Isa said, "If I were you, I would plan to get to the United States sooner rather than later. Europe is not likely to fare well this week."

"I will," Benny said. "Thank you, Isa."

Hanging up the phone, he picked up the antidote bottle and put it back in the box of possessions from his apartment. He rummaged a bit until he found the last unused vial of poison. Then a box of chocolates caught his eye. "Come here, you," he said to the sweet morsels. He popped one in his mouth as an idea formed. He took a particularly luscious-looking dark-chocolate-covered caramel from the box. His favorite. Using a pen, he made a slight hole in the underside of the chocolate and poured in a bit of the poison. Powerful stuff. "A little dab'll do ya," he sang, the lyrics from the jingle of a television commercial he'd seen in his youth.

He pressed the button for the guardsman to clear his tray. When the guard's eyes met Benny's, the new pope could see the soldier's surprise that he was well. That look was all Benny needed to know that this man had worked with the remaining cardinals to take him out.

"Clear this tray, will you?" he asked the man kindly.

"Sí," the man said with a slight bow.

Benny strolled to the desk and scribbled something on a piece of paper. Crossing the room in a gliding motion, he handed the paper to the soldier. "And would you be kind enough to deliver this for me with utmost urgency?" he asked with a sickeningly sweet smile.

"Sí," the guardsman said, clearly anxious to leave the room.

When the soldier left, Benny fell to the white couch laughing. It hadn't been such a bad day after all.

The buzzer rang and Benny admitted the guard. Seeing that the guard had accomplished the task laid out for him, Benny dismissed him with a piece of fine chocolate as a sign of appreciation. Behind the guard stood Michael, his disheveled face a mask of despair. Benny stifled a chuckle. "Come, now, Michael," he said drolly as he held out his arms. "Give your uncle Benny a hug."

"Don't get me wrong, Benny," Michael said softly. "I'm surprisingly happy to see a familiar face in all this madness." He hugged his uncle gingerly.

Like a newly engaged young woman, Benny flashed the papal ring in front of his nephew. "You may want to refer to me as Pope Peter from now on," he said with pride.

"In line with St. Malachy's prophecy of the popes, no doubt," Michael said with a look of sarcastic disdain. "But appropriate in so many other ways as well." He threw himself nonchalantly onto one of the facing couches. "So tell me, Benny, how did you manage to pull this one off?"

"The rap—" Benny began before remembering Isa's admonition. "The current pandemonium left several vacancies in the College of Cardinals just as they were about to consider the fallacious report Chris had filed about me."

"Fallacious! Huh!" Michael huffed.

"Remember your manners, Michael," Benny chided. "A very curious illness took hold of all remaining. I just so happened to have the antidote." Benny held up the empty vial with a shrug and a grin. "They were more than willing to elect me pope when I offered to share it with them."

Benny chuckled as Michael wiped his face in disgust.

"So, you're the pope now," Michael said, shaking his head dismally. "This really is the tribulation."

"Oh, Michael, you sound like Chris and your brother. You don't really believe all that trash, do you?"

"As a matter of fact, Benny, I do," Michael said with a grin. "I've seen the error of my ways, and I've given my heart to Jesus."

"Well, unfortunate as that may be, Michael," Benny said smugly, "you've given your life and your service to me."

"I don't understand," Michael said, much to Benny's annoyance.

"The guardsman who brought you here tried to kill me earlier. It appears the cardinals have buyers' regret regarding their decision to elect me as pope."

"Small wonder," Michael quipped.

"Really, Michael, your wit knows no bounds," Benny said sarcastically. "The bottom line is this: we may not have always agreed—"

"*May* not?" Michael aped.

Benny grimaced his disapproval and then continued. "But we're family, and we're all that we have left. Frankly, Michael, you're the only person in the world I trust not to kill me. That's why I've made you my camerlengo."

Michael jumped up from the sofa, putting his face inches from Benny's. "A dubious honor. What makes you think that I would ever consent to something like that?"

Benny backed up a step. "Well, for one, listen to the pandemonium outside. The world has turned upside down. There's only one way I can keep you alive, and that's to keep you close."

"Really?" Michael exclaimed. "You're doing this because you love me?"

"In my own way, you know I do, Michael!" Benny yelled back. "And it's certainly not for your winning personality, either. It's because your mother was the only person in my life who honestly gave a damn about me."

Michael's demeanor softened, and he returned to the couch. "She truly loved you, Benny. I'll vouch for that."

"That's not all," Benny said, collapsing next to Michael on the sofa, his face suddenly wrenched with pain and fear. He began to speak, but the words were caught in a sob. Fanning his face, he continued in a hoarse whisper, "I saw your mother." Then tears began to flow.

"It's the time we're in, Benny," Michael tried in an awkward gesture of comfort. "The prophet Joel said there would be a lot of dreams and visions in the Latter Days. I'm guessing now that our family members have resurrected bodies, the Lord allows them to enter our lives on occasion. I'll tell you a secret."

"What?" Benny whined through tears.

"I had a dream about Chris and Gabe. But it was more than a dream. I saw them, heard them, and touched them as if they were really there. I understand you when you say you saw Mom."

"It wasn't all that pleasant for me, Michael. In my dream, she was covered in light and power—beyond anything I've seen before, including Isa." Benny looked pleadingly into his nephew's eyes only to see him bristle at the mention of Isa's name.

"She made me agree to look out for you and the kids ..."

"The kids!" Michael choked. "Gabe and Chris mentioned them too. I was sure they would have been taken." Michael sat next to his crying uncle, tears welling in his own eyes. "I polluted Michele's mind with my pretend gospel. She must have gotten to young Chris too." Michael's shoulders heaved.

In a rare moment of shared compassion, Benny saw the younger priest as the little boy he had once held and sang to. Softly he said, "Michael, all I can tell you is this world is in for horrendous times before things get better."

"I know," Michael gasped.

"Isa has granted my desire to keep my family from the flames. Don't make me fail your mother this one last time, Michael."

"I can't. If I don't do everything in my power to protect the kids, I'll be failing Gabe yet again." He coughed, wiped his face, and said, "You're right, Benny, we're all we have left now. I'll work with you for the protection of the kids, but you have to understand that the kids and I will fall on the Christian side of this battle."

"I understand." Benny grinned, wiping his own eyes. "Let's face it—we have a lifetime of experience with vehement disagreement stifled to protect those we love. So, we'll continue on a bit longer."

Michael laughed. "I know nothing about being a camerlengo, Benny. I'm hopeless at organization, and I've spent my priesthood trying to avoid the hierarchy of the church, but I'll do it. I know it's what Chris and Gabe want, and I have to look out for the kids."

"Good man, Michael!" Benny cheered. "And for what it's worth, you bested me in a negotiation when you weren't even ten. Put those Grandpa Stan genes to work and you'll be fine. I have a little wine left. Should we drink on it?"

"I'll take a sip," Michael said with resignation. "So, what's next, boss?"

"Well." Benny's eyes gleamed as he poured two glasses of wine. "At some point we'll have to do a coronation ceremony announcing me to the world. So, I'll need you to work with me on a press release to make me sound the part. You know, growing up with a silver spoon but eschewing worldly things to serve others—all the stuff people like to hear in times of trouble."

Michael giggled at the sheer lunacy.

"Don't underestimate your abilities," Benny said, handing him a glass. "You did a good job reinventing Jesus in the Gospel of St. John. You can find something good to say about me."

Michael winced.

"There, there," Benny chided in a condescending manner. "It's water under the bridge now, Michael. We have to play the hand we've been dealt."

Benny took a sip of his wine only to be blown off his feet by an enormous explosion. As he fell, he saw the fireball rising from the darkened garden. Instinctively he lay facedown and covered his head with his arms. The lights went out as shards of glass from the picture windows blew over him. He heard Michael's screams over the shriek of shattering glass and the rumbling thunder of the explosion.

"Michael, are you all right?" he shrieked.

"I ... I think so," Michael replied. "I managed to shield my face from the glass. One shard took a good nip at my leg, but I think I'm okay. What about you?"

Benny could barely hear his nephew over the cacophony of screams from the crazed crowd below. "I'll be fine!" he bellowed as Michael rolled off the sofa to take a place beside him.

"Come on, Benny, let's get you to your feet," Michael said, half carrying him away from the windows. Then the closer sound of screaming and fighting rang from the hallway.

"This isn't good, Benny. It means they've breached the Vatican. We have to get out of here. Keep your head down."

Michael led him to the office door. He listened for a moment and placed his hand on it. "This way is no good. They're torching the place!" Michael's face contorted with concern for their welfare.

"We'll have to go by the servants' entrance," Benny said decisively. In the dim flickering light of fire from the gardens, they ran to the other end of the room. This time Benny felt the door. It was cool to the touch. After opening it, he stumbled through and tripped on something. Michael came barreling after him, and both fell.

"Agh," Michael yelled with disgust as he looked into the dead face of the guardsman who had brought him to the office.

In the dim light, Benny could see the half-eaten chocolate on the floor beside the man. "Forget him, Michael!" he yelled. "We have to get out of here."

As they proceeded, the hallway grew from long shadows to utter darkness. They felt their way along the walls, listening for noises from the crowd, not knowing if they were headed toward the rabble or away from it. Michael took the lead as Benny clung to the sleeve of his cassock.

It was all too much for Benny. The courage he had shown at the initial explosion was giving way to feelings of immense self-pity. "Just my luck," he blubbered. "I worked so hard to get here, and I never even got to enjoy the place."

"Yeah," Michael said derisively as they inched further into the darkness. "Of all the things to feel bad about in the world right now, that's got to be top on my list too."

"I'm hurt, Michael. Can't you show a little compassion?"

Michael stopped short. Benny felt his nephew's arm pinning him to the wall. "Listen up, Benny. Our lives are in danger. Can you *please* pull your swollen head out of your colossal butt long enough to work with me here?"

It worked. Taking hold of his emotions, Benny said, "You're right. Although you have a lot to learn about how to address a pontiff."

"That will be second on my list of things to feel bad about, Benny. Let's get going."

"Where will we go?" Benny asked.

"We need to get to your plane. Hopefully one of the pilots is alive and sane. We're going home, Benny."

"To Georgia?"

"To Georgia."

FIVE

The setting sun cast long shadows as Will White finally made it to the outskirts of Atlanta. Looking back over his beloved city, he was reminded of the old novel *Gone with the Wind*. Atlanta was burning again. Smoke billowed from every corner of the city, and the fires were bold enough to cast an orange-red glow on the clouds of smoke hanging low over once-stately buildings. Screams from citywide rioting blasted through the night. He had fought hard to get this far, but he needed to rest. He would have to find nighttime shelter soon. Looking at the area around him, he spied a grove of pine trees. They were thickly needled and would provide good cover if he could rest inside them.

He pushed through the prickly branches to the center and piled up some of the soft underbrush to form a makeshift mattress. He lay down on his back, his crossbow and an arrow across his chest. Things were too wild now. He decided to shoot any intruder, animal or human.

He was incredibly tired, more tired than he could ever remember being, but he knew it would be a long time before he gave way to sleep. Unaccepting of this horror, his mind ran over recent events in a continual loop as if it could make sense of them.

Will was a magician and an entertainer. He had grown up poor in the backwater end of the state, raised by a grandmother who tried her best but who was old, tired, and more than a little disillusioned with life. Her daughter, his mother, died not long after he was born, and his father was mythical, just someone his mother had known briefly. The circumstances of his conception were shrouded in his grandmother's disapproval of his mother's views of premarital sex. So, he only knew a bit. His mother had saved her Winn Dixie earnings fastidiously after high school to have her dream vacation, a Caribbean cruise. There she found herself infatuated with a man who was only interested in a casual encounter. What's the phrase? Two ships that passed in the night. Nine months later William Marron was born. At least that's the last name his mother remembered when she filled out the birth certificate. His grandmother tried to find his father. She contacted the cruise line, but there had been no passengers or staff using that surname on his mother's cruise.

His entire young life was about shame. He carried his mother's shame in a tiny town that knew everyone's business. He carried shame of his very existence from his grandmother's constant complaining of how unfair it was for her to raise a child at such an advanced age. He carried the shame of being poor and never having the things other kids had. Even when there was money, there was the hurdle to get past Gram's contention that newfangled stuff was the ruination of society.

His retreat was found in the forging of a new character. In grade school, he convinced Mr. Hawthorne to let him work after school in his convenience store. Mostly, Will swept the floors and cleaned the toilets, but every two weeks he received his pay—cash money. Gram didn't believe in banks either. Her family had been rich, she claimed, until the Great Depression. "Then the banks up and took it all. All of it!" she would harangue.

At first the money bought a few comic books. And then one day he saw an advertisement for a magic kit. He had to have it. Saving for months until he finally had enough, he sent away a money order and received in return a box that changed his life. He found that he was very good at the tricks. As he got better, his confidence increased. Finally he began to do tricks at recess. It was simple stuff, like pulling a nickel out of a girl's ear, but the kids ate it up. Magic had given him an identity beyond the disastrous Marron heritage.

By the time he was in junior high school, his magic tricks were fairly sophisticated. He staged events at local talent shows and worked tirelessly in Gram's old barn to design, build, and paint props and sets. It was great for him until the fair came to town and he saw a danger act. A man performed motorcycle stunts Will had never even imagined. He knew there was no way he could afford a motorcycle or any of the sophisticated toys he had seen at the fair, but there had to be something. Then one day he came across his grandfather's old crossbow, at which point Will White, magician and crossbow entertainer, was born. He practiced with the crossbow nonstop until he was a veritable William Tell.

By that time, puberty had set in and girls began to notice his thickly muscled body and flashing green eyes. The crossbow carried with it a sort of medieval mystique. He capitalized on it by making for himself a sleeveless leather tunic and fringed leather wristbands to wear when he performed. To finish the look, he grew his hair long and pulled it straight back from his angular face. He was Robin Hood, and many a young girl fantasized about being his Maid Marian.

Despite their intentions, he wasn't much of a mover and shaker. To be sure, he was very attracted to the opposite sex, but he lived in fear of becoming like his unknown father. He refused to let carnal desires put him in a place where he would have unwanted children running around. This was just fine with his girlfriend Allison. She was a Christian girl who believed in waiting for marriage. He didn't share her belief in God. Frankly, he thought that if God existed, surely He had abandoned him as carelessly as his father had.

But he liked Allison. She was great company and great to look at. Her dark complexion and high cheekbones from her Cherokee heritage coupled with the light blue eyes and blonde hair from the Norwegian side of her family gave her an exotic beauty. Just as important to Will, she had a high passion for adventure. It was only natural that she would join him in Atlanta to perform after they graduated high school. They were doing pretty well too. Will wasn't a headliner, but he sure was a spellbinder and quite a draw. Most of his act centered on daredevil feats with the crossbow. He shot blindfolded, hitting an apple balanced precariously on Allison's head, or shot backward with the aid of a mirror. Just last year, they had developed their most popular trick. He would strap her onto a spinning wheel. At each stop of a clock was placed a balloon, with Allison spread out in the middle like some sort of circus Jesus. He would spin the wheel and then block his view of it with a large paper drumhead bearing his name in broad strokes. He would shoot effortlessly into the paper, twelve shots in succession, as the audience held their collective breath. When he was done, he would pause for effect and shake his head a bit as if he suspected something had gone wrong. Wincing slightly, he would remove the paper to reveal burst balloons and Allison spinning slowly with a big smile. The crowd always erupted with cheers and applause.

Will had nerves of steel and a precise aim, but he always hedged his bets on the side of Allison's safety. First of all, there were carefully taped marks on the floor to which the drumhead had been carefully aligned. Once in place, he knew there was six inches of give from the edge of the drumhead to the point where an arrow could harm Allison. As long as he stayed within that six-inch boundary, his love would be safe. As for hitting the balloons? Well, the wheel made clicking sounds as it spun. The balloons were always placed where the tabs of the wheel hit the paddle at a different angle, enough to change the sound of the click. Fear of what might go wrong always put the audience in entranced silence. Will simply counted clicks to know when to fire.

Will and Allison had repeated the trick for probably the hundredth time at tonight's show. Everything went off without a hitch, but a huge volley of thunder rocked the old theater at the moment of the great reveal. First, one woman in the audience screamed. Will looked toward the direction of the scream, but the stage lights blinded him from seeing into the dark audience. Not really knowing what else to do, he continued the act, flamboyantly rolling away the drumhead to reveal ... an empty spinning wheel. Allison was gone! She had been securely fastened to the wheel for her own safety. In disbelief, he ran to the wheel as another, and then another, person in the audience began to scream. He grasped at the bindings that had held Allison to the wheel. They were bound and intact. How could she have gotten off the wheel without loosening the straps? More importantly, he knew she would never do such a thing. She was as dedicated to their success as he was.

As he pondered the situation, he paid little attention to the rising clamor in the theater. What had begun as isolated screams turned into a full-fledged cacophony of horror as the panicked crowd herded like cattle to the exits. He ran to the side of the stage to turn on the house lights, hoping they would help bring calm. At the edge of the stage, he was hit solidly across the back. Falling forward in a flash of pain, he looked behind him to see Ronny, the stagehand, raising a metal folding chair over his head to dash him again. Will pushed through his pain to roll out of the way and used his legs to trip the young man. Ronny fell forward on his face, the chair crashing to the stage. Immediately, Will was on top of him, putting him in a chokehold and trying to speak sense to him. Ronny calmed, and Will let up only to find it had been feigned capitulation. Ronny threw Will off and rose to his feet. Will could see no sense of reason in the young man. They had worked together for months now, but Ronny looked through Will with not even a hint of recognition. Like a wild animal, he foamed at the mouth and lunged as Will managed to tuck and roll out of reach.

Scrambling to his feet, Will ran across the stage to his crossbow. He shouted a warning to Ronny, telling him to stay away, and then yanked an arrow from the spinning wheel. The man stared at him blankly for a moment, as if searching for sanity to make sense of the situation. Then his face contorted into a grotesque mask of rage and he charged. Will's arrow was true, striking Ronny in the heart. He fell. Will's mind spun, refusing to accept the brewing catastrophe. Just seconds before, it had been an ordinary night. Now all hell was breaking loose. Literally. He could feel the tenor in the room change as if some insidious darkness had inhabited the area.

He collected his wits, resuming his original track. At the light panel, he dimmed the stage lights and turned up the house lights, hoping to quell the panic. Looking out over the audience, Will estimated about a quarter of them had exploded in inexplicable rage, as they punched, hit, kicked, and bit at anyone near—imitations of the rage in the man he had just killed. Killed! The very thought of it left Will dead in his tracks.

At some point, one of the sane, terrified members of the audience sought the exit behind the stage. She ran past Will, who stood motionless with his bow raised in case the woman had the mind to attack him. Seeing her run past, others bolted onto the stage as well, followed by their mindless pursuers. Will knew he had to get out before another crazed one took after him. Running to the spinning wheel, he yanked down each arrow and shoved them into his quiver, fearing he would need them before he got to safety.

And he did, on two occasions. He realized that, for the most part, the insurrectionists were mindless. Like enraged wild animals, they fought anyone in sight. Will managed to avoid them by staying close to buildings and hiding in the shadows. With his back to a building, he would slide along it and wait at its end for a lull in the crowd, during which he would run at full speed across the open space to the safety of the next building. The strategy worked well for him through the relative calm of the business district. When he made it out of downtown and to the more residential areas, things got tougher.

Employing the same strategy, Will made his way through a street of row houses. He heard gunshots and explosions just ahead of him as people shot out the streetlights. The suddenly dark neighborhood filled with endless screams—screams of rage, screams of agony, and screams of betrayal—as loved ones suddenly became mortal enemies.

He kept his mind focused on only one thing: getting the hell out of the city. He shut down his thoughts to make sense of the situation, to determine a cause for the sudden plunge into insanity. There were no answers. Sliding off the side of one brownstone, he hurriedly took the few steps to the cover of another, where he paused to survey the area around him. Without streetlights, there was no real telling where he was, but he sensed he was heading in the direction of the airport. And that was fine with him. A plane to anywhere would be fantastic.

With inhuman speed, a window behind his head was thrown open. He didn't have time to duck out of the way before a set of hands seized his neck from behind. In stunned shock, he tried to turn to see his attacker, but the vicelike hands squeezed relentlessly.

Will tried to speak, but no air left his throat. And no air entered. His lungs burned as the hands tightened their Herculean grip. Arms flailing, Will lashed backward at the man accosting him, making solid connections with the arms and head. But the psychotic attacker held on tight. Will's flailing left hand found his quiver. Taking an arrow, he pointed it behind him and thrust it at the attacker's head. The arrow stuck, and the man howled like an animal. And still he held on. Will stabbed again and again, feeling each time the first tight resistance followed by a yielding of flesh to the arrow. Finally, the tension around his neck gave way. He fell forward to the ground and lay there gasping for air. He turned to see the face of his dead attacker. Repeated thrusts with the arrow had left it looking like so much chopped meat hanging from the window. Turning away, Will vomited into the street. Barely able to stand, he ran haphazardly to the next building.

As he moved farther into the suburbs, things quieted down. There was still the occasional scream of terror, but the sheer reduction in the number of people in the streets made passage much easier. On a particularly quiet street, Will felt safe enough to pause for a second. He grabbed his cell phone. Maybe he could call 9-1-1, the police, or someone he knew. If nothing else, maybe he could get a news feed to find out what was happening. The phone was dead. The battery was charged, but there was no service. He tried to click into his photos just to get a glimpse of Allison, but the screen was frozen on the No Service announcement.

"Damn," he muttered just before he heard the sound behind him. He turned quickly to see a shirtless bald old man charging him. He screamed a warning, not wanting to hurt the old fellow. But the man was seized with the madness and hatred twisted his face.

"Stop!" Will warned as he quickly cocked an arrow into the cross-bow and backed away. He thought he could easily put distance between him and his aged pursuer, but he was wrong. With almost inhuman speed, the old man leapt at him, screaming in a foreign language. To Will, it sounded like German. He barely managed to duck and roll out of the man's way, spilling the arrows from his quiver.

His aged attacker sprawled to the pavement as Will found his footing. Quickly gathering the arrows, he pushed them into the quiver and ran from the man at full speed, but the old fellow gained on him. Will's breaths became heavy. He turned to look behind him and saw that the man hadn't tired. "Impossible!" he exclaimed with a shallow breath. Finally, he knew he would have to make a stand. He pushed with all his might to gain as much distance as possible and then stopped short, throwing himself down on one knee.

He screamed at the man in a panicked plea as he loaded the bow, "Stop, old fellow. Stop!"

The man screamed back gibberish and kept coming.

"Stop! Please!" Will pleaded to no avail. Taking aim, he fired and brought the man down.

Lying on his pine-needle bed, Will wept. He had never been a violent person. He had never even hunted with the crossbow. He had honed his aim only for show, never to kill. Yet in the past few hours he had been forced to kill three people. How could he ever live with that? He rolled over to a fetal position and heaved in huge sobs. Eventually the sobs subsided, his pain giving way to troubled sleep.

———————————

"Will, it's time to wake up," the voice called. "Come on, Son, wake up."

Will awoke with a start. He found himself on a plush velvet sofa in an immense wood-paneled drawing room. At the entrance to the room, a man beckoned. Will stood groggily and walked toward him. As he got closer, he realized it was almost like looking in a mirror. The man was a bit taller and more thickly built, but the flashing green eyes could have been his own.

"Where am I?" he asked with a half grin.

The man's half grin matched his own. "It's where I grew up," he said as the grin broke into a full-blown smile. The love and care pouring forth from this man was palpable. Will could swear he saw shimmering light surround the guy.

"Come on, I'll show you around and tell you a little bit about myself." Will followed him through a grand foyer. His eyes followed the glistening mahogany of an intricately carved staircase rising one, two, three stories from the ground floor.

"This is the formal part of the house," the man said dismissively as they passed the large dining room with its highly polished inlaid floor and gargantuan table. Will quickly counted twenty chairs around it. "And those are the offices," he said, pointing to a suite of rooms.

"Offices?"

"At first, my mom used them just for the family business. But when I got older, I also used one to manage a network of orphanages. But this isn't the comfortable part of the house."

"House?" Will asked. "I'd call it a mansion!"

"We just called it 'home.' It was always a haven for us. When the world was crazy, there was always this house, which my mom filled with love." He led Will to the back of the house, where there was a room with a wall full of windows overlooking a finely manicured garden. Through the windows, Will could see a much smaller building with stained glass windows. He was captivated by the sense of peace in this room dominated by a large off-white sectional couch and two leather easy chairs.

"That's our chapel," the man said with pride. "I wasn't much into religion at first, but by the time I was in my thirties, I fell in love with Jesus and spent a lot of time with Him there."

"I wouldn't know," Will said with a shrug. "I've always been pretty much an atheist."

"That's not exactly true," the man said with a knowing smile. He sat in one of the recliners and motioned for Will to take the other.

"What do you mean?" Will asked defensively. "You don't even know me." He tilted his recliner back. The soft leather cradled him, and he blew a sigh of relief.

"You've had a tough life, and you've come to believe God couldn't exist or else He would have helped you out a bit."

"That's true," Will said coldly.

"But deep down, it's more than that. You believe in God as a heavenly Father who abandoned you to an uncertain life."

"If you say so," Will said nonchalantly to hide how the man's statement had hit home. He returned the recliner to the seated position.

The man slapped Will's knee. "I'm hungry. And if I'm not mistaken, my mom probably has some cherry pie in the kitchen. She makes the best pies. Are you hungry?"

"Famished," Will said with a smile.

"Well, come on, then. There's a coffee brewer on the counter and cups in the cabinet above it. Why don't you pour us each a cup of coffee while I plate up some pie?"

Will did as he was told. After the day he had had, the coffee smelled heavenly. He thought to himself, *I must be dreaming ... but everything seems so real: the coffee smell, the clean smell of the "house," the softness of the leather recliner.* He took the coffee to the kitchen table, on which the man was placing two plates of cherry pie and vanilla ice cream.

Will tasted his pie after he seated himself at the table. He had never tasted anything so good. "Your mom sure does make a great pie," he said as he took another bite.

"To tell you the truth, she's my adopted mom," the man said. "My birth mom met up with a guy who was only serious about one thing. He wanted nothing to do with her when she turned up pregnant."

"Nice freaking guy!" Will said. He could hear the anger at his own father in the statement.

"I'll say. Anyway, Michele, my birth mother, got into drugs and prostitution. She was strung out a lot. It was tough going for me until I met a boy named Michael. We just had this connection. Have you ever met someone and it was like you'd known that person forever?"

"Not until just now," Will said with a sheepish grin and a mouthful of pie. "I've been pretty much a loner."

The man put his arm on Will's shoulder. An overpowering sense of love enveloped Will. He had never felt so cared for.

"Well, anyway. This kid became my best friend. We did everything together. This is where Michael lived." The man swept his arm to indicate the estate. "I was here one weekend when Michele overdosed. Michael's mother adopted me and made me one of the family."

"Wow," Will said, thinking how he would have been very happy to have someone save him from his surroundings when he was growing up.

"You know the weirdest thing?" the man asked.

"Weirder than having some rich woman swoop in and give you a mansion to live in?"

The man grinned. "Even weirder than that. It turned out Michael and I had the same deadbeat dad. We really were brothers."

"So that was the connection you felt," Will said, absorbed in the story.

"Yep," the man answered. "And we lived a happy life here, although I went through some rough growing pains. The family was pretty religious, but I wasn't. I liked to live on the edge. Then in my thirties, I had an encounter with Jesus. I realized He wasn't a concept or an idea, but a real person—or, to be more precise, a real personal God who came to earth to die for my sins."

"I can't relate," Will said.

"Not yet." The man smiled and continued with his story. "I married a wonderful woman. We had great kids, a boy and a girl. I ran orphanages and wrote books about the end times."

"My girlfriend used to talk about the end times. She said there would be a rapture and ..." Will dropped his fork. Allison had been taken in the rapture. He knew it now. The reality struck him hard. She had told him of the horrible darkness that would befall the world after Jesus took His own to heaven with Him.

"The rapture was a real event, Son," the man said, looking deeply into Will's eyes. "One minute I was doing my thing, and the next I had been transformed into a resurrected body."

"So, you're like, what, a ghost?" Will asked.

"No." The man grinned. "I'm as real as I ever was. More real, in fact, but the resurrection body can operate in more dimensions than the four I used to inhabit."

"This is all too weird for me," Will said, suddenly wishing he could awake from this dream.

"I understand," the man said softly. "For just a few brief moments, the Lord allows us to visit with those left behind in dreams and visions to accomplish His will."

"And His will is that I have cherry pie with you," Will said in sarcastic disbelief.

The man chuckled. "Yes, but there's more. Will, when I was your age, I was a bit of a cad. I chased alcohol and the ladies pretty hard. I signed onto the crew of a cruise ship. I used to think I was doing young girls a service by providing them with fantasy sex."

Will stared in horror at the eyes that were so like his own. He had a sense of where this conversation was going. This man to whom he had connected so easily was his father.

The man continued. "With those women, I used the last name Michele gave me, rather than my adopted name, to keep the women from finding me. I used the name Marron."

Tears flooded Will's eyes. He jumped up from the table and stormed out the back door. He didn't know where he was or where he was going, but he knew he needed to get away from the man he had hated most of his life. Ahead of him, beyond the manicured garden brimming with multicolored rows of tulips, the chapel windows shone in the sun—radiant hues of garnet, azure, and emerald. With no understanding of why, he ran to it. Throwing the doors open, he fell into the small building. He looked behind him at the doors he had just come through and threw the deadbolt, locking out the man who had abandoned him. Then he turned to find that the man was standing behind him.

Hot tears stained his cheeks. "How could you live here in all this luxury knowing you had a son out there?"

"I didn't know," the man said passionately. "Will, if I had known, I would have swept you into my arms and brought you here to live with me. It pains me that I let you grow up without a father, without all of this." He took Will by the shoulders. When he did, that overwhelming feeling of love surrounded Will again. He fell into his father's embrace in a flood of tears.

"The worst thing of all," his father said, "is that I could have introduced you to Jesus. You could have been with me on this side of heaven if only I had known."

"So you didn't abandon me?" Will sobbed.

"Never," the man said. "I would never, never have abandoned you had I known about you."

"You have no idea how much it means to hear that," Will said with his head buried in his father's chest.

The man said, "My name's Gabe, by the way, but my other kids call me Dad."

"I'd love to call you Dad," Will said as he awoke on his bed of pine needles. Early morning sunlight danced through the surrounding pines. Sitting up, he said to himself, "Whoa! That was some dream."

"Maybe," a voice said behind him. He turned to see Gabe silhouetted in the sunlight.

"Dad," Will said softly, as if saying it too loudly would break the spell.

"Yeah, Son," Gabe said with a half grin.

Will rose to meet him, staring into the face so much like his own.

Gabe said, "You understand I can't stay with you, right?"

"Sure," Will said, unable to hide the disappointment in his voice.

"Look, Son, it's a long story, but my brother, Michael, wasn't taken in the rapture. You guys are going to need each other."

"How will I find him?" Will asked.

"Just stay here for a few days until the madness dies down."

"Will it?"

"This anarchy is called the Dark Awakening. It will continue

59

for only a brief period of time. I want you to wait it out right here." Gabe jerked his head to indicate the area behind him and to his right. "There's a stream back there. You'll have water. Berries are growing along the bank, and there are plenty of fish."

"How will I know when it's time to leave?"

"You'll know; trust me," Gabe said with a smile. His form faded as he said, "I have to go now, Son. I think we have time for a hug."

Will threw himself into his father's strong arms. As he held him close, Gabe vanished. Will sat down on the pine needles. A forlorn look crossed his brow. "I forgot to ask him what my real last name is." But in some way, it no longer mattered. He hadn't been abandoned. Years of anger, fear, and loathing had been exorcised from his psyche. Relieved of the psychological burden, he felt as light as a feather. Now he knew he had a dad who loved him. On the worst day of his life, Will felt better than he had ever felt.

He sat in the early morning light, thinking … and waiting.

SIX

t was a stifling hot day in Houston, Texas. It was also humid. But the oppressive heat was only a mirror of a greater oppression gripping Gloria. The past few days had rocked her world. She was lost in despair as she sat in her bedroom. Her husband, Zack, wasn't home. At least she could be thankful for that. She needed time alone to think, to sort things out. Her mind ticked through recent events.

After returning home from a weekend in Georgia, her mother and stepfather had come to Gloria's mansion to confront Zack about his infidelity. It wasn't just any infidelity; it was with Michael's creepy uncle Benny—and in the chapel on Kim's estate no less. The very thought was lunacy to Gloria. There was definitely a dark side to Zack's character, but she didn't believe him to be capable of such actions. And then, poof, her mother and David were gone in a flash of lightning.

When it happened, Gloria's mind reeled. Her father, a missionary to Africa, used to talk a lot about end-times prophecy and how his generation was the one that would see the return of Jesus. Unfortunately for him, he was murdered during the fall of Idi Amin's regime. Any serious consideration of the rapture and tribulation events died with him in Gloria's mind. She had taken the pain of that tragedy and turned it into a disdain for the theology that had, to her mind, contributed to his murder.

Her life had been a series of actions to flee from the events of Africa. She had married Zack and wholeheartedly adopted his brand of Christianity that emphasized the here and now—not the there and then of the gospels, and not the where and when of eschatology. It was easy to buy into. His ministry had catapulted them to the kind of fame and glamour traditionally held for the Hollywood elite. She looked around at the exquisitely appointed master bedroom of their mansion on the Gulf of Mexico. The fresco-painted walls in pastel colors invited the deep blue of the Caribbean Sea to nestle snugly between floor-to-ceiling white linen drapes. To call it beautiful would be an understatement, but she would trade it all for the opportunity to undo the horrible decisions that had gotten her here.

Tears ran down her face, marking her perfectly applied makeup. She wiped at the tears and noticed the mascara and foundation on her hand. Jumping off of her bed in an angry refutation of the bowl of porridge for which she had sold her Christian birthright, she stormed into the master bath and scrubbed furiously at her face. She wanted to lose every bit of it, every microscopic tinge of tint that had so blinded her to the reality of who she had become. The scrubbing was compulsive and fierce. Finally, when her face stung from the abrasion and she had removed all of the makeup, she fell to the floor. Pulling her knees to her chest, she sat with her head down and thought about the past few days.

Immediately after her mother and David had disappeared, she looked around the house in stunned disbelief as the loudest thunderclap echoed around her and Zack, shaking the mansion. Fear and panic took over as her mind filled with her father's teachings.

"Oh, Lord!" she screamed as she fell to her knees. Looking up, she saw a smug grin form on Zack's face, where horror and agony should have resided. "Zack!" she screamed. "It was the rapture, and we weren't taken!"

Zack laughed heartily. "Calm down, Gloria," he said with nearly mechanical precision. Something had overtaken him, as if a previously hidden dark part of his personality had exploded to the surface. He offered his hand to help her stand. She ignored it. His eyes darkened from light blue to black as he grabbed her and yanked her to her feet.

"Stand up!" he screamed. She had never seen him like this.

"Zack!" she yelled back. "You're hurting me!"

He cupped her face in his hands. The action could have been tender if his hands weren't holding her with vicelike tension.

"I need you to calm down, Gloria," he said softly. "Everything will be fine."

"How can you say that?" she moaned.

"Because it's the beginning of a new world. We talked about this. We knew this time would come. Now we'll see an expanded gospel. Our son will come with healing in his wings." Zack grinned and stared into the distance as if having a beautiful vision. For Gloria, it was the unfolding of a nightmare. She had long since put out of her mind the strange pregnancy that had resulted in the hybrid alien being Zack referred to as their son. She winced at the thought of interaction with the Lady, the strange alien being that had so easily beguiled Zack. She pushed her hands to her ears.

"Stop it, Zack!" she screamed. "I don't want to hear this. I can't take it right now." She broke into a primordial wail as thoughts of her father's preaching rang in her ears.

Zack removed his hands from her face and drew her into a tight hug. He held her close out of habit, but she couldn't sense any love. His harsh demeanor was a warning. She placated him and yielded to his body.

He stroked her hair for a few moments and spoke softly to her. "We knew the old Christian paradigm was dying, darlin'. We've been preaching for years about a softer, more inclusive gospel with power to unite the world. Your parents, and mine for that matter, could never really accept it. They were taken out of the way, that's all."

"I don't follow," she said calmly into his chest as her mind raced.

"Maybe some of that old rapture talk was more than a bunch of superstition. Maybe Jesus knew a time would come for some revision and that the people holding back the message would have to be removed. You're reacting fearfully because you think you've been left behind to endure terrible judgment. It's simply not the case." He released his grip.

She backed away from him to the camelback cream sofa in the formal drawing room. Forcing herself to move calmly, she sat gracefully. He sat next to her—very close. Looking deeply into his dark eyes, she asked, "So, you think maybe it was the rapture but that it's not bad that we weren't taken?"

"It's just a changing of dispensations," he said softly as he took her hand in his. "Think about it. When the Dispensation of the Law was enacted, the Israelites couldn't really accept it. An entire generation had to die off in the desert before they could move ahead to the Promised Land. When Jesus came to introduce the Dispensation of

Grace, many of the people of His day couldn't accept it. It's how God's revelation unfolds, Gloria."

She shook her head involuntarily, caught herself, and stopped. "You're saying we're moving into a new dispensation?"

He nodded vigorously, wide-eyed. "I'd call it the Dispensation of Enlightenment. We've learned the lessons of law and grace. Now it's time for us to move ahead."

"Dispensation of Enlightenment," she said thoughtfully. Her mind was yielding to him. He could be very persuasive. "But what about Mom and David?" she asked, a catch in her voice.

He patted her hand and smiled. "I'm sure they're fine."

"Do you think they're dead?" she asked.

"No, probably just moved out of the way. They served God the best they could, and I'm sure He rewarded them. But their mind-set didn't fit our new understanding of God." His voice rose with passion. "What were your parents preaching? Self-sacrifice. Self-debasement in the hopes of becoming like the Jesus of history. Instead they should have been like the overcomer Jesus who took control of His surroundings. We're all destined to ascension, Gloria. That was Jesus's message."

"Zack, there's a two-thousand-year history of people believing something different."

"No, Gloria, there's a two-thousand-year period where the original message got distorted. Christianity became a political device of division. Do you really think Jesus intended the Crusades, the Inquisition, or the constant bickering that came out of the Reformation?"

"Probably not," she conceded.

He squeezed her hands and looked deeply into her eyes. "No. Jesus taught us to overcome all of this. The world is ready to take a quantum leap forward."

"Do you really think so?" she asked. His hands felt soft and warm. She felt herself being lulled further and further into his way of thinking.

"That's what our child is all about. He's going to usher in a golden age for humanity. And we're a part of it."

"We don't even know where he is ... or who he is."

"I'm not so sure of that," he said with a grin. I've been waiting for him for years, and I've been watching. Keep your eyes on this guy from Turkey, Isa Kurtoglu. I think he's the One."

"How do you know?"

"It's more of a feeling than anything else. Time will tell." He punctuated his pronouncement with a nod and a huge grin, the same expression he fed the cameras when recording a sermon.

They spoke for over an hour as he pulled her in line with his train of thought. There was little doubt he was manipulating her, but she took such comfort in his words. For years she had been hurt that Jesus had taken her father too early. Now He had taken her mother too. Zack offered hope. If she believed in the old paradigm, she faced damnation. It was too much to bear.

Later she and Zack made love, and she fell asleep in his arms.

They were wakened early in the morning by screams, the furious ringing of the doorbell, and an incessant pounding at the front door. Zack jumped up and pulled on some shorts while Gloria pulled on a robe. They ran from the master suite down the stairs and into the grand foyer. Gloria recognized the voice of Bonnie, Zack's secretary.

As Zack swung the door open, Bonnie fell into his arms. "They're gone! My kids are gone, Zack!" she screamed as she buried her head into his bare chest, caressing it as she cried. Gloria cringed. She moved closer to comfort the younger woman and to pry her from her husband.

"No, Gloria!" Bonnie screamed as she pushed her away. "This is between Zack and me." Gloria stepped back in shock to assess the situation as Bonnie turned again to Zack.

"Feel my stomach! Our baby is gone, Zack! He disappeared with my other kids."

"Our baby?" Gloria screamed, yanking the girl away from her husband. "Zack! What is she talking about?" she demanded in a shrill voice.

"Not now, Gloria," Zack said through clenched teeth, not looking at her.

"Yes. Now!" she screamed in reply.

"We were pregnant," Bonnie spat. "All along Zack has been in love with me, Gloria."

Zack held Bonnie fiercely at arm's length. Turning to Gloria, he protested with wide eyes, "I have no idea what she's talking about!"

At that remark, Bonnie shrieked in grief and threw herself to the floor. "You told me you loved me, Zack. Only me," she moaned.

Gloria felt the blood pressure ringing in her ears. "How long has this been going on, Zack?" she snapped, gesturing to the wailing woman on the floor.

"It's not what you think, Gloria," he said sheepishly. "There was a brief encounter. That's all. Bonnie got pregnant, and I told her to have an abortion."

"I'm supposed to be comforted that you tried to cover infidelity with murder?" Gloria shrieked.

"Not like you said it," Zack pleaded. "I would never put our ministry—all of this—at risk."

"You said you loved me, Zack," Bonnie moaned. "Gloria, he told me it was over between you and him years ago. I swear!"

"And it didn't dawn on you, Bonnie, that Zack and I were still together? *Were* is the operative word here, Zack," she barked. Covering her face with her hands, she forced back the tears. She wouldn't give into Zack's ego to let him see two women crying over him.

She bent down and offered Bonnie help to stand. "Is it true, Bonnie? Was this just a brief encounter?"

"No," Bonnie answered with a bit more composure. "It's been going on for years. He told me you had stopped sleeping together, that the marriage was a sham for the sake of the ministry."

"Well, that was a bald-faced lie, Bonnie," Gloria said, staring a hole into Zack.

Bonnie moaned deeply. "I'm beginning to see that."

Gloria spat, "Yeah, well, I'm beginning to see a lot of things too. You can kiss your precious ministry good-bye, Zack. I'm done!" She stomped to the stairs.

Zack caught her in seconds. Spinning her around, he erupted, saying, "You should know by now, Gloria, that I'll do whatever it takes to protect this ministry. If I do it without you, it will be because I'm a widower." He shook her fiercely. "Do you understand me? Do you?"

She pushed him hard. He fell back a step and then punched her solidly in the face. She reeled, stars in her eyes. Turning to the stairs, she held the bannister to get her balance. Zack stomped away from her.

"Do you want to see how far I'll go, Gloria? Do you want to *see*?" he raged. In two quick strides, he stormed to Bonnie and clamped his hands around her neck. Bonnie struggled to get away, but he held her more fiercely, jerking her back and forth like a predator with its prey.

Light-headedness from the punch began to dissipate. Gloria ran to Zack's side, suddenly becoming the protector of the woman who had tried to usurp her.

"No, Zack!" she yelled as she yanked at his arms to pull him from the gurgling woman.

"Back off, Gloria!" he screamed as he threw his elbow to her face. The second blow knocked her to the floor. For a brief second she passed out. When she came to, Zack was standing over Bonnie's lifeless body.

"Zack," she moaned. "What have you done?"

"What I should have done a long time ago, Gloria," he snapped. He took a step toward her and kicked her hard in the side. She doubled over in pain, assuming the fetal position.

Speaking in a shrill staccato, he tried to justify his actions. "Sure, the affair with Bonnie was a mistake. I was trying to manage it, trying to move past it." He strode around the large foyer like a caged animal. "You don't understand the pressure I'm under! Every once in a while, Bonnie gave me some relief. That's all. I only ever loved you. Don't you see that? Don't you see that?"

He bent to grab a handful of her hair and pulled her face millimeters from his. His hot breath assaulted her. "We are together, Gloria. And we will *always* be together. Till death do we part, darlin', so get used to it." He released her, and she staggered to her feet.

She bitterly said, "I never knew you," and turned from him.

One more time, he grabbed her by the hair and pulled her to him. His hands folded around her throat and applied increasing pressure as he spoke. "I'm going to dispose of that trash, darlin'," he said as he motioned over his shoulder to Bonnie's lifeless body. "When I get back, I want to see you dressed. And I want some by-God makeup covering the bruise forming on your cheek. Do you understand me?" He increased the pressure, making it hard for her to answer.

Slowly, deliberately, she gasped, "Yes."

He let go of her and stomped over to Bonnie's body. He kicked it once for good measure, threw it over his shoulder, and headed to the garage.

Stunned and disillusioned, Gloria did what Zack had told her to do. She dressed and put on makeup. As the shock wore off, she found her resolve to scrub it away.

"Oh God, what am I going to do?" she cried to the empty bathroom.

"There's only one answer," came a familiar voice. She looked up to see her father, young and vibrant as he had been years before in Africa. Beside him stood her mother, beautiful and young.

"Oh, Daddy," she cried as he helped her to her feet and held her close. She remembered every detail of the man: his scent, the softness of his skin, and the kindness of his embrace. Slowly her hand played with the soft blond curls at his collar as she had as a child.

"Gloria," Fran said as she rubbed her daughter's back, "only Jesus can save you now."

"Oh, Mom," Gloria cried as she used one arm to pull her mother into their family embrace. "Can you ever forgive me?"

"No grudges in heaven, sweetheart," Frannie said with a smile. It was a line she often used on Gloria when she was growing up.

"But I was so wrong. And I was so rude to you and David."

"I'm sure David forgave it all," Fran said kindly.

"So, Zack and I have been wrong all these years?" she asked through sobs.

"There's no salvation outside of Jesus," her father said decisively. "You knew that when you were little, but you just couldn't get over my death."

"I never thought I'd see you again," she whined.

Tom moved a bit of hair from her face. "Do you remember what the prophet Joel said about the Latter Days?"

"That there would be dreams and visions?" Gloria asked.

"That's right, pumpkin." He smiled. Her heart leapt at the sound of his nickname for her.

"Your mother and I are here only by the grace of Jesus. We have a short time to talk with you and to invite you to be with us in heaven one day."

"Gloria, words can't describe the beauty, peace, and love there," Fran said.

"I was disappointed not to see you, pumpkin. So were Grandma and Grandpa."

Gloria began to cry deep, heaving sobs. What she wouldn't do to go back and change things.

Pulling away from her father, she looked into his beautiful blue eyes. "Daddy, I don't know if Jesus can forgive me. You see, there was this baby and—"

"You weren't a willing participant," Frannie said with the ferocity of a mother lion protecting her cub. "Zack tricked you. And there were some very powerful spiritual beings pulling strings."

"I don't know," she said. "After a while I bought into it, Mom."

Fran nodded and smiled. "I agree, sweetie, but I can assure you of one thing: if it were too late for you, Jesus wouldn't let us be here."

In the distance, they heard the front door slam. "Gloria?" Zack bellowed from the foyer.

"There won't be many more opportunities for you to set things right," Tom said forcefully.

"How do I know this isn't just some hallucination?" she asked, confused.

"Gloria?" Zack called, running up the stairs. His pull on her was amazing.

"We're not a hallucination," Fran said in the type of kind but stern voice that only a mother can muster. "Gloria, I don't want to live in eternity without my baby."

There was a pounding at the bathroom door. "Gloria!" Zack screamed. "Don't do it! We have so much to look forward to."

"Easy words from a man who has cheated on you, beaten you, and tricked you with seducing spirits," Tom said sternly.

"Is it really as simple as the Sinner's Prayer?" Gloria asked.

"Yes," Tom assured her, "but you have to mean it."

The pounding on the door had given way to huge thuds as Zack attempted to break it down, all the while furiously screaming Gloria's name.

"Father," Gloria prayed, "You know how I've betrayed You and Your Son. I know there is nothing I could ever do to make it up to You. I know now there is no salvation outside of Jesus. I ask You to accept me into Your family through the blood that Jesus shed for me on the cross. And I promise, Lord, never to forsake You again. I ask this in Jesus's name."

"Amen," said Tom as he swept her into his arms.

"Amen," Fran echoed joyously.

"Oh, Mom," Gloria cried out as Tom handed her off to her mother. She cried, this time tears of unspeakable joy as the Holy Spirit flooded into her. As she peered at the events of her life from a perspective of eternal forgiveness, she could see how misled she had been. The clarity of mind astounded her.

The wood of the bathroom door began to splinter in the barrage of Zack's blows. She could hear the Lord in the voice of her father as he said, "God has made a promise not to remember your sins. You are white as snow in His eyes now, pumpkin."

"I know," she said with assurance. "I can feel it, Daddy." For the first time since she had been a child she felt totally at peace. The entire room had a soft glow about it. "I can't wait until I'm with you guys and Jesus for good."

"Well, the good news is that it won't be long before everything changes for the better on earth," Tom said. "But the next several years are going to be terrible, Gloria. You need to steel yourself against the tide of deception with the Word of God. Really get into the Bible."

"And pray constantly," Fran said. "Even though things are going to look bad, know that they will come to a wonderful end."

"Play the hand you've been dealt," Tom said. He hugged her, and an instantaneous download of information flooded her mind. She knew what she had to do.

"I love you," she said to Tom. "Mom, I love you so much. Only now do I appreciate how much you went through to raise me without Daddy around."

"I waited a lifetime to hear those words." Fran smiled warmly as she held her daughter close.

"But we have to go now, pumpkin. Trust Jesus," Tom said softly.

Zack was frantic. He had been pounding the door with a chair for minutes. The wood on the door had splintered, but the door itself never gave way. What a horrible day this had been. He and Gloria were supposed to come through this as the hottest ministers ever to hit the stage. He could see all the money and fame going down the tubes if he lost her. He feared he had pushed her to commit suicide.

Why else would she have barricaded herself in the bathroom, refusing to answer him?

If only he had let Bonnie die of poison when he had the chance, none of this would have happened. He would be sitting pretty right now, strategizing the future with Gloria, forever out of the gaze of that disapproving shrew of a mother-in-law.

He had to stop Gloria. He had to win her back to the cause at any cost. There was too much to be lost. As he swung at the door another time, it was thrown open. A man with a fierce expression stared at him malignantly. From photos, he recognized the man to be Gloria's father. Behind him stood Fran, the old battle-axe, herself, staring at him smugly. It was just a glimpse of them before they turned into bright, hot, white light. Energy erupted from them in a tremendous burst that knocked Zack to the floor.

Horrible fear gripped him as Gloria strode through that light—more confident and self-assured than he had ever seen her. Looking down at him, she said sternly, "You're wrong, Zack. You've *always* been wrong."

SEVEN

Michele instinctively rolled to the ground at the sound of the second shot. With only her knowledge of the terrain, she ran in a crouched position toward the dim flickering candlelight in the windows of the chapel. She had to get to the bunker. Mimi had stocked it with weapons. Although Michele had never shot a gun, she felt sure she could do so if pushed.

"Jesus, please help me," she prayed as another shot rang out. She cringed at the breeze of a bullet as it whizzed past her head. How could the intruder see her so well in the dark? She dove for a row of hedges and stayed among them as she made her way to the chapel's entrance. She yanked on the door. It was locked. Feeling her pockets, she hoped against hope she hadn't returned the key to its place earlier. Nothing there.

Although she had paused only briefly, it was all the time her pursuer needed. Hearing a feral growl, she turned to find the demonically distorted face of a teenage boy. Her mind raced. Dad had believed in the ability of Christians to confront evil. It was her only hope.

"Stop in the name of Jesus!" she screamed with authority. The boy stood still, tilting his head as if a saner part of his personality had struggled to the surface. He threw the gun at her.

"Kill me!" he screamed. "Kill me before I go crazy again."

Picking up the gun, she pointed it at him. "I … I can't," she cried.

"Aaagh!" the boy screamed. "It hurts so bad. Kill me. Please."

"I can offer you peace of mind," she said with deliberate calm. "Jesus is your only help now."

At the mention of Jesus's name, the boy's face contorted again and his voice deepened to a growl. "Jesus? We hate Him. He's the enemy of everything we love."

"No!" Michele screamed as the madness returned to him. "Fight the temptation. Don't let this thing ruin you."

He grabbed at the gun. She sidestepped. He charged her. Although he was only slightly bigger than her younger brother, his strength was tremendous.

"Give me the gun," he howled.

She tossed it with the hope he would leave her to find it.

A torrent of curses ensued. "I'll kill you with my bare hands," he screamed. In an instant he was on her, furiously pounding at her. Her hands found his throat. Putting her head down to shield it against the blows, she squeezed with all her might, vowing not to let go, and prayed as the barrage continued.

"I don't want to kill you!" she screamed, tightening her grip. Everything moved to slow motion as adrenalin raced through her. She intended to choke him until he passed out, and then run back to the house.

He coughed, gagged, and threw himself into her, slamming her into the chapel door. Her head hit hard; her grip on his throat loosened as she struggled to maintain consciousness. Before she could fall to the ground, he pinned her to the door with the full weight of his body. She closed her eyes against the visage in front of her. She felt the heat of his breath on her neck as his hands found their way to her breasts. *He's going to rape me!*

She began to pray. "Jesus. Jesus, help me ... please!" Managing to free one hand, she yanked furiously at the boy's hair, pulling out handfuls. He was impervious to the pain. She began to cry. He laughed, spurred on by her fear.

Over his shoulder she saw movement in the moonlight. Jimmy! He stumbled but remained amazingly quiet. The thing on her began to claw at her pants. She had to hold the boy's attention to give Jimmy time to act. Using her free hand, she gouged at his eyes.

He yelped and then screamed, "It's only gonna make it worse for you." He slapped her hard on the face and then kissed her furiously. The heat of his rancid breath assaulted her. She resisted. He slapped her again. As her mouth opened in pain, he found her. The taste of his mouth nauseated her. She bit ferociously down on his tongue, tasting hot, salty blood. He backed his head away and howled in pain as she spit out the piece she had bitten off.

"Am onna kill ou!" he screamed, unable now to form full words. Jimmy was standing directly behind the boy and to the right. Michele watched in horrified relief as Jimmy slowly placed the gun to her tormentor's temple and fired.

The boy's head jerked to one side, and Michele's head jerked to the other as it was pummeled with the spray of his blood and brains. He fell with a sickening thud.

Jimmy stepped over the body to catch Michele as she fell with relief. "Are you okay?" he asked as he held her close.

"I ... I don't know." She cried long heaving sobs against his shoulder as the adrenalin faded and reason returned. "Are you?"

He pointed to his left arm. "Bullet grazed my arm. Hurts like hell, but I think it'll be okay."

"Let's go back to the house, Jimmy. We can wait until daylight to deal with this," she said, motioning to the bloody corpse on the chapel steps.

They limped back to the house, wounded, weary, and war-torn. She showered to shed the intruder's blood and afterward bandaged Jimmy's arm before the two of them fell asleep in the reclining chairs of the family room. Jimmy slept with the intruder's gun on his lap.

After a few hours of sleep, they both awoke before dawn. Michele brewed coffee and doled out Advil for their pain.

"Thanks." Jimmy winced against the ache in his arm. "Michele, I'm sorry you weren't taken in the rapture, but I'm happy to have someone to talk to."

"I know what you mean."

"I should have listened to your parents," he said, pushing at a stray lock of brown hair that had fallen over his hazel eyes.

"We both should have listened to them. Where were you when it happened?" she asked, noticing the brightness of his teeth against his heavily bearded face. She had always found him to be particularly attractive. She remembered how her mother would grin knowingly when she turned up her hair and makeup a notch when Jimmy came to the house.

"I was in the gym refereeing a basketball game between our boys and the boys from the Gray's Woods orphanage. All of a sudden there was this burst of lightning. When the brightness faded, only Billy Watt and I were standing there. Then the thunder knocked us to the ground."

"I'll never forget that moment," Michele said with a faraway expression.

"Immediately, I knew what had happened. Your parents had been trying to get me to give my heart to Jesus since I was ten. And, of course, I read all of your father's books. But for some reason, I couldn't do it, especially after your uncle found that version of John's Gospel."

"Same here," she said. "I just thought my parents were old-fashioned and that they would come to their senses someday. It looks like I was the one who needed to come to her senses."

"Billy had come from a bad place. His parents worshipped Satan. He was a tough number when he came to the orphanage. Not only did he refuse to accept Jesus, but also he refused to claim anyone other than Lucifer as lord. With enough love and encouragement, your parents convinced him not to try to influence other kids."

"I was so busy growing up, I never really paid attention to my parents' work," she interrupted.

"Well, I can tell you this. I know of at least a hundred people who are in heaven right now because of your parents' work."

"And only God knows how many more due to my dad's books," she said, wiping a tear from her eye. "They're something else."

He nodded his agreement and continued his story. "Once the thunder subsided, I went to make sure Billy was okay. He's the guy who attacked you last night—you saw the expression on his face. He hit me so hard, it knocked me off my feet and I'm not a small man."

She took full measure of him. He was solidly built—handsomely built, in fact. "No, you're not."

"Michele, I'm telling you, Billy had some weird kind of otherworldly power. I'll admit I was afraid of him. Before I knew it, he grabbed the whistle around my neck and tried to strangle me with the cord. I had to fight like a wild man to get free. After that, I ran to the equipment cage and locked myself in. He threw himself against the cage over and over again. Then, suddenly, he stopped and left. I waited for a bit to make sure he was gone. When I heard a gunshot, I had no doubt he was coming back for me, so I ran."

"You ran all the way here?" she asked, knowing it was about a seven-mile drive.

"It's shorter when you go through the woods. I've camped, hunted, and fished in those woods. I know them pretty well. Plus, I could hear gunshots and screams from the road. I figured there were more like Billy out on the streets.

"Anyway, when I got here, the house was unlocked. I called out for everyone. Nobody answered. I figured everyone had been taken."

"I was in the chapel," she explained.

"I went to your dad's office and started reading one of his books. I figured I needed to brush up on what was going to happen so I could stay one step ahead. I guess I fell asleep.

"I had this dream about your parents. They told me Billy had followed me and that you were in danger. When I awoke, it was dark and I heard rustling noises in the hedges behind your father's office. I looked out the window, and there was Billy toting this gun and running in the backyard. I needed to find you in order to let you know we were in trouble."

"That's when I heard you and panicked," she said, filling in the pieces.

"I didn't want to call out to you because I was afraid of alerting Billy. Then I heard the alarm system shutting down. I ran after you to try to get you back in the house, but Billy found me."

She looked at their empty coffee cups. "I could use another. How about you?"

"Absolutely," he said.

"We have some eggs and bacon in the fridge. Are you hungry?"

"Absolutely," he said again with a grin.

"How do you like your eggs?"

"Over easy," he answered.

"Well, with my mother and Mimi doing all our cooking, I didn't learn a lot. I'll try for over easy, but they may turn out more like scrambled."

Michele finished digging the hole in the garden. Jimmy carried Billy's body over his shoulder, steadying it with his good arm.

"I've hunted deer, so I've been around dead things before. But it wasn't like this." He grunted as he unsuccessfully tried to lower the body gently into the hole. It landed with a thick thud.

Michele looked sadly down at the troubled teen's bloating body. The morning was already hot, and the body smelled of released bowel and bladder. "I'm going to need a few minutes before we finish this," she said.

"He's not going anywhere. Take all the time you need."

"That's the problem, Jimmy. We know where he's going. Yet everything inside me says we should give him a proper burial. I'm uncomfortable just throwing a pile of dirt on him."

"Have you made the decision to follow Jesus?" he asked.

"Yeah. That's pretty much what I was doing when you arrived yesterday."

He shrugged. "Well, you're more qualified to say something than I am."

"You haven't done it yet?" she asked as she sat on the grass by the flower bed. She inhaled deeply of the sweet scent, happy for a brief reprieve from the lingering smell of death.

"Well, to be fair, I've been a bit busy," he said, skirting the issue. He sat next to her.

"Really? Is that the only reason?" she asked, giving a slight chuckle at how much she sounded like her mother.

"I heard it too." He grinned. "Here's the thing. I felt so abandoned when my parents died. Even though your mom and dad took good care of me, I was mad at God. And now somewhere deep inside, I feel abandoned all over again."

She rubbed his thick shoulder. "Jimmy, He didn't abandon us. We abandoned Him. He did everything to save us, and we chose not to accept it." His shoulders heaved as tears flowed.

She spoke softly. "But we've been given another chance. There will be horrible times ahead, but He'll bring us through them to be with the people we love."

"I guess I still need more time," he said resolutely, wiping at the tears.

"I hear you. But remember this, Jimmy—the Bible predicts a deception to lead people away from Christ. It will never be easier than it is now to commit your life to Jesus."

"Now you sound like your dad," he teased. Standing, he grabbed the shovel with his good arm. "For health reasons alone, we probably should get Billy buried. What do you want to do?"

"Well, I know God is good, and He's gracious. Hopefully Billy had some clarity of mind and called on the Lord before his spirit left his body."

"I think that's wishful thinking," Jimmy said sullenly.

"No, just hopeful thinking. I'm going to pray for him." She bowed her head; Jimmy followed. "Father, we don't understand Your ways. You're too far above us. But we know Your compassion and Your grace, so we commend Billy's spirit to You. If there is a way, Lord, bless him. If not, at least know that we forgive him. Most importantly, we trust You and want to serve You well. We pray in Jesus's name. Amen."

"Amen," Jimmy echoed. With difficulty, he managed the first shovel of dirt. It made a fluffing sound against the body.

Michele wiped at her face. She desperately didn't want to cover this boy over, but it was obvious that Jimmy couldn't physically maneuver the shovel with one arm. "How about giving me the shovel?"

"Nah," he said awkwardly. "I can't let you do this by yourself. It's messy business."

"I have a funny feeling it's all going to be messy from here on out," she said, taking the shovel. "Take a rest."

He sat on the ground, and she threw her first shovelful of dirt. It made her weak in the knees to hear it hit the body. But it had to be done. She swallowed hard and willed her emotions to some back corner of her mind. Then she shoveled rhythmically and methodically until the task was completed. She was in a zone, and Jimmy didn't interrupt. If he had, she would have asked him to be quiet.

They continued in silence until the hole was filled. She smudged some dirt on her face when she wiped away a tear at the end of her task. Leaning against the shovel, she looked at Jimmy with a bittersweet smile. "That was hard. I'm happy it's over."

He opened his mouth but couldn't speak. He swallowed hard and tried again. "I've been thinking while watching you. A few days ago you were a goofy teenager, not a care in the world. Just now you acted with a strength and resilience I've never seen in anyone. It's like I can see the Spirit of God working in you." Her mind flashed to Grandpa Chris's frequent quoting of St. Francis, "Preach the gospel always, and if necessary use words."

"You sound like you're ready to commit to Christ," she said encouragingly.

"I am. Would it be okay with you if I spent some alone time in your chapel?"

"Absolutely." She smiled. As he stood, she walked to him and gave him a hug. He put his arm around her as they walked to the chapel. It felt very good to be in his embrace.

They stood at the chapel doors for a few seconds. She took his hand and said, "I'll be out here waiting for you." He nodded, offered a tentative smile, and went inside.

She sat on the chapel steps, letting the warm sun heal her. She would have given anything to do over the last couple of days, making the commitment to Him before the rapture. She was thankful to know Him now, but she missed her family so much! Grandpa Chris used to say, "Forgiveness of sin is God's gift through Christ, but the effects of sin can still impact our lives. Our actions and inactions still have consequences."

She sighed loudly, knowing she would have at least seven years to live through the consequences of not accepting Christ when it would have been easy to do so.

Looking over the manicured gardens of the estate, she took comfort in her memories: playing tennis with her brother Chris, swimming in the pool with her mom and dad. She hoped she could keep this enclave of peace during the harsh times to come.

She tilted her head to let the healing rays of sunlight fall on her face. The sky was unusually blue and clear. Her father had railed for years against chemtrails, the ominous streaks leaked constantly from the tails of planes. It seemed as if it had been years since she had seen such a crisp, unspoiled sky.

"Well, I guess the world is too messed up for them to cover up the sky today, Dad."

She took it all in with gratitude, knowing that prophecies told of a time when the atmosphere would be filled with smoke and haze. There would be a time when it would look as if the sun had lost the ability to shine.

"Get it while you can, girl," she told herself. She reveled in every detail, building a memory to keep her in the tough times to come. Then her eye caught sight of something unusual. She blinked and shook her head slightly to be sure it wasn't some trick of light and shadow. To the right of and below the sun, there looked to be a blue disk. It was almost unnoticeable against the blue of the sky. Smaller than the size of a full moon, its shape was barely visible, but it was there.

Staring at it and trying to decide what it could possibly be, she shuddered against a chill of incredulity and fear.

EIGHT

sa stood basking in the glow of the golden sun on the balcony of the Turkish presidential palace. In the square below, nearly a million people chanted over and over, "Mahdi ... Mahdi!" The Dark Awakening in the Middle East had taken the form of a sea of humanity demanding the return of the caliphate. Problems between Shiites and Sunnis evaporated as the tide for Isa's reign took effect. In Sunni eschatology, the Mahdi was to be a political figure that would prove himself by his ability to unite Islam. Shiite eschatology called for a more spiritual leader, a direct descendant of Mohammed. It was very easy for Isa to manipulate records to depict himself as descended from the Prophet through his wife Fatima. His unusual abilities sealed the deal for the Sunnis. His political prowess had built Turkey into the sole hegemonic power in the region, and his modern ways and European charm endeared him to other world leaders who were only too willing to back him as a stabilizing influence in the region.

The Dark Awakening's violence in the Middle East was targeted at the existing governments, freeing the way for the rise of the caliphate. A new supranational identity was formed over the course of hours as cries rang out for the restoration of the once-glorious Ottoman Empire.

"I promise you," he screamed into the microphone, "I will never dishonor your choice. My caliphate will rule the world!" He paused for an uproar of cheers. "Our days of being seen as the third world are over, my brothers and sisters. We will be the pinnacle of political unity, we will be the best society has to offer, and we will set the course of human history. We ... will ... be ... victorious ... throughout ... the ... ends ...

of … this … earth!" he screamed at fever pitch, thereby invoking even greater cheers from the ravenous crowd.

He motioned for them to be quiet. They dropped to silence as if he were the conductor of a faithful orchestra. "Don't be dismayed, my brothers, but there is still much work to be done," he said in a hushed tone. "The West is falling as we speak. Governments are toppling. We must remain strong and united to fill the resulting vacuum. Therefore, I call on all here to solemnly pledge your allegiance to me." The crowd began to murmur, with first a few, and then more, people saying, "I swear allegiance," until it grew to a chant and then to screams of faithfulness to the new caliph.

Once he had dismissed the crowd, he hurried down the hallway to the palace's large ballroom. The immense room with gold-overlaid intricate molding and Persian rugs of cream, gold, and gray had been fitted with rows of cloth-covered tables. Assembled before him were some of the top scientists of the world who had been gathered at a conference in Geneva when the Dark Awakening fell. The Turkish Air Force had rescued them and brought them to the palace. Still charged with the energy of the crowd below, Isa strode into the room.

"Gentlemen," he said as he moved to the podium. The scientists had been briefed and were told to prepare a presentation for him. At first they had refused, given the highly classified nature of the information, but these giants of science were easily broken with the pedestrian methods employed by Isa's security force. "I believe you have prepared a presentation for me. I know your respective governments have placed you under strict vows of silence, but your governments are in shambles. It is incumbent on me to assess your knowledge and, where appropriate, to enhance it." He took a chair at the head table. With a wave of his hand, he ordered a screen to be lowered. Huge chandeliers hanging from the frescoed ceiling dimmed as the screen descended. The American scientists handled the presentation, as they had been at the forefront of a decades-long scientific study.

A dim red ball of light appeared on the screen as an unkempt elderly man took the podium. "President Kurtoglu, you are looking at an infrared image of a brown dwarf star. This star formed along with our sun. They are twins, born out of the same stellar nursery." The presentation moved to a video clip depicting a large gas cloud in space. At either end, the gas began to swirl and coalesce into opposing whirlpools. The right side of the cloud grew at a more accelerated pace, pulling more and more of the gas in its direction. Eventually, the right side ignited with a huge flash. The resultant percussion blew the remaining gas toward the left whirlpool. Then the gas began to redistribute. Some of it formed a disc around the new sun on the right. A smaller amount formed a disc around the smoldering mass at the left. "As you can see, in the stellar nursery, our sun was greedy. Its weaker twin, which is called Nemesis in the scientific community, grew into a large body with great heat but not enough mass to ignite the nuclear firestorm of a regular star. It is referred to as a brown dwarf. It emits a significant amount of infrared heat but very little light. Its inability to emit light has kept it hidden from us for generations." On the screen, the two bodies began an awkward dance, the larger one moving slightly while the smaller swung around it in an uneven arc. "The two bodies technically orbit the center of the combined system's mass. Our sun moves only a bit because it is much heavier and the center of mass resides closer to it. The smaller is forced into a far-flung orbit of varying speed. When it is farthest away from the system's center of gravity, it slows, only to speed up again when its orbit brings it closer."

Isa had known as much from the Lady, but he needed to bring the world's scientists into his camp, so he feigned great interest in their crude presentation.

The old scientist continued. "As you can see in our illustration, planets formed around each star. Nemesis has a grouping of rocky planets comprised largely of iron. When the stars are far from each other, their respective planets do not interact. However, when the stars are closest, their solar systems intersect one another." The video moved to show fully formed solar systems. When the stars came to their closest points, the planets of each whizzed past one another. "On one of the passes, two worlds collided in a fireball that cooled to chunks of debris in an orbit around our sun between Mars and Jupiter, the asteroid belt."

The presenter yielded to another. This man, in his midforties, bore the dark leathery complexion of a man who had spent years in the sun. Isa looked at the meeting agenda to learn that the man was a very respected archeologist. "President Kurtoglu, my specialty is antiquities. Although it has been hidden from the public, we have unearthed substantial evidence of a prehistoric advanced civilization on earth. We believe this civilization perished when Nemesis passed through the solar system."

The first presenter explained, "Our assumed orbital trajectory for Nemesis has it coming perilously close to the inner solar system at periodic intervals. We can only estimate the time frame because each passing causes gravitational disturbances that alter the orbit. Sometimes the alteration is slight, when the gas giants are on the other side of the sun. When it passes close to Jupiter or Saturn, the perturbation of Nemesis's orbit is greater."

The second presenter picked up where the first had left off. "Similarly, the incursion of Nemesis has differing effects on Earth depending on where it is in its orbit around the sun at the time of the passing. At the time of Noah, Earth was in the bull's-eye and most life on the planet perished. At the time of Moses, Earth was not nearly as damaged. Ancient Sumerian records point to Nemesis's planet Nibiru as the cause of much devastation in the ancient past."

"I presume you are coming to a very uncomfortable point," Isa said, almost cheerily.

"President Kurtoglu, our scientists first noticed the Nemesis system in the 1950s. Its signature was faint, but there were some indications that it was heading toward Earth from the south of the ecliptic, the plane in which our sun's planets orbit. As time went by, more studies were conducted, the *Pioneer* probes were launched, and infrared observatories were built in Antarctica. As the data poured in, the conclusions were inescapable: Nemesis is inbound."

"And when do you see this happening?"

"Again, it is hard to know for certain the exact timing or the extent of damage because each incursion into the solar system destabilizes the orbit of Nemesis and its planets. Nibiru is the planet that has the most interaction with Earth, but its movement can and has been affected by the gravity of the gas giants. Even when it was distant, we witnessed its effects."

The astronomer continued. "We have chronicled this effect on Earth under the guise of global warming and climate change. In actuality, the entire solar system has been heating up. The atmosphere of Pluto has gone from a frozen slush on its surface to a gaseous envelope;

there have been storms on and rotational shifts in both Uranus and Neptune; the weather patterns of Jupiter and Saturn are particularly violent; and there has been a mean increase in the global temperature of Mars since we started landing probes there."

A soft-spoken geophysicist picked up the conversation. "On Earth, we have seen a steady increase in volcanic and earthquake activity accompanied by climactic imbalances generating the most violent and unpredictable weather patterns in recorded history. There is also an effect known as the Schumann resonance frequency. Think of it like a hum emitted from the center of the Earth. Throughout history, this frequency has vibrated at about 7 to 8 hertz. Within the last decade, it has jumped through the teens and now stands at about 20 hertz."

A biologist joined the group, introducing himself briefly. "We are not completely sure how the brain responds to the Schumann resonance, but we have catalogued increases in personal and societal anxiety as the frequency rises. Throughout much of the recent past, we have been able to minimize societal disruption with a class of drugs known as selective serotonin reuptake inhibitors."

"Prozac and the like," Isa said with a shake of his head to indicate he knew of their function.

"Yes," the biologist continued, "but as this frequency heads above 20 hertz, this class of drugs is falling behind in their ability to compensate."

"Which brings us to the recent mass outbreak of violence," Isa said, barely able to contain a smile. These men were singing exactly the song he needed to hear from them.

"Yes, sir. The frequency peaked at nearly 30 hertz a couple of days ago but has been steadily decreasing. As it decreases, societies around the world are stabilizing."

"But we are at the whims of this effect," Isa said. "Are you telling me we could see a repeat of this type of violence any time the frequency increases?"

The biologist shrugged. "At the moment we are at its mercy. Barring the invention of a new class of drugs, people will have to be tightly controlled to prevent them from hurting themselves."

"So, you're advocating martial law," Isa concluded with a tight grin.

"At least for a time. The current uprisings will more likely than not kill off those who are most susceptible to the effects. But if we go higher than 30 hertz, there's no telling how many more people will be affected."

"I see," Isa said gravely. "But people can't live under martial law forever. We'll need a long-term solution."

"And we are working precisely to that end from a biological standpoint, sir. But I think I should point out that it would not be forever in any event. Nemesis will make its pass, and then it will storm away, taking with it these ill-effects."

The astronomer picked up the conversation and clicked the screen to set the video in motion. The screen showed the dark star careening into the solar system and then whipping back out. "We believe we are about seven years away from its closest passing. But once it passes, its effects will diminish rapidly, due to its acceleration and the fact that it will once again leave the ecliptic."

"But we're not sure of the time or the level of devastation," Isa said, taking care not to reveal his inner joy.

"No, sir. Think of Earth's orbit as having four quadrants. There is a possibility that Earth could be in quadrants two and four during the inbound and outbound phases of the crossing. In this scenario, Nemesis and its planets would pass on the other side of the sun, shielding us from the most dangerous effects." He paused the video at an image of Earth's orbit with a graphic dividing it into quadrants, with the Nemesis system lurking in the background.

"So, global warming continues, there are more earthquakes, and the Schumann resonance frequency continues to increase," Isa said.

"Yes, sir. More of the same with a bit of increase in the frequency and duration of each event."

"But if Earth is in quadrants one and three?"

The astronomer answered, "If Earth is in quadrants one and three, we'll be in the middle of a battle of suns. Magnetic attraction between the two bodies will form a powerful electromagnetic field that is subject to discharge. There will be space lightning between the sun and Nemesis as they try to dissipate the magnetic imbalance between them."

"Like the worldwide event a few days ago?" Isa asked.

"Exactly. That discharge was huge and violent but not devastating.

However, as the two objects come closer, the magnetic arc between them will become a pathway for solar ejections. Superheated plasma from the sun, possibly larger than Earth itself, hurling along the magnetic lines between the two suns."

"If Earth is caught in the crossfire?"

"There would be nothing left," the scientist said grimly. "Our planet would become a cinder."

"An extinction level event to be sure," Isa said. "But there's no certainty a discharge will strike Earth, right? Nemesis has been orbiting for millennia and humanity is still here."

"That is true, Mr. President, but even if we aren't in the direct path of a coronal ejection, the magnetic field will play havoc with Earth's magnetosphere. Nemesis will zoom into the solar system from beneath us and exit above us. As it does, its poles will attract the poles of our sun's planets. If Earth finds itself in quadrants one and three, there will be tremendous crustal displacement as its poles try to align themselves with the intruder's."

"The coming polar shift conspiracy theorists have been warning about," Isa muttered.

"Yes. Depending on the proximity of the approach, we could see Earth flip upside down at the worst, or wobble to and fro at the least. On Earth these events would be experienced as global earthquakes. Sudden shifts in the mantle would slosh the oceans in their basins, creating ongoing global tsunamis."

"So, in quadrants one and three, even if we aren't burned to a cinder, we face the risk of extinction from Earth's reaction to the passing system. Well, gentlemen, let's hope for quadrants two and four."

"Mr. President, if I may," the astronomer interrupted. "Even in the quadrants-two-and-four scenario, there are tremendous dangers. From violent exchanges with our solar system for millennia, Nemesis has acquired a huge trove of orbitals, debris ranging from the size of a grain of sand to that of an asteroid. This debris follows along behind it in a tail. Any debris in Earth's path creates a strong probability of bombardment. If Earth is fortunate enough to encounter only the smaller sediments, rain would cleanse them from the atmosphere. Given the high iron content, this would most likely result in a reddish pollution of water until the atmosphere is cleansed. If

Earth encounters larger objects, bombardment would have disastrous consequences."

"So, even the safest option is perilous," Isa commented.

"We estimate in either scenario the casualties could be in the billions, sir."

Isa pinched his own leg to stop a forming grin of glee. "Well, thank you, gentlemen. You certainly have given me a lot to think about. And I would like to return the favor. Please take your seats." As the scientists found their respective tables, Isa took the podium.

"There is an aspect to this impending crisis you have not considered. The danger is greater than you have presupposed, but there are potential benefits as well. I have a special guest to explain the matter more fully. Would you welcome, please, the Lady, an emissary from another star system who has come to help us through this difficult time."

A huge collective gasp filled the room as the Lady entered wearing a golden floor-length robe. She gingerly mounted the steps to the podium, where Isa bowed slightly to her and lowered the microphone.

The Lady spoke in a high-pitched wheeze. "I can tell by the shocked expressions on your faces that you have not seriously contemplated meeting extraterrestrial life, although I imagine many of you have heard rumors of our interaction with your world's governments." A nervous chuckle followed her remark.

"To be clear, the universe is teeming with life, but intelligent life is harder to come by. For this reason, my society has sent me as an envoy to your world. The dark star Nemesis has given birth to an even darker society living on its planet Nibiru. To their society, this approach into your solar system is an opportunity to exploit the resources of your warm sun.

"They will rape this world of its atmosphere, its vegetation, and its people. In ages past, they found your world to be interesting, if you will pardon my expression, as dessert. There once flourished a civilization on the planet Mars. After millennia of culling its populace, Nibiru's warlike reptilian species decimated the planet. I'm sure you have all seen photos of the face and pyramids on Mars. They are all that remain of a once proud civilization.

"The operative word is *proud*. My species offered them advice as well, but they failed to implement the hard measures needed to defend themselves. We offer you the same counsel with the hope that you will take the necessary measures to withstand this attack."

Isa leaned into the microphone to talk. "Lady, please explain to them, as you did to me, why your species doesn't offer something more tangible than advice."

"My species is a member of a much broader collective. We have strict prohibitions against interfering with the development of other worlds. In extreme circumstances such as this, we bend the rules a bit to advise, but we cannot interfere. We can teach you how to build defensive weapons. And we can offer potential solutions to the frailty of your species, thereby providing a greater probability of survival.

"Be assured that if you follow our advice and wisely use the technologies we provide, your species will enter a golden age. Your ability to repair any damage wrought by the passage of Nemesis will be quantum leaps above the technology available to you now. And most importantly, you will have proven yourselves to our collective, and we will cordially and warmly welcome you into our ranks. Inclusion in our collective comes with many privileges, including access to our wormhole technology enabling transportation throughout the galaxy, full trade member status, and most importantly a military pact.

"In other words, if you do well, this will be the last time the marauders of Nibiru will rain havoc down on your solar system."

As Isa had anticipated, the room was pregnant with stunned silence. It was all too much for the scientists to take in. But each face wore an indelible smile at having interacted with alien intelligent life. The Lady was the undoubted fulfillment of every *Star Trek* fantasy these men and women had ever had.

Isa spoke. "You may be wondering why you have never heard of this malevolent species before. The fact is that you have. Sumerian records speak of a fierce race of individuals called the Anunnaki who tried to enslave humankind. The ancient Hebrew writings of Enoch tell of a group called Watchers who descended to Mount Hermon. Legend says they tried an advanced breeding program with the women of Earth."

"And not only your women," the Lady added. "They also manipulated the DNA of several other species in their attempts to create more palatable flesh. They come from a very iron-rich environment, as did the civilization on Mars. Simply put, to the Anu, the residents of Mars were tastier than the inhabitants of Earth." She paused as the audience exhaled an involuntary gasp. "On previous crossings, they sought the genetic manipulation of your species and several others, most notably bovines. Having planted the seed generations ago, they are coming back to reap the harvest."

Isa picked up the conversation. "The Lady assures me her race has much better science to determine the point at which Nemesis will encounter the inner solar system. The good news is that the encounter will occur at the cusp of the quadrants-two-and-four alignment. So we can expect events to be far better than in Noah's time, but a bit worse than in Moses's time. This implies that the geologic consequences will be manageable. But the consequences of interplanetary war will be devastating if we do not come together to face this challenge head-on."

"More to the point," the Lady interjected. Isa frowned slightly at the implication that he might not have been on point. He corrected his look immediately, hoping the Lady hadn't read his expression. She continued, "Admission to our powerful galactic alliance will bring benefits you cannot imagine. The collective relies on the sharing of consciousness. When the people of your world blend with us, they will seem like gods considering their current level of comprehension."

Slowly rising from his seat, a timid-looking man in the back called out a question. The place card in front of him identified his nationality as Swiss, a scientist involved in the CERN project. "I don't wish to appear impertinent, Mr. President and Ms. ... ah ... Lady, but I wouldn't be Swiss if I didn't think of the art of the deal. With so many wonderful benefits to come from inclusion in the collective, I can't help but wonder what the collective gets out of all of this. Surely there is some quid pro quo."

The Lady looked at Isa with a blank expression. Isa clarified. "Simply put, Lady, we have nothing of such value to offer in exchange. So the question is, what does the collective hope to gain from us?"

The Lady's face registered a pained expression as she attempted to smile. "We do this for two reasons. First, we believe we have a spiritual mandate, sort of a vow, to unite the intelligent species of the galaxy. It's our ... religion. Second, you do not realize the immense richness of your planet's biosphere. The taste of your fruits and grains alone would be of great value to our members."

The man seemed to be satisfied with the answer as he took his seat.

Isa concluded the session. "My friends, the Lady tires easily. And I daresay you have heard enough to blow even your great minds today." The people in the room chuckled as he smiled warmly. "I invite you to stay in this room for dinner, which will be served shortly. Afterward, I ask that you stay in the palace with us for a few more days while we iron out the tasks to be performed in this desperate hour. Then I insist that you accompany me to the United Nations, where the Lady and I will present these findings to the world."

On cue, the Lady looked admiringly at Isa. "A final comment before we leave you: President Kurtoglu possesses an entirely unique pedigree, the culmination of centuries of effort by my species' most brilliant scientists. He carries the full DNA of my species as well as his human DNA. In short, as an amalgamation of the best of our species, he is Earth's only hope to meet this challenge." She left the podium unceremoniously as the group stood to applaud her.

Isa followed her from the ballroom to his office. Once the door was shut, he laughed and said, "I think that went splendidly. Our story layered on top of their research was very convincing."

"You have a greater understanding of the human mind than I," she said as she took a seat in front of his large desk. "Do you think they suspect some underlying deception?"

"It is a scientist's nature to question," Isa said as he fell into the heavily padded leather chair behind his desk. He put his hands behind his head and looked up at the ceiling with a huge satisfied grin on his face.

"I worry about the one from Switzerland," she said flatly.

"Oh, him? I'm quite sure he'll soon have a fatal accident of some sort."

NINE

Michael pulled his cell phone from his pocket. It's screen still screamed, "No service," as it had since the rapture. "Damn," he said. "If we don't make it out of here, I would have liked the opportunity to talk to the kids."

"Is this really the time to be lamenting cell service?" Benny quipped.

"Just a reaction to the stupid screen," Michael said, turning the phone to light their surroundings. They were in the stairwell below the papal offices. The going was tedious, but the dim light of the phone aided their progress.

As they descended, listening to the endless screams of the Dark Awakening, Michael tried to push out of his mind the horrors the kids may be facing at this moment. "Oh, Lord," he prayed silently, "I am so sorry I robbed Gabe's kids of the opportunity to know You before the rapture." He wiped a tear from his eye, which caused the light from the phone to swing wildly above him and Benny. He heard a crash as Benny tumbled down a few stairs to the landing. Turning the phone toward the noise, he saw Benny sprawled out on the floor, obviously waiting to be picked up. Then the light fell on the cause of Benny's misstep. The horribly mangled bodies of two priests lay just ahead of Michael. He shuddered. Their blood flowed freely.

"Get up, Benny," he whispered sharply. "We have to keep moving or this could be us." Benny responded by raising a hand for Michael to help him up. Michael grabbed the old outstretched hand to steady his uncle, but nothing happened.

"Well, at least try to pull me up," Benny complained.

"I'm not lifting you, Benny. I'm offering a hand. If you won't try a bit on your own, I'm moving on without you."

"Fine," Benny hissed. He nearly knocked Michael over trying to pull himself up.

"I guess I didn't need that arm anyway," Michael quipped. His mind flashed on some saint's vision of a future pope leaving the burning city of Rome amid the bodies of fallen priests. "Listen, Benny," he whispered, "the presence of these priests is ominous. There's violence inside the Vatican. The crowds have breached our security. We have to get to the papal hangar at Fiumicino, and it's not like I can hail a cab. Are you up for this?"

"I am," Benny said with a resolve Michael had previously thought to be reserved for the dinner table.

"Okay," Michael said hopefully. "No complaining about the circumstances. We'll just put our heads down and gut it out. All right?"

"Yes."

"Good. We have one more flight of stairs before we're at street level. There's no telling what we'll encounter out there. One thing we have going for us is that nobody knows you're the new pope. I think we have to go incognito, Benny. What do you have on under your cassock?"

"Sweatpants and a T-shirt," Benny answered. Michael could hear the horror in Benny's voice as he anticipated leaving behind the fine linen garb he had fought and killed to obtain.

"We'll leave our cassocks here," Michael said as he removed his to reveal the black pants and shirt of a priest. He yanked free his clerical collar. Benny whined a bit, but he removed the cassock to reveal a white T-shirt, which had dark underarm stains, and sweatpants.

"I don't know what's happening outside, but I'm sure we'll be better off if we just blend in. Too many people know me from television appearances," he said, ruffling his hair to make it look more unkempt. "Until we get home to Georgia, call me Jake."

"Okay, Jake," Benny said with a touch of amusement in his voice. "And I think I'll choose the name … Luciano."

Michael rolled his eyes as Benny said, "Yes. Luciano it is. Lead on, Jake."

They quietly descended the last flight of stairs and pushed open the door to reveal unbridled savagery. People were literally at each other's throats as the Dark Awakening flung into full force.

Benny recoiled as a screaming woman mercilessly beat at a fierce-looking man. In one bold, uncaring swipe, he knocked her to the ground beneath their feet. Michael bent to help her up, and she bit at his hand. He yanked it away.

"They're rabid," he screamed to Benny so as to be heard over the din. He pushed his uncle to the right. The two men stayed close to buildings as they exited the Vatican and fell into the equally untethered society of Rome. The night was bright with an orange glow as fire lighted billowing clouds of smoke pouring from the Vatican. The only thing they had going for them was that there were no bystanders in this raging mob. Nobody was staying to the periphery to observe. Rather, everyone had rushed to the center, anxious to play a part in the bloodletting.

"Scoot along the buildings," Michael said, pushing Benny ahead of him.

"You first," Benny said, fear filling his voice.

"Fine," Michael answered, "but stay close behind me."

"Not to worry," Benny offered, grabbing tightly the back of Michael's shirt.

Michael worried about their ability to make it to Fiumicino. He also worried about Benny's ability to walk the fifteen miles to the airport. Benny had never in his life walked that type of distance. Right now Benny was running on adrenalin, but Michael seriously doubted they could reach their destination. He had to find another way. He halted at the edge of a building for a few moments to think. The frightened Benny clutched at him.

"Take it easy, Benny," he called over his shoulder. "I just need a few minutes to think ... and pray. Lord, I really could use a good idea right about now," he said softly, sure that Benny wouldn't hear him over the din of the crowd. His mind flooded with an image from his youth. On a visit to Rome when they were ten, he and Gabe had come to love Benny's heroic assistant Father Chris. On the last day of their visit, Chris took them to Piazza Navona to meet one of his friends, Father Vinnie. The images coming to Michael's mind were vivid and as fresh as if he were seeing them for the first time through his ten-year-old eyes. He scanned the piazza, smelling the fresh-baked bread in the damp early morning air. He tasted the fresh mozzarella, basil, and tomato sandwich Father Vinnie had handed him as his eyes fell on a group of Vespas. He chuckled at the little motorcycles haphazardly parked at the end of the square. The image froze. He knew what he had to do.

"Thank You, Lord," he said softly. Calling to Benny behind him, he screamed, "We're going to Piazza Navona. Maybe we can find a few motorcycles there."

"Do you think you'll find one with a sidecar?" Benny ventured. "I've never driven a motorcycle."

"Great!" Michael countered. "Listen, it's not much harder than riding a bike."

"Can't say as I ever did that either." Benny shrugged.

"Well, you're about to learn," Michael screamed. He lurched forward, pulling his frightened uncle behind him.

The going was tedious. Every couple of steps, someone from the brawling crowd fell into them or in front of them. Oblivious to everything, they barely noticed as Michael shoved them away from the periphery and back into the seething crowd. Over the course of a couple of hours, the pair made it to Piazza Navona. The square must have seen one of the first outbreaks of the insanity. It was deadly silent, bodies strewn all over, the howling hordes having moved on.

Michael was at once relieved to be out of the fray and horrified to be in the midst of such carnage. Benny let go of his shirt. They surveyed the damage.

"The world has gone crazy, Benny ... uh ... Luciano," he said breathlessly.

"The crazies have always been here, Jake," Benny replied in stunned awe. "Tonight they've just made themselves known. Trust me, in the long run the world will be better off without them."

Michael swung around, fighting every carnal urge to take his uncle out. "Shut up! Just ... shut ... up!" he screamed as confused, angry tears filled his eyes.

"I'm not trying to be offensive, Jake. I just don't want you to be too overwhelmed by the circumstances. There's a plan. If you don't believe there's a plan, you'll go crazy yourself. And frankly, I need you to be in a stable frame of mind."

The Holy Spirit inside of Michael helped to quell the rage he felt toward his uncle. He had to be wise. There was so much at stake. And although it wasn't as Benny had meant it, there was indeed a plan. Michael knew the Lord's will would be done. The world would get even more ugly as evil manifested. He would have to witness it, but he couldn't let himself be blown away by it.

"Fair enough," Michael said, wiping at tears that had formed in his eyes. "I'm not going to have a meltdown, Benny." He scanned the square in the light of the burning buildings on its periphery. There, just ahead of them in the far corner of the square, was a row of bikes. They just had to find a couple with keys. Not a very unlikely scenario considering that their former owners were not of a rational mind when they left them.

Finding the Vespas was not nearly as difficult as teaching Benny to use a clutch and to balance. For a full hour, he squealed like a little girl, going a few feet, stalling, and falling over. To Michael's surprise, however, he kept with it and finally got the hang of it. By God's grace, they were only interrupted a couple of times, but not by crazies. The interveners were just people who walked in stunned silence away from the frenzy overtaking their city.

They left the piazza, Benny following Michael. They had to make it to the E80, the highway to Fiumicino. The going was slow once they entered the fray. Again staying close to buildings, they drove slowly down the most passable streets, Michael clearing the path of bodies and debris with Benny following closely behind. Michael couldn't wait to be out of the city and onto the highway.

Finally they made it to the on-ramp, and there Michael's hopes were dashed. He hadn't been thinking clearly. The rapture had taken people from their cars. Driverless cars had crashed into others, leaving twisted piles of metal. Then the madness had struck occupants of other vehicles, and slaughter ensued.

They made slow passage between cars and trucks. Again, Michael led the way, stopping every few minutes to move a body just enough to allow their bikes through. The gravity of the situation had overtaken him when he moved the body of a pretty young girl, her face contorted in shocked horror in his bike's headlight. Moving her bloating body, he wept. He was spent. He couldn't do it anymore. The going was too slow in the dark, and he needed to rest. He led them to an exit and motioned Benny to pull up alongside him.

"We'll make much better progress in daylight, Luciano. I'm physically and emotionally exhausted. Let's put up here for the night and grab some sleep near that grove of trees."

"I'll be happy to get off this contraption, Jake. Lead the way," Benny said with a burst of enthusiasm. To Michael's delight, they had stumbled upon an orchard. As Benny gracelessly and arduously dismounted, Michael plucked a few apples.

"What I wouldn't give for a piece of meat right now," Benny said, scowling at the slightly sour taste of the underripe fruit. "I'd even settle for a piece of one of the dead motorists."

Michael gasped as he sat in the grass to taste an apple. "Let me guess: besides everything else, you're a cannibal as well."

"Don't be rude," Benny said, taking umbrage and sitting next to his nephew. "One course of *uomo marsala* does not a cannibal make. And besides, it was a prepared dish. I didn't know what I was eating until after I had eaten it."

Michael wiped his hand over his face in disbelief.

"And before you ask, it was very tasty," Benny said defensively.

"Just shut up and eat your apple. I don't want to hear any more about it," Michael spat. They sat on the ground silently eating as Rome burned in the distance.

"Benny," Michael finally spoke.

"Luciano," Benny corrected.

"Luciano, I'm concerned. Even if we make it to the airport, we may find nothing more than bodies and debris. I don't know what we'll do ..."

To Michael's shock, Benny pulled a small satellite phone from his pocket, dialed it, and spoke a few sentences in Italian. Benny knew Michael had been trying desperately to get hold of Gabe's kids, yet he hadn't offered use of the phone! Michael threw his apple to the ground and paced as Benny finished the conversation.

"Italian troops have secured the airport," Benny said. "The papal plane can take us to Atlanta. All we have to do is get to the gates tomorrow and security will meet us. They're prohibited from leaving the airport, so they can't come to rescue us."

Michael stomped over to him. "You knew I was heartsick about Gabe's kids, Benny!"

"Luciano," Benny corrected.

"Shut up! Give me that phone!"

Benny chucked the phone. "Have at it, Jake. It won't do you any good. It transmits on a government frequency to other government agencies. But you won't believe me, so try it yourself."

Michael dialed each of the kid's cell phone numbers and then the house's main number. True to Benny's word, each number drew an "unauthorized service" response.

He handed the phone back to Benny.

"You can say thanks any time now," Benny said harshly.

"For what? For you hiding that from me while I dragged your fat butt through Rome?"

"For arranging the flight," Benny said scornfully.

Michael reined in his temper. He had dealt with Benny long enough to know how to handle him. "Listen up, Benny."

"Lu—"

Michael drew a finger to his lips to stop Benny from correcting him. "Circumstances have put us together in the worst parody of the *Odd Couple* to hit real life. But here's the deal: You have to come clean with me about everything if you expect me to be your camerlengo. No more lies. I want to know everything." Michael never expected Benny to comply, but he had to express his outrage.

To Michael's surprise, Benny spoke kindly. "I suppose I should bring you into my confidence. After all, I'll be relying on you to give me the public image of a tortured saint of a man trying his best to help humanity through its darkest hour."

"So you think I'm going to help you perpetrate that fraud to the whole world?" Michael asked, aghast.

"Sit down, Michael," Benny said sternly. "Your indignant outrage seems a bit out of place for a man who foisted his forged gospel on an unsuspecting world."

Michael sat beside him. The full gravity of his participation in this madness struck him anew. He remembered every painstaking stroke to forge the revised Gospel of John. "I can't tell you how much I regret my actions," Michael said breathlessly.

"Now, now. No need to get all emotional about it," Benny said. "I know you miss your family, and you think they were right about all this Jesus stuff, but you did the right thing. In time you'll realize that, Michael. And in time, you'll realize that we are birds of a feather, you and me."

Michael had to force down the bile in his throat. He hated to admit it, but he, like St. Paul, was chief among sinners. And yet, a scant forty hours ago, Jesus had forgiven him and made him a new man. Benny would never understand.

"Because you are my closest living relative, I'll tell you my story." Benny sighed. "Your grandpa Stan was a mean, heartless man."

"So you've told me about a million times—he said boo-boo words to you and didn't leave you an inheritance. It's ancient history."

"You know he died in a horrible car accident, but did you know his brake lines had been cut?"

"So you're telling me you murdered Grandpa Stan?" Michael asked. Long ago he thought that nothing Benny could do would surprise him. He had been wrong.

"Murder. Cannibal. There you go again with the judgmental terms, Jake. At some point you'll have to understand a basic truth. Mankind is a biological mistake that oozed out of some long-forgotten primordial pond. The only higher moral imperative is survival of the fittest. There's really nothing else."

"We'll have to agree to disagree," Michael said tersely. "Was that the first time you killed someone?"

"Oh, heavens no," Benny said with a wave of his hand. "Your grandfather was no good, but I would never have known him if my mother hadn't married him."

"You killed Grandma? I thought she died of a disease."

"Let's just say your grandfather was remiss in not ordering a toxicology report," Benny said offhandedly. "Do you know why I'm telling you this, Michael?"

"To make the worst day of my life even worse?" Michael asked in awe.

"Even though I wanted the estate, the money, and the power, I could never even think about killing your mother. We both know that, in a lapse of judgment, I thought about killing you, but I couldn't go through with it."

"Are you trying to convince me you have a conscience?" Michael asked in annoyed disbelief.

"Don't be so obtuse. I couldn't kill you because in my own unconventional way, I love you, Michael. I may never say it again, but it's the truth."

"With the crap you've pulled all my life, you want me to believe you love me because—"

"Because I let you live," Benny said somberly. He yawned and put his head back. "I have to rest," he said, followed quickly by the steady breathing of sound sleep.

Michael lay back as well, his head spinning.

The dream was especially vivid. He was in the pope's office. On the facing white couches in front of the huge bank of windows sat Benny's predecessor, along with Chris and Gabe. They spoke softly but with a sense of urgency.

"This is a hard stance for me to assume, my young friend," the pope said to Gabe with a slight grin. "For years, the church has taught that we are now the heirs of promises made to Abraham."

Michael wondered if he was dreaming or having a vision of a previous encounter between the three. He walked past the coffee table between the two couches and waved his hands in front of Chris and then Gabe. They were oblivious. Clearly they couldn't see him. He sat down next to Gabe to witness the remainder of the conversation.

"I'm familiar with those beliefs, sir," Gabe said tenuously, "but a more literal interpretation of scripture would most likely lead to a dispensational viewpoint, one that tells us the age of grace, also known as the age of the church, will at one point end. Then the Lord will resume with His plan for the nation of Israel."

"Again," said the pontiff gravely, "this would imply that the new nation of Israel is the fulfillment of ancient prophecies rather than the fulfillment of men's desires. As an institution, we must show prudence, restraint, and reverence. It is not an easy task to abandon theologies held for centuries."

"That was before Pope Benny the man-eater," Michael said,

followed by a chuckle. Nobody heard him. He longed for the days of banter with Chris and Gabe.

The pope continued. "Chris, I wholeheartedly agree with your suggestions to add more weight in the liturgical readings to St. Paul's Letters to the Thessalonians and the books of Daniel and Isaiah. The curia will not burden itself with items so mundane as the readings selected for Mass. They view me as a biblical egghead, and they're more than happy to let me putter with scripture." Chris and Gabe chuckled.

The pope continued with a grin. "That view will help me prepare our sheep right under their noses."

The men exchanged glances. Michael could see that, in the confines of this office, world government was a foregone conclusion. The wealth, power, and political might of the world's elite were too strong to challenge. Those facts didn't stop the pope from trying to hand them a hollow victory.

Chris smiled at the logic. "So, Holiness, while they're building a larger sheep pen, we'll rescue the flock from them."

"Absolutely." The pontiff laughed. "But we have to make the most of the time we have, gentlemen."

Gabe turned to Michael. "Did you hear that, bro?"

Michael was startled. "You can see me?"

Gabe tilted his head back to laugh loudly. "Yeah. Smooth move, McGoo, waving your hands in front of our faces like that."

Michael laughed hard. So did the pope before he disappeared, leaving only Gabe and Chris.

"With all the languages he speaks, *that's* how he tried to get our attention," Chris added with a snigger. "Do you catch the bigger picture here, Michael?"

"I think," Michael said, noticing how unsure he sounded.

Now serious, Gabe said, "God has let you occupy a unique position. As Benny's only blood relative and confidant, you'll be able to snatch some of the flock from him and Isa."

Chris picked up the conversation. "Look, Michael, for years I took care of mundane matters for Benny while feeding information to the pope so he could sidestep whatever crazy plans Benny and Luciano Begliali were hatching. Benny lacks the organization skills to keep an office flowing. If you have his trust, you'll be shocked at how much access you'll have."

Michael grimaced. "I don't know about this, guys. I've done so many horrible things."

"All under the blood of Christ now, Michael," Gabe said. "Those things don't exist on this side."

"You don't know how much I wish I were on your side right now," Michael said with a sigh.

"We do too," Gabe said, patting his brother's shoulder.

Michael bolted awake to the spatter of water and the rustle of leaves near his head. The sun was coming up, and Benny was relieving himself. He quickly rolled out of the way.

"Benny!" he shouted. "Move away from the camp when you want to do something like that. And while we're at it, never, *ever* unholster that thing in my presence again!"

Benny chuckled at the thrill of Michael's discomfort. "Here, have some breakfast," he said, chucking an apple toward Michael.

"No thanks," Michael snapped, batting it away. "I know where your hands have been." He jumped up and picked an apple for himself. "It will be daylight soon, and we probably have a good eight miles to Fiumicino. Once I finish this apple and move a *respectable* distance from the camp to attend to my needs, we should get going." He ate the apple quickly in big bites. The first taste was sour, but he grew to like it as he ate.

The road conditions were the same nightmare they had been the day before, but at least it was daylight. The visage wasn't pretty. As far as the eye could see, cars were in a tangled heap. It was an apocalyptic nightmare worse than any Michael had seen in the science fiction movies he loved as a kid.

"It will be slow going," Michael said as they mounted their bikes. "At least we can choose the path of least resistance. There's less wreckage on the median strip, but we'll have to be careful of bodies. It looks like everyone moved to the center to duke it out when the Dark Awakening hit."

"They'll smell by now," Benny offered, turning up his nose.

"Well, then you won't be tempted to eat them," Michael snipped as he put his bike in gear.

It was as he had suspected, slow going. And as Benny had predicted, it was nauseating. The smell was nearly unbearable in the rising heat of the day. Michael was forever swatting at flies drawn to the stench.

Those were the good moments. Too many times people had died in bunches. The only away around was to move the bodies. Their smell and the pudginess of their bloated flesh assaulted Michael every time. His eyes stung, but he feared to wipe at them after touching the rotting bodies. Of course, Benny stayed on his bike, waiting for Michael to clear the way. Michael wanted to challenge him to help, but then he asked himself, *What's the use?* Benny had never helped at anything other than finishing the last bit of dessert. Benny: Pope Peter! What a disaster!

When they got to ride a while without having to move bodies, Michael's mind inevitably went to the circumstances that had left him here with the most evil man he had ever known ... well, the second most evil man. There was always Isa, the beast who shared his DNA. Each time he got to this point, he would force himself to think about something else.

At times he would pray for the souls of the dead people around them, victims of a plot too insidious to even mention. "Lord, are their souls responsible for the things done by multiple personalities forced upon them?" he would ask. He doubted he would come to know the answer this side of heaven.

They were able to proceed at a pace of around a mile an hour. Neither wanted to stop for a rest in the stench. They just kept on keeping on until they finally found themselves at Fiumicino Airport. It was eerily silent as they found the main entrance. The doors were locked, and military vehicles were parked all around the structure.

Benny pulled out his satellite phone and dialed. Hanging it up, he said, "Our pilot will be out to get us in a few minutes." He crawled off his bike and rubbed his backside. "If I never do that again, I won't be too disappointed."

Within a short period of time, a golf cart appeared at the airport's glass doors. The driver looked to be about fifty years old and had a deep receding hairline, graying at the temples. He jumped from the cart and spoke briefly to a stern-looking soldier, who then opened a door and motioned them through. The man with the cart looked them over and introduced himself as their pilot.

Michael became suddenly aware of how ragged he and Benny looked. He buttoned the top button on his shirt and inserted the plastic priestly collar. It didn't do anything for the mud and grass stains or the smell of decay rising from him, but at least it identified him as a priest. Benny looked even worse in only a mud-stained T-shirt, but when he extended his hand to reveal the papal ring, he garnered instant respect.

"I'm Enrico Passamente, Holiness. You look as if you have been through a tough time, but not to worry. You are in good hands now." He led them to the cart. Michael took the catbird seat, and Benny lumbered into the back.

"These are interesting times, are they not, Father?" Enrico asked as they sped through the airport. He spoke English well, with only a slight accent and the occasional peppering of an Italian word.

"Yes," Michael said distractedly. His attention was drawn to servicemen in masks unceremoniously filling body bags and moving them to a growing pile at the other end of the concourse.

"There was an uncontrollable mob in the public spaces," Enrico said as he saw Michael's expression. "The only way for the military to secure the space was to shoot them."

"This is horrible," Michael said. The magnitude of destruction hadn't ceased to amaze him.

"Fortunately, the insanity did not reach the hangars. The Vatican plane is safe, as am I and your copilot, Annamaria DiCenzio. The runways didn't fare so well. When the panic started, some planes were taking off and some were landing. Most made it through all right, but some, suddenly without pilot or copilot, crashed." He lowered his voice to a conspiratorial tone. "Some people I know say they vanished. Poof. No more pilot. Sounds *impossibile*, but that's what they say."

"We had some vanishings at the Vatican as well," Michael said. He looked over his shoulder to see that Benny's eyes were shut in a catnap.

Enrico looked closely at Michael and nodded. They rode in silence for a few seconds. "Anyway," Enrico said, picking up the conversation, "the army cleared two runways—one out and one in. Atlanta is pretty much the same, but they think they will have two more open by the time we arrive."

"Air traffic will be pretty jammed up then," Michael said.

"What traffic?" Enrico said, waving his arm. "Only government flights are permitted now. We have clearer skies than ever since I've flown. And that's a long time now, *signore*."

"So it sounds like Atlanta got hit by the same madness," Michael said with a wince and a prayer that Gabe's kids were okay.

"Same. Maybe a little worse. America got hit hard. Everyone in government but the president got killed by the crazies."

"What?" Michael asked in astonishment.

"Sí. It's true. Nobody but the president left. When America coughs, the world gets the flu, Father. Between you and me, most Europeans think this president's a little bit *pazzo*—crazy in the head—but we're happy to have him around. Somebody has to get control of all those nukes."

"He's the only one left? That's unbelievable!"

"But believe it. Two days ago, I wouldn't have believed any of this, but it's a new world, Father."

They exited the terminal. Enrico drove the cart up to the Gulfstream's stairs, where copilot Annamaria waited for them. She had long blonde hair and a kind smile.

"Holiness," she cooed, "let me help you." She took Benny's hand and stumbled a bit as Benny let her lift his bulk from the seat.

"Times are tough," Annamaria said, "but we managed to find a hot meal for you and a bottle of wine. You will feel better with something in your stomach, no?"

Benny's expression lightened significantly at the mention of food. Michael realized that he was famished as well. In short order, they were seated in plush, leather-clad club seats. With no traffic, they took off immediately and reached cruising altitude quickly. Before they knew it, there was a steaming bowl of pasta and a glass of wine in front of each of them.

Annamaria smiled broadly as she said, "I have to go back to the front to help the pilot. If you need anything, feel free to help yourselves. Everything in the galley is unlocked."

"One thing before you go," Benny said before downing his glass of wine. Raising his glass toward her, he said, "Could you bring the bottle, please?"

Once she left, Michael shook his head. "'Bring the bottle, please?' You are going to need one heck of a makeover, pal, if you plan to pull off this pope thing."

"I learned a little bit about charming people from Luciano. And I've been practicing a pious face. Let me know what you think." He tilted his head back and made his eyes as wide as saucers, folding his hands as if in earnest prayer.

Michael chuckled. "Well, clearly we have to buy you a mirror, Holiness."

"No, seriously, Michael, what do you think?"

"It looks cartoonish and contrived, Benny. Normally, people in media training would tell you to just be yourself, but we both know that's not going to work."

Benny snarled and poured another glass of wine. To Michael's dismay, it rekindled Benny's litany of unkind acts. Michael fell asleep sometime around a tryst with a leather-clad man named Bruno in New York.

The Atlanta airport hadn't fared much better than Fiumicino's. The hangar for private planes was in good shape, so Enrico and Annamaria planned to stay there until the flight to New York in a few days.

"You're going to New York?" Michael asked Benny when he heard them discussing the plan.

"No. *We're* going to New York. Isa wants me there when he addresses the United Nations. It will sort of be my coming-out party. The whole world will get a first taste of their new pope."

"Aw, Benny, haven't they been through enough?" Michael wisecracked. "You won't need me there, will you?"

"Of course I will," Benny huffed. "I only have an entourage of one, Michael: you."

"Note to self," Michael said sarcastically. "Buy Benny an entourage."

There was no golf cart service at this airport. Michael's and Benny's shoes made lonely clattering sounds as the two men wound through the terribly silent hallways. Mangled, bloodied bodies filled the place. The air-conditioning had slowed the decay and kept the smell down compared with the road to Fiumicino, but the harsh glare of the fluorescent lights caught every distressing detail. Michael willed himself not to look so as not to imagine the circumstances behind their deaths, but every once in a while he would happen on the horror-struck face of some innocent, the wide-eyed expression of a sane person who happened to be in the midst of lunatics when the Dark Awakening hit. At one point he found himself staring with compassion at the sight of a teenage boy frozen in a death struggle with an older man.

"We can't help them, Michael," Benny said with more compassion than Michael had ever heard him muster.

"I know." He shrugged. "Some of them really get to me, though."

"I know," Benny said as they resumed their fateful journey to the car rental counters. He gingerly patted Michael's shoulder. "Something had to give on a planet that could no longer sustain its population. I've long endorsed the view that any mass event would ultimately benefit mankind. I guess I still do, but to see it and smell it is more difficult than I had imagined."

Michael just shrugged. He was ambivalent. Part of him was happy to know Benny was at least sane enough to relate to the world's suffering as something other than an inconvenience. Part of him was angry with the man who had actually longed for such an event. Whatever. He was too tired to challenge Benny—tired of self-recrimination, tired of this seemingly endless push to get home, tired of death and despair. And most of all, he was tired of Benny. But if working with his lunatic uncle would help some find their way home to Jesus, then so be it. He would have to suck it up, buttercup, as his mom used to say.

The bodies were literally piled up at the rental car locations. It looked as if the sane ones had rushed the counters to get cars out of the place when the insanity took over.

"This doesn't look good, Benny," Michael said as he jumped behind the counter. All the keys were gone. He hated to do it, but he rummaged through the bodies until he found a set of keys for a car on the first floor of the parking garage. "Let's see if we can find the Taurus in space 105." They walked through the automatic doors to the lot only to see another shambles of death and destruction. Some cars were totally destroyed. Some were crammed with people who had tried to get out only to be stopped by the ravenous crowd.

Benny and Michael found space 105. The Taurus clearly had seen the brunt of some collisions during the rush to leave, but it still looked better than the others. And Michael really didn't want to have to pry some dead person's hands from the steering wheel of one of the other cars. He unlocked the Taurus's doors and said to Benny, "Hop in."

"I hope this thing can get us the thirty miles to home," Benny said doubtfully.

"It's the best choice we have. Even if it takes us partway, it's better than walking." The front end had been smashed, but if the car ran, then Michael would take it. He pushed the ignition button. The vehicle started with a whine, and it shook horribly while idling, but it ran. They were both startled when the radio came blaring on: "This is a message from the emergency broadcast system. Due to unforeseen events, the United States is in a state of emergency. All residents are ordered to shelter in place until a proper assessment of damages can be completed."

Benny turned the radio off. "Tell us something we don't know," he snarled.

Michael eased the Taurus from its slot. There was a lot of twisted metal between them and the exit, but he thought he could squeeze the car through an opening between a steel girder and a pileup of three cars. He inched forward and came to an abrupt stop. He almost hadn't seen the body in front of him. Everything inside of him wanted to just drive over it, but he couldn't. Throwing the transmission into park, he held his breath and grabbed the portly man in a business suit under the arms and dragged him to the side, praying for the poor fellow as he did so.

When Michael got back in the car, Benny turned up his nose and said, "That one smelled ripe." Michael didn't know whether to laugh or cry. He just said nothing and threw the transmission into drive again. Inching the car slowly ahead, he felt and heard the grinding of metal as the Taurus sacrificed its side mirror to the steel girder. He winced, and drove on until the car came to an abrupt stop. It was stuck between the girder and the pileup. Michael panicked at the thought of being trapped. He floored the engine, sending the car careening forward as sparks flew where the metal of the car grated against the metal of the girder. Michael and Benny both winced at the piercing shriek of metal-on-metal grinding. Finally the tangle of cars yielded, and they were free.

"The old girl has some pickup," Michael said with a smile as he looked at the girder in the rearview mirror and proceeded out of the parking lot. The first hurdle was down, but he had to open the parking lot gate and lower the pavement spikes.

Inside the booth at the gate, the body of the unusually large attendant lay over the desk inside. "Oh, Lord," Michael prayed, "I'm so tired of moving bodies." He twisted the door handle, but the booth was locked. Of course it was. The poor feckless attendant had probably locked himself in against the raging hordes, but a bullet found him anyway. Michael could see the bullet hole through the Plexiglas window and the dried blood that had oozed from the man's head onto the console before him. Jumping back into the car, Michael rammed the door of the booth three times before it gave way—Benny screaming in panic the entire time. Michael then jumped out of the car and shouldered the remnants of the door to gain passage. The body had rotted in its sealed coffin. The resultant smell was atrocious. He thought he could get to the button without actually having to move the body, but he would have to reach around it, meaning making nearly full body contact. He couldn't bring himself to do it. Stepping back outside for a breath, he inhaled deeply and returned to the booth. Using both hands, he yanked the oversized man hard by his belt. The body fell backward from the console with a nauseating splat. Michael quickly found the button and raised the gate.

Stepping out of the stink-hole, he took a deep breath and assessed the situation. Home was about thirty miles away. He had grown up in Georgia and knew he could snake around back roads for about twenty of those miles. The first ten, though, would have to be on the highway. He surveyed the tangled mess of metal and flesh ahead of them and began the arduous journey. He would be able to drive a few feet, and then he would have to leave the car to move a body or another vehicle.

Most of the cars had been left running when the Dark Awakening hit, emptying their gas tanks. When this was the case, he had no choice but to put the vehicle in neutral and push against the driver's-side frame while steering. It was slow, tedious work. A lot of the vehicles were abandoned, but in quite a few, he had to remove a body from the driver's seat to get the car running.

After the fifth vehicle and less than a quarter mile of passage, he got back into the Taurus to see Benny crunching on something. "What are you eating?" Michael asked.

"Nothing," Benny said through a full mouth.

Michael grabbed Benny's cheeks until his mouth popped open. "Don't lie to me, Benny," he said angrily.

"Fine," Benny said, pushing him away. "I raided the candy and crackers from the plane."

Michael slapped the steering wheel. "And you weren't going to share, right? You just wait for me to get out of the car to shove something in your mouth."

"Michael, I couldn't possibly eat in front of you when you smell like all those bodies. Seriously, have you even considered the germs you must be carrying?"

"What?" Michael demanded as he pried Benny's hand open and took the crunched remainder of a package of peanut butter crackers. "Are you *trying* to annoy me, Benny?"

Benny smirked and said calmly, "There are so few entertainment options available."

Michael slammed the car into drive and inched down the road. He wondered if God would mind a lot if he just offed Benny right then and there. Of course he knew he couldn't do it. In fact, he felt the Holy Spirit check him immediately. *I hear you, Lord. But Benny is a body I wouldn't mind moving right now. Just saying.*

"Michael, you're tense," Benny said in an approximation of a conciliatory tone. "Let's take your mind off the task at hand. We really should be using this time to talk about crafting my papal image. I need to look pious but strong, leading a troubled world to a brilliant future."

Michael put his hand to his face. Benny was right; the smell was disgusting. "You'll have to change just about every mannerism, Benny," he said.

"Not really a problem. I've always considered myself a bit of a thespian, you know."

The absurdity of it all was suddenly amusing to Michael. He choked back a chuckle. "So, let's say you can pull off the act. What do you need me for?"

"I'm going to need a bit of a theology rewrite. You have the most practice of anyone I know, and you already have the world's admiration for your fine work," Benny said with no small amount of pride. Michael was sickened by the thought that he had been an unwitting tool in the creation of this monster and also by the more disturbing prospect that his most heinous act had earned Benny's esteem.

Benny continued. "I need to be someone who transcends mere Christianity. So the first thing to go will be the title Vicar of Christ. It's just not inclusive enough. In the new world, I don't think I want to be associated with Christ."

"Finally something we can agree on," Michael shouted. "I don't think you should be associated with Christ either, Benny."

"Here's what I'm thinking," Benny said. "You can write me an encyclical to bridge the old religion to the new. It will go something like this: Jesus died on the cross to take away sin. Therefore, sin no longer exists. None of this give-your-heart-to-Him stuff. Everyone is saved."

"All right, let's get something straight, Benny. I'll haul your water, but I won't do any dirty work that denies Jesus. Got that? Consider me ... Chris the second."

"How boring! At least Chris was eye candy. He had that sort of rugged build you could just ..."

Michael threw the car into park and jumped out to move a body that was lying in the road. Suddenly the road work didn't seem so bad.

Returning to the car, he said, "Benny, I can't concentrate on your career right now. And to be clear, I never want to hear you talk about Chris like that again. It gives me the heebie-jeebies."

"Fine. Just understand that what I said is perfectly acceptable in the post-sin world."

Michael stared ahead and put an extended index finger to his mouth. "Shh," he said.

"Fine," Benny huffed. They proceeded to the next stalled car as Benny repeatedly sighed.

As the day grew hot, so did the car. The radiator had sprung a leak. In each car he entered along the road, Michael looked for a full tank of gas, thinking they would have to abandon the Taurus at some point. Until then, he had to turn off the engine periodically to let it cool.

"Time for a break, Benny," he said, turning the car off. "The car's heating up. Stretch your legs for about twenty minutes while it cools down." Michael popped the hood to air out the overheated engine, and then he moved forward to look for another vehicle. He checked car after car to no avail, but he was able to clear a few out of the way.

"Come on, Benny." He motioned as he started the Taurus. The engine still registered a bit hot, but it was clearly an improvement.

As Benny entered the car, Michael said, "From now on, I'm going to have to turn the car off when I clear the road. We'll have to keep cooling it down. Hopefully, I'll find another car ahead of us that has some gas. Then it's adios to the Taurus."

"Whatever," Benny said as he turned on the air-conditioning. "I'm surprised I didn't have a heat stroke just now."

Michael briskly turned the air-conditioning off. "Open your window, Benny. No more air-conditioning for this car."

Benny cussed—a lot.

"That's something that will need to change in your new role, Benny."

"Shouldn't you be calling me Luciano? If not that, you could call me Holiness."

"Well, *Luciano*," Michael said through clenched teeth, "open your window."

The heat and humidity were stifling. Wavy lines rose from the scorching pavement. But they proceeded. They had made it about three miles in eight hours. If he weren't loaded down with Pope Potty Mouth, Michael would have abandoned the Taurus and walked until he could find another car. He had to consider their options. The sun would soon set. Certainly the Taurus would fare better once the sun set, but he seriously doubted he could clear the way in the dark. At some point they would have to find shelter.

Scanning the horizon, Michael saw a grove of trees about a half mile ahead. If worse came to worst, they could camp out there. Or at least he could. Benny had already made it clear that Michael smelled too bad for the two to pass the night in the car together. He put the car in park and turned off the engine.

"Here's the deal, Benny. I'm going to try to clear the road up to that grove of trees and let the car cool down while I get to work. I just hope I can clear it before dark."

The work was slower than Michael had anticipated. He hadn't considered how tired he had become. He noticed how his strength had waned when he pried the driver, a particularly heavy woman, from an incongruously small Volkswagen Bug. In the back was an empty child's car seat. "Thank You, Jesus, for not leaving any kids behind to suffer this."

In the distance, he heard windows smashing and the howls of a couple of crazies. Pausing to listen, he heard another sound of shattering glass. It sounded closer, just over the next hill. *This can't be good.* With the driver's door open, he threw the Bug into neutral, put his shoulder to its frame, and pushed. Gravity took over, at which point he guided the car to the left until it coasted into an SUV.

He sat down on the guardrail to rest and to listen. There was no doubt about it: the marauders were closing in. He could hear two distinct voices. He and Benny might have to make a stand. Two against two. Who was he kidding? His only chance was to offer them a Pope Porky roast. Then a plan formed. He and Benny should be able to hide underneath the Taurus until the evildoers passed.

Slowly and quietly raising himself from the guardrail, he took ginger steps toward the Taurus. That's when he heard it, a sharp pop and a gushing sound. Damn! Why hadn't he taken the Taurus's keys with him? Of course, Benny had turned on the air conditioner! Of course the car overheated! And of course, the sound had attracted the crazies who charged over the hill in Michael's direction! He broke into a run, but they gained on him, urged on by some primordial predator gene.

"Oh, Lord." He panted as he ran. "What do I do now?" The first one hit, tackling him. Michael lost his wind as he slammed to the pavement. The second fell over them both, giving Michael an opportunity to jump up and breathlessly resume his beeline to the Taurus. His pursuers righted themselves and gained on him. He made it to the Taurus and grabbed the door handle just as he heard the doors lock.

"Benny! Let me in," he screamed. Benny's face was frozen in fear as he looked past Michael to the approaching beasts. Michael turned to face them. Their faces barely looked human, little more than swollen masses of bruises. Their black eyes lacked even the remotest hint of human understanding. He braced himself and balled his hands into fists.

He swung hard as the first one attacked. The blow was enough to divert the attack, but the second creature fell on Michael. Like some twisted animal, he clutched at Michael and bit down on his cheek. A burst of pain clouded Michael's vision, and then he felt the beast arch his back in a howl as he fell to the pavement. The other beast went down beside the first, each felled by an arrow.

Looking to the hill along the road, Michael saw a physically powerful man in a hooded leather tunic pointing at him with a crossbow. He looked like something out of the Middle Ages. The weapon was loaded.

"Aw. What fresh new hell is this?" he muttered.

TEN

An eerie calm had settled over Houston—over most of the country, in fact. As the riotous destruction dissipated, shocked residents peered outside their homes to assess the damage. It wasn't pretty. Gloria had watched the burgeoning news coverage in disbelief. All over the nation, buildings had been torched, people had been savagely brutalized, and infrastructure had been wantonly destroyed. Skeleton news crews ventured into the damage and brought endless videos of similar destruction across the globe.

Silence had fallen over the Jolean household as well. Zack was courteous and expressed his relief that his wife was okay. He told her how he had feared she had tried to take her life in the locked bathroom. She tried to bring up the subject of her parents. She knew he had seen them too, but he vehemently denied it.

Earlier in the day, he said, "I'm going to try to make it to the church to assess the damage." In response to her silence, he added, "Wish me luck."

"Good luck," she said bluntly. Yet now she regretted her callousness.

Her feelings for him were so confusing. She had loved him once; at least she had told herself so. But could she ever have loved a man who could so callously murder another as she had seen him do to Bonnie? She shuddered at the thought of that horrible moment. If it weren't for the all-too-apparent bruising on her own face, she would have thought it all some horrible nightmare. As it turned out, though, her life with him was the real nightmare. Just a few moments with her parents had made that abundantly clear. She had helped Zack turn Christianity into a media circus full of magic, lights, and music, but devoid of content.

"Oh Jesus, I am so sorry for what I have done. How could I have been so blind?" She felt the instantaneous warmth of His presence. How had she lived her life without it all those years? Now that she knew nothing could separate her from His love, she would do nothing to hinder its expression. That was not going to sit well with her husband.

And so her thoughts turned to him. Had he been part of the madness? Was Bonnie's murder a part of the madness that had also befallen the rest of the world? If so, could she hold it against him?

She had to figure out what to do. She wandered to the bedroom where her mother and David had stayed and rummaged through Fran's suitcase to get an article of clothing, anything that smelled like her. She grabbed a blouse and held it to her nose, vividly recalling the recent warm hugs with her parents. She never thought she would be able to feel her dad's strong embrace again once he died in Africa. Now she knew he and her mother were waiting for her. It made all the difference. Missing the rapture was a horrible fate she wouldn't wish on anyone. Finding Jesus in the aftermath was a blessing beyond belief, a second chance.

And back to Zack. Did he deserve a second chance? She stared at her mother's journal sitting in the suitcase. Since their hasty departure from Africa years before, her mother had kept a journal. When Gloria was little, she had asked about its contents. Fran told her that parenting was a two-person job and that when she felt like she needed to talk to someone, she would release the pressure by writing to Tom.

Gloria opened the journal to its last entry. A little thrill came at the sight of her mother's handwriting. "Tom, I don't have high hopes for today. Between you and me, I've never trusted Zack. But to have to tell Gloria about him and Benny ... I can't even bring myself to imagine what Chris saw, let alone break the news to Gloria. Of course, this whole affair brings back my recurring fear that Zack did away with Mack and Sarah. They wouldn't have just sailed into the sunset without so much as a good-bye. They would have had a big televised party, for crying out loud! David says I need to leave it in the past while we deal with the current situation. He's right, of course."

Gloria closed the journal. She thought about the disappearance of Mack and Sarah. The circumstances were odd, but Gloria had been too caught up in the emotion of her pregnancy to question it. Meemaw knew, though. Her mind filled with memories of the dear old woman trying to warn her about Zack from her deathbed. At the time, Gloria attributed it to dementia.

At least Meemaw had confided in her. Why hadn't her mother shared her concerns? The answer was obvious. Gloria had been a brat with her mother. She had bought into Zack's false gospel and challenged her mother and David any time they expressed even a small measure of concern. Her love for Zack had made her unapproachable.

She shook her head. That wasn't the only reason. Zack had convinced her they were on the cusp of a new revelation from God to be brought about by the child she had carried. And she believed it. Well, in her own defense, she had carried the child. It was real enough. To believe it was anything other than a miracle of sorts would be tantamount to saying she was participating in a horrible evil. And now she knew she had.

She wiped at the seemingly unending tears falling down her cheeks. Zack had used her. Plain and simple. And while she couldn't prove it, he had probably killed Sarah and Mack to get his hands on their ministry. Her body convulsed in sobs as it became clear how she had been duped. Zack only cared about the fame and fortune, and he would do anything to protect it. He would kill her as easily as he had killed Bonnie.

Would it be so bad to die? She could avoid the impending doom and be with Jesus. But in her spirit, she knew He was telling her it wasn't her time. There was work to do, a chance to right some of the wrong—the opportunity to offer others the second chance Jesus had offered her. But Zack wasn't likely to go along with it. She needed leverage.

Rushing from the guest bedroom, she quickly went to his office, his inner sanctum. She knew Zack well. He viewed himself as a creative person. Passwords and the like were a constant aggravation to him. As she entered the wood-paneled space, she looked at the rich mahogany desk atop the ornate Oriental rug. A few days ago, she would have relished the décor, the perfect window treatments, and the fine leather furnishings. Now they were nothing more than a witness to all the wrong decisions she had made over the years.

Turning on his computer, it was as she had expected: no password protection. Why should he protect his files? There were only the two of them, and she *never* invaded his space ... until now. She typed "Mom and Dad" into the search bar. Easy enough. He had a folder of files dedicated to them: letters they had supposedly written from Grand Cayman, and letters from the Grand Cayman authorities that Mack and Sarah had gone missing. All had been typed by Zack on his computer. Her head throbbed. It was one thing to suspect it, but it was another to see the proof.

Next she typed in "Benny." Another folder appeared, this one containing correspondence about payments made and a tryst in New York. She clicked on an old file: a letter shortly after the cruise. As she read in horror, she could string together the pieces. Benny had helped Zack kill his parents in return for a cut of the profits from the ministry. This just kept getting worse and worse.

Gloria ran to her office to get a flash drive, her tears flowing all the while. As quickly as she could, she downloaded the first few files. If she was going to do what she planned, she would need a way to keep Zack at bay. The first part of the plan was to retrieve the information. The next would be to secure it somewhere he could never get to it. Then she would tell him what she knew. She would demand concessions from him, but she had to be cautious. Clearly, Zack and Benny were not above murder.

She heard the front door open. Turning off his computer, she grabbed the flash drive and escaped the office quietly. By the time Zack made it back to the kitchen, she had managed to pour a cup of coffee and sit at the table as if she had been there a while.

"How did the church look?" she asked with convincing concern and more affection than she had shown before he left.

"Minimal damage," he said, but his expression was grave. "But there were dead bodies in the parking lot, Gloria. It was one of the worst things I've ever seen." He choked back a sob.

To Gloria, it looked like a parody of true emotion. Had he always been this transparent? Well, maybe not to her, but to her mother and David. It was so easy to see now, whereas it had been nearly impossible before she had given her life to Christ. She knew she couldn't tip her hand that she was onto him. She got out of her chair and hugged him.

"That's not all. I'm afraid I have some bad news." He pulled out of the hug and looked deeply into her eyes. She could feel him probing at her mind. Had it always been like this?

"Whatever it is, we'll get through it, honey," she offered.

"It was Bonnie's body in the parking lot." His voice broke, followed by more furious wiping at his eyes, struggling to produce tears. He pulled her close. She gasped, not at his news, but at the realization that he was trying to plant a false memory in her mind. He was more devious than she could ever have imagined.

Real tears formed in her eyes as she vividly recalled Bonnie's death at the hands of the man who held her. *Oh, Mom, I owe you such an apology the next time we meet.*

"That's horrible news, Zack!" she exclaimed, hoping it wasn't too dramatic. "I wonder if her husband knows ..."

"I saw his body there too," Zack offered weakly.

She sighed with the certain knowledge that Zack had killed him too. "Well, at least the kids were spared all of this in the rapture."

He pulled away from her abruptly. "Gloria, you don't actually believe Jesus came back to take His own out of the world, do you?"

"How else to you explain it, Zack? One minute we were talking with Mom and David. Then there was a flash of light, and they were gone."

"They succumbed to the madness, Gloria. Don't you remember how they ran out of here when the lightning hit?" She could feel him trying to plant the false memory. How would she have responded to something like this in the past? She had to make it look believable.

Pacing the kitchen as if mad with grief, she cried, "We have to find them, Zack. For all we know, they're lying in the street somewhere ... hurt or maybe worse!"

"All I saw out there was death, sweetheart," he said as he gently caressed her upper arms and put his face close to hers. "When they ran out of here, they sealed their fates. Even now, National Guard troops are gathering bodies out of the streets. You saw the news; anyone missing will be presumed dead by the government. They simply don't have the resources to catalog each body and notify next of kin."

She forced an expression of horror at the thought. It wasn't too hard. She knew her mother and David were safe, but Zack's scenario would become reality for most of the world. He responded by hugging her again. Her immediate sensation was revulsion, but she quelled it, allowing herself to be comforted.

Pulling out of the hug, she said, "Zack, what are the odds that both of our parents would just disappear without a trace? First Mack and Sarah, and now Mom and David?"

He bristled. Maybe she had pushed it too far. She had to be careful not to tip her hand.

"Losing Mom and Dad was one of the worst things that ever happened to me," he said gravely. "But you were here for me, darlin', and I plan to be here for you."

She buried her head in his shoulder and heaved as if sobbing. In her mind's eye she saw the inevitable smug grin on his face. She was beginning to understand that her penance over the next seven years would be to live with the monster to whom she had cast her lot years before.

He led her to the table. "Drink your coffee, darlin'. I'll fix us something to eat."

"I don't think I can eat right now." She sighed heavily.

"Force yourself, then. You have to keep up your strength. There are tons of people out there hurting, and our job is to help them through it."

"Tell me something, Zack," she said. "How do we help people whose lives are ruined?"

He offered a sad smile. "We'll just love them through it. I know things seem tough right now, but I can't shake this feeling that these events are the prelude to some wonderful things to come. Our son—"

"Do you think we'll ever meet him?" She cut him off as her mind raced with a cacophony of self-recrimination for her part in that misadventure. She pushed it aside.

"I sure hope so," he said.

She lay still in bed, waiting to hear the steady breathing that would signal Zack's having finally fallen asleep. She carefully slid out of bed and then cautiously and slowly left the bedroom to return to his office.

Inserting the flash drive into the computer's USB port, she began to download the remainder of the files. As they downloaded, her eye was drawn to another folder, this one labeled "Isa." After opening it, she saw articles about the young Turkish ruler.

She read of his meteoric rise to power in the wake of his father's death. An article extoled his political acumen in establishing Turkey as the central player in all Middle Eastern affairs. Quotes from US and European sources praised him as the next best hope for the war-torn region. Even the Israeli prime minister hailed him as the only real chance for negotiating peace in the Middle East.

"So Zack thinks you're our son, Mr. Kurtoglu," she said to the screen as she zoomed in on his photo. A soundless *O* of astonishment formed on her lips. There was no denying it; this man had Michael's eyes.

She downloaded the "Isa" file to the flash drive and then pulled up dim, dreamlike memories of her alien impregnation. Michael was there, as was Zack. What had the Lady said? Something about their needing DNA from all three of them, and that it would be attached to a third stand of DNA from her leader. "Well, we know who her leader is, don't we?" she asked the empty room.

She heard footsteps upstairs. She held her breath in fear, but then she sighed in relief as she heard the bathroom door close. A few moments of reprieve. She stared anxiously at the screen as the files were saved one by one. Done. She pulled the flash drive from the USB port and turned off the computer.

She winced as the computer gave the musical signal that it had shut down. She hoped Zack hadn't heard it, but there was no way to be sure. Rushing silently out of the office, she ran again to the kitchen, quickly poured some milk into a pan, and put it on the stove.

"Couldn't sleep?" Zack startled her from the kitchen doorway. How had he come down the stairs so silently?

"No," she offered weakly. "I thought maybe some warm milk would do the trick."

"Throw some cocoa in there and I'll join you," he said with a leering glance and a half smile. She knew his intentions.

"You know, that sounds good to me too," she said, turning to the pantry. She deftly stashed the flash drive behind a box of rice and emerged with the cocoa.

As she stirred the milk, her husband stood behind her, his body brushing against hers. "I know something else that might help you sleep." He put his arms around her waist. For years she had thrilled at his touch. Now it produced a nearly uncontrollable urge to run and hide. She had to keep up the ruse.

"I bet you do," she said in a sultry voice.

As he kissed the back of her neck, she said, "I've been thinking a lot about what you said, Zack. This crisis has rocked the world. There are so many needs for us to meet."

"Mmm," he said in agreement as he nuzzled her ear.

"So, I was thinking that I'd like to develop my own program. Kind of a kitchen setting. I could give tips on how to get households back in order."

"I like the way you think. It could end up in all kinds of endorsement deals and advertising revenue if we plug products." He gave her butterfly kisses.

"So you'll allow me to do it?" she asked.

"Allow it? I encourage it," he said as he held the full length of his body against hers.

"It's a deal then," she said. He couldn't dream she would plan to do straight gospel teaching on her show. All have sinned. Jesus died to pay the price for those sins. There is no other way to the Father. She couldn't let him know until she had safely hidden the flash drive—someplace where he couldn't get to it—with instructions to release all information to the press if she disappeared or died suddenly.

She turned and deeply kissed the man she once loved but now reviled.

ELEVEN

The war ended nearly before it had begun. In the madness of the Dark Awakening, before the rioting populace killed their government leaders, Israel's neighbors launched a coordinated attack. Syria, Lebanon, Egypt, Jordan, Saudi Arabia, and Iraq all joined Hamas, Hezbollah, and ISIS to squash the tiny nation from all sides. Israel was not unprepared. For decades it had planned for such an attack and armed itself to the teeth with special atomic weapons. The conventional wisdom had been that fallout from even strategic nuclear devices would be too hazardous to risk deployment in the small geographic area of the Middle East. The world had relied on Israel's restraint for years, but restraint fell victim to chaos in the Dark Awakening.

Israel's choice weapon was the neutron bomb, with an atomic blast that channeled its immense power into producing neutrinos. These heavy subatomic particles ravaged enemy bodies while leaving all infrastructure intact. In a word, the Arab conventional forces hadn't known what hit them. With most Israelis in shelters, the bombs did their work, leaving in their wake eerily silent cities. The very dense neutrinos dissipated rapidly, allowing Israel to precisely calculate fallout zones. It was a small matter for Israel to mop up in an all-sides landgrab to include the Sinai Peninsula, all of Lebanon, southern Syria, western Jordan, and southwest Iraq.

Israel's victory was so sudden that the Arab world could only gasp—most of the Arab world, that is. In the Turkish presidential palace, Isa Kurtoglu laughed with wild abandon. The tensions between Israel and its neighboring states would have been a constant source of aggravation in his new caliphate. The war had produced three highly desirable outcomes: it relieved the tension that threatened to eclipse the birth of the Islamic state; it toppled the Middle Eastern governments most likely not to go along with his plan; and it galvanized the remaining people to throw their support behind him. All in all, it had been a good day for Isa. Sure, there were casualties, but in a world with billions of people, nobody would miss the victims of this exchange.

The war was not without its destruction, however. The largest neutron bomb had been dropped into the center of Damascus. While the weapons were not built for the destruction of infrastructure, their immediate blast zones were still annihilated. Then, of course, there was the Dome of the Rock. Shells from the Arab confederacy had all but destroyed it, leaving behind a pile of rubble with occasional glints of gold from its once magnificent dome. Its destruction was the height of embarrassment to followers of Islam. The world would never know that Turkey's sole missile fired in the fray was responsible for that piece of damage.

While addressing his growing crowd of followers, Isa appealed to the Islamic tradition of *taqiyya*, the creation of a false peace with one's enemies only in order to arm oneself for the next confrontation. The crowd saw the logic in his reasoning at once. Just as the policy had worked for the Prophet, it would work for them. And even though the peace would seem humiliating, there was a price to be paid for the al-Aqsa destruction.

It was all done but the peace accord, and Isa was on his way to a meeting with the Israeli prime minister. As he entered the room, he greeted the man warmly. "Mr. Prime Minister, welcome. I hope you don't in any way believe I endorsed the attack on your nation."

"No, Mr. President," the prime minister said softly. "I know you to be a man of peace. And I know Turkey had no role to play in the most recent attacks."

"Excellent," Isa said with a winning smile. "As luck would have it, Mr. Prime Minister, the Arab world is calling for the reestablishment of the caliphate with me at the helm."

"We have been busy with this war, but I can assure you our intelligence forces have devoted ample time to the analysis of the current situation."

"Then you no doubt agree with me. We are in an historic position, Mr. Prime Minister. The individual nations who attacked have lost most governing authority. As caliph, I can negotiate with you a fair and lasting resolution to this conflict."

"With all due respect, Mr. President," the prime minister said, "Israel's sound thrashing of its attackers has put us more in the frame of mind of forced armistice rather than peace treaty."

Isa laughed heartily. "You misunderstand me. By the end of the week, I will announce the formation of my caliphate. Israel will be an island nation surrounded by me. There is no ragtag coalition of the vanquished for you to impose peace upon."

A sullen look passed over the prime minister's face as he considered the implications of being surrounded by another, single nation. The risks to Israel would be great.

Isa continued. "You also have to remember the considerable number of weapons at my command. The arsenals of Turkey, Iran, and Libya have not been used. On the other hand, my resources tell me Israel's most powerful strategic arms are depleted. Is that a fair assessment?"

"It would be a fair assessment," the prime minister said sullenly.

"The good news for you, Mr. Prime Minister, is that I have no designs on Israel. I am prepared to offer you complete autonomy in the center of my caliphate. Your nation will exist as my protectorate."

The prime minister winced.

Isa continued. "I know it sounds unmanageable, but I truly believe we have the opportunity to bring lasting peace to the Middle East. Think of the peace dividend to Israel's economy once it is freed from the financial burden of defense spending. Add to that the economic impact of free trade with the rest of the region. It will be a golden age for Israel."

The prime minister grinned. "I admit it all sounds like a dream come true, but the notion of protectorate status presumes a loss of sovereignty that my nation can't accept. Islam's concept of *taqiyya* is well-known to the rest of the world."

"But old paradigms are dying fast, Mr. Prime Minister. Let me ask you something. Why didn't the United States offer assistance in the recent round of battle?"

"The United States military ignored our requests for aid." The prime minister bristled, and spoke with downcast eyes in a vain attempt to conceal the rage still smoldering within.

"Well, surely you called the American president, did you not?" Isa asked smugly.

Looking up with flashes of uninhibited fury, the prime minister nearly shouted, "He refused to take my calls."

"It would appear you have lost your major ally. Some would say your only ally, but I disagree. Once your nation lies within my new Islamic Republic, you will be protected on all sides. Anyone trying to get to you would have to go through me.

"Think of the possibilities for your people. Rather than seeing Israel as surrounded by its enemies, you need to embrace the similarities Israel will have with Switzerland. That nation has done very well as a financial powerhouse at the center of the EU."

The prime minister gained control over his temper and sat deep in thought. Isa could see him warming to the idea. Israel was too small to go it alone. If he rejected Isa's offer, his nation would be adrift with not a single ally in the world. It needed to secure strategic defense measures with a stronger power, someone to fill the vacuum left by the United States. Where was he to turn—Russia? Even the thought was ludicrous. Isa said nothing, letting the man think it through. And he thought none too quickly in Isa's estimation.

The prime minister began softly, weighing his words. "I think the issue, Mr. President, is that unlike Switzerland and the EU, we have an unstable history of uneasy peace punctuated by untethered brutality. I personally see the value of your proposal. And let's be frank, you offer me two alternatives: to be surrounded by an enemy or to be surrounded by a benevolent dictatorship. Obviously I choose the latter, but I may need something to offer my people to get them behind this deal."

Isa laughed and slapped the desk with his hand, his exuberance startling the exhausted prime minister. "I think we both know where you are going with this line of reasoning. Let's cut to the chase. I am prepared to endorse Israel's construction of its longed-for temple."

The prime minister's smile covered the entire width of his face. He was too excited to remain seated. Pacing the floor of Isa's office, he said, "The temple *and* peace with our neighbors. It would be a dream come true for my people."

"After the events of the past few days, peace will be the dream of every person in the world. I have some information to present to the United Nations next week in New York. While I cannot go into details with you about it now, let me assure you that I will present a very powerful rationale for the world to unite in peace. It will help my cause tremendously if you will join me there. Our new relationship will serve as an example of how even the most ancient of enemies can find peace if they really seek it."

"It would be an honor to join you in New York," the prime minister said. "In the meanwhile, may I brief the Knesset leaders as to the nature of our agreement?"

"Under the strictest of confidence, I assume." Isa nodded gravely. "Absolutely."

"Then you have my blessing," Isa said. The two exchanged an uncomfortable hug before the prime minister left the office.

"That went even better than expected," Isa said to himself after the prime minister left. He strode exuberantly to the bar and poured himself a glass of scotch. He thought of how marvelously his plans were coming together. The notion that one man could bring the entire planet under his control in a matter of days was not considered even a remote possibility by the unsuspecting world. But then again, Isa wasn't the typical man. He pondered his own nature. His human side gave him tremendous insight into the people he would rule. But it was his alien nature that made him capable of such rule.

He marveled at the frailness of humanity and, by comparison, his unmitigated strength. His ability to see beyond Earth made him different from everyone who had come before him. Long ago he realized that his greatest strength was not in his genetic partnership with humanity but in his distinction from it. He had no emotional attachment to a species as different from him as they were from apes. Despite the fact that he shared their physiology, to his mind the human population was little more than unproductive herds foolishly feeding on the valuable resources of this beautiful world.

He knew how to feign human emotion and human connection. That was how he manipulated the bipedal beasts. At his core, however, he was so far above them mentally and spiritually that even in his most benevolent moments he could see them as little more than pets.

He didn't look on everyone with such disdain, however. There were a few who captured his imagination and tickled his spirit. The new pope, for example, was a sterling example of unabashed selfishness and ambition, two qualities that spoke to Isa's heart. And then there was Father Michael. The DNA they shared and the priest's sterling intellect combined to make him one of Isa's favorite pets.

As for peers, Isa had none. This bore itself out in his sexuality. He had no more desire to mate with these hairless apes than an owner wished to mate with his dog. It had been a bit of a concern for the elder Kurtoglu. The old man had urged him repeatedly to dive deep into the pleasures of the flesh. To the reckoning of his father, a man truly ungifted mentally, this lack of desire was an indication of homosexuality, anathema to the strict rules of Islam. It was years before his father realized that the lack of sexual interest was based on an absolute disdain for humanity on a grand scale.

"Oh, Father," he said aloud with a smirk, "too bad you couldn't live long enough to see the emergence of my empire." He chuckled at the sarcasm of his remark. The elder Kurtoglu had meant nothing to Isa other than a name traceable to the lineage of Mohammed.

Isa longed for the day when the human herd would be adequately culled to five-hundred million suitable men and women. From this remnant he would build a society rivaling the Lady's. The Lady! He couldn't wait to thank her for her work and then wrap his hands around her scrawny little neck. It galled him that she acted superior to him. He had no more attraction to her race than he had to humanity. It was the synthesis of the two that made him truly beautiful among all of creation. The undeniable human spirit combined with the multidimensional intelligence of her species made him stronger, better, and more capable than any member of either species.

Drink in hand, he sauntered over to the mirror. Even he couldn't believe the physical perfection afforded by this unlikely pairing of species. If the truth were to be told, his reflection was the only beauty to which he was physically attracted—the line of his face, the crystal blue color of his eyes, his swarthy complexion, his thick black hair worn long and straight off his face. And what a face it was with high cheekbones that bore just a hint of ruddy color, full red lips, and a perfect smile of dazzling white teeth.

The human response to being unique among all in the world would be a feeling of isolation and loneliness. Isa's response was exuberant exultation. It was good to be king! He looked at his watch: time for his scheduled call from the Russian president. The phone rang just on time.

"Hello, Vladimir," he spoke into the phone. "I assume things are going well for you now that you reign without the constraints of the Duma."

"Yes, my friend," the Russian president responded. "I have been drawing up plans to expand my territory."

"Ah, but remember our agreement. You may have the Balkans and eastern Europe, but the Islamic republics will be first-tier members of my caliphate."

"To be honest, Isa, they were difficult to reign anyway. You may have them with my blessings as long as you allow unfettered access to the Black Sea."

"Of course, Vladimir. When my vision is complete, the world will be free of petty restrictions on the flow of goods."

"You have not really shared this vision with me," Vladimir prodded.

"You will be fully briefed during next week's meeting at the United Nations. Trust me when I tell you, however, that it will be revolutionary."

"A beautiful word to an old Soviet." Vladimir chuckled.

"Indeed. Speaking of communism, have you had any luck persuading your Chinese counterpart that his support of my cause is the only sane option for him?"

"I'm afraid he doesn't see the value in submitting to the will of Turkey. He has spent many years honing a fearsome army and a devastating nuclear arsenal. I don't believe he thinks you have anything to offer him."

"Did he not accept my offer of Taiwan and South Korea?"

"No more than a tourist would believe someone trying to sell him the Burj Khalifa." Vladimir laughed loudly at his own joke. Isa did not see the humor. He didn't like to be treated so dismissively. He had made overtures to the Chinese ruler but was rebuffed. That's when he decided to enlist the aid of the Russian president, but to no avail.

"And you reinforced my message that it was I who controlled the Dark Awakening?" Isa asked skeptically.

"Again, Isa, he sees that as insane posturing on your part. He refused to believe you had any role to play in the uprisings throughout his country. And he said he was too busy with quelling the revolt to take seriously your offer."

"I can imagine it would be difficult to contend with the pent-up rage of a billion angry Chinamen." Isa chuckled as he turned to his computer to see coverage of the devastation rocking China. That was just the beginning of sorrow for the hapless Red leader. It was time for Isa to play hardball. He could barely contain a self-satisfied grin of anticipation.

"Ah, well, it is time for me to deal with him directly then, Vladimir. On the off chance the Chinese attitude has influenced your way of thinking, I invite you to keep your eyes on Shanghai. Something momentous is about to occur."

"I will do that, Isa. And let me assure you that I see the value of our partnership, and I am very grateful to rule my great country as a monarch." Isa knew he was lying, but he enjoyed the butt-kissing. It may be feigned at this point, but the time would soon come when Vladimir and the rest of the so-called ruling elite would bow to him in honest and unforced worship.

"Good, Vladimir. I'm happy we see eye-to-eye. I must end our call now. I have pending business with China."

———

The general was seconds away from a briefing with the Chinese leader. He didn't have a good story to tell. The army had made some headway in quelling the riots, but every city and every village was under siege. It would take weeks to bring order back to the troubled nation, and then months or even years to clean up the damage.

As he was shown to the president's office, his satellite phone rang. He felt conflicted. Loath to show rudeness and disrespect to the nation's leader by answering it, he was at the same time hopeful it was some piece of good news to soften the blow of the hard message he was about to deliver. He looked at the phone. Isa Kurtoglu. He paused to take the call.

"General," Isa said cheerily. "You are entering a briefing with the president, are you not?"

How could Kurtoglu know this? The man had amazed the general with his intelligence capabilities over the past couple of days. At some point, when the rebellion was quelled, he would have to plug the security breach that afforded the Turkish president such uncanny insight.

"I am," he answered cautiously.

"Good. Give him my regards and tell him to look at his computer. I have a message for both of you." The line went dead.

"Mr. President," the general said to his leader as he holstered the satellite phone and entered his superior's office, "I have just received a phone call from President Kurtoglu. He asks that we turn our attention to your computer screen."

"Him again?" the president asked with disdain.

"His intelligence network gives him incredible access to our affairs. There's no telling how much he knows unless we engage him. And for what it's worth, Mr. President, he has offered to help us in this time of crisis."

The president huffed, turning his chair to the computer console behind his desk. Once he looked at the screen, Isa's image appeared.

"Good evening, Mr. President," Kurtoglu said with a smug smile.

"How did you manage to take control of my computer?" the president demanded.

"Actually, that's not the topic at hand. I have dealt patiently with you and even engaged the services of your Russian counterpart to convince you I am the one in control of your rebellion." The president said nothing, staring angry darts at the screen.

"Now I think a little show of strength is in order. You see, Mr. President, the Dark Awakening goes deep into your military. At this very moment, your nuclear silos are opening, and a hydrogen bomb is acquiring its target—Shanghai."

The general's satellite phone rang. It was a report confirming what Kurtoglu had just said. "Mr. President," he said gravely to his leader, "it is true. The silos have opened."

"But only I have the final sequence to the launch code," the president said smugly.

"Well, you *and I*," Isa said cheerily. The president cursed loudly as his computer screen filled with urgent messages that the missile had launched. It reached its target in mere moments.

The horror of the situation was lost on the general. He felt as if he were losing consciousness, losing himself. As if watching from a distance, he saw his own hand reach for his sidearm. In a matter of seconds, the president lay dead in his chair as blood oozed from the fresh hole in his head.

Looking at the president and then at his own pistol, the general dropped it in horror. Isa's face reappeared on the computer screen. "Very well done, General," he cheered. "Or should I call you Mr. President?"

"Mr. President," the general answered. "The People's Republic of China is at your service," he added quickly, to affirm that he would not make the mistakes of his predecessor.

"Of course it is." Isa grinned.

TWELVE

Michael slowly raised his hands in the air, trying to make sense of the Robin Hood bearing down on him with a crossbow. He caught a shimmer out of the corner of his eye, and then he heard Gabe's voice saying, "It's okay, buddy." The man moved the sights of the crossbow slowly to the left, where Michael had seen the shimmering light. Had he seen it too?

The man slowly lowered his weapon. Michael slowly lowered his hands. Moving lithely down the hill, the man called out to him. "My name's Will White."

"Jake," Michael said, offering no surname. As Will neared, he pulled back his hood. Michael's heart leapt at the sight of him. There was a strong resemblance to Gabe in his eyes and ease of movement. Michael stared for a moment.

"What?" The man grinned.

"Nothing. You just remind me of someone I really miss." The men shook hands. Then Will bent to recover the arrows he had spent. Using his foot to steady each body, he pulled sharply to extricate the arrow. Michael winced at the slushing sound when the bodies gave up the instruments of their deaths.

"I know," Will said sympathetically. "I can't believe this happened either. Trust me. I've never used the crossbow, not even to hunt, until the craziness of the past few days."

"I owe you a thank-you for saving my life," Michael said as he watched the young man wipe the arrows clean in the grass.

"Well, you needed help," Will said softly. "Why are you out in this mess?"

Michael offered a wry smile and an exceedingly condensed version of his travel with Benny. "Trying to get home from Italy. I was able to get this car out of a rental garage, but it's pretty beat up."

Will returned the arrows to his quiver as he said, "There's a Hummer about a quarter mile up the road. And it's got gas. We'd be better off using it. I've been scoping it out."

"Why didn't you use it?"

"Nowhere to go," Will said as an expression of pain darkened his brow. "Besides, I had this feeling I'd know when it was time to move on."

"And you want to move on with us?" Michael asked, happy for the help.

Benny rolled down the window. "Jake, it's hot as hell in this car! If you two can break up your coffee clutch, I'd like to know what we do now that we don't have any transportation."

"This is my uncle Luciano," Michael said with a smirk. Then he added, "Everyone calls him Lucky."

"Nice to meet you, Lucky," Will said, shaking the older man's hand.

"We'll see about that," Michael said, chuckling at the horrified expression on Benny's face. Clearly he detested the moniker Lucky.

"You're certainly a strapping young man," Benny said with too much of a leer, still holding Will's hand. Michael pulled Will's hand free and opened the car door.

"Get out, Lucky," Michael said tersely. "Will spotted a Humvee about a quarter mile up the road. We're going to use it to get home."

"Where is home?" Will asked.

"About twenty miles east of here," Michael responded.

Will asked, "Will there be room for me to spend a night or two? I sure could stand to sleep in a bed."

"Room we got," Michael said with a smile, slapping the young man on the back. He couldn't believe how quickly he had come to like Will. They had an instant rapport. As they walked along the side of the road, Michael asked, "So, what do you do for a living, Will?"

"I have a magic and daredevil act. Basically, I do trick shots with the crossbow." Will wrinkled his brow. "Trust me, I don't dress like this as a fashion statement."

Michael chuckled. "I can't complain about your attire. I can assure you, Lucky and I have seen better days."

"Fashion is more than clothing," Benny huffed from behind. "It's an attitude, Jake." He strode past them as if walking a catwalk.

Will laughed at the entertainment and began to respond when Michael cut him off. Looking sharply into Will's eyes, he shook his head slightly and mouthed, "He's serious."

Will responded with a look of surprise and a suppressed giggle. Michael's eyes narrowed as a huge grin crossed his lips.

"I know you're making fun of me, Jake," Benny said over his shoulder.

"Never in a million years, *Lucky*," Michael tried to say, but it was garbled with a laugh as he pronounced Benny's new name.

"How about you guys?" Will asked. "What do you do?"

"I'll level with you. We're priests."

"You mean, like, 'Bless me, Father, for I have sinned' kind of priests?" Will asked skeptically.

"That's an old viewpoint," Benny began to lecture.

"Not the time for theology, Lucky," Michael said with what he hoped would look to Will like a playful slap to the back of his uncle's head.

"But why are you here?" Will asked.

"Why is anybody here?" Benny responded. Michael clipped him on the head again. Benny glared at him.

"No, I mean the rapture and everything. Why aren't you in heaven?" Will asked.

Benny made a groaning noise but said nothing.

"You know about the rapture?" Michael asked.

Will answered with a far-off voice as if describing an ancient memory. "My girlfriend was a Christian. She was also my assistant. She disappeared during our act, and then all the craziness started to happen."

"Kind of the same for me. My family believed in the rapture too. I made fun of them until my brother vanished in front of me."

"So, were you a bad priest?"

"Yes, from the standpoint that I didn't believe in Jesus as my Savior. I'm also a scientist. I put all of my faith in science to save mankind. The deeper I got into it, the more convinced I became that humanity was its own savior. I know better now. How about you?"

"My girlfriend tried to convince me, but I just couldn't believe in a loving personal God. I was a bastard child raised by a tormented grandmother in a tiny town. I used to fantasize that someday my father would find me. As it turned out, he wasn't even looking. I guess I ascribed those same attributes to God."

"Your father abandoned you?"

"It's not even that pretty." Will shrugged. "I was nothing to him, not even a second thought."

"Does it still hurt you?" Michael asked cautiously.

"Until the rapture it did. My escape from downtown was pretty horrific—made me question everything. Then I met my father in a dream. He only found out about me after he was taken to heaven in the rapture. He told me he loved me, and they weren't empty words, you know? I could feel it."

There was a clicking sound of disgust as Benny sucked at his teeth.

"Are you okay, Lucky?" Michael asked as an implied threat rather than a true inquiry.

"Fine," Benny said sullenly. "Don't mind me. I'm just a little old to be out walking like this. How long until we reach this mythical transport to safety, Mr. White?"

"Just a few more minutes, Lucky." Will grinned. Michael watched Benny's shoulders bristle when Will used his name. It brought yet another quick chuckle.

"So you gave your life to Jesus, then?" Michael asked.

"I'm not there yet. Being a magician, I would have told you a week ago that most of Christianity was little more than a variation of the sleight of hand I perform every day. Now I'm not so sure."

"Well, it's a start," Michael commented. "So what did you do after meeting your dad?"

"I just hung out in the woods. My dad called this craziness the Dark Awakening. He said I'd be safer to wait it out in the wild. So I hung out and fished for food. When I saw those guys coming after you, I figured it was my time to move on."

"Interesting," Michael muttered. His mind wandered to what seemed to be a distant memory. Even though it had been less than a week prior, he had to concentrate to pull into focus a dream he had. This guy was in the dream … nightmare was more like it. Isa forced Will and Michele into submission in the gardens of the family estate.

"Jake. Jake!" Will called.

Benny nudged his shoulder. "That would be you."

He returned with a start from the memory of the dream. Behind him, Will called to stop him. Lost in thought, he had nearly walked past the Humvee. He looked at Will in silence for a few seconds. There was no doubt about it: this was the man he had seen in the dream.

"Dude," Will said with a wry grin. "What were you doing? Sleepwalking?"

"I guess I was." Michael returned the grin.

"See what I have to put up with?" Benny asked Will.

"Our chariot awaits," Will said, motioning to the bright yellow Hummer H2. He grinned as he opened the back to reveal several containers of gasoline. "I'm guessing the owner was planning to be off-road for a while. Looks like we have a tank or two of gas in these cans."

"One of the most beautiful things I've seen in a while!" Michael exclaimed, happy to have left the Taurus behind.

As Benny crawled into the backseat and stretched out, Michael and Will filled the gas tank.

"It'll be dark soon," Will said. "There's a break in the guardrail a little way up the road. I'm thinking we could make it there and catch some z's until daylight."

"Sounds good," Michael said, wiping his brow. The idea of clearing more bodies and cars from the road was like a punch to the gut, but it had to be done. He and Will worked easily as a team. Michael was impressed by the younger man's strength and intestinal fortitude as he effortlessly carried bodies out of the way. The H2 came in really handy in removing vehicles blocking their way. After saying a prayer over each body they removed, Michael would sit in the driver's seat of the disabled vehicle and throw the transmission into neutral. Will would nudge the vehicle forward with the H2 as Michael steered it to the side of the road. The only problem was the width of the H2, as it required more space to be cleared. Still, the two worked seamlessly together, each anticipating the other's moves.

When the last car was cleared, Michael joined Will in the H2 to the loud sounds of Benny's heavy snoring. Out of habit, he checked his cell phone, only to remember that it had long since run out of juice.

"Lucky's been sawing logs for a while now," Will said with a mischievous grin.

"Trust me, we're the lucky ones when he's asleep," Michael said.

"That bad a fellow, huh?"

"Seriously, Will," Michael said with a stern tone. "The worst. You can never trust him."

"Sounds like you don't like him much."

"He's my mother's older brother, and I have sort of a family obligation to him, but I don't trust him for a second."

"You said he was a priest too, right?" Will asked as he drove the H2 through the break in the guardrail.

"In name only. You just have to trust me on that," Michael said as he nestled into the soft upholstery of the passenger seat and felt the day's fatigue overtake him.

Will parked the H2 and exited it to retrieve his crossbow from the rear. Upon his return, he patted Michael's shoulder and said, "I'll take the first watch. Get some sleep."

The next thing Michael knew, bright rays of early morning sun filled the vehicle. Benny was snapping at his head with his index finger. "Don't you have something better to do?" Michael demanded irritably.

"Not really," Benny said with too much glee for Michael's taste. "Come to think of it, I could pee. My bladder isn't what it used to be."

"But then again, what is?" Michael asked sarcastically.

Will chuckled at the exchange as Michael rolled out of the H2, wiping the sleep from his eyes. "You didn't wake me for my shift," he said to Will.

Will shrugged. "You were so beat that I let you sleep. Besides, our only weapon is a crossbow. Have you ever shot one?"

"No," Michael said somberly. "I wouldn't have been much of a protector."

They were interrupted by a high-pitched scream as Benny came scampering toward them, waving his hands at ear level, his fly undone, his equipment in the breeze. Will raised the crossbow.

"Snake!" Benny yelled. "I saw a snake!"

"Did I mention Lucky is high drama as well as high maintenance?" Michael asked drolly. Benny glared at him.

Will stifled a chuckle as the three of them got into the H2. Will drove; Michael navigated. Benny fell back to sleep. They made good progress across the fields alongside the highway. For a long time they rode in silent awe at the devastation—cars and bodies bound in an unending death march along the highway.

After a while, Will pointed out the driver's-side window to the highway. There, on the crest of a hill, were soldiers with bulldozers plowing a single lane clear on the road's right shoulder. "Maybe the Dark Awakening is over," he said happily. "America's finest to the rescue."

Michael grabbed Will's hand as he raised it over the H2's horn, intending to beep his support for the troops.

"Just keep going," he said. "We have to be under martial law. I'm guessing they would arrest, or at a minimum detain, people out and about."

"Good point," Will said. "We don't want them to think we're the rear guard of the Dark Awakening."

"What's going on?" Benny asked groggily.

"Talk about Dark Awakening," Michael said under his breath as Will grinned.

"We're only a few miles from home," Michael answered Benny. "Will, you need to turn due north from here. We'll cut through the fields up there for a couple of miles. Then you'll see a high fieldstone wall. Drive along the wall for about a mile to a gate."

"Then what?"

"Then I open the gate and we drive a mile along the driveway to the house."

"Sounds like some house!" Will exclaimed.

"It's a bit Old South for my taste," Benny said with a broad smile, "but I'll be ecstatic to see the old gal!"

———————————

Will was in awe as he drove the H2 up the long driveway. He had never known anyone who had a fence, let alone a key-coded gate. The driveway was lined with willow trees, beyond which were small orchards: peaches to the left, apples to the right. Before long, he saw it. The estate rose gracefully from the fields as if it had always been there. The architecture was Georgian with a huge canopied front porch and white clapboard shingles on the main section. Main section! To either side were stone wings, set back slightly from the front. He counted the windows. It looked like it had four floors. "You live here?" he asked in awe.

"Well, I grew up here. It's been in the family for generations." Jake grinned. "I actually live in a five-hundred-square-foot apartment in Rome."

"I've never seen anything like it," Will said admiringly. "At least not in real life. On TV maybe."

"I told you we'd have room for you," Jake said. "You can stay as long as you want, Will. We wouldn't have made it here without you."

"I just may take you up on that, Jake," Will said as he stopped the Hummer at the front porch steps.

"About my name," his new friend began as they mounted the porch stairs. The front doors flew open, and a pretty teenaged girl flung herself into Jake's arms. Both cried hysterically as she screamed, "Uncle Michael!"

"Uncle Michael?" Will cried. For a second he saw the image of his father and knew he was home. He fell to the porch floor in tears of his own.

THIRTEEN

Michele clung to her uncle Michael. She didn't think she had ever been so happy to see someone. She buried her head in his shoulder while he buried his head in her hair.

"I'm so sorry, Michele," he said through sobs as he held her tight.

"We make our own choices, Uncle Michael," she said through tears of her own. "I chose not to believe in Jesus. But I've taken care of that already."

"Thank God," he croaked.

She pulled back from him. He looked terrible. His face was sunburned and bruised. His right cheek bore a swollen scabbed row of punctures as if he had been bitten. His hands were dirty and scarred as well. His shirt was torn and filthy, and he smelled of death and rotting flesh. She could only imagine what he had been through. But there was something else about him. Despite the obvious signs of trauma, he had an air of peace and contentment she had never seen in him before. She hugged him again.

"You've given your life to Jesus too!" she exclaimed, barely aware of Uncle Benny huffing into the house. She would have to make amends for slighting him later.

"Uh-huh." He sighed before a torrent of fresh apologies poured out of him. "I was so wrong about everything, sweetheart. I've hurt so many people, including the most precious little girl in the world." She hugged him tightly at the mention of his pet expression for her. Then she let him cry on her shoulder. It was only as his tears subsided that she noticed the strangely dressed man who had collapsed into tears on the porch. Pulling away from Michael, she nodded in the direction of the man whose shoulders heaved as he held his face in his hands. His long hair had fallen forward to cover his hands.

"This is Will White," Michael said as he knelt down beside the man.

"Marron," Will said through tears. "White is a stage name. My real name is Marron."

"Marron?" Michael asked in disbelief.

Will pulled his hands from his face and pushed his hair back. Michele gasped. He looked so much like pictures of her father when he was young. "My mother had a one-night stand with a guy who worked on a cruise ship. He told her his name was Marron."

Michael sat beside Will as he continued. "When I met my father the other day, he told me about how his mom died and how he was adopted by this rich woman. He told me how much he loved his brother Michael."

"Marron was your dad's birth name," Michael said in a breathless sigh. "Later he took our family name—Martin."

Will nodded. "I figured it out when this girl called you Uncle Michael."

"This girl is your sister Michele," Michael said with a half smile. "Michele, this is your older brother Will."

She didn't know how to handle this information. She missed her brother Chris so badly, but to have another brother sprung on her like this was too much. She backed away as Michael hugged Will and said, "You're home now, buddy. You're home."

"I don't know how to feel about this," she said softly. Just then she felt an arm around her shoulder. Turning, she saw the dazzling green eyes of her father.

"It's okay, Michele," Gabe said to her. His assurance caused a burning inside as if she were feeling her father's love for the son he had never known. She stepped closer to Will and gently brushed away the hair from his face to see his eyes, so much like her father's. Then she gently kissed his cheek and said, "Welcome."

He smiled at her, his smile also reminiscent of her father. She hugged him and Michael for just a second before hearing angry screaming from inside the house. Will stood abruptly and rushed into the house ahead of her and Michael.

They entered the foyer to see Benny with arms raised. On the second-floor landing stood Jimmy with her father's rifle, aiming down at him. Will stood in front of Benny, blocking Jimmy's aim and glaring.

"Jimmy!" Michele screamed. "No! This is my uncle Benny and my … brother." The word stuck in her mouth. It would take some getting used to.

Jimmy lowered the rifle and snapped the safety. He smiled with relief and ran down the stairs to her side.

"Lucky's real name is Benny?" Will asked.

"Who's Lucky?" Michele asked.

Michael laughed and patted Will's shoulder. "There's so much to learn. Why don't we shower and get some fresh clothes before we share stories? Michele, we'll need to find some clothes for Will."

"We're a little short on medieval attire," she said in her first real appraisal of his costume. "But you look like you'll fit into my dad's … uh … our dad's clothes."

While the guys showered, Michele headed back to the kitchen to stir up something to feed the weary travelers. As she passed by Mimi's office, she heard a familiar ping. It sounded like the Internet was back. She was at once thrilled to see a return to normalcy, however modest, and struck by the loss of her family. She had to face it: there would be no such thing as normal anymore. She peeked into Mimi's office. Her computer beeped and glowed as e-mails loaded.

Repeated e-mails from Naomi DeRance spoke of plans to run the company on an emergency basis. Michele had known she would have to get into the family businesses at some point, but she didn't think it would be this soon. Thankfully, she had Uncle Michael here. DeRance's most recent e-mail sounded like she was taking over.

Moving to the kitchen, Michele concentrated on what she had learned of the family's businesses in the days following the rapture: a behemoth of a food company; a natural resources business that included gas and oil drilling, processing, and distribution; and an aircraft manufacturer with a lot of government contracts. The last was the business built by her great-grandfather.

As she began to heat some of her grandmother's canned stew, Jimmy entered the kitchen. "Penny for your thoughts?" he asked.

"Internet's back." She smiled. "There are already e-mails coming in from our company's execs. I have a lot to learn in a short amount of time."

Jimmy turned a chair around and sat with his arms across its back. He laid his head on his arms and asked, "What about this sudden brother thing? How does that make you feel?"

"Well, I haven't had time to process it, but he has a greater physical resemblance to my father than either Chris or I do. I saw my dad just now on the porch ..."

"Really?" Jimmy asked quizzically.

"It's not the first time. Daddy confirmed that Will is his son. I'm lonely for family anyway. So I'd say that finding him is a miracle, or a blessing at least."

"I have a confession to make," Jimmy said haltingly. "I kind of liked it when it was just you and me. For a couple days, I felt like I belonged somewhere."

She turned to face him. She had never really considered what it would be like to live as an orphan. The devastation of losing her family made it clearer now. Jimmy had never known any kind of safe, happy family life. His eyes glistened and he wiped furiously at tears forming there, an action in sharp contrast to the masculine look of his steely eyes and heavy beard. She knew in that moment that she could fall in love with him.

"Jimmy, you have a place here. As you can see, we have plenty of space."

"I just thought now that your family's here, you wouldn't need me," he said, not meeting her gaze.

"Jimmy, look at the world we're now living in. Of course I need you." She smiled reassuringly. "We need each other." She rubbed his bicep, a strong muscle sheathed with soft skin. He stood, smiled, and wrapped her into a hug.

"Ahem." Michael coughed at the kitchen entrance. "Do you two need a chaperone?" he teased.

"Uncle Michael!" Michele blushed. Jimmy moved immediately to the other side of the kitchen to get plates.

"What have you managed to scare up for food?" Michael asked.

"Well, you know how Mimi was a pack rat."

"She was a worrier," Michael mused. "She wanted to be prepared for any contingency."

"Well, today we have her homemade beef stew. She just canned a batch a couple of weeks ago. I've got water on the stove to boil some noodles."

"You'll never know how good it sounds to have Mom's beef stew." Michael grinned. Then turning serious, he asked, "Michele, are you okay discovering you have a brother you never knew about? I know it can be a shock, but I have to tell you that finding your father was the highlight of my life. I hope it will be the same for you."

She chuckled for a moment as images of her father and Uncle Michael flooded her mind. "I'm fine with it, Uncle Michael. I saw Dad on the porch just now. It was just for a second, and then my heart was flooded with feelings of love for Will. It'll be great to have him around."

She hesitated a second before continuing. "Speaking of which, Jimmy has been a great help, and I want him to stay here as well. No monkey business." Jimmy gave her a mischievous grin.

"No monkey business," Michael repeated in a stern voice reminiscent of her father's.

"Uncle Michael, we've both given our hearts to Jesus, and we know where the world's heading."

"I understand completely," Michael said. He walked across the kitchen and extended his hand to Jimmy. "Welcome," he said as he warmly shook Jimmy's hand.

"Thank you, Father," Jimmy said respectfully.

"Just call me Michael. We have to re-form our family now. And you're part of it."

Michele hugged her uncle fiercely. She had always loved the handsome exotic priest, but his simple act of kindness toward Jimmy made her love him all the more. As she pulled away, she remembered the e-mails. "Uncle Michael, the Internet has come back online. Mimi's been getting e-mails from Naomi DeRance."

"That old battle-axe!" Michael exclaimed. "What's she trying to do, take over the company?"

"She's calling for an all-hands meeting of the executives tomorrow at company headquarters. The company's helicopter can pick us up."

"Wow, I've had my hands so full, I hadn't even considered the business." He paused. "I hate to ask, but ... do you think you can keep an eye on things?" he asked sorrowfully.

"If you had asked me last week, I would have said no. But the world has changed, Uncle Michael. The company is huge, and we could use its resources to help people who have been hurt by this madness."

He grinned. "Now you're talking my language. But some of the execs there are pretty tough, Michele. Take Naomi for example. She smokes stogies, drinks her business partners under the table, and has enough testosterone for two men."

Michele giggled at the description. Jimmy laughed out loud.

Michael continued. "But she's great at what she does. Through her, our businesses developed the most sophisticated cash-pooling techniques on the globe. We literally set the standard for efficient use of working capital. She's also great at negotiating mergers and acquisitions."

"Sounds formidable," Michele said with a grimace.

"But a great ally when kept on a short leash," Michael concluded.

"And I'll be at the other end of that leash?" Michele asked. This was starting to sound like a challenge she didn't need. Nonetheless, she knew it had to be done.

"Yes." Michael winced. "I wouldn't wish that on anyone, but—"

"To tell the truth, Uncle Michael, I've studied up on the businesses over the past couple of days, and I have some ideas."

"Really?" Michael asked with a look of amused pride.

"Yes. We can use our food processing and distribution to feed a lot of people. We have a mothballed oil refinery we could open up again. From reading Mimi's files, it looks like we shut it down because we couldn't compete. Mimi wasn't willing to take shortcuts that could hurt the environment, but I'm not interested in making a profit."

Michael laughed heartily. "I love where you're going with this, and I've got to tell you, your mimi would be very proud of you."

"*Is* very proud of me," Michele countered. "I refuse to talk about them like they're dead when I know they're more alive than we are." She offered a wry smile.

"Whatever you're serving, it smells heavenly," a freshly scrubbed Benny called from the kitchen doorway.

"Mimi's beef stew, Uncle Benny," Michele said with a smile.

"Your grandmother's fare was always a bit pedestrian for my taste," Benny said haughtily, "but today it seems like a miracle to have it." In a rare moment of sentiment, something Michele had never seen from Uncle Benny, he wiped at a tear. "I never really thought of life without Kim. She was always a bedrock of sorts for me."

"More like a well," Michael said with good-natured sarcasm.

Benny rolled his eyes and proceeded to the table, giving Jimmy a wide berth and a glaring look.

"I'm sorry about what happened earlier," Jimmy said, extending his hand. Benny ignored the hand and the comment.

Michele intervened in the awkward moment. "Jimmy, could you drain the noodles for me?" He gratefully moved away from the table as Will entered the kitchen. Michele was taken aback. Out of the stage costume and in her father's clothes he looked amazingly like Gabe.

"Smells great," Will said as his emerald eyes inventoried the well-appointed white kitchen and stainless steel appliances.

"My grandmother's ... our grandmother's beef stew." She grinned. "There's so much I want to tell you about your family."

"I'd love to hear it. I saw some pictures when I was changing in your parents' room. It looks like you all had a nice life here."

"Well, not all of us," Benny intoned.

"Let me save you some time," Michael said, jumping in. "We all loved growing up here, except Benny. My grandfather wasn't nice to him when he was growing up."

"Well, it's a little more dramatic than you make it sound," Benny said gruffly.

"Anyway," Michael continued, "we should say grace and get ready to enjoy this treat Mom left for us." Jimmy brought the noodles to the table, and Michele brought a serving dish with the stew. Michael said grace.

They ate well, happy for a bit of normalcy. In turn they told their stories—where they had been when the madness started, how they found their way to the estate. Michele could see the pain in both Will and Jimmy as they spoke of having to kill in order to survive. The world had changed, and it was about to get a lot worse. Michele was thrilled to hear how her father and Grandpa Chris had told Uncle Michael to take care of them.

When Will spoke about meeting her father, walking through the house with him, and eating some of Mimi's pie, she walked to the refrigerator in the pantry with a grin. Carrying a cherry pie to the table, she said, "Mimi made this a couple of days ago. I had forgotten about it."

She plated the pie and watched as Will took his first bite. Mimi had a way with pies, and cherry was her best. Her secret ingredient was just a touch of chai tea spice. When the fork hit his mouth, Will grinned and then tears flowed. "This is exactly the taste from my dream!"

Benny gobbled his pie, leaned back in his chair, and patted his stomach. "If you will all excuse me, I think this full belly would like a much-deserved sleep."

"Sounds good to me too," Michael intoned.

"I'm afraid you have work to do, Michael. I'll be taking over your mother's office tomorrow. You'll need to clear her things out of there tonight. Castello Pietro needs to get up and running."

Michael moaned as Benny left the kitchen.

"Castello Pietro?" Michele asked with a smirk and a furrowed brow.

"Sort of Vatican West, I assume," Michael said with a grimace. "Did I forget to mention your uncle Benny's the new pope?"

Michele gasped.

Will dropped his fork to the plate. "Lucky's the freaking pope?"

"It wouldn't be the tribulation any other way," Michael quipped.

FOURTEEN

Michael sat in the red leather chair behind his mother's desk. The scent of her perfume lingered in the office, and for a second he just sat there and drew deep breaths. His mind flooded with memories of growing up in the estate and the times he had taken comfort in the fragrance of her perfume. His heart was heavy, but inside there was a steady joy that he would see her again soon. If Gabe was right in his interpretation of end-time prophecies, there would soon be a peace agreement with Israel. That agreement would set the clock ticking for a seven-year period of Isa's reign. It wouldn't be pleasant. In fact, it would be horrific, but there was a foreseeable end when Michael would be reunited with his family. Until then, he had a job to do.

He cleaned out the drawers of her desk in little time, leaving pens, notepads, and other office supplies. Anything of significance was contained in the combination-locked file room behind her desk. After dialing the combination—Grandpa Stan's birthdate—he opened the room and set about emptying the built-in filing cabinets. The first few were filled with documents regarding the family businesses: contracts, agreements, and details of mergers and acquisitions, all filed neatly and each bearing her handwritten notations. He would have to help Michele understand the details. He didn't envy her the work she would need to do to come up to speed.

A full filing cabinet was dedicated to employment agreements and performance reviews of the company's top staff. Michael familiarized himself with the players and their compensation in anticipation of the upcoming meeting. Another was filled with family documents:

Gabe's adoption papers, Michael's and Gabe's high school and college diplomas, Gabe's marriage license, the kids' birth certificates. Michael contemplated each. He had wasted so much time in a dungeon beneath the Vatican when he could have been enjoying this wonderful family.

As he emptied each drawer, he used the service elevator to carry its contents to his suite of rooms on the third floor. His rooms would be a mess until he could get everything put in place, but the important thing was to leave nothing for Benny's prying eyes. Michael thought of a lifetime of family conflict stemming from Benny's attempts to make off with the family fortune. Serving Benny would be the worst of the upcoming years, but Michael had had years of practice at thwarting the man's patently evil plans. In so many ways his entire life had been a preparation for what was about to take place.

When the file cabinets were finally emptied, Michael went to the wall safe. He knew its contents would be stock certificates for the family's vast holdings. He had a safe in his room that should handle most of it. Tucked away amid all of the legal documentation was a solitary manila envelope with a question mark written on it. Carefully unfolding the metal tabs holding it closed, Michael opened the envelope to reveal an aged photo and its enlargement displaying a group of adults and children lined up at what appeared to have been some sort of picnic.

Michael looked carefully at the photo. It seemed inconsequential at best. Why would his mother have kept it hidden away in her safe? He studied the faces. One of them was definitely Grandpa Stan. Turning the enlargement over, he saw script in his mother's fine hand: "Daddy. Me. Mom. Benny. Chris? Fran? Father Vinnie?" He turned the photo over again, looking more carefully. A young boy in the front had Chris's unmistakable eyes. They hadn't met Chris until he was an adult, yet the child certainly looked like Chris, down to the slightly crooked smile. He turned the photo over again to see which person she had identified as Fran. The little girl in the second row definitely looked like her. He went back and forth, looking first to the list of names on the back and then at the photo itself. A young man in a black shirt and with a wisp of black hair certainly looked like it could have been Father Vinnie.

What was the likelihood that all of these people could have been together at the same time, at the same picnic, years before they met? Michael shook the envelope, and a piece of paper fell out—Kim's notes to herself, basically mirroring the same questions running through Michael's mind. Kim's handwriting grew large toward the end of the page, where she had written, "No memory of this *at all!* What else don't I remember?"

It was a mystery. Michael carefully placed the original photo in the billfold section of his wallet and returned the enlargement and Kim's note to the manila envelope. After carrying the files to his room, he studied the photo again. What were the implications? Could it possibly be that some unseen hand, other than the hand of God, had manipulated their lives and the lives of their friends so completely? He shivered at the thought.

By the time he had moved all the files, it was nearly dawn. He decided to finish up the night by saying Mass in the chapel. He had said Mass since becoming a priest, but it was a rote matter until now. Now that he had given his heart to Jesus, every word, every gesture, took on so much more significance. He found himself in utter joy to celebrate the Lord's Supper in his family's chapel. He was so enrapt by the beauty of the moment that he didn't notice Michele in the last pew until he had finished the celebration.

"When did you get here?" he asked as he strode from the altar.

"Right around the time you were taking Communion." She smiled. "You were so into the experience, I didn't want to disturb you."

"I've never felt so happy to say Mass." He grinned.

"I'm happy I found you here, Uncle Michael. There's something I need to show you." She led him to the back wall of the chapel, where she pressed several stones in sequence and then paused. Nothing happened. She tried it again. This time, a section of the hardwood floor opened to reveal stairs. "Wait until you see this," she said with a grin as she bolted down the stairs.

Michael followed, the floor to the chapel automatically sealing behind him after he had descended into an underground shelter.

"Mom and Dad showed me this place shortly after the rapture. Mimi built it sometime before I was born."

Michael looked around in awe at the expansive shelter, thinking, *It must take up the entire back garden.* "I remember when she renovated the estate and the gardens. I thought she just had some kind of redecoration bug. To be honest, I blamed it on change of life ..."

"Typical man," Michele said, rolling her eyes. "She's got a setup to grow plants and fish. Now that the Internet is up again, I'll order the fish and start it up. The place is powered by generators in the room over there, and there's an office," she said, pointing to a closed door.

"Let's take a look in the office," Michael said, opening the door. "Maybe she left us some information on how to run this place."

As he spoke, a voice came from the computer on the desk. "Voice verification. Father Michael Martin. Birthdate please."

Michael looked at the computer screen and shrugged. He gave his birthdate.

"Brother's birthdate," the computer asked. Michael complied.

"Grandfather's birthdate," the computer intoned. Michael answered. The screen went blank for a moment before returning with a video of his mother. The sight of her brought tears to his eyes. He turned to see the same reaction in Michele.

"Michael, it's my greatest hope that you will give your life to Jesus before the rapture and never have to see this video. If you are watching me now, then we've gone to heaven without you. Before I do anything else, I want to encourage you to give your life to Jesus.

"You can pause this video at any time just by saying the word *pause*. Use the word 'resume' to start it up again. This system is very interactive. If you have given your life to Jesus already, say so and we'll skip to some information I need to give you."

"I've given my heart to Jesus," Michael answered. The screen went blank for a moment and then returned with an image of Kim smiling.

"I'm so happy to hear you've made the right decision, honey. Now to the matter at hand. First of all, I should apologize to you and Gabe. I sort of violated our standing agreement about all three of us authorizing expenditures over $250,000. The businesses were doing so well, and you and Gabe didn't seem interested in them anyway. Well, I took some extra money and invested in small companies I thought would hold the keys to the future of technology. Imagine my surprise when I learned that a lot of the companies were doing highly secret research with the Vatican. Naturally I thought of you.

"Here's a list of the companies." Michael read the list in awe. She had invested in many of the alternate energy, communication, quantum computing, and small pharmaceutical companies to which he had parceled out information he had gleaned from the alien disc. He let out a slow whistle. "Your grandmother was an absolute genius!" he exclaimed to Michele.

Kim continued to speak. "In each of these cases, I own at least 51 percent. You know me: if I don't have a controlling interest, I don't want it." She laughed heartily, bringing a smile and a nod of agreement from both Michael and Michele. "But only as a silent partner. The people running these businesses have never met me. All communications and funding are done electronically. One of the great benefits of owning the controlling interest in a quantum computer think tank is that all communications go to a dummy site in the Cayman Islands and then are quantum-encrypted before reaching me. The anonymity of our investments is about as secure as it can possibly be."

"Pause," Michael said to the computer. He turned to Michele in excitement. "Michele, do you know what this means?"

She grinned at him vacantly. "Not even a clue."

He waved his arms excitedly and paced the floor as he spoke. "For years, I worked in a secret Vatican lab translating information on a disc from an ancient advanced civilization ... at least I thought it was at the time. Now I realize it was most probably fallen-angel technology. The science on the disc was centuries more advanced than ours, total sci-fi stuff. Over the years, I've been parceling out the concepts to research labs in an attempt to benefit mankind with this crazy science: energy created from the very fabric of space–time, faster-than-light travel and communications, DNA-enhanced immunity."

"From fallen angels," Michele said cautiously.

"Well, yes," Michael said as his bubble burst. "But the science is real, Michele. Only now I realize I was a pawn. All the information on the disc was meant to be a tool for the Antichrist to enslave humanity." A thought so vile stunned him to the point that he lost his footing. Falling to the floor, he grasped his head in his hands.

"Uncle Michael," Michele called. "Are you all right?"

"Yes," he croaked. "But I've just now realized how incredibly diabolical this technology can be. Michele, the stuff I've been working on for the past twenty years isn't meant only to enslave mankind. The fallen angels are hoping to develop technology to help them in their fight with heaven."

"So, what?" she asked sarcastically. "They want to nuke God?"

"I think they believe they can create weapons to defeat Jesus's return … or at least devastate creation at such a fundamental level that He'll have nothing to return to."

"Wait a minute," Michele uttered slowly. "What technology could defeat God?"

"None," Michael said gravely. "But the fallen angels must be insane at this point—"

"Knowing their time is short," Michele finished with a paraphrased Bible quote.

"Exactly," Michael said. "The most they can hope for is the destruction of humanity and the devastation of earth. And I've helped them bring the technology to light." The weight of his actions combined with his lack of sleep to leave him emotionally and physically drained. He put his arms around his knees and buried his head.

"But Mimi has bought up controlling interest in the technologies," Michele said carefully.

"Yeah?" Michael raised his head.

"There are some possibilities. Maybe we could find a way to sabotage the technologies."

"Michele, this is really complicated stuff. I don't think we could …" He stopped speaking as he remembered a meeting with the pope years before. He had been afraid the pope would remove him from his work on the alien technology, so he created a back door for himself. He had forgotten all about it. But to get access would still be impossible without the programmers. Another thought struck him. Using his mother's quantum encrypted protocol, maybe he could hack the companies to manipulate the data undetected. It wouldn't be as powerful as manipulating the Lady's database, but it was workable.

"Michele, your mimi isn't the only genius in the family!" He jumped up from the floor and hugged her.

"I'm not done, Uncle Michael." She smiled. "These companies stand to make a fortune. Half of that money will come to us. We can use it to care for Christians during the tribulation."

"Hah! You're right!' Michael exclaimed.

"Jesus is going to win this battle in the end," Michele said. "We just have to find a way to live through the next seven years. Between this information, your ability to spy on Uncle Benny, and the family businesses, we're poised to help a lot of people get through this."

"Right again!" Michael yelled. He felt like jumping up and down.

"And late," Michele said with a slight frown. "The company helicopter will be here to pick us up in an hour."

Michael looked out of the chopper with bleary red eyes. Even though he had just come from Atlanta the day before, he could not believe the amount of devastation when he saw it from a bird's-eye view beneath roiling clouds threatening at any moment to cast away their contents. There was slow progress removing thousands of cars from expressways. Unbattled fires had taken huge swaths of several neighborhoods. But the most devastating thing was the quiet. They saw very little activity other than rescue crews and bulldozers trying to gain passage on the snarled roadways. People were simply too afraid to venture out. They hunkered down, sheltering in place.

"It's awful," Michele yelled to him to be heard over the drone of the chopper. "I can't imagine what it must have been like for you to find your way home."

"I can't believe we actually made it." He offered a tired, wry smile. "From this vantage point, I can see how bad things really were. When you're in it, it's overwhelming, but you keep a false belief that the circumstances will be better somewhere down the road, around the next turn."

He felt a tear forming. Michele reached up to wipe it away. "From what I hear, it's a cardinal sin to show a sign of weakness to Naomi and the gang," she said.

"She's pretty tough, but I bet these circumstances cracked even her hard exterior," Michael said. "Did she say who else would be there?"

"John Santos, the CFO."

"Oh no," Michael moaned. "John's such a nice guy. I hoped he would have been raptured."

"His wife used to come by the house every once in a while. I heard her talking to Mom about Dad's books one day. She said John liked the books, but he refused to make a commitment to Jesus—something about wanting to be around to fight the Antichrist."

"I wonder how he's taking it now. I bet he's devastated at the loss of his family. They meant everything to him," Michael commented.

"Alan Anderson, the chief operating officer, will be there along with Tanya Schilling, head of human resources, and Pak Song, from risk management."

"I've known Alan for years. He's a pretty good guy. Very anal, but then again his entire career is making sure things run smoothly. Tanya is a single mom with a happy disposition and genuine concern for the employees. I don't think I've ever met Pak."

"Well, you will soon enough." Michele grimaced as the chopper approached the headquarters building in a large, manicured industrial park. In a matter of seconds, it placed them squarely on the front yard of the sprawling five-story edifice that had been built by one of the food companies subsequently purchased by Kim. Some people referred to it as the Taj Mahal because of the huge domed section at its center. Others said it looked like a spaceship that had landed in an industrial park.

Naomi stubbed out a cigar as Michael and Michele exited the chopper. To Michael's surprise, the burly woman wrapped herself around him in a bear hug. He realized at that moment how profoundly affected she had been by recent events.

"Thanks for calling this meeting, Naomi," Michael said as she released him. He coughed slightly against the smell of her cigar.

"I'm shocked your mother didn't call it. I'm guessing she didn't make it."

"She's in heaven now," Michael said quickly.

"How did you manage to get here from Rome?" she asked as they headed into the building.

"You don't want to know." Michael grinned. Then it dawned on him how dismissive Naomi had been toward Michele. In fact she hadn't acknowledged her.

"You remember my niece Michele," Michael said as they entered the elevator to the fifth-floor executive suites.

"Of course," Naomi said warily. "How are you, dear? Is Uncle Michael babysitting you today?"

"No," Michele said lightheartedly, not playing her hand. *Good for you, Michele!*

"Truth be told," Michael said to Naomi, "our family has been pretty devastated. Michele and I are all that's left."

"I see," Naomi said glumly.

The elevator doors opened on the fifth floor. A smile crossed Michael's lips as he realized that his mother's penchant for redecorating hadn't been confined to the estate. She had taken a drab office environment and made it light and airy with a soft palette of earth tones. Subtle gray carpeting and light beige walls were accented with colorful landscape paintings and wide Queen Anne moldings painted a soft white.

Naomi caught his expression. "I know," she said curtly, "I feel like I work in a damned spa."

They entered the conference room dominated by a huge walnut table and white leather chairs. A portrait of Grandpa Stan stared over the table from the opposite wall—a formidable-looking man. Michael's eyes first fell on John. He was disheveled. His eyes were swollen and red from too many tears and too little sleep. Tanya wore a ton of makeup that couldn't conceal the worry, stress, and grief etched into her face. Alan, who always looked like Wally Cox to Michael, looked today like an even sadder frail little man. In contrast, Pak Song looked nearly joyful.

John stood to shake Michael's hand. "Hello, Father. I'm sorry to see you under these circumstances." Then he hugged Michele hard. Michael remembered that John's daughter was about Michele's age. The others said hello from their seats.

"You remember Kim's granddaughter Michele," Naomi said, forcing the issue. Pointing to the waiting area outside the boardroom, she said, "There are some magazines outside on the table, honey. Make yourself at home while we have our meeting."

Michele moved to the head of the table, pushing Naomi's portfolio to the side. "I'll be attending," she said with an ersatz sweet smile.

"We might as well get right down to it," Michael said, pushing the little power struggle to the side. "Alan, have you heard anything about the condition of our factories and distribution?"

"It's all anecdotal, Michael. In some parts of the world, we've been able to get hold of employees to take a look around. In other parts of the world, we haven't established contact."

"I can imagine how difficult it is," Michael said. "I've just gotten in from Rome."

Alan sighed and looked down through a pair of reading glasses to his notes. "We've been able to establish contact with about 40 percent of our factories and probably 30 percent of our US distribution depots. So, all my information comes from less than half of our US manufacturing–distribution footprint. I have nothing substantive from our international operations. Based on what we've seen, there's a lot of damage, but it is recoverable. In the food-manufacturing plants, unattended machinery made a mess and ruined the work-in-process inventories, but there doesn't seem to be much structural damage. Aircraft manufacturing is unfazed.

"The oil and gas wells kept right on pumping, so we're on pretty good ground in the energy businesses. Distribution is another matter, though. The depots are all pretty much fine. Some minor damage in the rioting, but they're pretty boring places if you're a looter. But the trucks? There's just no way to tell. I'm sure you saw how the roads looked on your flight here."

"I traveled them yesterday." Michael rolled his eyes.

"But it must be different in different time zones," Michele said softly.

"What?" Michael asked.

She spoke more loudly. "The trucks aren't on the road 24/7. On the East Coast they would have all been out, but on the West Coast, some of them wouldn't have been rolling yet."

Michael looked at Alan. He grinned. "She's right. To tell the truth, we haven't made contact with any distribution centers in the West yet, but it stands to reason."

"So we may have a skeleton crew of trucks once the dust settles?" Michele asked.

"We might," Alan conceded. Michael grinned and winked at his niece.

"What does it look like from the financial side of things, John?" Michael asked.

John looked up at Michael with heavy eyes. Michael reached out to pat the man's shoulder. John said, "I'm sorry, Father. My wife tried to tell me we were living in the time of the rapture. I had this vain idea that I would rather stick around and fight evil … some sort of knight fantasy. I was so wrong."

"Enough with the rapture crap," Naomi yelled. "Michael, you're a priest. For God's sake, tell him he's wrong!"

Michael drew a sharp breath. He hadn't thought that the meeting would move to this place, but now that it had, he wanted to put his cards on the table. "Naomi, a week ago, I would have said that the rapture was a figment of the imagination. But now I believe it happened."

Naomi and Pak were visibly disturbed by Michael's statement. Naomi threw her reading glasses to the table. Pak chuckled nervously. Tanya and John were now in tears. Alan sat as rigid as a stone, his eyes darting from Naomi to Michael.

Michael continued, "I was hugging Gabe when it happened. His body just transformed in a second. I've seen him since then in his resurrected state."

"It sure would help me to know that my wife and kids are okay," John said softly.

"They're better than okay," Michael said compassionately. "They're living more fully and more vividly than we can imagine right now. If you take the time to let Jesus in your heart, you can join them in a few short years. I've made that decision."

"I have too," Michele said boldly.

"I have too," John said. Then he punched the table. "How could I have been so stupid to wait?"

"I've heard enough," Naomi screamed. "I don't have to work in this type of hostile environment!"

"You're right. You don't," Michele said sternly. Naomi threw herself back in her chair as if slapped.

"Calm down," Michael said deliberately. "Nobody's trying to insult you, Naomi. But in the end, this is a family business. We're just telling you what the family believes."

Naomi said nothing, but she didn't walk out. Michael thought his niece had done a pretty good job of asserting the family's authority with a few short words.

"For what it's worth," Pak said, "I've never been happier. My wife hounded me constantly about getting right with God. I don't believe for a minute she was taken in the rapture. I just don't believe in it … or in God. Nonetheless, my life is much nicer without her."

Naomi chuckled. Michael stared, aghast. Collecting himself, he moved the conversation back to the business. "Go ahead, John. Tell us what you know."

"There will undoubtedly be huge write-offs for destroyed inventory and infrastructure. It's not likely we'll show net income this year. That's the bad news. The good news is that compared to our peers, we'll have a sterling report. Kim was stockpiling cash for an acquisition. We have plenty of funds to keep the doors open, service our debt, and pay dividends until things stabilize."

"Let's not worry about the dividends for now," Michele said decisively. "The family's not hurting for cash."

"There's an employee stock program," John said tentatively.

"Maybe we can declare a special dividend to just that class of stock," Michele offered.

"That could work," John said. "Our stock is nonvoting and really amounts to little more than a profit-sharing plan."

"Let's look into it," Michael said. "Naomi, what do you think?"

"The cash will come in handy, but I don't think we should dismiss Kim's original acquisition plan out of hand."

"Fair point," Michael said. "I'm only now getting an appreciation for how prescient Mom could be when it came to selecting acquisition targets. What was she looking into?"

"Survival foods," Naomi said with a chuckle.

"If nothing else, the technology could come in real handy," Michele said to Michael with a knowing look. "The more shelf-stable our products are, the better for the remnant."

"The remnant?" Naomi asked.

Michele covered her answer a bit. "This most recent crisis, whatever you want to call it, will have a lot of people focusing on storable food. A long shelf life will be a benefit to our consumers."

"Not necessarily good for business," John said. "In the long run, it's better to keep them coming back to the store. It gives us a more predictable, steady revenue stream if we keep near-term 'best by' dates."

"Probably a moot point in the new world, though," Michael said thoughtfully. "Pak, how do we stand with insurance coverage?"

"We're pretty heavy up on insurance. Our entire infrastructure is insured to replacement cost value. Our business-interruption policies have been outlandish from a premium point of view. I used to argue with Kim that we were overinsured. It may turn out we're fully covered."

"Only if the insurance companies remain solvent," Naomi said disparagingly.

"Probably not likely without some sort of government bailout," Pak agreed. "That having been said, our lifetime of heavy premiums and small losses should put us in a good place when they decide how to dole out whatever funds they come up with."

Michael continued with his questions. "Now the hard part: the employees. Tanya, do you have any feel for how we've been affected?"

"It's flat-out too early to know anything, Michael." Tanya offered a weak smile. "The few government reports we've seen indicate we may have lost up to 20 percent of the US population. It's hard to know what the rest of the world looks like.

"I want to caution you about what I'll say next. It will sound heartless, and I don't want it to. My heart is breaking right now. But there's an underlying fact to be considered. If there has really been such a heavy decrease in population, there has been a corresponding decrease in consumers. If we lost people in proportion to the general population, we may not have to take any layoffs. There will be some cost to reeducate or backfill on critical positions though."

"I see," Michael said softly. He hoped that most were taken in the rapture and not murdered in the Dark Awakening. He sighed wearily.

"There's also the possibility that we wouldn't need to replace much of the lost infrastructure, considering the smaller consumer base," Alan thought aloud.

"This has been really helpful," Michele said thoughtfully.

Michael rejoined the conversation. "I'll be very busy with Vatican business as time proceeds. So, Michele will hold my mother's role." Again, Naomi threw herself back in her chair.

"Thanks, Uncle Michael," Michele said. "There are only a few short years left, and I want to run this company with that perspective. Our primary goal will be to offer aid and assistance to the downtrodden. Financial benefits, profits, EBITDA, and all other business measures will take a backseat to humanitarian efforts. With that in mind, I want to know as soon as our factories are up and running. We'll donate as much food as we can to the relief efforts. And I think it's time to take the oil refinery out of mothballs."

"You have no idea what you're saying!" Naomi screamed. "Michael, it's time for you to bring some sanity back to this meeting."

"On the contrary," Michael said with a slight grin. "The world has gone insane, Naomi. Rational responses will be resounding failures. Michele and I plan to think outside the box."

"I've heard about all I want to hear from you two," Naomi chided. "Kim would not appreciate your approach. Kim was a formidable businesswoman. Kim …"

"Is not here!" Michele cried out. "I'm here, and this is what we're going to do. So suck it up, buttercup."

There was dead silence for a second, and then Michael started to laugh. His mother had used that expression frequently. John laughed as well, and then Alan and Tanya joined in. Pak, a relatively new employee, looked bewildered. Finally, Naomi cracked and joined in the laughter.

"Kim may be a lot more present than you think," Naomi said. "You've got your grandmother's spunk. I heard the stories of when she took over from your great-grandfather. The old fogies didn't want to listen to her, and they were wrong. I almost became one of those old fogies just now. But I'm beginning to think that history may just repeat itself."

The laughter released the tension everyone had brought into the room. Michael was relieved, and more than a little impressed with his niece.

The chopper had no sooner landed on the estate's front yard than Benny had come charging out of the house, followed by forlorn-looking Will and Jimmy.

"Michael, thank God you're here! These two buffoons are useless. My eggs were runny. My toast was cold. My coffee was weak. To top it off, Will is nearly useless as a secretary. Can you please get in here and get Zack Jolean on the phone? I need to plan for the United Nations briefing."

Michael winced. He couldn't wait for this day to end.

FIFTEEN

t was a bright, sunny day in Texas, with the deep blue sky offering just an occasional puffy cloud as an exclamation point. Most of the Riverside congregants had come to clean up damage done to the church in the Dark Awakening. Gloria took a look around. The damage was minimal: a few broken windows, some graffiti, and human waste that had been flung at the building. In the long run, there was nothing that couldn't be repaired or scrubbed away with a hard day's work.

The turnout was huge. Gloria winced. The number of people present was a stunning rebuttal of the good she thought she had done. For years she and Zack had shepherded this group to damnation, teaching them to ignore a relationship with Jesus in favor of chasing money and power. And here they were like cattle looking at the damage and wondering what had happened to the world.

Zack spoke powerfully to the group about how positive attitudes would carry them through this temporary setback. He cried openly as he told the crowd about discovering his secretary and her husband dead in the parking lot, an apparent murder–suicide brought on by the mysterious insanity that had overwhelmed the globe. "I was shaken to the core to see this lovely young mother and her handsome husband lying dead in front of our church. It could have shaken my faith, but it didn't. Do you know why?"

"Why?" the crowd cheered back as if it were a normal Sunday service.

"Because I saw what was happening on television. The entire world was caught up in some kind of lunacy that defies description." He smiled knowingly. "You saw it too. Didn't you?"

163

"Uh-huh," murmured the crowd.

"When I saw what was going on out there in the world, I realized we're doing something right at Riverside. Make no mistake about it. The deaths of my secretary and her husband were devastating, but that was the extent of the tragedy at Riverside. Compared to the images we've seen from all over the world, we came through this with barely a scratch. And do you know why?"

"Why?" echoed the enrapt crowd.

"Because we know how to attract the good things in life. We don't let ourselves get bogged down in the things that drive most people crazy. You know what Jesus said? He said to be in the world but not to be of it. He was partly right."

Gloria tried to hold back a shiver. How could she have bought into this ridiculous theology for years? She forced a good-preacher's-wife smile for the group. She had to be smart about how to proceed. If she worked behind Zack's back, she might be able to save some of them. If she challenged him outright, she would lose the opportunity.

"Jesus meant to say, 'Be *above* the world.' That's right. You heard me. We can rise above, and we have. The stats prove it. I heard on the news today that there are estimates of as many as 20 percent of Americans who have been lost, but we are faring much better than the national average. Look at the news reports and then look at the comparatively little damage done to Riverside. Seriously, take a moment to look around you."

The crowd, now spellbound by a message of hope they longed to hear, did as they were told. Gloria followed suit. Her eye caught something in the sky—a patch of blue just a little darker than the surrounding sky. She winced into the glare of the sun to focus. It was not a patch; it was a circle. She wiped her eyes and looked again, seeing a sphere a bit smaller than the size of the moon. A cloud passed by and obscured her view.

Zack continued. "Now look at the people around you. Look at your husbands, your wives."

"What about our children?" a distraught mother shrieked. "Where are my babies?" The crowd fell momentarily out of its stupor. Gloria had not considered a world without children. How terrible could that be? She stared at Zack. The question threw him for a second.

"You've seen the news reports. The governments of the world are telling us they foresaw this crisis and removed the children to safety. It's not the first time this has happened. During the bombings of London in World War II, children were sent to the countryside, out of harm's way. A similar thing has happened here."

"When will we see them?" the distraught mother asked, followed by others in the crowd.

"I'm sure that when the danger has passed, you will be reunited with your children," Zack said calmly. "In the meantime, we have a once-in-a-lifetime opportunity to build the world we want for them. I know a lot of people worry about the rapture and the end times. Well, folks, I'm here to tell you that they got it wrong. Look around you! Look at what we've accomplished for the Lord. Do you really think God would have left you behind?" Zack's voice grew soft and deep. "No, my brothers and sisters. That teaching was only ever a heresy. That's why I never taught it. The truth is that we are a blessed generation. We are the people to build the kingdom of God on top of these ashes." He closed his eyes looking for inspiration. Gloria felt a chill as if an evil arctic blast had swept over the proceedings.

The newly calmed crowd stood at attention, awaiting instruction from their inglorious leader. After a few long moments, Zack opened his eyes and said very softly, "So, now it's time for us to do our part." His voice rose in volume and pitch. "We can rise from these ashes to form a better world, a great place for our children when they return. It's on us, people. We can turn this tough time into an opportunity to make lasting changes to this world!" The crowd erupted into cheers. Gloria forced a smile on her horror-stricken face. *Somehow Zack has managed to chase away the pain of lost children. Unbelievable!*

Zack continued. "Now let's start by cleaning up our church, our source of comfort and inspiration in these trying times. I've placed baskets at the doors for your donations. We can and will be a positive force to build a better world. Are you with me?"

The crowd erupted in applause and cheers for their leader. Gloria had no doubt the baskets would be filled to the brim with offerings from people who now had nothing—their families, loved ones, and salvation itself stolen from them by the monster beside her.

Zack put his arm around her waist, drawing her close. He waved off the applause and yelled enthusiastically, "Now let's get to work!" The crowd dispersed to their tasks. Zack smiled broadly and pulled Gloria close. "Could you feel the power, darlin'? Isn't it exhilarating?" She returned his embrace as her skin crawled.

Before starting her cleanup tasks, Gloria made a point to hug the young mother. "I'm so sorry you miss your children," she said softly. "But I'm sure they're in a much better place, no doubt having the time of their lives right now."

The young mother looked at her distantly. "Oh yes. I think so too. The sooner we rebuild this world, the sooner they'll be back with us." She moved away from Gloria and busied herself with picking up trash from the church parking lot.

Gloria joined in, her mind racing. The horror wasn't only the man with whom she shared her bed. The horror was that she had been his partner in the fleecing of these poor, misguided people. She sat on the ground a few moments to wipe tears from her eyes.

"Lord, I am so sorry for my participation in this crime against You and against them. Please show me how to make amends." With that simple prayer, a desire grew to a passion in her. They had to hear the truth, and it had to be kept under Zack's radar for now. She had to be careful for the sake of her ... flock.

Gloria was happy to shower away the grime from the day's cleanup activities. The shower felt so good. She had been tempted to linger in the hot water, but she felt the urging of the Lord to move quickly. Zack's personal hygiene regimen took exactly one and a half hours. It never varied. At least she could count on some time to herself to read the Bible. She had no sooner opened to the Gospel of Matthew when the phone rang.

"Hello?"

"Hello ..." the caller fumbled, clearly confused. A sigh. "Gloria, it's Michael. I didn't expect to hear your voice."

"You thought I was taken?" she asked.

"Yeah," Michael said glumly. "At least I hoped."

"Sorry to hear your voice too," she answered. In truth, her heart leapt at the sound of his voice. If only she had met Michael before she met Zack, they both might be in heaven now.

"Well, I've punched my ticket for heaven," Michael said. "Too bad I waited until it was too late to get the first train out."

"Same here," she moaned. "Michael, how could we have been so blind?"

"I don't know." She heard a catch in his voice. "For me it was the lure of science … and some demonic intimidation in the form of what I thought to be an alien."

She gasped, flooded with long-repressed memories. "The Lady," she said breathlessly. "Michael, sometimes that all seems like a dream. Could those events really have happened?"

"Oh yes. We were used in a horrible experiment. I can barely bring myself to say it, but the Antichrist shares our DNA."

Hearing those words knocked the breath from her as surely as if she had been punched in the stomach. "Michael, I can't bear the thought of it. Are you sure?"

"His name is Isa Kurtoglu. I've met him."

"The president of Turkey?"

"The embodiment of evil … with my eyes," Michael said with despair.

She wiped at a tear, amazed that she had any left to cry. "I'm already having a hard time dealing with how many people Zack and I have hurt. But this? How can I live with it?"

"I'm worse than both of you, Gloria. I led the world to believe that the Bible is a piece of fiction. I can barely look at myself in the mirror … and yet." His voice broke. He continued after a long sob. "And yet Jesus forgave me and came to live in my heart. I'm overwhelmed by His power and grace. The very idea that He would forgive me compels me to make the most of these next few years."

"To save as many from the fire as possible," she said knowingly. "Same here, but I have to be careful of Zack. He's given himself over to evil, Michael."

"I'm sorry to hear it. But I'm not surprised given his association with Benny."

"I was defending him to my mother and David when the rapture occurred."

Michael told his story. "I had just made up with Gabe. I told him I would probably give my heart to Jesus before the day was out. We hugged, and then he disappeared in my arms."

Gloria tried to offer comfort. "We'll be with them soon enough anyway, Michael. The tribulation will be horrible, but at least we know it's only for a defined period of time."

He agreed. "Right. Let's face it, the worst thing that can happen to us is death—and that's an upgrade."

"I hear you. Still, seven years can be an awfully long time ..."

"But we have so much to do in such a small amount of time. At first I was overwhelmed by it all, but I can see the Lord's hand in events since the rapture. For instance, I just got through a meeting with the execs at the family business. I watched an incredible transformation in Michele."

"Oh no!" Gloria exclaimed. "Michele wasn't taken?"

"No. And her uncle Michael's theology is to blame," Michael said glumly. "But on the positive side, I just witnessed this seventeen-year-old girl blossom into a tough woman. She took control of the business and laid out a plan to use it and its cash flow to help others. It was absolutely amazing. Not only that, but Gabe has a son he never knew about. His name is Will." He told her about miraculously meeting the young man on the way from Rome."

"You made it all the way from Rome in this confusion?" she asked with surprise. She had been watching the news. There is no way Michael could have traveled that distance in the Dark Awakening without the direct hand of God.

"Yeah. It was a horrifying experience, but we made it. I would have thought it impossible, but God led us through."

"Praise God!" Gloria exclaimed.

"Well, that's the good part. The bad part is a penance of sorts. I've been made camerlengo to the new pope. The old pope went in the rapture."

"Michael, that could be a tough position. The new pope could well be the prophesied False Prophet," Gloria cautioned.

"Tell me about it. The new pope, Peter, is none other than my uncle Benny."

Gloria let out a gasp and then a nervous chuckle. Benny was

singlehandedly the foulest individual she had ever met. The idea that he would be a world religious leader was laughable.

Michael chuckled as well. "I know. My role is to stay close to him and Isa and save as many Christians as possible from their upcoming satanic tirade."

"I don't envy you, Michael, but I have to tell you that I'm in pretty deep myself." Gloria tried to speak, but she broke into tears as she thought of her current situation. Regaining her composure, she said weakly, "Zack's secretary was pregnant with his child. When the child left her in the rapture, she freaked out. There was a confrontation in our foyer and ..." Her voice broke. "Zack killed her, Michael. And now he's acting as if nothing happened. He's very dangerous."

"You have to get out of there, Gloria. Come live in Georgia. We'd be happy to have you here." Gloria felt her heart lighten at the thought of being with Michael.

"No, Michael. The Lord really dealt with me today about our church. We have thousands of congregants and millions of television viewers. Zack and I have hurt them, depriving them of the true love of God. I have such a heart to make things right for them. This is what the Lord wants from me in the remaining years."

Michael cautioned, "If Zack killed his secretary, Gloria, what makes you think he won't do the same to you?"

"I'm under no delusions, Michael. He would kill me if I got in his way. But I have a plan. I've been doing a lot of digging into his records. I could pretty convincingly prove he participated in his parents' deaths to get the ministry."

Michael sighed. "That doesn't make me feel any better regarding your safety."

"I've already planted the seed that I want to do my own show, sort of a 'coffee in the kitchen' show. He thinks it's a great idea. I plan to make it straight gospel."

"He'll never allow that message ..."

"I have the goods on him, Michael." The thought hit her like a thunderbolt. "You can help me tremendously."

"Name it. I'll do it," Michael answered.

"If I gave you all the incriminating evidence and you agreed to go public with it in the event of my death, it would back him into a corner."

"He's a dangerous man, Gloria. He'll try to find a way around it."

"True. But Benny has been able to control him for years with this information. The fact that someone stands ready to denounce him publicly on my behalf would give me the upper hand."

Michael asked, "Can you have the information in the next couple of days?"

"I have it now on a flash drive. Why?"

"Isa and Benny are convening a meeting of the United Nations on Friday. As Benny's glorified secretary, I'm calling to arrange Zack's attendance. Come with Zack and bring the information with you."

A sigh of relief escaped her. She hadn't realized how alone she felt in this endeavor until she finally had someone on her side. "Oh, Michael," she cried. "You have no idea how good that sounds to me. Once I have this information in a safe place, I can begin my ministry— my real ministry. And it will be so wonderful to see you."

"Same here," Michael said. "The downside is that Isa will be there. You'll have to steel yourself emotionally to see him. It's horrifying to be around him knowing his parentage."

In a few short days, she would face the nightmare in person. Not a very comforting thought.

"Gloria?" Michael asked.

"I'm here," she said softly. "What's he like?"

"He's handsome and brilliant, and evil beyond words. He sucks the positive energy out of the room and has this weird way of entering your mind if you're not careful."

Zack entered the room. "Who are you talking to?"

"Michael," Gloria said defensively.

"What does *he* want?" Zack snarled.

"Still as charming as ever," Michael said in her ear.

"You'll never believe it," she said, ignoring both of them. "Benny is the new pope." She paused for a moment to let it sink in. "Michael is calling to invite us to be with Benny when he and Isa Kurtoglu address the United Nations on Friday."

"Isa Kurtoglu?" Zack grinned as if having a beatific vision.

"Yes. Michael's trying to set up the details …"

He grabbed the phone from Gloria's hand and spoke warmly. "Michael! So glad to hear you and Benny are doing well."

SIXTEEN

The blades of the chopper roared and echoed through the man-made canyons of New York City. Even though the helicopter was equipped with a silencer to baffle the sound, the noise was loud in the cabin. Benny stared at the burned-out buildings and piles of trash and debris. Road crews worked feverishly to clear the snarled traffic jams, but the job would take months. Everyone attending the convocation of nations had to fly into the nearby private airports in Westchester, New York, or Teterboro, New Jersey. From there, the UN employed a veritable army of helicopters to ferry attendees and supplies to the auspicious meeting.

Benny knew he should be appalled at the devastation and anarchy below his feet, but he just couldn't be. This meeting would be his unveiling as Pope Peter Romanus. Freaking pope! He had hoped all his life and worked tirelessly for this day, enduring years of pain at the hands of pedantic bureaucrats like Cardinal Bilbo and the emotionally abusive Luciano Begliali. Well, too bad they couldn't see him now from their perches in hell. Then again, maybe they could. He stuck out his tongue and waved his middle finger on the off chance they could.

"Nice," Michael said with disgust.

"I've waited a long time to stick it to the world that has treated me so cruelly," he said defiantly.

"Not buying it," Michael snapped.

Benny's first response was to be annoyed, but then he took a close look at his nephew, who was staring down at the destruction through tears. He was moved to console the younger man.

"Look, Michael. I know things must seem very confusing to you right now. The world is changing in dramatic ways, but the world needed to change. Too many people. Too few resources. We've been teetering on the brink of disaster for the past fifty years. Now that it has come, we can rebuild. We really can make a better world."

Michael turned to him with a pained expression. "The saddest thing is that you actually believe the world will get better, Benny."

Benny sighed. "The world couldn't get a lot worse. Anything Isa brings to the table is likely to be an improvement."

"Has he shared his plans with you?" Michael asked cautiously.

"Actually, he hasn't," Benny said defensively. "He told that me all would be made known when I met him in New York. He's quite mysterious, you know."

"That's an understatement," Michael said glumly, returning to the window.

"Michael, you miss the family. I understand that, but there's nothing you can do to bring them back. You can mope around pining for them, or you can choose to throw yourself into the task at hand."

"What if I view my task differently than you do?"

"Well, to a certain extent, you will have to bend to my will since I'm your boss. But I'd like it a lot better if you could embrace your new role."

"Point well taken, Benny," Michael said, never turning from the window. Benny knew the man well enough to know he had won no ground. He sighed loudly and shook his head.

Within only a few minutes, the chopper landed between the United Nations building and the East River. As two security guards rushed to greet them, Benny was overcome with the rank odor of rotting flesh and trash. The slow cleanup effort left tons of refuse, human and otherwise, to decay in the hot autumn sun. He covered his nose and mouth with his hand and followed the guards as the chopper roared off to escort another round of dignitaries.

When they were safely in the building, one of the guards, a gray-haired portly gentleman, said, "Holiness, President Kurtoglu is waiting for you in the Dag Hammarskjöld Library. Follow me." He led Benny and Michael through a waiting area to a narrow room with a curved, cave-like wooden ceiling on one side and floor-to-ceiling windows on the other. Just as the security guard left, closing the door behind him, a door at the other end of the long room opened. In strode Isa Kurtoglu, perfect in every way. On his arm was the Lady, dressed in a gold lamé robe that bunched at her skinny shoulders and tented out to the floor. Huge sleeves grew like cones from the shoulders, masking her frail arms. She was a delight for Benny to see in the flesh, and he nearly wanted to kneel before her. Nonetheless, he was acutely aware of his newfound position. The pope does not kneel before anyone.

"Isa, I am so happy to see you," Benny oozed. "And, oh, my Lady, you look absolutely regal in that gown."

Isa smiled his greeting. The Lady stared at Michael. It was only then that Benny realized Michael had not extended a greeting. He looked over to see his nephew overcome, as if seeing a ghost. He whispered tersely, "Get hold of yourself, Michael. Offer a greeting. These are the two most powerful people in the world ... hell, probably in the solar system!"

"Hello," Michael said weakly as Benny made a tsk sound and shook his head in disbelief.

"Hello, Michael," the Lady said with a leering grin as a tiny sliver of saliva dropped from her nearly nonexistent lip. "We really need to get together sometime."

Michael whined, "Uh-hum." He shut his eyes. If Benny hadn't known better, he would swear the man was praying.

"I'm afraid the proverbial cat has caught my nephew's tongue," Benny said as he stared at Michael. "I'd be honored if you could one day teach me how to silence him so effectively."

Isa laughed heartily, and the Lady let out a high-pitched whine that Benny assumed to be an alien laugh.

"Benny, we mean no disrespect," Isa said ceremoniously, "but it would be in our best interest if Michael does not participate in our meeting."

"I understand completely," Benny said. "Michael." No answer. "Michael," he said more loudly. No response. Finally, he smacked the younger man's chest with the back of his hand. Michael snapped to.

"You need to wait outside, Michael," Benny said sternly.

Still looking a bit dazed, Michael muttered, "Of course," and left the room.

"Good help is so hard to come by these days," Benny joked nervously.

"He's just a bit overwhelmed," Isa said charitably. "The Lady has appeared to him ethereally over the years, but meeting her in person is an entirely different matter." A muted sense of rage filled Benny as he thought of his many sexual encounters with the Lady. He thought their relationship to be unique, yet something in the tone of Isa's voice led him to believe otherwise. He bristled.

"Come, Holiness, sit down. We have much work to do." Isa motioned to a chair. It was a bit small and a bit low to the ground for someone of Benny's girth. He eyed it suspiciously, and then tried to lower himself gently. When he thought his legs would bend no further, he fell unceremoniously to the seat below him. The arms of the chair dug into the flesh around his middle. Opposite him, Isa and the Lady sat as well. She balanced herself on the edge of the cushion so that her gold-slippered feet touched the floor.

"I assume you want to discuss your plans for the world," Benny began. "I have some ideas I would love to share. I studied world religions quite extensively for Luciano Begliali ..."

The Lady stared at him with her huge, watery eyes. "He is so willing, yet so incapable," she said briskly. The remark stung.

"We have a saying," Isa offered. "The spirit is willing, but the flesh is weak."

"Very appropriate for this situation." The Lady chuckled in her high-pitched squeal.

"I'm not sure I like the tone of this conversation," Benny said defensively.

"Not to worry, Benny," Isa said graciously. "We are not looking to criticize you. We merely want to help your external appearance so that others are more easily drawn to you."

"I've always prided myself on my appearance." Suddenly Benny was frightfully aware of how snugly he fit into the chair.

"Of course you have," Isa continued. "But the stakes are very high, my friend. Take, for example, that ill-fitting priestly garb."

"Oh." Benny smiled with relief. "I can explain this. I had to leave Rome in a hurry, so I wasn't able to bring any papal attire. This is a vestment Chris wore when he said Mass at our family's estate. It's all I had." Benny fiddled with the vestment, suddenly consumed with its wear and poor fit.

"Understandable. The thing is—it is not only a bad fit, but also it carries the wrong message. Benny, I want to proclaim you today as the pope who will unite the religions of the world. You must not limit yourself to concepts of Catholic dogma, or even Christianity. You have to take on a persona to draw men and women of all faiths. For that reason, I have taken the opportunity to redesign the papal attire." He moved to a closet in the room and produced a robe similar in construction to the one worn by the Lady, but this robe buttoned down the front like a clerical cassock. "I hope you like it," he said as he handed the garment to Benny.

The simple beauty of the robe immediately struck Benny. It was woven of white linen and spun silver yarn. It shimmered brilliantly in the light from the windows. Its buttons were crafted from diamonds, each weighing several carats. He let his hand glide over the softness of the robe. He didn't think he had ever seen anything so beautiful.

"It's really very beautiful," he said as he held it out. It was then that he noticed the cut. The shoulders were broad, and it tapered to a narrow elastic waist before expanding out to a bell-bottom just barely above the floor. Benny grimaced. There was no way this garment would fit. His shoulders would swim in the excess material at the top, and his waist would stretch the elastic to breaking point.

"Isa," he said apologetically, "I don't think I'll be able to wear this. The fit is for a much younger man with a more masculine physique."

Isa laughed. "Not to worry, my friend. This is the body shape you will have once I ... 'adjust' you."

Benny grew suspicious, not being thrilled with the idea of being 'adjusted.' "What do you mean?" he asked cautiously.

The Lady explained in her wheezing voice, "We quite like your spirit and your willingness to support the New World Order, but surely you know others find you to be off-putting."

"Off-putting!" Benny snapped. He couldn't believe this grown bug would have the audacity to call *him* off-putting.

"Come now," Isa said with a stern edge to his voice. "There's no need for histrionics, Benny. You are proving our point." Benny threw himself back in his chair. He didn't like Isa's tone. It scared him. His mind flashed to Isa's murder of Luciano Begliali. Benny hadn't thought of it in years. And he didn't believe he thought of it now. Isa was in his head, calling forth the horrible night when he sent Luciano to hell.

"Perhaps I was rash," Benny said softly, offering his attempt at a cute, disarming smile.

The Lady mocked, "Perhaps you were."

"Listen," Benny pleaded. "I meant no disrespect. It's just that I can't see how I'll ever pull off a tunic like this, lovely as it is."

"And …" the Lady led.

"And I see your point," Benny awkwardly conceded. "Sometimes I make people uncomfortable. In an odd way, I always considered it to be part of my charm."

"And it is," the Lady cooed, apparently happy with Benny's admission. "There are those of us who find you incredibly charming, but we can't rely on the world at large to share our eclectic tastes. For you to perform your role, you need to be changed."

"I think that is the hard part for me to understand," Benny said with downcast eyes and a humble tone. "What is the process to 'adjust' me? Will it hurt?"

"Not much." Isa chuckled. "We will merely call on an ascended master to inhabit your body and transform it."

Benny swallowed hard. His heart raced. "You … you want me to share my body with another consciousness?"

"In a word, yes, but it's not as mysterious as it sounds."

"Will my consciousness be present? Or are you just interested in my body as a vehicle?"

Isa laughed scornfully. "Trust me, Benny, we are not interested in your body. In fact, we want to change it."

"But that doesn't answer the question of what will become of my consciousness."

"Oh, right," Isa said. "For a time you'll be aware of another personality. But after some initial adjustment, your consciousness will merge with his to form a blended entity."

It didn't sound like such a good time to Benny. He had to find a way to reject the offer without offending his hosts. "The thing is, Isa, I've always been kind of a loner. I've never really felt the desire to share my life … or to share anything for that matter. I really think I'm not a good candidate for this 'adjustment.'"

"To the contrary," the Lady said, wheezing, "you are the perfect candidate. It is as if you have been saving yourself all this time. Sort of a virgin bride."

"Who has no romantic delusions of the wedding night," Benny offered. "I'm afraid I'll have to decline your most gracious offer." He wriggled out of the tight chair, planning a steady march to the door. He would get Michael and get out of here.

"Not so fast," Isa said sternly as Benny was walking away. Benny felt his legs go weak under an unseen pressure on his shoulders. He fell to his knees.

"Funny, I thought the pope kneeled before nobody," Isa said curtly, mocking Benny's thoughts at the beginning of the meeting.

Benny tried to look into Isa's eyes, but the pressure now formed around his head, forcing it to stay bowed. "Please, Isa," he muttered.

"I'm afraid there is no other path for you, my friend," Isa retorted. "You were bred for this moment. I advise you not to fight it. That could be … painful."

"And if I don't fight it?" Benny asked.

"It won't be so painful, and the rewards will be immediate."

"What rewards?" Benny asked woefully.

"For starters, you'll fit into your new attire. Your body will be transformed. You will also retain the spiritual powers of the ascended master." Benny began to relax. If Isa were telling the truth, this 'adjustment' would make him everything he had longed to be—a handsome powerful man in his own right. Well, not exactly in his own right. He would have to share his body with whatever the hell it was Isa wanted to inhabit him. His mind swirled for an answer.

"Could I meet this ascended master first?" Benny asked. "I mean, we're going to be very close. I'd like to meet him."

"A willing spirit. Much appreciated," the Lady cooed as she clapped her four-digit hands. Benny noticed that they didn't produce the flesh-on-flesh sound of human clapping. It was more like a rattling of bones.

"I agree, Lady," Isa intoned. "Benny, you may return to your chair."

Benny felt his body follow the command, although he, himself, had not willed it to move.

In a voice that reverberated throughout the room, Isa commanded, "Nergal! Come forth!" The room's temperature dropped suddenly, sending a shiver through Benny's spine. Light in the room dimmed next to Isa as a shadowy figure began to take shape.

Benny drew a sharp breath as the shadow coalesced. At first it was an outline of a tall being. Benny guessed him to be about seven feet. A huge chest descended to a tiny waist. *Well, I understand the tunic now.* The outline continued to fill in, and Benny became increasingly disturbed. The being was definitely reptilian. Slanted, far-set eyes and a hornlike nose sat above a lipless mouth. The creature's gray-green face sat on a thick neck. The being stared at Benny with eyes displaying perpendicular slits for pupils. Benny's heart raced. There was no way he could let this inhuman thing live inside him.

"Isa," Benny spoke breathlessly, "I don't think I can go through with this. It's … it's all too much."

Nergal growled, and the Lady scowled. Isa grinned as if the fear in Benny's eyes was the thrill of his day. "I'm afraid you have no recourse, old friend."

Benny moaned. His mind flashed to countless actions and conversations in his past. He had really believed that Luciano and his powerful friends were out to bring good to the world—well, at least to the few chosen to survive. Now, for the first time, he was seeing the hidden truth that he had been manipulated, that he had been a pawn in the age-old battle between good and evil. His selfishness had been the hook to pull him to the wrong camp. He wanted to pray, but he knew it was too late. Instead he muttered a low guttural groan as Nergal approached.

Outside in the waiting area, Michael had collected his thoughts. The overwhelming power of evil in the room, and his past nightmares of the Lady, had left him stupefied and powerless. He resolved in future encounters to stay in prayer, letting the Lord's power prevail. He busied himself with the autobiography Benny dictated to Will and Jimmy while he and Michele were at corporate headquarters. The combination of Jesus and Superman presented in the bio had not even the slightest resemblance to the Benny Michael knew.

He was rocked by a bloodcurdling scream, long, drawn-out, and terrified. It was Benny's voice.

SEVENTEEN

The library was deadly quiet after the bloodcurdling scream. Michael concentrated to hear anything else, but only silence filled the air. Eventually, he returned to Benny's autobiography.

He read how Benny raised his half-wit half-sister. Michael shook with anger as he read how Benny taught her the family business when he decided to throw off worldly pursuits to serve the Lord. In this version of history, Benny saved Kim from a life of promiscuity, prevented her from having an abortion, and then practically raised her child. He even arranged Gabe's adoption in this new account.

Michael was so consumed with anger at Benny's casual tossing of his family under the bus that he had barely noticed the opening library door.

"Michael, has Zack arrived yet?" he heard Benny call from the opening door.

"I don't know, Benny," Michael said tersely as he shoved Benny's ridiculous autobiography into his briefcase. It was only then that he looked up at the older man and felt momentarily faint. Benny had been transformed. The heavy build? Gone in favor of a lithe, maybe even muscled, torso hiding behind a form-fitting papal robe. The bald head? Now pillowed in a tuft of brilliant white hair. The dark, black-circled eyes? Now replaced with younger skin and eyes that glistened beneath long lashes.

"Benny ... what happened to you?" Michael gasped.

"It's the new me," Benny said without joy. For a second, Michael saw the old Benny in the new man's eyes. Benny was afraid. He shivered as if caught by a chill, and then the old Benny was gone. The eyes were now bright, and the new slender face stretched a smile from prominent cheek to prominent cheek, revealing dazzling teeth. It was clearly intended to be calming and disarming, but to Michael it more closely resembled the mad smile of the Joker. Michael prayed silently for help and protection from the thing that had taken control of his uncle.

"Michael," Benny said menacingly, all the while never losing the gross characterization of a smile, "never mind about finding Zack. I can feel him coming down the hallway."

"Okay," Michael muttered, still staring at Benny in disbelief.

"You'll get used to it, Michael," Benny said more warmly.

"I guess I'll have to," Michael said cautiously.

"Come on now, even you have to admit this is quite an improvement."

"I'm not as concerned about the look as I am with *who* you've become," Michael said, eyeing the being cautiously.

"It will take a bit of time for two very distinct personalities to become one," Benny said softly. He pointed at Michael and said, "You look almost frightened. Why?"

"The smile is just too big," Michael muttered. "It looks fake, menacing."

"Well, it's not as though Benny had much practice smiling before I met him. How's this?" He dialed the smile back to a loving grin, his eyes radiant.

Even with the power of the Holy Spirit in him, Michael was drawn to the warmth expressed. He cleared his throat. "That's … that's much better," he fumbled.

"Good," Benny said warmly, clapping Michael on the shoulder. "Zack is about to arrive, so I have just a bit of time to tell you that your belief in the old regime of the Nazarene does not threaten me. I have plenty of time to prove you wrong."

"I see," Michael said in a strong voice. "And if you can't?"

"I'm still Benny. I'll still honor the promise I made to your mother."

"Because you fear the mere presence of a person who has been glorified by Jesus," Michael said. This time it was Michael who wore the grin.

Benny turned on his heels to reenter the library. "Think what you like, Michael. Zack is here. Show him into the library."

As the door to the library closed, a member of the security team entered the waiting room with Zack and Gloria in tow.

"Michael," Zack said sternly, his only salutation.

"Zack," Michael offered tersely. "Benny's in the next room with Isa and the Lady. They asked me to send you straight in." Zack proudly strode to the door, gave it a little knock, and fairly ran into the room. Michael quickly closed the door behind him. He wished he had a key to lock them all in.

Wasting no time, Michael crossed the room in a few strides to hug Gloria tightly. He felt her shoulders heaving with sobs. He began to cry as well, but only for a second. He released Gloria from the hug and offered her a tissue.

"We have to stay strong," he said to her in a hushed tone. "Isa and the Lady sent some very powerful demon to indwell Benny. You won't believe when you see it. They've turned him into a handsome, distinguished-looking guy with bright eyes and a warm smile. Pope Peter is about to capture the hearts of the world." He took Gloria's hand and led her to the farthest corner from the door to the library, where they took chairs facing one another.

"I just can't believe everything that has happened in such a short space of time," Gloria said, rubbing her arms as if chasing away a chill.

Michael looked at her, carefully cataloging the lines etched by grief and despair in her lovely face. "I know," he added. "The pain of losing so many loved ones to the rapture and the knowledge that we could have been spared this ... it's almost too much to bear. Or at least it would be if I hadn't finally given my life to Jesus."

"I agree," she said, taking his hand. "But sometimes I have trouble finding the will to live. I just keep thinking how much better it would be to die in Christ." She sounded forlorn.

"It would be, Gloria, if we didn't have work to do. By a set of circumstances that could only be viewed as miraculous, we're in unique positions to snatch some of their intended victims right from under their noses. I intend to work tirelessly to that end. My mother has set up some incredible infrastructure, and I think Michele is a chip off the old block when it comes to the family businesses."

Gloria smiled weakly. "She's a good kid."

"She really is," he agreed. "But I'm not fishing for a compliment about my niece. I'm trying to encourage you to follow through with what you told me about on the phone. Use Riverside's platform to point people to the one and only true God, Jesus." He could hear the excitement building in his voice. In years past, this type of passion had come from solving an archeological puzzle. Now it came from serving the Lord. For the first time in his life, he felt clean and transparent, devoid of secrets and ulterior motives.

"You're right." She smiled. "Maybe Michele and I could coordinate our efforts. I can get airtime, but I don't have access to the type of resources you guys command."

"That's my girl," Michael exclaimed. The outburst was followed by an awkward silence as he pondered what could have been, and how such an inappropriate exclamation could feel so right in their current situation.

Breaking the silence, Michael said awkwardly, "I'll have Michele give you a call."

"Thanks," she said with downcast eyes as the door opened at the other end of the room. Michael raised an eyebrow at her as both stood and walked toward the door.

Zack exited first, looking shell-shocked and robotic. Benny followed. In the few moments he had been away, the two personalities had begun to merge. Michael saw much more of Benny's pride in his walk, and his smile now had a bit of the sardonic quality Benny had carried since Michael had known him.

"Hello, Gloria," Benny said with a grin.

"H ... hello," Gloria said awkwardly. "I know so little of Catholic protocol. I don't know how to refer to you." Michael could see her scrutinize the new Benny. Her legs weakened for a brief second in what could easily have been mistaken for a slight curtsy.

Zack came to her side. "I think the proper term is 'Holiness,' darlin'."

"Our families have known one another for a long time," Benny said graciously. "I have no problem if you refer to me as Benny within the small confines our family unit."

"Thank you, Benny," she said, recovering. "And may I say that you look fabulous."

"Why, thank you! I feel fabulous," Benny said as he gave a muted pirouette to offer Gloria a 360-degree view.

Michael couldn't suppress a grin. *That was definitely a Benny move. That demon may have bitten off a little more than he could chew when he went after old Benny!*

Benny came out of the turn to address Michael. "The show's about to start. You and Gloria better take your seats."

The General Assembly's meeting room in the United Nations building was packed. Despite restricted travel and nearly impassable roads, leaders of most of the world's nations joined their UN ambassadors at their designated tables. The gallery was filled with reporters. The world had gone crazy, and everyone was looking for an answer. In the center, directly in front of the podium, sat a group of world-renowned scientists, many of whom Michael recognized.

At the front of the room in the center of a large circular area stood the iconic granite desk. Usually three chairs stood behind this desk, but today they were reduced to two. A large screen hung from the ceiling behind the desk, a speaker's podium in front of it. To the right of the podium was a small riser of chairs designated for the heads of state from the Security Council. To the left of the podium was a similar riser of chairs designated for selected religious leaders of the world.

Michael and Gloria took assigned seats in the first row behind the delegate desks on the left side of the stage. The world's delegates chattered incessantly at their desks until the lights dimmed. Then all attention focused on the stage. First, the religious leaders took their places. Zack filed in with this group, looking like the cat that swallowed the canary. Joining him were a Native American shaman, a Jewish rabbi, Sunni and Shia imams, a Buddhist monk, a Hindu pandit, and an African tribal shaman. Michael noticed a woman dressed all in black sporting a huge amulet around her neck. He guessed she was the Wiccan delegate. Following her, the parade became increasingly bizarre as six more individuals followed. Their attire was so strange that Michael couldn't associate them with a religion. They looked like participants at a Comic Con. Curiously absent in the delegation was Catholic representation. Michael guessed that Benny would fill that role. He rubbed his eyes. It was going to be a long day.

Before sitting, the grinning Zack offered a quick wave to Gloria. "This is going to be so bizarre," she said to Michael through a clenched smile as she returned the wave.

"And it's just beginning," Michael said as the Security Council heads of state took their places on the opposite riser. Finally, Isa and Benny strode to their places behind the large granite desk at the center. Michael wondered about the behind-the-scenes politics and dirty dealings needed to convince the world's leaders to take subservient positions to these two. Michael had to admit they were an impressive pair following Benny's makeover. They exuded confidence and a caring nature that beckoned to the weary crowd.

"Do you feel that?" Gloria whispered.

"Yes," Michael said. A tone of rapt devotion filled the crowd. They were entranced even before Benny and Isa had taken their seats. Michael could sense the demonic pull to worship them, but to him the feeling was like bugs crawling over his skin. The assembly fell into total silence. Isa sat for a second, little more than a dramatic pause, and then proceeded to the podium. The strobe of camera flashes made it look as if he walked in slow motion.

Isa took the podium with a command-and-control attitude, and the crowd simply acquiesced. They applauded him until he raised his hands in a gesture to stop them. Then they fell immediately silent.

Finally he spoke. "Ladies and gentlemen, we are at a crossroads. The world as we have known it is gone. We will never be able to return to the level of innocence we enjoyed just a week ago. What I'm about to share with you will seem fantastic and unbelievable. You will wish it weren't true, but you only have to look at recent events for confirmation.

"For years, scientists have been aware that our sun, like most stars in the galaxy, did not form alone. It has a twin, a muted twin not large enough to erupt into fusion reactions common to most stars. Instead, it smoldered as a dark massive object at the edge of our solar system. Scientists have long observed this object's gravitational effect on the outer planets, but because it is dark, a brown dwarf star, it could not be seen in normal light. It was only after the launch of infrared telescopes that they were able to get a look at this star and the planets surrounding it." He paused for a moment as the screen displayed a red and black smoldering mass surrounded by one large blue orb and four smaller points of light.

"This is the object. In the 1980s, scientists' measurements indicated a slow but definable orbit bringing this small solar system close to our sun."

The screen moved to an animation of a large disk and a much smaller one in orbit around a center point of their mass. He continued, "As you can see, when a very large object and a much smaller object are gravitationally locked, they actually orbit around their center of mass. Because our sun and our solar system are much more massive than the solar twin, there are periodic incursions of smaller solar system into the midst of ours.

"As time went by, archeologists were drawn to historical records describing strange events in the sky followed by devastation on Earth. For years, people thought these ancient tales to be fanciful. A closer inspection revealed a description of the effects of the solar twin's entrance into our solar system. Scientists have taken to calling this failed star Nemesis."

The crowd was still enrapt, but Michael could sense a change in the room's energy. These people had come for a quick answer. They shifted uncomfortably in their chairs at the dawning revelation that the world's troubles were far from over.

Isa continued. "As you have probably assumed, Nemesis is inbound. In fact, its largest planet, Nibiru, is faintly visible as a blue patch slightly darker than the sky. You probably haven't seen it because your leaders have engaged in a pattern of deception, spraying the sky with chemicals specifically to obscure it."

The crowd gasped as Isa gestured to the heads of state to his right. "These men, with the best of intentions, believed nothing could be done to avert the coming crisis. Rather than worry you, they chose to lull you into having feelings of security while building for themselves underground bases in which they planned to ride out the storm."

The heads of state looked shocked at Isa's stunning betrayal of them. Murmurs filled the room, and Isa let them percolate for a few moments before quelling the feelings of distrust he had sown.

"To be fair to the world's leaders, they felt they had little choice. To disclose these facts would only result in worldwide panic. They wished they could save everyone, but they didn't see it as an option.

"However, they were wrong. There is an option that will allow the world to survive the coming storm. I will have to take a few moments to describe the coming events before I tell you how we will survive them. I hope you will allow me to continue."

The crowd fell silent again. Isa continued. "There are two major threats arising from this passage. They come from the intense magnetic radiation of the Nemesis system and from a race of beings in that system that has proven itself to be hostile."

Again the room uttered a collective gasp and broke into panicked muttering. Isa motioned for them to be quiet.

"First, let me speak to the magnetic effects. They have the potential to unsettle most of the electronic equipment on the planet. Fortunately, we have a full seven years before the radiation becomes intense enough to do serious harm. If we dedicate sufficient resources to securing our infrastructure, we'll be able to endure the magnetic storms with minimal disruption."

A breath of fresh air, a feeling of hope, spread around the room.

"We have a simple choice. Either we go on the way we have been going and lose everything within the next decade, or we devote ourselves wholeheartedly to a last-ditch effort to save the world. The UN Security Council has abandoned their ostrich-inspired methods in favor of my plan to save as many as possible."

The room broke into spontaneous applause. Michael was stunned by the ease with which Isa was painting himself to be the savior of the world.

Isa motioned for silence. "That is the good part. However, the magnetic radiation will impair the functioning of the human brain well in advance of destroying our infrastructure. I'm sure you all witnessed the huge flash of lightning that enveloped the world a week ago. We were caught in an electromagnetic discharge between our sun and Nemesis. There is no predicting when these discharges will occur or if they'll pass Earth, but we now understand the impact to society. In short, those people most susceptible to the radiation lost their minds last week. This is the sole cause of the recent mayhem. As the magnetic imbalance subsided, so did the insanity, but the cost in terms of lost lives is still being tabulated.

"There's good news, though. We have friends in high places ...

literally. We have made contact with an ancient race of extraterrestrials desiring to develop our world as a trade partner for our natural resources. This gives them a vested interest in securing our world against the coming devastation. To that end, they have offered to show us how to build weapons that will be effective against the warlike population of Nibiru, the largest planet in the Nemesis system."

The room was stone-silent as the attendees considered the gravity of the situation and the offer of salvation from an advanced race. Isa continued, to the shock of his incredulous audience. "We are fortunate to have with us today two representatives of this race. The first is a being that prefers the name Lady when dealing in English. She'll tell you of their plan and about the second representative. Please offer a welcoming round of applause for the Lady."

The audience applauded as they had been told to do. Michael looked at the expressions of awe on every face as the Lady moved from the wings to the podium beside Isa. Her very presence sent a chill up his spine. He winced a bit as Gloria squeezed his arm in a vicelike grip. She was having the same reaction.

Isa lowered the microphone to the Lady's height before yielding it. The Lady spoke in a wheezing voice. "Thank you for the warm welcome. I find your atmosphere to be a bit cumbersome, so my remarks will be brief. I come from a star system in this galaxy. We are part of a much larger federation of spacefaring societies engaging in trade throughout this quadrant of the galaxy. For a long time, we have admired your abundant biosphere. We have anxiously awaited a time when your people would evolve to a planetary form of government and spacefaring capabilities so that we could admit you as equal partners in our trading alliance. Unfortunately, your world has been stopped short of attaining these minimum standards by the incursion of your solar twin. Its magnetic properties wipe clean your best minds. Its gravitational effects drive global catastrophes. And worst of all, its inhabitants rape your world with each passing. Finally, our federation has decided to waive the basic criteria for accession into our ranks with the hope of helping your world protect and defend itself.

"A perspective from outside your solar system gives us a very clear indication of the effects of each passing. The severity of the impact is determined by where your planet lies in relation to the sun when the

Nemesis system passes. In some incursions, Earth has been on the opposite side of the sun, shielded from the worst of the magnetic output and from direct contact with the race calling itself the Anu from planet Nibiru. Unfortunately, in the coming passage, your sun will not be between you and Nibiru."

Grave faces filled the arena as one after another of the attendees considered the prospect of war with a planetary intruder.

"Our organization has a strict policy of neutrality. However, we have worked for generations to develop a vehicle of hope. Through countless fertilization projects we have modified the genetic code to one end—the creation of a being that is fully alien and fully human. As an alien, he has access to all our knowledge and technology. As a human, he is able to direct the manufacture and distribution of weaponry to defend your world. Thus we have offered you the tools to defend yourselves."

Isa approached the podium to stand beside her. *Here it comes,* Michael thought. He glanced at Gloria, who had set her face like stone, and then at Zack, who grinned broadly and bounced in his seat as if he could barely contain his excitement.

The Lady continued, "This most wonderful being, the best of both our societies, is none other than the man you know as Isa Kurtoglu." Isa smiled warmly toward the audience. She finished speaking with a final admonition. "Listen to him. He is your best hope." Then the Lady took the seat next to Benny, who fawned over her and helped her into her chair.

Isa raised the microphone as he smirked over a quip he was about to make. "Thank you, Lady. If I had just told them I was a representative of the federation, they would never have believed me!" The crowd let go of pent-up tension with a loud round of laughter. Isa let it go for a while, and then he drew the crowd's attention to a new image on the screen, a time line.

"Folks, we have about seven years to get ready to stop an Anu attack. It isn't a long time, but it is enough time if this august assembly will vote to unite behind me in this most valiant effort. Through the most recent discoveries of scientists working on the Large Hadron Collider at CERN, we have access to powerful energy derived from the very fabric of space–time—energy to power directed-beam weapons to thwart an Anu invasion.

"We believe the Anu would most likely try to invade us at the absolute center of the world's landmass. From there they would radiate outward." The screen resolved into an image of the Middle East from space. "The geographic center of our world is the city of Jerusalem. Perhaps there is some hidden understanding at the very recesses of our collective consciousness that is attuned to this fact. Perhaps that is why we have lived with millennia of anger and tension regarding the control of that city.

"But we can no longer afford to be divided over this marvelous city. To that end, my caliphate has made a peace agreement with Israel. As part of that agreement, Jerusalem will be an international city and a home to all our major religions—the best of humanity—and we will defend it to the best of our ability against invasion."

Michael whispered to Gloria, "There's the prophesied peace agreement with Israel."

The room erupted in applause. Michael had no doubt that the assembly would give Isa dictatorial control. He shook his head over the speed with which Isa had accomplished all of this.

"We need to liberate Jerusalem from the shackles of religious division in order to save our world. Thankfully, I've had the privilege to work with the newly elected pope. We have been friends for years, and I have recently come to learn that the Lady has trained him for years in preparation for this time. Please join me in welcoming Pope Peter II."

Benny strode gracefully to the podium in what Michael found to be a decidedly manly gait as the members of the assembly applauded. Most seemed only vaguely aware that a new pope had been elected in the tumult of the Dark Awakening. Benny looked handsome and in total control of the situation. As he stepped up to the podium, Isa hugged him warmly and said, "Welcome, friend."

Benny adjusted the microphone and spoke in a warm, rich baritone. "Thank you, Isa, and thank you, United Nations Assembly, for your warm welcome. I have the displeasure of telling you that we lost our last pope to the magnetic madness that overwhelmed our planet. In a very decisive and quick action, the College of Cardinals appointed me to fill his role in this time of great trial."

"It's hard to believe that's Benny," Gloria whispered.

"At least in part," Michael whispered in return.

Benny continued. "We have indeed come to a crossroads, my friends. It is time for us to put aside our petty grievances and religious differences. Over the years, I have learned that the nature of God transcends the individual tenets of the world's religions. We are inherently spiritual beings. Our very DNA vibrates at a frequency that allows us to 'tune in' to the universe. Through the mechanism of quantum entanglement, the subtle science of which eludes me, we are one in a mystical way—mystical, I say, but proven by science nonetheless.

"It is this mystical union we feel when we pray or meditate. It is this mystical union we feel when we come together as a group with a united purpose, whether it be in a church, mosque, synagogue, or sports arena. The shared consciousness of such moments is the feeling of unity that undergirds every religion on earth. Over the centuries, we have tried to use human intellect to define this mystery. But as the Lady's presence in this room will attest, this mystery is universal and far beyond the purview of the human experience. Arguing over Buddha, Mohammed, or Jesus only muddies the water. Spirituality is at the very heart of the DNA molecule and is, at its very essence, a connection to the universe and all it contains."

Benny paused for emphasis, allowing his comments to sink in. "In a perfect world, we would be free from the encumbrances of religion to express a more pure profound spirituality that surpasses all ritual and rhetoric. The Lady tells me her race needed the passage of three generations after their first encounter with other intelligent life forms to figure it all out. We have a scant seven years.

"It is no accident that Christians bound inextricably to the Bible were among the most affected by the recent magnetic anomaly. Over their lifetimes, their strict religious beliefs kept them from experiencing the broader realm of spirituality. In the simplest of terms, their narrow-mindedness prevented them from attaining a higher consciousness. Their DNA vibrated at a lower frequency, one that was most susceptible to the magnetic flux."

Michael wanted to stand up and scream the truth, and yet he felt constrained by the Holy Spirit. The Bible had predicted a spirit of delusion over the world. He was witnessing it.

Benny continued. "Lest any of us who remain feel smug, I should point out that they were just unfortunate enough to be at a frequency most prevalent in the recent anomaly. There is no guarantee that any future magnetic fluxes will carry the same frequency. It could be Muslims, Jews, Hindus, Buddhists, or the adherents of a more ancient religion to go the next time. The point is this: all such beliefs hinder the spiritual evolution we need if we are to survive this impending catastrophe. We *must* rise above our individual belief systems to the truth resident in all of them."

An unexpected fresh round of applause burst through the room. Benny paused and flashed a grateful smile until the applause subsided.

"We can't get to pure spirituality overnight, but we can start down the path to true enlightenment. To begin, I will be working with representatives of all the world's major religions to find our common spiritual center. In the meantime, we must insist on a world order that accepts all religious beliefs. I'm not just talking of tolerance. We must, each of us, be open to the religious practices of all. It is only in the diversity of all religions that we will find the common core of unity." Benny's voice surged with passion to the renewed applause of the crowd. "To this end, I petition President Kurtoglu and the membership of this assembly to outlaw any religious practice that eschews the practice of other religions. As a sign of my serious intent, I have suspended all Catholic sacraments in recognition of their noninclusive nature. In addition, the Catholic faith now embraces *all* other inclusive faith practices. To my friends of different faiths behind me here on this stage, to anyone with an ear to hear, and to my atheist and agnostic brothers and sisters, I proudly and boldly proclaim: I'll see you in heaven!"

The crowd erupted in cheers as Michael's mind flooded with a prediction made by Bishop Sheen, a Catholic bishop who grew up not far from Chris in Illinois. He said the last pope would be very popular, but he would lead many astray with a Christ-less gospel. *You nailed that prediction, Bishop.*

The applause, now louder, continued. Benny waited for absolute silence. With a soft voice now, he added gravely, "But it won't be enough, friends. Unaided, we cannot accomplish the type of spiritual evolution we need in seven short years. We need more than a change in attitude; we need a global shift in consciousness. The Lady has shown me that there is a way to achieve this rapid growth through technology."

Here it comes, Michael thought. He raised an eyebrow at Gloria. She drew a deep breath. Just a few weeks ago, he considered Gabe crazy for believing such a thing could happen.

Benny continued. "Within a few short years, we will develop and manufacture nanotransmitters that can be injected into the world's population. These transmitters will bond with us at a cellular level, altering our DNA to a frequency too high to be affected by future magnetic anomalies."

Benny grinned at the hushed crowd. "But there will be side effects. Our studies lead us to believe we will see an average increase of fifty points in IQ within weeks of receiving this technology. Not a bad downside if you ask me." The crowd chuckled.

"Fully protected from the magnetic onslaught, we will be able to function as a cohesive society to produce the weapons needed to repel the Anu invasion. I call on the governments of the world to donate sufficient funds and resources to ensure the development, production, and administration of this nanotechnology to every man and woman on earth.

"I would like to close with a word of encouragement. We have at our fingertips the ability not only to survive this impending crisis but also to rise from it a stronger species ready to find our ultimate destiny. For once in our history, let us come together for the benefit of all."

Isa joined Benny at the podium. He raised the microphone and concluded the meeting. "So, you have heard our presentation, my friends. In summary, this world—the entire world—is faced with the most extreme threat. And yet we have been given the tools to meet that threat head-on. It will be the toughest period of human history as we deal with the environmental and geological effects of our sun's intrusive twin. But it also will be a time of valiant superhuman effort as we develop the technology to protect ourselves from a marauding alien race."

Michael leaned into Gloria and whispered, "These people are so sick, they actually think they can shoot Jesus out of the sky when He comes. They want to build hyperdimensional weapons they believe will kill the Son of God! It's sheer lunacy." Her wide-eyed expression told him of her shock and dismay.

The crowd erupted, getting to their feet as Isa continued. "Together, we can use this challenge to build a spectacular future. The road will be tough; the work will be arduous; the sacrifices will be many. But with the help of our galactic neighbors, we will ascend to a greater consciousness of spirituality, enabling us to join a federation of like-minded races, sharing and exploring the cultural and genetic diversity of the universe. Is it too much to give personal liberty a backseat for a defined period of time in order to give ourselves a liberty that extends beyond the confines of this one tiny planet?"

Isa had to shout to be heard over the din of the crowd. "I know what I am asking you to do is tough, but it is our only chance. Vote now, in this most profound assembly of humanity, to give me the global authority to put our plans to work. Let us seek together the only viable answer for our world. In a second vote, I ask you to confirm support for Pope Peter's initiative to outlaw any and all restrictive religions and to deliver the technology to protect the world from future magnetic anomalies. Again, it is our only hope, lest we, too, fall to the madness that recently nearly tore our societies asunder." The screen behind him changed to a live shot of the sky. The camera found a slight smudge of blue, just a bit darker than the sky. Then it zoomed in to show a sphere: Nibiru, the supposed home of the coming invaders.

"A beautiful future can be had, ladies and gentlemen." He motioned to the screen. "But we have to get past this. This is what stands between us and true happiness. It's time to let all political and religious sectarianism die in the dustheap of history. We must now choose to unite the human family as never before."

Michael felt Gloria's hand in his. He looked down to see she had given him the flash drive she had spoken of earlier—the dirt on Zack. "I don't even know if it matters anymore," she whispered somberly. "We'll be preaching against the great delusion. These people are swallowing Isa's message hook, line, and sinker."

Michael held her hand a bit longer, taking in the never-ending applause, Isa's broad smile, Benny's rapt adoration of Isa, and the Lady's toothless grin. Then he looked at Nibiru's image on the screen. He had never imagined world events could change so quickly.

He sighed, wiping at his eyes, at the tears for what he had lost in the rapture, tears for the vast changes to society in the past days, tears for the deluded masses, and tears for what was surely to come.

TIME

EIGHTEEN

The sun was just beginning to rise over Jerusalem. It was Michael's favorite part of the day. In the fresh smell of the wee morning hours, he could pretend the rapture hadn't happened two years earlier. For just about an hour each day, it was just him in prayer with Jesus as he walked the streets once walked by his Lord.

Michael pondered the changes in the past two years. Of course, the United Nations had granted Isa all he wanted. Nations continued to exist, but they formed amalgamations. Ten superstates reported through their leaders to Isa. The American president reported to Isa for the North American Union. The Europeans had a leader from the European Union. Eastern Europe and the former Soviet states reported through the Russian leader. Eastern Asia reported through the Chinese leader. Australia, Japan, and the Pacific Islands formed a group that reported through Tokyo. Central and South America reported through the Venezuelan ruler. Northern Africa reported through the Egyptian leader. The western part of Asia region that included Vietnam, Cambodia, and the islands between Asia and Australia reported through Indonesia. Sub-Saharan Africa reported through Johannesburg. And western Asia, which was essentially Isa's caliphate, was ruled directly by him.

The Vatican was still under repair, although progress had slowed to a snail's pace as the emphasis moved to Jerusalem. The new, improved Benny was adamant about bringing the three Abrahamic religions to heel in the New Order. He chose the Temple Mount to make his stand. He was building the Basilica of St. Peter II. Benny the saint! It would include a large courtyard connecting it to the new Dome of the Rock and the new Temple of Solomon. Together, they would be referred to as the New Vatican. Given that much of the world economy was now working to harden assets against attack around the globe, the New Vatican construction cost was little more than a blip on the radar screen of overall spending.

The construction proceeded on target despite daily insurrectionist speech by two prophets at the base of the Temple Mount. Michael had known, from his reading of the book of Revelation, that they would come. He hadn't exactly envisioned them in the modern era, though. Bearded and ancient-looking, they wore jeans and T-shirts, looking more like they had stepped off the set of *Duck Dynasty* than from the pages of history. Appearances aside, they were not to be trifled with. They spent their days calling out Isa as the Antichrist and Benny as the False Prophet. They didn't refute the reality of the approaching solar twin. Rather, they claimed it had been set in motion ages before as the instrument of God's judgment for the rejection of Jesus as Savior.

The sheer spiritual power of their presence brought to his knees anyone whom Isa sent to remove them. As had become his custom, Michael bought three lattes and walked in the early morning light to see them. While they made it a habit to speak boldly and broadly to the inhabitants of Earth, they rarely engaged in direct conversation. He approached them gingerly and smiled. Placing the cups on the ground about ten feet from them, he backed up slowly and said, "Good morning."

As usual, they smiled broadly and called, "*Todah,*" the Hebrew word for "thank you."

Michael waved to tell them they were welcome. Then to his surprise, a flood of words poured forth from the two. His mind raced as they spun through different languages. Their sentences would use a subject from one language, a verb from another, and conjunctions and modifiers from other languages. A key aspect to their dialogue, though, was the use of languages Michael understood.

"You're doing well, Michael," said the one Michael had always assumed to be Elijah.

"Thanks," Michael said, his knees suddenly weak. They had never spoken to him personally before.

The other spoke. "Two years have passed since the Lord came for His bride." Eleven words, eleven languages. Michael's mind spun to keep up.

Michael nodded in acknowledgment. "I just wish I had known about the Lord before He came. I was so arrogant."

The second one looked deeply into Michael's eyes as his own green eyes remembered a hurt far in his past. "I wish I hadn't struck the rock in my anger." So this one was Moses!

"I am so honored that you have spoken to me," Michael began.

Moses cut him off. "I regret hitting the rock and not being permitted to enter the Promised Land." This time he spoke in the paleo-Hebrew of his time. Michael could barely make it out, but the archeologist in his personality thrilled at the experience of actually hearing an ancient language spoken. Moses smiled as if he could read Michael's mind. He continued, "But the Lord used it to His glory, preserving me for this task at the end of time."

Michael nodded, not really knowing what to say. He wondered where Moses was going with this conversation.

Moses didn't let him wait long. "In His grace, the Lord has also preserved you for such a time as this. As with me, it has always been His will that you should share in this great end-time ministry."

Michael's knees buckled a bit, but he managed to stand before these incredible men of God.

Elijah now spoke. "The world has known relative peace as it has coalesced around the Beast's vision. In short order, he will face opposition from within. He will prevail, but the consequences will be dire. Many will be killed."

"Ezekiel's war of Gog and Magog?" Michael asked.

"Yes," Elijah said. "Russia, Iran, and even Isa's homeland of Turkey will revolt against the caliphate. They will desire to control Jerusalem, thinking they alone can offer a sufficiently savage response to the coming invaders."

"If I may ask," Michael began tentatively, "are the Anu real?"

Moses answered, "The ones coming to Earth are none other than Jesus and His bride. As to the real Anu, they are a demon horde. Many are here already. Many will come later, when our work here is complete, but yours will continue."

Michael took a drink of his own latte and then nodded. "It's going to be bad. I know."

"But you are blessed by the Creator of the Universe, Michael," Elijah said with a kind smile. "He, in His wisdom, has prepared you to help His people through the turmoil."

"I understand," Michael said, buoyed by Elijah's confidence.

The two suddenly stiffened, looking formal and foreboding, as they had been before the conversation. Elijah glanced behind Michael and motioned to Will, who stood there in the festooned Swiss guard attire Benny made him wear as head of his personal security team.

"He has much anger," Moses said.

"I have tried to get him to turn it over to Jesus, but he is as stubborn as his father," Michael said.

"And his uncle," Elijah said with a slight smirk.

"I worry about his salvation," Michael said somberly.

Moses assured him, "Do not worry for this one. Like you, he has been preserved for this time."

The two returned to their statuesque positions in front of the Wailing Wall and began to cry out their message that Isa was a false savior of humankind.

Michael took it as his cue that their conversation had come to an end. He turned and walked the thirty paces to his nephew, a smile of greeting on his face. "Good morning, Will! You wouldn't be spying on your old uncle now, would you?"

"As if you were that interesting," Will declared in the voice of his father.

"Spoken like a clown in a clown suit," Michael said as he gave a playful yank to the ponytail holding Will's hair close to his head.

"Nuh-uh. Not the locks, Jake," Will chided with a smile.

"So why are you following me?" Michael asked.

"More like looking for you. Lucky woke up early and wants to talk to you about his schedule."

The reference to the fake name that Michael had given Benny always drew a chuckle. "There's a lot of the old Benny in there," Michael said. As time went by, Benny had found a way to keep the resident demon in the background. Only in public appearances and in the presence of Isa did he let the evil entity hold sway.

"More and more," Will agreed. "Whatever got into him, he's keeping it in check."

"Benny's a tough old bastard, Will. If it were possible, I'd even feel a bit bad for the demon who thought he could control Benny."

They both laughed. Michael asked pointedly, "Do you believe he's been inhabited by a demon, Will?"

"Something surely changed him. I'm not the idiot you suppose me to be," Will said defensively.

Michael could sense Will bristle against his preaching. "I never thought that of you. I just wonder how you can see all that has transpired and not want to throw yourself into the loving arms of Jesus."

"I'm not as far away as you may think," Will said with a half smile. "I have the head knowledge, but not the heart knowledge."

"It's because you're angry."

"Damn right I am!" Will countered. "If even half of what you say about Isa and Benny is true, they're a scourge to humanity."

"But that's not the only reason you're angry," Michael said somberly.

"Uncle Michael, I was always angry with my father. He was an evil myth in my mind, the cause of all my despair. I used to daydream that he was some wonderful guy who would come to rescue me from my circumstances, but he never came."

"But he appeared to you once he knew about you, Will."

"I know," Will said, wiping with brisk annoyance at a tear on his cheek. "And I'm grateful to know you and Michele. Finally I have a family. But ..." He shrugged his shoulders. His mouth moved, but no words came.

Michael looked deeply into the pain-filled eyes of his nephew. "You won't hurt my feelings, if that's what you're worried about. Just say what's on your heart. Trust me, your old uncle is going to love you anyway."

"He should have come earlier, Jake. If I had known my family before the rapture, maybe I wouldn't be here right now. In the middle of all this mess. Wearing a clown costume and working for the two most evil men in history.

"I'm mad at my father, mad at my circumstances, and frankly a little bit mad at God. It's like I wasn't allowed to find out about Bible prophecy until it was too late for me to do anything about it."

Michael put his arm around the younger man's shoulder as they walked to Benny's temporary home in what used to be the Church of the Holy Sepulcher. "Have you ever read about Moses getting water from the stone in the desert?"

"I've heard of it. The Israelites had no water, so Moses hit a stone and water came out."

"That's part of the story. The Old Testament establishes the rock as a symbol of the Messiah. The first time Moses was to get water from the rock, he was told to strike it. This was a symbol of how Israel would treat the Messiah during His first appearance. The second time, God instructed Moses to call forth water from the rock. Moses was so mad at the Israelites that he struck the rock. He blew the symbolism because of his anger, and God kept him from entering the Promised Land."

"So you're telling me this to warn me not to let anger cause me to miss my chance to enter the Promised Land?"

Michael chuckled. "Actually, that's a pretty good application of this tale, but it's not what I was going for. Moses's anger was a sinful and defiant act, but the Bible tells us that God uses all circumstances for the good of those who love Him. Moses was eventually allowed to enter the Promised Land, but not until now." Michael pointed with his thumb over his shoulder to indicate the place near the Wailing Wall from which they had just come.

"One of those guys is Moses?" Will asked incredulously.

"Yep. Darker hair, green eyes, white T-shirt, and jeans." A broad grin filled Michael's face.

"No way!"

"Yes way. He was just telling me how God took that most embarrassing moment of his career and used it to save him for his most important work. You see, buddy, I can get bogged down with self-anger pretty easily because I refused to listen to your father and Chris. I become livid with myself about the people I led astray with that fraudulent gospel."

"But you've leaked findings showing it not to be real," Will defended.

"Not until after the rapture, and I feel horrible about it. Moses was trying to tell me not to get too bogged down in what could have been. Instead, I should take hold of God's opportunity to use me in this time and this place. Maybe I was born to play the role I'm in right now. My delayed acceptance of Jesus was part of the preparation. Does that make sense?" Michael asked tentatively.

"Are you saying God didn't let you find Christ until after the rapture? If so, you're proving my point."

"No. If I had given my heart to Jesus, He would have found someone else to fill my current role. But He is redeeming the time for me and using me to His purposes, when I am probably the least fit among men. It's so right, so biblical, that He would work this way!"

"I have to admit, it's pretty neat." Will grinned.

"Moses also said God has a plan for you, Will."

"He mentioned me? Specifically?"

"Yep." Michael beamed as the two made their way to Benny's quarters.

"What are you two smiling about?" Benny asked indignantly.

"Nothing in particular," Michael answered nonchalantly.

"If you two don't need me, I'll resume my post," Will said. Then he quickly left the room.

"Lucky man," Michael chirped as Benny scowled over a report. He chucked it from his desk, which used to be the altar of the iconic church. It fell to the floor, where Michael retrieved it.

"What's this?" Michael asked.

"A report from that two-bit computer company to whom you farmed out the Lady's technology. They should be ready with their quantum computer application, but they're behind. Michael, I've told you this before. The chip technology won't work to save mankind unless the chips feed and receive RFID signals from a central computer. I *must* have a functioning quantum computer to deal with all that information in real time."

Michael looked through the report from one of the companies secretly owned by his mother. He had been successful in corrupting the data from the Lady's disc. The result was a very unstable quantum environment. As he fanned through the report, he realized the company had hit upon the problem. Michael sighed. He had only been successful in delaying the advent of the technology.

"Well, Benny, it's not entirely hopeless. They think they've found the problem."

"Yes, Michael, but the problem is structural. They'll have to start all over again. We won't have a live, working system for another year and a half. Do you have any idea how horrible Isa will be with me when he hears this?" Benny yelled.

"I can only imagine." Michael grimaced. He continued to look through the report. "But it's not your fault, Benny. They think the Lady's information is to blame."

"Do you really think he'll buy that from me?" Benny asked sarcastically.

"Maybe this data was right millennia ago when it was recorded to the disc, Benny, but a lot has changed since then. For instance, the post-Flood world doesn't have the benefit of a water vapor canopy to shield the planet from cosmic radiation. That alone could be enough to upset something as sensitive as a quantum containment system."

"Do you really think it's a viable excuse?" Benny asked in a whine.

"Yes," Michael fudged, knowing full well he had changed the specs of the system to employ an alloy other than the one indicated on the disc. "I know Isa has a time frame he's working under, but we can't assume full responsibility when things get behind. After all, you would think the Lady could have overseen the project."

"She's pretty useless in person," Benny said with a tsk. "I thought so much of her in the early years when she visited me in an ethereal way. In person, she's smelly, whiney, and critical. I'm amazed Isa can put up with her."

"Well," Michael countered, "maybe her repulsiveness—and to be clear on this, Benny, I *always* found her to be repulsive—will make Isa appreciate his human heritage a bit more." Michael knew it wasn't so, but the days with Benny were long. He often looked for conversation that played to the gossiping side of Benny's personality rather than giving the older man time to examine his subversive efforts.

"A heritage you played a part in … or so I hear." Benny smirked.

"Trust me, Benny, I was no willing participant." Michael frowned.

"And yet your parentage is as clear as the crystal blue eyes you both share." Benny's smirk grew to a haughty grin.

Michael knew Benny enjoyed this topic because it got under Michael's skin. "Don't remind me of it, Benny."

"I should think you would be proud. I'm proud. Trust me, the qualities the Lady chose in you came from my side of the family."

"And that's supposed to make me feel better?" Michael asked.

Benny chuckled. "Hardly. I'm not about making people feel better—except in my official capacity, of course."

"Isa should be happy on that front. You've pretty much destroyed religion in favor of this personal spirituality voodoo you're promoting."

"He is, and no thanks to you, I might add."

"Benny, you know full well I play for the other side on this issue."

Benny forced a pained grimace. "Yes. Yes. I know. You're too old and too unimaginative to forgo loyalty to a man who has long ago turned to dust. We've had this conversation, Michael. It bores me."

"Let's stick to the facts, then. You've given Isa what he wanted. Strict adherence to any exclusive religion has been outlawed throughout the world."

"Yes, but I think there are a lot of people like you who worship the old gods in private. We have to bring that under control or else the world will face repeated anarchy if we're caught in more electromagnetic discharges between Nemesis and our sun."

Michael rolled his eyes. He knew full well that the lightning on the day of the rapture was none other than Jesus removing His people from Earth. No electromagnetic discharge and no subsequent psychotic episodes.

"Cat got your tongue?" Benny interrupted his thoughts.

"Benny, in your heart of hearts, do you really believe Mom, Chris, Gabe, and Tina disappeared into the murderous throng that terrorized the world?"

"It's the party line," Benny said wearily. "There's an old saying, Michael—history is written by the victor. This war isn't over yet. Isa has plans. When he wins, your mother will no longer be able to terrorize me into protecting you. At some point you're going to have to kiss my ring, my boy."

Michael frowned. He had pushed the conversation too far. Benny was losing control to the demon within. Soon the conversation would turn to vehement rants against God, Jesus, and the heavenly host. Good old Nergal would promise restoration of the kingdom to Lucifer. Michael had heard it all and didn't plan to listen to it again today.

"Benny, I want to remind you that I'll be leaving for Georgia later today. Michele and I have a board meeting at the end of the week. We have to keep the company running."

"Fine with me," Benny huffed. "I need you far less than you imagine, Michael."

"In that case, maybe I'll stay through the weekend."

"Fine," Benny replied, grunting.

"I would like to take Will with me. He hasn't had a break for a long time."

"He can go, but I need you both back here for work on Monday morning. Give my regards to Castello Pietro."

Savario Scharpacci had just showered to get ready for work. He was on the afternoon shift this particular day, but that was all he knew. In fact, it was all he could remember. He knew only that he was a computer programmer and that he worked for the Vatican, but literally nothing else came to mind. Ever.

He assumed he was good at his job. The paychecks kept coming. He looked at friends who were stressed by their jobs and counted himself lucky. He never had the late-night e-mails or phone calls from the office. It was as if the office didn't exist when he wasn't there. And yet there was a nagging feeling that he should at least be able to remember what he did in a day. He could only ever recall entering and leaving the secured facility, nothing else. For a while it had bothered him, especially when people asked him about his job. He began to answer briefly, saying he worked for the Vatican on things of a very confidential nature. With the advent of the new pope, people just assumed he worked on the global peace initiative. Maybe he did. He didn't know, but it was nice to think he served a greater purpose in his work.

He stood in front of the bathroom sink brushing his teeth. Brush, brush, brush. Head down. Spit. Head up.

"What the hell! Who are you?" he screamed at the man staring back at him from the mirror.

The man never answered. He pulled a handkerchief from his pocket and held it over Savario's face. He struggled briefly against the intruder before fumes from the cloth left him unconscious.

NINETEEN

Gloria nervously pulled at a lock of her hair as she read through the plan for today's show. Her office at the studio was large, with a private bath and a small bedroom. Nothing was too much for Zack's little star. When she had come up with the idea for this show, she had no idea how successful it would be. Given the dire circumstances in the world, people gravitated to the nurturing nature of her show. To keep Zack at bay, she styled the show around a cooking segment. Everything took place on her kitchen set, where guests would pop in to enjoy a recipe. Gloria had a talent for subtly promoting the lordship of Christ with homespun tales and humor during these interviews, but it was risky business. Public reference to the exclusivity of Christ's claims now constituted a hate crime punishable by imprisonment. Gloria only got away with proclaiming her message because her show was associated with Zack's feel-good ministry, which had bent over backward to embrace all forms of spirituality.

Church services at Riverside had become pale imitations of the sideshows they once were. Bad as Zack's message had been in the past, at least it had the pretense of Christianity. In the new world, though, all pretense was abandoned. Mediums and spiritualists were a constant presence. The music had moved from glory and praise songs to transcendental sitar strains accompanied by mantra chants from the audience. On top of that were sermons about Master Jesus or Master Mohammed or Master Buddha. Every message supported Benny's "one god, many paths" doctrine. Zack and his congregation had expanded their minds. Now they worshipped the nameless, faceless, unknowable god of the Lady's race.

Fortunately, Gloria had been able to maintain a very low profile at the Riverside services. She was too busy with her own show. It purported to be a show that found good for its audience in the growing hardship experienced by the world. Erratic weather patterns had resulted in very poor farm results in the two years since the rapture. Supermarkets that once boasted aisle after aisle of choices now offered bulk supplies of whatever crop had performed well that year. Thankfully, the wheat crop had been good this past year. All of Gloria's shows over the past few weeks had dealt with wheat processing, storage, and recipes. She often had to be pretty inventive given the lack of dairy products, but when it was all said and done, she usually came up with some tasty recipe alternatives.

And wheat was a great sermon topic. As she cooked, she told Jesus's parables about the man who sowed grain on different types of soil. Then she would explain the text nonchalantly—just good friends talking in the kitchen. So far, the censors hadn't complained and Zack seemed happy.

And now this had to happen! She picked up the report on her desk, looked at it again, and threw it back down. The latest ratings had come in. Her show ranked higher than the Riverside services, which was great for getting the Word out, but bad for drawing attention of the censors. And worse still, it was likely to stir up Zack's cutthroat competitive nature. If he felt threatened by her show, he would look for ways to sabotage it. He would scrutinize it and see it was laced with old-school Christianity. She raked her hands through her hair. There was bound to be a confrontation.

She couldn't think of it anymore. Whatever would happen, would happen. She wasn't about to change her message. She turned on the television and began to flick through just to get a sense of the news articles and editorials she would try to place in a Christian perspective for her viewers.

On every channel she saw Isa's grinning face. He applauded efforts at factories grinding out the high-tech multidimensional weapons he planned to use against the Lord at His return. His hubris was astounding—and thought-provoking. Gloria had given her life to Jesus; she would never recant. But deep inside she worried and questioned. She didn't know enough about the spiritual world to understand the new weapons Isa and the Lady were producing, but she wondered why they thought these weapons would be effective. Were they so delusional as to presume they could actually kill God's Son? Or was there a possibility that Jesus had retained some remnant of His human nature they could actually harm?

She shivered at the thought. If they could actually harm Him, would it change her view of Him? She laughed at the thought. He had been hurt pretty hard at the crucifixion, only to be glorified. If there was even a chance they could harm Him, He would still be the victor.

She flicked the channel again to see the government aid camps for people devastated by the crop failures. The news report showed a FEMA camp. Its occupants worked in the new munitions factories in return for food and lodging. The news report extolled the humanitarian benevolence of the new serfdom. She shook her head in disbelief. And then she saw it: just a small glint of light off the neck of one woman as she marched with the others to her factory post. It was a cross.

"Lord," Gloria prayed, "show me how many of these people are Christians." As she watched, she saw a slight glow on the woman wearing the cross. Then another person glowed, and then another. In seconds most of the marching detainees were glowing. "Oh, Lord," Gloria moaned as she held her hand to her mouth. She knew the day would come for Christian incarceration, but she always assumed it would be after the administration of the biochip, the production of which had seen quite a few delays.

She picked up her secure cell phone, compliments of Michele's quantum encryption company, and dialed. As soon as Michele answered, she said, "Michele, turn on CNN."

"I saw the piece about the FEMA camp, Gloria," Michele said sorrowfully.

"How are your plans going?"

"Uncle Michael is coming this week for a board meeting. I want to take him through everything so I can ensure proper coverage with the powers that be if we get caught."

"But your camps are ready?"

"All of our old orphanages have been surrounded with barbed wire fences and fitted with guard towers. Jimmy has done a good job duplicating the FEMA signage, so we're ready to go on that front. But we haven't been able to get a look at their documents. It sure would help if we could get some letterhead to duplicate and a hack to their system, just enough to make us look official when people deal with us."

"I have an idea, Michele. What if a television personality—say, a minister's wife with a cooking show—decided to film a segment from one of the camps?"

"Brilliant!" Michele yelled.

"I'm sure we'll have to do a lot of paperwork to get it accomplished. And if I'm careful enough or persuasive enough, I may even be able to con some letterhead out of the staff."

"We sure could use them. Do you think you can get into one of the camps?" Michele asked.

"It may take a bit of a bribe. Considering that I do a cooking show, a donated trailer full of food products would be an appropriate gesture. It will look as if we're supportive of the global initiative and extending compassion to those harmed by the crop failures."

"I can get you the food. To be honest, Gloria, the crop failures aren't as bad as the media portrays them to be. Our company is more affected by government quotas of how much raw material it can store and how much product it is allowed to ship."

"So, the shortages are contrived?" Gloria asked.

Michele hummed for a second as if thinking of what to say. "There was some horrible weather, but a lot of the GMO crops pulled through it just fine. Of course they have half the nutrient value of their non-GMO ancestors, but bellies could be filled."

"So the shortages are a sham to bring the FEMA camps online—to look like a compassionate initiative rather than internment camps." She felt a touch of anger blush her cheeks.

"That's what it looks like from my perspective, Gloria. My company gets a lot of crop reports and buys a crazy amount of raw materials. The good news is that the new government threw together its reporting requirements in a rush. We've found some loopholes enabling us to buy, hold, and produce more than is officially sanctioned. Our only real constraint is the risk of detection if we go too far overboard."

"So the food is there, but only Christians are victims of the shortages …"

"More to the point, the shortages are contrived to give the government cover while it's gathering up the Christians," Michele said.

"All under the guise of human kindness."

Michele caught her breath. Gloria could tell the younger woman's brain was looking for even more loopholes. "Gloria, their guise of human kindness may be our best cover."

Gloria smiled. "I'm listening."

"If you can get into one of the camps to do your show, I'll get you the trailer of food products. Then I'll be so moved by your compassion for these poor individuals that I'll offer to donate food on an ongoing basis to the FEMA camp system."

"And we'll do it publicly so they'll look like the crumbs they are if they refuse your offer," Gloria said with a laugh. She liked where this conversation was going.

"Yes!" Michele squealed. "I can be a guest on the broadcast and be so moved that I'll make the offer on air."

"The only problem with that is getting a live feed," Gloria said, deep in thought. "The censors don't like live feeds anymore. Too much risk that real news will get out. But there may be a way around it, Michele. I have to submit my shows for comment two days before they air. To tell the truth, they've never questioned me because Zack is so devoted to their cause. I'll submit a copy *without* your generous offer for their review, but I'll air an updated show *with* your offer as a sort of last-minute addition to the story."

"The censors may watch you more closely after that," Michele cautioned.

"I know, but consider the upside. We'll be able to feed the Christian detainees and hopefully get enough information to avoid the detection of your dummy camps."

"If we can pull this off, my camps will be prayer centers, not detention centers."

"It will be hell for us if we're caught," Gloria said somberly.

"We're two years into the tribulation, Gloria. Hell is coming to earth no matter what we do. We might as well try to support the saints, bring as many to the Lord as possible, and maybe throw a few wrenches into Isa's plans."

"You're right. But I have to tell you; the old world seems so far away and long ago. We still have five years to endure!"

"I know," Michele said with a touch of despair. "When my dad would talk about these times, I thought they might be exciting—kind of cloak-and-dagger, "Tribulation Force" stuff. The reality is so different. Leading a double life is exhausting. Constantly covering my tracks leaves me feeling mentally fatigued. I can't wait until a day when I can relax and let my guard down."

"That's not likely to happen for a while. But you can't let yourself burn out either, Michele. Take the advice of someone much older. If you get too burned out, you'll be no use to any of the people you're trying to help."

"I hear you." She chuckled. "A few short years ago, my mother would have told you I'm the least likely person she knew to suffer burnout. I was always a bit of a coaster before everything changed."

"I'll tell you what: how about I join you guys at the end of the week? We can discuss our plans with your uncle and maybe have enough time for some relaxation."

"I'd love that," Michele said gratefully.

"Consider it done *if* I can make the arrangements."

Zack entered her office without so much a warning as a little knock on the door. An exaggerated inquisitive look passed over his face, and he mouthed, "Consider what done?"

She held up one finger to tell him she would be only a bit longer. Into the phone she said, "Thanks again, Michele. Zack just came into my office. I'm probably late for a meeting. I think this can really be a great show. If I can get there this week, I'd love to iron out all the details. Uh-huh. I'll tell him you said hi. And thanks again. Bye-bye."

"What was that all about?" Zack asked with an uncomfortable grin.

"It was about an opportunity to really do something to support the global effort," she said with a huge smile.

"That sounds interesting," Zack said as he pulled up a chair, "and totally out of character. Tell me about it."

"I saw a CNN report today about how families have been ravaged by the food shortages. FEMA has pulled together some camps to help the poorest of the poor, but frankly their lives don't look so good.

"I can't sit around a studio pretending everything is fine when people don't have enough to eat. My show is mostly about food, for crying out loud! I keep imagining these poor, hungry people seeing my show and wishing I was making something to feed them."

Zack grinned in a condescending manner. "*That* sounds like you," he said with a smirk. She knew he viewed her as vacuous and driven solely by emotion. *Good. Let him think that.*

"Anyway, I got this idea. Maybe I could do a show from one of the camps and put out a really nice meal for these poor people, maybe at Thanksgiving—" she corrected herself to use the new term—"ah, Harvest Fest. So I got this idea. If I could get Michele to donate the food—"

"We'll look very devoted to the common cause," Zack said, completing her sentence.

"Not look like it, Zack. We'll *be* devoted to the common cause. I'll admit I'm still a little bit stuck in the old mind-set. Old habits die hard. And call me a silly blonde, but I don't like to think about an intruding dark star and a space enemy. That doesn't mean I think the cause isn't important, though. I'd be a fool to think that."

"Not if you clung to the old beliefs and were just trying to exist through the tribulation." He stared at her, clearly trying to discern if she were being truthful with him.

"I'm in two camps on all of that stuff, Zack. Maybe all of this is a fulfillment of Bible prophecy, and maybe it's not. All I know is that the current threats are real and the current food crisis is real. I can help people. I know I can." She paused to choose her words carefully. "And so far, the new order established by Isa hasn't been so bad. Crime rates are practically nil; people are united in a common cause for the first time in history; and there's honest-to-goodness peace in the world. Can all that be bad?" She was really working it. She hoped, and guessed, that he would buy into it. His mind was predisposed to worship Isa and his progressive agenda.

He looked at her intently, pushed his chair back, and put his hands behind his head, weighing her words. She looked back at him with an open, honest expression and a little bit of a grin. "I know. I know. I'm a hard sell, and it's about time I got on board. But better late than never, right?"

"Right." Zack grinned. She thought she had him convinced, but Zack was inherently duplicitous, so she couldn't know for sure.

"So you agree with my show premise?" she asked.

"Yeah. Especially since it's something you can get behind. I've been afraid you would be defiant of the new order. You know, some of the things you say on your show—"

"I know," she said apologetically. "They sound old school, Zack, but it's just the terminology. I'm sure there are lots of people like me who will come to this at a slower pace."

"Lots and lots, apparently," he said. "Have you seen the latest ratings sheet?"

"Yes. And I want to say up front that I know the success of my show is only because I'm your wife. Let's not be competitive, okay?"

"Gloria, listen to me. It's my ministry. You participate in it and support me, but it's not the other way around." His words were harsh, but his tone was still soft and caring. She believed she could work him around. She would have to if she intended to put this plan into effect.

"Not only do I get it," she said with a smile, "but also that's the way I want it. Seriously, honey, I don't know how you put up with the pressures of your ministry. I'm no longer cut out for that. A cooking show and reaching out to hungry people—that's where my talents lie."

His look softened, and he broke into a grin. He said in a half-hearted tease, "Good. Because if your numbers keep going up, I might have to consider you my biggest competition."

"Not competition, Zack, partner." She offered him what she hoped would be construed as a loving, adoring look. She knew she would never—could never—feel that way about him again. The blinders had come off, and they weren't going back on.

"That's my girl," he said with a schoolboy grin. She had him, but she had to weigh very carefully what had just transpired. Either she had played to his unbridled ego sufficiently to quell any fears her show could somehow eclipse him or he was scamming her, letting her believe he bought into her lie. Only time would tell where he really stood.

"So," she continued, "if you don't need me, I thought I would go see Michele for a day or two to get things lined up."

"You can't do it over the phone?" He scowled.

"These things can be tricky. Do I need to remind you of your mother's disaster when she fought with that lady in the Thanksgiving food line?"

He raised his hands in submission. "Enough said." He rolled his eyes. "Mom was probably set up, but once the cameras caught that squabble, their ministry was toast."

She nodded her head in agreement. "I think it's better that Michele and I plan for every contingency. The last thing I want to do is bring that kind of scandal back to Riverside."

Sporting a sardonic grin, he said, "Go … with my blessings. When your plans are all set, let me know. I can hype it on my show."

"Great." She smiled broadly. "I might be able to use your help to gain access to a camp. You have a lot of sway with people ever since you were on the stage at the United Nations."

He leaned back in his chair. His eyes had a faraway look. "It certainly was one of the best days of my life, darlin'. But it wasn't only being up there on that stage with Isa; it was knowing that I, that we, had a hand in the creation of this amazing person. I think I now know what it is like to be a proud parent."

She smiled at him, trying to mimic his enchanted faraway look. "It was a day to remember," she said dreamily.

"I only have one regret, darlin'. It's that you had to sit in the servants' section with the pope's no-account nephew." She could feel his pride at being able to cast Michael in such a harsh light.

"It wasn't that bad, Zack. I was just honored to be there and proud of you."

"That's mighty gracious of you."

"Well, to be honest, at first I was a bit disappointed, considering that Isa grew in my body." She hoped he couldn't see her gulp the bile at the back of her throat. "But then I realized you were the one with the vision. I could never have had the strength to make a deal with the Lady."

"That's very generous, Gloria, but—"

"But nothing." She smiled. "If I'm sure of anything in my life, Zack, I'm sure you deserved to be on that stage."

He beamed.

"You deserved it," she repeated as she made her way around the desk. She stood beside his chair and stroked the back of his head, letting her fingers comb through his hair.

TWENTY

Your caliphate isn't as loyal as everyone would assume," the Lady droned with her characteristic toothless smirk.

Isa wondered if she could possibly appreciate how much she got on his nerves. She was a constant nag, an incessant whine, and a perpetual naysayer. "Yes. Yes. I know. The Russians and Iranians are planning to stage a coup. Well, let them try, Lady. Let them try!" His voice raised with a mixture of anger at their hubris and sheer disdain for her rubbery stick figure.

"Your hatred for me is showing," she said with a slight tilt of her head.

She actually enjoys aggravating me! "Hardly, Lady. I don't hate you. But surely you'll pardon me if I point out that the human side of me is the fun side. You raise fear and loathing to an art form."

"Don't be so quick to sell out your alien heritage," she said smugly.

"I'm not," Isa said, matching her tone. "But extended time with you since your materialization in this world has shown me I am so much more than either of the constituent races from which I hail. I truly am a marvel, Lady."

"Keep telling yourself that," she mused. "But a day will come when your humanity will give way to your foreign nature. You will be far less an amalgamation of two species than a human shell, sort of a human mask to obscure your darker nature."

"Huh!" He paraded to the bar and poured himself a scotch, not so much because he wanted it, but because it annoyed her.

"Alcohol won't solve anything," she chided. "The only course for you is to yield to your darker nature."

"And become a pathetic miscreant from a dying race, like you?" He snorted.

"Believe what you will. Time will vindicate me." She swept out of the room as Isa fell again into his nearly constant daydream of strangling the life out of her. He wanted to wring her miserable little neck like a chicken's.

In fact, he mused, *maybe I'll fry that disgusting body to see if she tastes like chicken.* He laughed aloud and then calmed himself.

Enough laughs for the moment. Undoubtedly the old bird was right. He had always entertained the likelihood that the Russians would someday strain at the bridle. And the remaining Iranian mullahs were too dogmatic to buy into Isa's claims to be Mahdi. Truly, it was easier to convince Israel that he was their political savior than to get those gray-bearded, turbaned idiots to see the expediency of his reign.

So, they were expected to betray him, and they had. But what of the Kurtoglu family? His father's family had been in the middle, brokering the deals between the Russians and the Iranians. They thought they were the rightful heirs to the caliphate. Fools! They had no idea the old man was only given power to provide a political base for Isa. No Isa, no Kurtoglu family. It was that simple. It was Kurtoglu's real sons, Ishmael and Rahim, who riled the Turks against him. Well, they would pay with the most painful deaths he could imagine, but for now, he needed them to play their part.

Russia had to make its move, but the timing was crucial. He pressed the intercom key on his phone and barked for his secretary to connect him with his top scientist.

"Dr. Kartoff, have you managed to fine-tune your findings?"

"Excellency, as you doubtless know, we have seen a season of unexpected calm. That having been said, the gravity of the approaching bodies has caused significant disruption in the asteroid belt."

"Yes, we've been over this," Isa said with a hint of annoyance at the scientist's constant need to rehash data. "The changes have thrown a fairly large asteroid in our direction, but we have pulverized it with lasers from our space-weapons platform."

"Correct, Excellency. The pulverized asteroid has become a swarm of meteors that, unfortunately, will rain down on Earth fifteen months from now."

"And that is why I called. When last we spoke, you believed their orbit path had stabilized sufficiently to pinpoint a specific date, time, and place of the bombardment."

"Yes, Excellency. Barring any further disruption, they will fall precipitously on your caliphate, in the north of Israel, 403 days from now, between 3:00 and 4:00 in the afternoon."

"Plenty of time to harden our assets then," Isa said hopefully.

"There will be great devastation, Excellency," Dr. Kartoff said gravely.

"Then the key will be to place in that area only those things we can do without," Isa said with a slight chuckle.

"Ah … yes … Excellency," the scientist muttered in confusion. "I … I don't understand your point, sir."

"Not to worry, Doctor. We have different perspectives is all."

"If you will allow me, Excellency, I would like to take this opportunity to point out that this event will be merely the beginning of tragedies as the Nemesis incursion progresses."

"Yes, Doctor," Isa said with an annoyed sigh. "I know all about the impending disasters. I am the one tasked with bringing this world through them, am I not?"

"You are, Excellency. I apologize. Will there be anything else?"

"Yes. Has news of the coming bombardment been kept secret?"

"Yes, Excellency. As per your instructions, all telescopes operate solely under the strict control of your government. None of the former nation-states have access to the data from any observatory in the world or in orbit."

"Thank-you, Doctor. Have a nice day." Isa cut the call short as the doctor was trying to say good-bye. *An annoying sod of a man.*

Isa picked up the Bible—a travesty of a book, but it did have its usefulness. Turning to the book of Ezekiel, he read about a prophesied attack on Israel from a group of nations headed by Russia. In that prophecy, God promised to smite the alliance with fire from the sky.

"Indeed God will stop the invasion." Isa chuckled to himself. "And that God will be me. I just have to maneuver the chess pieces into place on the right date."

"Vladimir, how kind of you to join me," Isa said as the Russian president was shown into the private dining room of the Turkish royal palace. "How fortunate I am to have caught you while you were in town."

The Russian president offered his hand. "It was a quick trip, Excellency, a little bit of shopping and relaxation. All undercover. I am shocked you knew I was here." Of course, the Russian had been in town to meet secretly to strategize with the Kurtoglu brothers. Isa could feel the Russian's fear that he had been found out. It tantalized something deep in Isa's nature.

"Shopping, you say?" Isa asked as he grasped the Russian's hand. The man's fear and doubt were palpable. Isa licked his lips and released the hand.

"Just some baubles. I have found that my new young wife requires more tangible expressions of my commitment than my first wife." He rolled his eyes as he took his seat.

"Buying affection can become a particularly tiresome treadmill, Vladimir. Personally, I would prefer to rent it if I were so inclined."

The small talk put the Russian president at ease. His famous hard-nosed persona returned. "If you were so inclined?" he asked.

Isa grinned. "My hybrid nature puts me at odds in finding a connection with either race."

The Russian laughed. "There is something wonderful about physical passion, my friend, but I admit a certain envy at your ability to rise above it."

"Human interaction is so complicated," Isa said. His mouth pattered on, but his mind had found entrance to the Russian's. He effortlessly moved through the data and memories stored there, all the while maintaining the conversation, which would be recorded, of course.

Then a thought crossed Isa's mind: maybe a little bit of fun was in order. He moved the Russian's hand to grasp his own, and then moved the man's mouth to say, "Maybe you just haven't met the right person yet."

"Vlad, are you making a pass at me?" Isa asked, aghast.

Isa sent the Russian to his knees, making him say, "I'm yours, Isa. Take me."

"Sorry, Vlad. I'm afraid you're not my type," Isa said, pretending to help the man off the floor and back into his chair. "Let's just forget this happened. No harm done."

The president took his seat. Isa could barely contain a chuckle at how embarrassed the Russian bear would be if the footage ever got out. Isa returned to the matter at hand, namely, planting in the Russian's mind an overwhelming urge to attack Israel at the precise time to make Isa's plan a reality.

They chatted through dessert before Isa released the president's mind. When he did, the man slumped wearily in his chair. Isa called for his security team to assist the Russian monarch to his limo, explaining that he'd had too much to drink. As the team carried Vladimir away, Isa chuckled. The Russian's only memory of the evening would be his rejected proposition.

Isa looked through the reports from the Large Hadron Supercollider. The results were encouraging. In the very near future, the team would isolate and contain a significant amount of strangelets and the elusive dark matter necessary to power weapons to repel the Anu.

The Anu! The very idea made Isa want to laugh. He was planning something far more devastating than the destruction of some mythological alien invasion. If he understood his mission clearly, then he was bound to tear at the very fabric of time and space. When he was done, all of creation would be held hostage to the devastation he could bring. Then the Lady's race and all other intelligent beings in the galaxy would submit to him.

He wasn't exactly clear on the details yet, but more and more had been revealed to him in dreams. He saw the coming invasion, and its leader appeared to be none other than Jesus. A few years ago, he would have said the messiah myth had served its purpose and run its course. But in the dreams, He seemed so real, not as an extension of the Creator, but as a usurper—not a deity, but a being clearly vulnerable in higher dimensions.

Isa rubbed his forehead and poured himself a glass of scotch as he considered all that had been revealed to him thus far. First, there was indeed a creative force that brought about the universe. Second, this force had favored certain individuals in this world and others. Third, the most favored, Lucifer, had been dealt a terrible blow by the usurping spirit inhabiting the body of Jesus. This spirit was treacherous beyond all knowing and needed to be destroyed.

That much he knew for sure. In addition, in his dreams he had seen the evil Jesus spirit disintegrate in the dark matter beam. Once that spirit was annihilated, the entire universe would be free of oppression. Peace, real peace, would reign. And Isa would be king.

Returning his empty glass to the bar, he picked up the phone to call one of the few humans he enjoyed.

"Excellency," Benny screamed into the phone. Isa held the receiver away from his ear.

"Calm yourself, Benny." Isa chuckled.

"To what do I owe the pleasure of your call?"

"A status update, Holiness. I've heard there has been a delay in the manufacture of the identity chips. I cannot stress to you the importance of these devices."

Benny sighed heavily. "The data regarding quantum containment from the Lady's disc is old, Isa. I don't know if it is corrupted with age or if it represents a science that worked better in the environment of antiquity. Either way, the alloy specified on the disc is too fragile."

"Have our people found a more suitable alloy?"

"I'm happy to report they have, Isa."

"Very good. It's worrisome that the data from the disc was bad. Could there also be a problem with the programmers so carefully reduced to robots by your nephew?"

"I don't know. I could get Michael to take a look at things."

"No, Benny. I don't want him near that disc. Have the programmers prepared interfaces to transfer the disc's data to the quantum computers?"

"I'm told that they have, Excellency."

"Good. A lot rides on that system."

"Excellency, all is back on schedule to begin production with the new alloy."

"A man after my own heart, Benny." Isa chuckled when Benny gasped at delight in the compliment. "How are things on the Temple Mount?" Isa asked.

"Everything is going according to schedule," Benny intoned with pride.

"Good," Isa said a bit sternly. "We cannot go beyond the drop-dead date I gave you."

"We'll be ready. And we'll have a glorious opening ceremony."

"You have no idea." Isa chuckled. "In fact, I just ordered the fireworks display."

TWENTY-ONE

Will put out an arm to prevent Michael from stepping into the limo sent to retrieve them from the Atlanta airport. Michael rolled his eyes in protest, but Will ignored him as he carefully examined the driver's documents. When he was satisfied with the driver's credentials, he raised his arm, allowing Michael to enter.

Michael offered a long, pronounced sigh. "Seriously, Will. I'm a big boy. I got along just fine for a long, long time before I met you."

"First of all, it's my job, Jake," Will said with a grin as he joined Michael in the back of the limo. "I've got to keep up appearances as a tough bodyguard for you and the pope."

Michael interrupted, "And may I say the pope is far more prone to attack than his erstwhile assistant?"

"Yeah, but the erstwhile assistant is my connection to a father I always wanted to know."

Michael chuckled. "Is that your convoluted way of saying you love your old uncle Michael?"

"Well, *love* is a strong word," Will teased. "Let's just say you're an acquired taste and I'm slowly getting used to you."

"Yeah, yeah. I've heard it all before from your father. You two really are cut from the same cloth."

Will smiled at the thought. "I really wish I could have known him. But you'll have to do as a pale imitation."

"I probably am a pale imitation of your dad. But you also have Michele."

"It's neat to have a sister. I'll admit it."

"And you have your uncle Benny," Michael quipped.

"*You* have your uncle Benny. If I have my curious genealogy figured out correctly, you bear the sole distinction in our family of actually being related to Pope Petey."

"Thanks for pointing that out." Michael winced.

Will chuckled and then grew quiet for a few moments. He looked out the window as they passed Georgia fields shorn for the approaching winter. He loved his uncle Michael for sure, but he was developing a terrible disdain for Benny.

He raised the privacy guard so the limo driver wouldn't hear. Removing his cell phone from his pocket, he consulted an app to ensure they weren't bugged. "Seriously, Jake. I'm afraid Benny is a really evil man."

Michael laughed sarcastically. "You're warm but not even close to hot, buddy. By definition, Benny is the second most evil man to have ever lived."

"If my dad's ideas on prophecy were correct," Will challenged. He knew he should accept the end-of-days scenario, but despite all that had transpired, he couldn't envision coming events.

"He was right, Will. You'll come to that realization yourself. But don't wait too long. I would be a much happier man today if I had heeded your father's advice years ago."

"Uncle Michael," Will said earnestly, "I earned a living making people believe things that weren't true through sleight-of-hand magic."

"And you don't want to fall for sleight-of-hand spiritual truths," Michael challenged.

Will shrugged. "An occupational hazard. The more you learn about creating illusion, the less you believe in anything but flesh-and-blood reality."

"Looks like I'll have to rely on God to touch your heart. Just promise me you won't turn away when He reaches out to you, okay?"

No answer.

"Okay?" Michael asked more vehemently.

"Okay," Will snapped. They rode in silence. Will appreciated his uncle's concern, but he wasn't ready to make that kind of commitment, no matter how much Jake pushed the issue.

The limo made its way past festooned Swiss guardsmen at the gates to the estate. A large granite sign declared it to be Castello Pietro, a province of the Vatican. Benny had made it independent of the United States, sort of a Vatican embassy. Will laughed as Michael made an annoyed *tsk* sound when he saw the sign. The guardsman waved them through. Will saluted him.

"I guess Benny didn't tell you the national status of the estate has changed," Will said.

"Neither did you. Neither did Michele for that matter," Michael snapped.

Will laughed at his uncle's annoyed expression. "If I had known I would enjoy your annoyed reaction so much, I would have told you earlier."

"Yeah. Yeah." Michael waved him off.

The limo made its way to the roundabout in front of the estate. Michele and Gloria waited for them. Will noticed a catch in Michael's breath when he saw Gloria.

"You two have a history?" Will asked, wide-eyed.

"In a different time, in a different place, maybe we could have been a couple. But we weren't. No history. No future," Michael said gloomily.

"Come on. Get your morose butt out of the car," Will said with a grin once the limo pulled to a stop.

Michele hugged him hard. It was very nice to have a sister. He had long ago come to view the estate as his home. Michael and Gloria hugged. Then Michele hugged her uncle.

"I'd ask why you have such a sour expression," Michele said with a grin, "but I'm guessing you saw the sign at the entrance to the estate."

"Benny shouldn't have done that without telling me," Michael said sternly, "and you two should have told me."

"He would have done it anyway," Will said defensively as he put an arm around Michael's shoulders and led him into the house.

"And there are some advantages to being an independent state," Michele added. "I think I can use my Vatican citizenship to repatriate our company. In effect, we'll be free from the government's rules."

"And subject to Benny's," Michael challenged tersely, shaking his head.

"Come on," Will said. "Benny's got the whole world doing his bidding. What will he care about us? This offers us protection from the local governments. That's all."

Gloria added, "Things are beginning to look restrictive here in the States, Michael. They're already populating the FEMA camps."

"Fine. I guess I have to go along with the new international status of Castello Pietro." He fairly spat the new name of the estate. "But the companies stay outside of Benny's purview. He'll take them for no other reason than to best my grandfather."

"Fine," Michele said briskly.

"Not fine," Michael answered sternly. "From now on, I need to know immediately about any changes Benny tries to make. This is as far as it goes."

"Okay," Michele said, eyes downcast. "And I'm sorry I didn't tell you. I just assumed you knew, given that you're Benny's assistant."

"Ditto," Will said softly.

Michael spoke more calmly. "That's my point. If Benny weren't up to something, I would have known about it. But I concede there's still an advantage to living where the local police have no jurisdiction."

"There also would be some serious tax advantages to changing our company's country of incorporation," Michele said. "Naomi showed me that we could be effectively tax-free."

"Naomi?" Michael asked. "How did she know about it?"

"She received a notification offering tax-free status if we incorporate there. Vatican letterhead. Papal seal. I'm guessing she figured you were behind it."

Will could definitely see Benny's hand in this, but to what end? "So Benny is trying to get the estate and the company under Vatican control. What does he get out of it?"

Michael led the way to the kitchen and poured himself a cup of coffee. "Coffee, anyone? This is a long story ..."

When everyone was seated around the kitchen table, Michael began his tale. Will listened with fascination. "Michele, your parents and I shielded you and Chris from some of the family's more colorful history. At Mom's birthday party, before the rapture, your dad and I talked about the fact that one day we would have to fill you in on how despicable Benny is."

"We always knew he was eccentric, but he was also goofy—kind of funny," Michele said.

"Wow! That's a bigger illusion than Will could pull off!" Gloria exclaimed. Will grinned.

Michael chuckled. "We were protecting you and, to some extent, your mimi. She always tried to see the good in Benny, or at least to understand him. She felt a sort of personal guilt for some ugliness that happened between Benny and my grandfather. I never met him, but I understand he could be pretty fierce. When he married my grandmother, she was widowed with a son—Benny. When Mimi came along, Benny felt left out. Grandpa Stan didn't like him much and refused to adopt him."

"The forgotten son. That much I understand," Will said thoughtfully. He could easily imagine being the bonus child in this mansion.

Michael put an arm around his shoulder. "Not like you, Will. From what I understand, Benny was a horror as a child."

"Makes sense," Gloria said. "He's been a horror the entire time I've known your family."

"Speaking of which," Michael said as he pulled an old photo from his wallet, "I found this in Mom's office. Look at the people in it. This little girl is your mimi. There's Grandpa Stan, and that pudgy boy with the scowl is Uncle Benny." Will stood behind Michele, looking at the photo with her.

"Here's the strange part," Michael continued. "This handsome young boy is Chris."

Gloria leaned into the mix to examine the photo. She chimed in quizzically, "And this girl is my mother. This boy is my father. And here are Zack's parents. That is so strange ..."

"But the families didn't know each other back then," Michele pondered aloud.

"It gets weirder," Michael continued. "This middle-aged fellow is Father Vinnie, Chris's friend."

"He's not in clerical garb," Will noted.

"No. Neither is the guy beside him, but I'm pretty sure he's a priest named Micah Morton. A very sketchy fellow. Knew a lot of Vatican secrets. He died mysteriously after threatening to disclose Vatican corruption. Some say in his younger days he did some undercover work for the Vatican secret service."

"Do we really have a secret service?" Will asked with a raised eyebrow. He had heard rumors but had seen no interaction with the group in the years he headed Benny's security team.

Michael nodded. "We sure do."

Gloria shook her head as she summed it up. "So our families are intertwined in a way, but we don't know how. Weird!"

Michael nodded. "I don't think any of them had a recollection of knowing each other back then. In Mom's notes, she considered it a mystery."

Gloria nodded. "I'm sure my mother would have mentioned it if they had been friends all those years before. As far as she was concerned, we met on that cruise."

"Well, the mystery just got deeper," Michele said as she blinked her eyes and stared closely at the photo. "Do you see this boy in the back?"

"Yeah," Michael said. He took the photo and held it closely to his face.

"Look at the nose and the peculiar hairline," Michele directed. "I'd be willing to bet it's Naomi."

"So, that boy's actually a girl?" Gloria asked. Will looked over Michael's shoulder. He would have sworn it was a little boy, and a tough little fellow at that.

"You've never met Naomi," Michael quipped with a chuckle.

Will stood and paced the kitchen as the implications exploded in his mind. "So the executive pushing to repatriate the companies was at this picnic nobody remembers."

"Looks like it," Michael said.

Still pacing, Will said gravely, "But she may be in cahoots with Benny. Michele and I need to know everything about Benny—about all the family secrets."

"Cahoots?" Michele asked with a grin. "Sounds like another stage word, drama king."

Will smiled. Michele often teased him about the way his highly dramatic stage talk crept into his day-to-day conversations.

Michael sighed and motioned for Will to take a seat. Once Will sat, Michael began. "In the long run, Benny and Grandpa Stan couldn't get along. Benny wasn't included in the will. Everything went to Mimi. She felt guilty and indulged him. Pretty much she gave him whatever he wanted. But soon she realized he was insatiable."

Michael drew a hard breath. "There is a long, convoluted story, but the upshot is that two young girls were seduced by the same man. They had children he never wanted. I was one. The other was Gabe. Maybe it was the genetic connection, I don't know, but we were best friends the moment we met in grammar school. When Gabe's mother died, Mom and I adopted him. When Mom saw Gabe's birth certificate, she realized we had the same father."

"Another strange mystery of coincidences," Will said.

"True enough. Anyway, Benny was really upset about another heir entering the family. I cut a deal with him—a hundred-million-dollar loan that would grease the skids for a Vatican appointment if he left Gabe alone."

Will whistled as he raised one eyebrow. "So Lucky might never have been pope if you hadn't bribed his way into the Vatican?"

Michael wiped his face with his hands. "I never thought of it that way. Well, there's another horror to add to my résumé, but to my defense I wasn't quite ten at the time."

"No, Uncle Michael," Michele said, patting his arm. "You protected your brother. It was a loving act. What Benny did after is on him."

Michael held Michele's hand for a moment and then continued. "Benny didn't live up to his promise. In fact, he tried to have Gabe and me killed while we were taking college courses in Germany. If it weren't for Chris and Father Vinnie, we wouldn't be here."

Rage exploded in Will. He stood again to pace the kitchen. "How can I work for someone like that? Be his personal guard?" he demanded.

"Sit down, Will," Michael said sternly. "We're in strange times that require us to do unusual and hard things. I don't like working for him either." His voice softened as he coaxed, "Come on, buddy. Sit down."

Will calmed himself and took his seat. Michael continued. "That was Benny's most open display of hatred. After that he sparred with Gabe and me, but it never really got dangerous. In fact, he was the one who got me the job at the Vatican."

"The job where you inadvertently helped that monstrous bug enter our reality," Gloria said with a scowl.

"Damn!" Michael exclaimed. "You're right. I've been played all this time!"

"Don't be too hard on yourself, Michael," Gloria said with quiet self-reflection. "We've all been manipulated."

Michael's eyes were red as if he were about to burst into tears. Will felt a sudden wave of compassion for his uncle. He couldn't imagine a life filled with Benny's disdain and constant interloping. He reached out to hug the older man. "You don't have to tell us the rest if you don't want to, Jake."

"N-no," Michael stammered as he wiped tears from his eyes. "Gloria, do you want to do the honors?"

She sighed and then picked up the tale. "For years, Michael and I separately had a series of nightmares about the Lady taking us aboard her spaceship and using our DNA to create a hybrid."

"The Lady who's on all the magazine covers did this to you?" Michele asked.

"One and the same," Gloria said with a scowl. "She created a hybrid and implanted it in my womb." An expression of intense pain crossed her face. Will felt as if his heart would break for her. She swallowed hard to push away tears, and then forged quickly forward with the story. "They harvested the child and raised him for a while before placing him in the household of the Turkish prime minister."

"You're Isa Kurtoglu's mother?" Will asked incredulously. His mind reeled. He was having a difficult time processing all this information. He threw himself back in his chair.

"Parents," Michael choked. Will remained silent. He had no words.

"That would explain the resemblance around the eyes," Michele said, shaking her head as if she couldn't believe it. "So, we're related to the Antichrist?" she asked incredulously.

"Well, technically, Gloria and I are." Michael raked his hand through his hair.

"But you're also related to the False Prophet," Michele said with a furrowed brow.

"Quite the pedigree, I know," Michael offered in a weak voice.

At that moment, the back door swung open. Jimmy entered with a big smile. "Sorry I'm late, babe," he said to Michele as he made his way around the room, saying hello. "Did I miss anything?"

"No. Just catching up," Michele said breezily, casting an eye at the group. Will nodded slightly. He agreed that Jimmy didn't need to know all the sordid details.

It was a fitful night for Will. His sleep was interrupted endlessly by nightmares. In a dream he saw vivid details of the events Michael had told them of earlier. It was as if he were there, seeing the scared child confront the intimidating evil priest. He awoke feeling afraid, like the boy in the dream. He checked the clock, punched his pillow, and rolled over.

In the next dream, he was in a dark alley. He saw younger versions of his father and Uncle Michael, beaten and drugged. He screamed at them to awaken from their stupor, to fight off their attackers. They couldn't hear him. His father offered one brave attempt but was easily overcome. A handsome priest in a cassock appeared unexpectedly at the entrance to the alley. He fought with the attackers. Flailing as if fighting them himself, Will awoke. The covers were off the bed. He pushed the long hair back from his face and remade the bed as he contemplated the dreams. The images were more real than a dream. It was as if he had lived those experiences.

He sat on top of the covers for a few moments to examine every detail of the dreams. He now had a good idea of the depth of Benny's evil nature. He shivered at the thought of working for the man, but he knew he had to do it. He could use his position to stand between Benny and the rest of his family. Technically his job was to protect Benny. In reality, he would use the job to protect his family.

Eventually he drifted off to sleep again. Again he dreamed in incredible detail. He was performing his stage act, shooting the crossbow at balloons surrounding his assistant. As in his actual act, the assistant was tied to a spinning wheel behind a screen. He fired with confidence through the screen. He had done the trick time and again. He grinned as the audience gasped. Removing the screen, he found to his horror that some of the arrows hadn't flown true. His assistant lay pressed up against the wheel by seven arrows. Panicking, he ran to the wheel to help her, but it wasn't her face he saw. It was the grinning face of Benny Cross. Will's panic gave way to a sense of overwhelming relief that the monster was dead.

TWENTY-TWO

Unable to sleep, Michael went to the kitchen to make some cocoa. There he found Michele and Gloria talking excitedly. Looking at his watch, he asked, "What drove you two to get up this early?"

"Actually, we haven't been to sleep yet." Gloria grinned. "We've been planning something, and we want to run it by you."

"Okay, shoot." Michael wiped at the need for sleep in his tired eyes.

Michele made the cocoa for him. Michael inhaled deeply of the rich elixir. She had made it with very little sugar and added a touch of cinnamon and cream, just the way he liked it. He grinned his thanks as Michele began. "Jimmy has been taking road trips to reclaim and repair the orphanages run by Mom and Dad. Uncle Michael, we can house a lot of people in those orphanages."

Gloria continued. "Also, the government has begun to move Christians into the FEMA camps. Well, technically, they are places for the homeless. It just so happens that the homeless are all Christians who have refused to recant."

"It just so happens ..." Michael rolled his eyes.

Michele jumped in. "The government now requires us to screen applicants for new positions. If they won't sign a sworn statement disavowing the exclusivity of their faith, the government won't give a tax deduction for the salaries and benefits paid to them.

"And it's not just the tax deduction. It's the recordkeeping and IRS audits. When it's all said and done, most companies just opt not to hire Christians. Tanya tells me she thinks the sworn statement thing will apply to current employees at some point."

Michael spoke softly as if thinking aloud. "History repeating itself.

Just like Hitler did with the Jews: first demonize, then isolate, then eliminate."

Gloria picked up the conversation. "The government shows its 'kindness' to the poor unemployed families by giving them temporary housing inside FEMA camps ostensibly created for emergency response. It just so happens that Isa's new weapons factories are built within marching distance from the camps. Christians are marched to the factories, where they work in exchange for food and a barracks cot."

"Provided by the largess of the world government," Michael said. Nodding, Michele brought a cake and some plates to the table. She cut a slice and offered it to him. He held up his right hand in protest.

"Exactly," Gloria confirmed, taking the piece of cake. "I've been pretty good at sneaking in the gospel message during my 'cooking' show. I get a fair amount of e-mails from Christians who can't buy into the New World Order. These people are definitely being targeted by the government and are in a lot of pain."

"Which brings us to our proposal," Michele said with a mouthful of cake. "Jimmy and I have fenced in all of the orphanages. We've been very careful to match the fencing and signage of the FEMA camps."

The idea hit Michael like a ton of bricks. "You're going to make dummy FEMA camps?" he asked incredulously.

"Not going to, Uncle Michael; we have. From the street you couldn't tell one of our centers from one of the government's. Granted, a lot of the thanks goes to the government's use of existing buildings for their newest centers. It makes just as much sense within each of the communities to use an abandoned orphanage as a mothballed Walmart."

"It's brilliant," Michael said cautiously. Gloria and Michele highfived. Michael bristled at their exuberance and then continued. "But it's too dangerous. You'll have to do more than look good from the street. Somehow you'll have to get into the system so that your facilities are recognized."

Gloria took Michael's hand. "We were kind of hoping to enlist the services of someone who could get the information into the appropriate database."

"Me?" Michael asked with astonishment.

Michele chuckled. "Don't take this the wrong way, Uncle Michael, but you're the only one we know with a proven track record of computer hacking and fraud."

He winced. "Not the legacy I hoped for."

Gloria continued. "Here's what we're thinking. If we move the orphanages under the Vatican umbrella, they'll fall out of the purview of the local government. That way, local governments would have no jurisdiction over day-to-day operations."

Michele picked up the rationale. "It makes sense that the Vatican would have reeducation centers for the most virulent Christian offenders."

Michael thought aloud. "So our facilities will go on the record as being for the most reprobate Christian population."

Michele turned to Gloria. "He said 'our facilities.' That's a good sign."

"Well, let's not put the cart before the horse," Michael said judiciously. "There's bound to be more to it than a computer ID and a few well-placed signs."

"When Jimmy was watching the real FEMA camps, he noticed that the workers carry electronic clipboards from which they read instructions, approve movements of people and goods, and issue printed documents. We could pretend to carry these clipboards, but our cover would be blown the moment we had to give a receipt. As old-fashioned as it sounds, we need some of their stationery."

"More to the point," Michael said, "you need one of their electronic clipboards. Then it needs to be jail-broken and hacked."

Michele smiled. "If only we knew someone with contacts at a quantum encryption company. Those guys could break down the programming in a matter of hours."

"True," Michael said cautiously. "But our dealings with Mom's secret companies have never been forthright. It's kind of hard to trust someone you've never met to do such a favor."

"But that's our greatest advantage!" Michele exclaimed. "Even if they decide not to do us the favor, they don't know who we are except investors with money they want."

"They've issued another capital call?" Michael asked warily.

Michele answered, "Cash shortfall. They haven't been able to deliver on the system to support the government's chip technology. Something about having to start over with a different alloy."

"I know all about it," Michael said with a wave of his hand.

"So the company is under tremendous pressure," Gloria said. "Sounds like they'd be happy to do you one little favor when they need more capitalization."

Michael smiled. "It could work. But the obvious hole in your plan is that we don't have one of these tablets—do we?" He furrowed his eyebrow. One never knew with these two.

Gloria answered. "Zack has agreed to help me get into one of the camps to film a show. My crew and I will go in offering aid and comfort to the poor and displaced. We'll cook up a big meal with food donated by your company. And if a tablet happens to go missing, well ..."

"Well, that sounds pretty dicey," Michael interrupted, shaking his head.

"We're in the end times, Uncle Michael," Michele challenged. "Nothing is safe. We're Christians in a world rapidly looking to exterminate us." She was right, of course, but Michael hated to hear it. He wanted more than anything to keep his loved ones safe through the coming trials. He certainly didn't want them to go head-to-head with the new government. He looked to Gloria to help him with the argument.

Gloria raised an eyebrow. "I can't help you, Michael. I'm all in on this. Michele and I have a plan, and it's a good one."

"I just hate to see you put yourself in such danger," Michael said to Gloria.

"We won't be in that much danger," Michele countered.

"We?" Michael asked. "You're going to the camp too?"

"As the company representative contributing the food, I'll be an honored guest on the show," Michele said sternly. "Two of us stand a better chance at lifting a tablet."

"This is nuts!" Michael exclaimed. "You two aren't thieves."

"True that," Michele said, showing her youth. "But our production assistant, Jimmy, was sort of an artful dodger when he first came to the orphanage. He was pretty good at acquiring things."

"And there's nothing I can do to change your minds?" Michael asked with no small amount of exasperation. He hated what they planned to do, but desperate times called for desperate measures.

"None," Gloria said with a smile.

"Also, Uncle Michael, I probably should make it clear that we were asking for your assistance, not your permission," Michele said strongly. She softened it with a smile, but her intent was clear. Michael had to face it; she had grown up. Trying times had forced her to an early maturity. After all, she was his "man on the ground" at the family business, and she was doing a great job.

Michael grabbed Michele's hand. "I know you're all grown up, honey. God knows I rely on you more than anybody, and you're doing a wonderful job. I just hope you understand that you'll always be my little girl. I'll always be concerned for your well-being."

She kissed his cheek. Looking at her watch, she scowled and brought the conversation to a close. "We talked longer than I thought. I need to get a shower and don my executive-woman clothes. We'll be leaving for company headquarters in a couple of hours."

"Yay," Michael said with mock excitement as Michele left the room.

"I'm going to try to catch some sleep," Gloria said with a yawn.

"Gloria?" Michael said as she was leaving the kitchen.

"Yes?"

"Remember, she's just a girl. Be sure to look out for her."

Gloria patted his shoulder and then planted a chaste kiss on his cheek. "I'll treat her as if she were my own child."

"Thanks."

Michael picked up his cell phone. He worked his way through the directory to the number of Savario Scharpacci, probably the most affable of the programmers he had used when working on the disc technology. Michael would prefer to use someone more prone to secrecy to break the tablet. It would be ridiculous to blow their cover as the major shareholder in the quantum computing business if he could get one of the programmers to hack the clipboard. But he had to see if he still had any control over them. A quick conversation should tell him all he needed to know. He tapped on the number and put the phone to his ear. The phone rang several times before it was answered.

"*Pronto.*"

"*Ciao,* Savario," Michael said in an animated voice.

"*Qui é?*"

"Don Michael Martin."

"Father," the voice spoke in English. It wasn't Savario's.

"Who am I talking to?" Michael asked cautiously. He had been told to stay away from the disc technology. There was no way he could pass this phone call off as an invitation to lunch.

"Your friend from the Dark Awakening." Michael placed the voice. It was the agent.

"How did I manage to dial your phone?"

"You didn't, Father. You dialed the phone of one of your former programmers ... but you know that," the agent said gruffly.

"Oh," Michael said, not willing to give anything else away.

"Why were you calling, Father?" the agent asked suspiciously.

"Just saw his name on my phone and thought I'd give him a call."

"Interesting," said the agent.

"How so?"

"I'm at his apartment now. He hasn't shown up for work in days. Looks like there was a break-in. Nobody seems to know where he is."

"What?" Michael asked incredulously.

"And add to that the coincidence that you called his cell phone just as I was investigating."

"I don't see anything in the coincidence," Michael said briskly. "I'm concerned about his well-being though. Let me know if you find out anything, will you?"

"Father," the agent said in a halting voice.

"Yes?"

"You spent many, many years on the wrong side of things. Old habits die hard."

"I don't know what you are implying," Michael said gruffly.

"I'm implying nothing. I have a job to do. If I find that you have fallen back to your old ways, I will pursue you as I would any other criminal. *Capisce?*"

"*Capisco,*" Michael said. He began to offer more when the phone went dead.

This is turning out to be one heck of a day!

———

The meeting of the Executive Committee was pretty much standard fare. Michael was distracted by Naomi's appearance in his mother's old photo. What did these people have in common? How could they have found their way into each other's lives when each had no prior knowledge of having met? The likelihood of something like this happening by chance was miniscule. There had to be an underlying manipulation.

And what about Naomi? Could she be trusted? Michael watched as she scowled throughout the meeting. She had an ever-present disdain for the company's move to a philanthropic agenda.

"Well, despite our best efforts, we seem to be turning a profit," Michele said with a grin. "This means that we have more funds available to contribute to hunger projects."

"With all due respect, Michele," Naomi said sternly, "the world has recovered pretty nicely since we first adopted this strategic direction. Meanwhile, we have debt so far out of the money that it begs to be refinanced, or better still, to be repaid."

John apologetically backed Naomi. "I wouldn't have thought we would do so well, but here we are. Don't get me wrong. I'm all for our humanitarian efforts, but it may be time to reinvest in the business a bit. There are factory upgrade requests you've passed on ..."

"I understand," Michele conceded, "but I can't see myself approving capital expenditures for new buildings and equipment with fifteen- to thirty-year projected life spans."

"You're basing your decisions on the notion that we're in the tribulation," Naomi protested. "Meanwhile, the world is chugging along pretty well."

Michael interjected, saying, "Even if nobody here buys into the tribulation viewpoint, then you should at least consider what Isa Kurtoglu says about the Nemesis threat."

Naomi said decisively, "He says we can band together to meet the challenge, Michael. We're a food company, for heaven's sake. People will need to eat after the Nemesis passing and the defeat of the Anu."

"Assuming they can be defeated," Pak said glumly.

"Well then, I'm sure the Anu need to eat!" Naomi exclaimed in a huff, squirming in her chair and throwing her hands in the air.

Michael could see her point. If a person didn't have a biblical worldview, then the next few years would be speed bumps in humanity's progression, maybe only growing pains on the road to a bright galactic future. This was the great deception spoken of in the Bible. Michael offered support to Michele. "If I recall correctly, Michele approved all capital expenditures related to product safety and quality, as well as every near-term capital request from the aircraft business to keep up with our government contracts."

"I also approved all capital expenditures related to energy production, provided they have a fast turnaround," Michele said defensively.

"And the energy expenditures," Michael repeated in support of Michele.

"Yes. Yes," Naomi said sarcastically. "Your little girl is doing a good job, Michael."

"I take exception to that comment, Naomi," Michele said tersely.

"It wasn't so much directed at you as at your uncle," Naomi shot back. "He needs to get his head in the game. His blanket support for you looks patronizing."

"Now I'm the one who takes exception," Michael said gruffly.

"Can I call a break to this meeting while I speak to you and Michele privately?" Naomi asked. It was clear that she had asked only to be polite. In reality she was calling a sidebar.

"Fine," Michele said as she huffed out of the room.

"Sure," Michael said as he stood to follow his niece. "But I want to remind all of you that this is a family business. Michele is the family member designated to oversee the day-to-day ..."

"Save the preaching for Sunday, Michael," Naomi groused as she followed Michele out of the room. Michael gave a curious look to the others in the meeting. He found a bit of compassion in John's face but was shocked at the stony gazes of the others. He hadn't caught it before, but it was patently evident now that the members of the executive team were in Naomi's camp.

He found the two women staring at each other silently in the hallway outside the conference room. He said sternly, "All right, Naomi, you called this little sidebar. What do you want to discuss?"

Naomi spoke in a hushed tone, pointing to the closed conference room door. "The natives are restless, Michael. It's obvious to every member of the executive team that Michele's humanitarian efforts begin and end at the door of old-school Christian organizations. Our filings with the government are looking more and more suspect, especially when you consider we no longer get tax deductions for do-nations to these types of entities."

"Uncle Michael, I have never been circumspect about my inten-tions to help the church or about my belief that we are in the tribula-tion period."

Naomi picked up the argument. "I'm not questioning Michele's integrity, Michael. But she is young and impetuous. Nobody can fly in the face of government regulation for long."

Michael wiped his forehead against a migraine forming there. He had to think. Certainly Michele was young. She wasn't running the com-pany for the long term. She didn't have to. On the other hand, there was certainly wisdom in living to fight another day. And Michael couldn't shake Naomi's image in the photo. There had to be some significance. There was a sharp divide in the attendees of that long-forgotten event; they were either very good or very evil. Michael wasn't sure to which group Naomi belonged, but he had seen her behave with animal-like ferocity over the years. Either way, she was a force with which to reckon.

His knowledge of Naomi led him to believe that her ego needed to be assuaged constantly. She needed to believe, or at least promote, the idea the company would be helpless without her. Michele would do well to allow Naomi an occasional victory in unimportant issues to secure her loyalty in more important areas.

His head still in his hands, Michael asked, "What do you suggest?"

Naomi rose to the occasion, assuming the demeanor of a wise advisor. "Surprisingly little. I just need a bit of cover with the rest of the team."

"Meaning?" Michele asked with too much of an edge in her voice. Michael stared into her eyes and shook his head slightly.

"Meaning," Naomi said tersely, "that we have a history of wanting the best for the company. We've all given a tremendous amount of time and effort to make this company what it is—or at least what it was."

Michele sighed as if to say she had heard it all before. Michael glared at her. She seemed shocked by his expression. With her full attention, his eyes begged her to follow his lead.

"Naomi," Michael said softly, "we don't know where we would be without you guys, you in particular. You've been a loyal friend and advisor to my mom and to us."

"He's right," Michele said quietly. "I apologize if I haven't shown my appreciation lately, Naomi. But you need to know I'm very thankful for your hard work and good counsel."

Naomi softened. "You don't know how much it means to hear you say it."

Michele continued. "I know we're going in a direction that's uncomfortable to the team."

Naomi interjected. "Listen, you have loyalty with John and me, but not everyone around that table is willing to put their necks on the line for you when the government comes calling."

"Do you really think it's that bad?" Michael asked. "It's not as if we are without influence with the new world regime."

"Huh!" Naomi spat as she waved her hands in dismay. "Do you really think your relationship to the pope will help? Benny would have gladly taken everything from your mother over the years. What makes you think he would treat the two of you any better?"

"Certainly he wouldn't be any kinder to us out of loyalty or love," Michael conceded. "But he now has everything he ever wanted. I can't imagine he would even want the businesses."

"He was pope when he changed the nationality of the estate and named it Castello Pietro," Naomi said resolutely.

"True," Michael said. He didn't have the time or the words to explain to Naomi that Benny had been invested with a spiritual entity that had much larger plans than encroaching on the family business. He wouldn't explain it even if he could. If Naomi was honest, was one of the good guys, then the threat of Benny would keep her on their side. If she was not, then she was probably already working for Benny.

"Tell us what you want us to do," Michael said decisively.

"Set up a charity within the confines of your Vatican presence. I don't give a hoot what you do with the money or food once it's donated to the Vatican. All I care is that our books show tax-deductible donations to legitimate charities."

"We can do that," Michele said softly. "But it puts the donations under Benny's auspices."

"Not if I hide them from him," Michael said, glibly wondering if it was a sin to deceive the master deceiver.

"That is between you, Michele, and Benny," Naomi said resolutely.

"All I need to know is that the company is getting legitimate tax deductions for donations made."

"Fair enough," Michael said, but he wondered if he had just inadvertently put the businesses in Benny's hands.

TWENTY-THREE

The hajj presented a total security nightmare for Will. Seven times, the whining Benny would have to walk around the Kaaba in deference to Islam's significance to the new worldwide faith. Hundreds of thousands of Muslims were in Mecca for the annual pilgrimage. In fact, the pilgrimage had for generations been the exclusive purview of Muslims, but now in the new world, rare non-Muslim guests were permitted as a sign of Islam's new openness.

It was Isa's idea that Pope Peter make a pilgrimage to the mystical stone from outer space. Benny was excited at first, but then the realities of the arduous trek became clear. In the sweltering heat, Benny slowly progressed with the countless faithful. He was surrounded by Will's security team, who traded in their festooned Swiss Guard uniforms for the simplicity of *thawbs*, traditional Arabic white robes, out of respect for the ceremony.

"Michael, a drink, please. I'm parched," Benny cried. Will couldn't help but grin at the sour expression on his uncle's face as he opened a canteen, shoved a straw in it, and held it to the older man's lips.

"Not funny," Michael mouthed to him over his shoulder, which in fact made the situation all the more amusing. He signaled to his second in command to cover him as he moved forward to Michael's side.

Leaning over Michael, he said to Benny, "You're going to have to buck up, Lucky. This was just one time around the Kaaba. You've got six more to go, and we're looking at well over hundred-degree heat this afternoon."

"I'm sure you find this amusing, Will," Benny said with familial disdain. "Sometimes you're too much like your father."

243

"Never too much like your father for me." Michael grinned as he removed a white handkerchief from his pocket to blot his forehead.

"I thought the new order would bring an end to this barbarism," Benny quipped. Michael shoved the straw back into the older man's mouth to silence him.

"Keep your thoughts to yourself, Benny," Michael warned. There are still stampedes at these events. Let's try real hard not to start one with a callous remark."

"Fair enough." Benny sighed as he grinned and offered a weak papal wave to onlookers. "I'll be good. Let's just get through this day."

"Good," Will said decisively. "This is a security nightmare, Benny."

The next couple of passes around the Kaaba were without incident. Will remained vigilant in his constant surveillance of the crowd, but his mind wandered. Soon the world would be coming upon the third anniversary of the Dark Awakening, or the rapture, or whatever they wanted to call it.

The world had changed so dramatically since then, but it hadn't really been the nightmare Michael had predicted. In fact, things weren't all that bad. Life under Isa and his extraterrestrial worldview had brought peace to the world. There had been no armed conflicts in nearly three years. It had to be a world record. Add to that the fact that the world was actually working together to a common purpose. It was unheard of.

Of course, the common purpose was to avoid the hardship of the Nemesis passing and to repel the Anu. These were dire specters on the horizon, to be sure, but Isa had convinced the world that their efforts could indeed be fruitful and that the end result would be well worth the fight. The message played well with the world. It played well with Will. He could get behind the idea of fighting to bring about a better world.

But would the new world be better? That was the real question. He looked up into the blinding sun to see the shadow of Nibiru in the sky. As it revolved around its dark star, our sun's twin, it seemed to go away in the sky, only to reappear with a vengeance a few years later as its orbit had brought it back around, closer this time. It was there for all to see—no denying it. Isa had briefed the world about its hostile race intent on ravaging Earth. He showed demonstrations of powerful new weapons to successfully repel their advances, but he was a bit quiet about anticipated geological and environmental effects of the passing.

They were bound to be severe. As head of Benny's personal security force, Will was in a position to know that vast underground bunkers were still being outfitted throughout the world for the elite. These guys knew that something was coming but weren't sharing the details with the rest of the world.

That's where his father's books came to mind. When he first learned of his father, Will had devoured his books about end-time events. He wasn't so much moved by the theology as by a chance to know his father better. But now, in the stifling heat, his mind had time to wander. His father's books told of a mountain-sized asteroid crashing into the sea, earthquakes shaking the entire world, large tracts of land burnt in a solar storm, destruction of untold proportions. His father's books had spoken of all these events as acts of God. Frankly, the idea of an angry God chucking big rocks at Earth made him want to giggle. Although he appreciated the sincerity and passion in his father's books, he was finding it hard to buy into the scenario.

But what if the events described in the Bible, as recounted in his father's books, were less spiritual manifestations than physical descriptions of a future Nemesis crossing? If that were the case, then the globe was due to see near annihilation—a fact Isa consistently withheld from the world.

It made sense. The Nemesis crossing would disrupt the asteroid belt, sending God knows how many huge rocks hurtling toward Earth. How big a coronal mass ejection would it take to burn the trees and grass on the side of Earth facing the sun? According to Uncle Michael, it wasn't so much the size of the fireball as its trajectory. If a coronal mass ejection struck Earth, there would be devastation.

The prophets talked of Earth reeling like a drunkard and every mountain being moved out of place. Again, it was easy for Will to see these as vivid descriptions of Nemesis's magnetic field grabbing hold of Earth's and pulling the entire planet into a superfast pole shift.

His mind quickened to something ahead of them. A group of pilgrims at the Kaaba were unfurling a banner over their heads. This was unusual activity, to say the least. He tapped his lieutenant's shoulder and pointed. The group stood in a line, each holding a bit of the banner as it unfurled from right to left. Huge Arabic letters angrily declared something.

"Uncle Michael, are you getting this?" he asked under his breath.

Michael nodded subtly. "Yes. It's not good," he said quietly.

"What? What's not good?" Benny demanded.

"Shh!" Will chided.

"First part pretty standard," Michael said softly. "No God but Allah. But the next part calls for death to all infidels. I'm thinking that means us."

Will had coordinated the careful scanning of the crowd for weapons. They were likely to be protesters, not insurrectionists. "No weapons," he said softly.

"An incendiary crowd is the only weapon needed," Michael said softly.

Will saw his uncle's point, calculating the devastating odds if they were the subject of mob violence. "We can't fight our way out of this mess," he said severely.

"We might not have to," Michael said softly. "Benny, whatever is inside of you needs to bring his orator skills."

Will looked on aghast as Benny's eyes changed. The soft-willed, whiney expression changed to one of power and strength. This was too weird.

"I never thought I'd say this, but I'm happy to see you," Michael said staunchly to the entity glowing out of Benny's eyes.

"What's the plan to save your uncle?"

"Do you know Arabic?"

"I know persuasion."

"Then be prepared to repeat after me when we get close to the group with the banner."

"Will do."

Will's mind raced. Michael was having a conversation with someone other than Benny in Benny's body. "Michael, what's going on?"

"I'll explain it later. When we get in front of the group with the banner, give the order for your men to present arms."

"Are you sure you want us to wave our weapons? Won't that be inviting a fight?"

"Present them. Don't aim them," Michael said tersely, barely moving his lips.

"Fine," Will muttered as they neared the group. A few more steps. Three, two, one. "Present arms!" Will commanded. The men simultaneously held their crossbows out in front of them.

"Repeat after me," Michael said softly to Benny, the last words Will understood. Michael launched into a stream of Arabic, which Benny shouted out flawlessly to the crowd.

Although Will didn't understand the words, he picked up the feelings emanating from Benny. A spirit of peace flowed from him, maybe even a kind of religious ecstasy. Whatever it was, Will was not immune to it. He felt his mood lighten with the crowd's.

Benny continued to speak, now without Michael's prompting. The unsuspecting crowd cheered and reveled in his every word. Tears of unexpected joy poured down the faces of men and women of faith. It was all Will could do not to join them.

Then he looked at Michael, whose face was frozen in a mask of terror and disdain as if he were witnessing a horrific event.

"Uncle Michael, what is it?" Will asked.

Michael wiped his eyes. "He just prayed to release a horde of demons. Can't you feel it?" Michael whispered.

"I feel what the crowd feels," Will said, suddenly concerned that his perception, and therefore his effectiveness, had been compromised.

Michael put his hand on Will's shoulder, closed his eyes for a second, and said, "Father, please let Will see what I see."

Will shuddered against a sudden blistering chill. His mouth fell open in awe as the scene before him transformed. The brilliance of the sun was obscured by a smoky darkness engulfing the entire area. This smoke had substance, personality.

"Do you see it?" Michael asked.

Will was nearly too stunned to speak at first. He nodded. "Wh-what is it?"

"I really think it's thousands and thousands of demons."

Will's gaze moved between his uncle's dismay and the incongruous looks of ecstasy on faces in the crowd. He felt panic rising within him. There was no logical explanation for what he was seeing or feeling.

"Uncle Michael, how do we get out of here?" he whined softly.

Michael pointed toward Benny, his face filled with disdain. "He's just about to make the crowd part for us."

Still speaking to the crowd, Benny turned toward Will to confirm what Michael had said. Will's knees grew weak at the full-on view of the thing controlling Benny. He had never in his life seen such a contemptuous look of evil.

"I know. It's hard to see at first," Michael said under his breath. "But it's going to get us out of here."

Next, the Benny-thing raised its arms and shouted something. The crowd erupted in joyous shouts and applause. Benny's arms made a parting motion, and the crowd divided to form an opening for him.

"Stay close to him," Will said to his men as Benny moved through the sea of people along the path opening before him. They cheered and waved at him as he passed, his arms raised in a constant motion of blessing.

It seemed like forever as they inched through the undulating crowd. Will scanned each person, looking for potential threats. It was at times difficult to see through the smoky haze still permeating the area. Finally, up ahead, he saw an end to the crowd. A few more yards and they'd be through the worst of it. Then he could radio for a car to take them to their hotel.

Then Benny stumbled. Michael caught him. Will saw none of the fierce evil in the man who had spoken to the crowd seconds before. Now he looked more like the whining Lucky Will had first met on the Georgia interstate.

"Is he okay?" Will asked.

"Exhausted. Spent from the thing inside him taking control," Michael offered as he propped Benny up. The old pope looked like a rag doll, and Michael struggled to hold him upright. "Come on, Benny," he whispered tersely. "Just a few more minutes, and then you can sleep it off."

Will's men in front of Benny turned to help Michael, taking their eyes off the crowd. As the last of them parted, Will saw it. Fear made his mouth dry as he gazed upon the seven men on horseback in bedouin dress. He had been briefed on the resurgence of the Hashshashin in the wake of the world government's confiscation of firearms, but he had never seen so much as a photo of them. The details, however, were unmistakable. Seven bedouins sat atop massive horses, brandishing curved swords. In history, the Hashshashin were warriors who directly served the Persian king. They were notorious for their practice of *janna*, the art of quick death. They were known to drug themselves with poppy to numb their bodies against the pain of battle. Their use of poppy gave us the word *hashish*. Their brutal, mechanical style of murder gave us the word *assassin*.

"Jake," Will said somberly, taking Michael's attention from the floundering pontiff. Will saw terror fill Michael's eyes. Clearly he had heard of the group as well. They had arisen as a Muslim fundamentalist reaction to the merging of world religions. No doubt, the intrusion of the infidel pope to the Kaaba was an infraction punishable by death in their minds.

Michael called to the men in Arabic. They offered no response, just cold stares. The nostrils of their steeds flared. The crowd backed away, slowly at first, but then with more ferocity. Soon the air split with shrieks of people crushed in the ensuing stampede to avoid the Hashshashin.

Will drew his crossbow and ordered his men to do the same, but the men in front had too little time, their attention having been diverted to helping Michael prop up the faltering pope. The seven struck with a lightning-quick speed to hack three of his men to pieces. Will's men hadn't stood a chance. As blood spattered all over Michael and Benny, Will instinctively fired off two arrows in rapid succession. His aim was true. The seven Hashshashin were now five. Perhaps they had taken too many drugs or had never considered that some of their number could fall. Whatever the reason, the death of their compatriots left them momentarily confused. Will took full advantage of their lapse, killing two more and taking aim at a third. The men behind him followed suit, leaving one lone assassin, who surprised them by jumping off his horse. He wrenched Benny from Michael's grasp and stood with the blade of the sword against the nearly unconscious man's throat.

Will ordered his men to stand down, but he kept his bow aimed at the bedouin, who stared at him and barked a command.

"He says to drop your weapon," Michael interpreted.

"What if I don't?" Will asked. He was suddenly very confused. The thought kept running through his mind that the world would be so much better without Benny. What if a show of strength on his part gave the bedouin an excuse to rid the world of such vermin? Will felt moist tears coursing down his cheeks. He blinked his eyes hard, clearing his aim. The bedouin yelled again.

Michael spoke deliberately. "Will, it has all been prophesied. Benny will meet his end, but this isn't his time. Certain things can't be changed."

Will began to lower the bow when he saw the bedouin flinch. For the briefest second he had a clear head shot, so he took it. The arrow careened through the bedouin's eye to the other side of his head, but the man didn't die immediately. As he pulled on the sword to decapitate the pope, Michael grabbed the dying man's hand. They struggled for a brief second before death overtook the would-be assassin.

Will yelled to his remaining men to grab the bedouins' horses.

"The police will be here soon," Michael said as they heard the distant sound of sirens.

"Not with this crowd," Will said sternly. "Help me get Holiness on this horse, and then take one for yourself."

Will got on one of the huge animals and then reached down to grab Benny under the arms. He was dead weight, completely unconscious. Will pulled as hard as he could, but he couldn't get the man to the back of the horse. "I need you to push, Jake."

Michael bent down and squared his shoulders against Pope Peter's holy buttocks to push while Will pulled. "Well, this is one of the worst jobs I've ever had," Michael said breathlessly as he grunted against Benny's bottom.

"I hear you, Jake," Will said with a quick grin. "I hear you."

Back at their hotel suite, they put Benny to bed. After a thorough debriefing with local law enforcement, they changed out of their thawbs and stole into the living room. Will poured a glass of scotch.

"I hope you're not like your father in this one regard, Will," Michael cautioned, pointing to the glass.

Will shrugged off his uncle's concern. "Not to worry, Uncle Michael. I can't remember the last time I had a drink. But after today ... I lost good men out there." He shook his head somberly.

"I'm with you," Michael said as he joined the younger man at the bar and poured a glass of wine. They moved to the couch in silence. Michael sat first, throwing himself backward and extending his arms in a stretch.

Will sat beside him. The soft velvet fabric of the sofa cradled him.

It wasn't until that moment when he realized how tiring the day had been. He took a drink of the scotch, held it in his mouth for a second, and then allowed the liquid to burn down his throat. "I ... I don't know what we saw out there," he stammered.

"I told you before. At the UN meeting, Isa instilled some powerful demon in Benny," Michael said as he laid his head back against the couch, stretching his neck.

"Deep down, I'm not even sure I really believe in that stuff," Will countered, "but what I saw today wasn't Benny. That thing was scary!"

Michael chuckled sarcastically as he sat straight. "In many ways, Benny's scarier."

Will bristled at the immensity of the comment. "Seriously, Jake, you can't tell me the world wouldn't be a better place right now if the Hashshashin had killed Benny."

"You're right, Will. The world would be a better place."

"But ..." Will led.

"But it wouldn't have happened. You read your dad's books. You know Jesus will deal with the False Prophet in the future, but he's not going anywhere soon."

Michael's phone buzzed. He pulled it from his pocket to check the incoming text message. "Huh," he said, showing Will. "Another of the programmers went missing. That makes three of the five."

Will scarcely responded as thoughts swirled through his mind. He refused to believe they were powerless pawns in some end-time drama written by the apostle John. Surely it was incumbent upon good men to stand up to the kind of evil they had seen today.

If someone were to take matters into his own hands, he would have to be a person who could see the truth without being bound to the inevitability of Christian prophecy. To Will, the Christian mind-set left them powerless against the likes of Benny.

Will had seen a lot of things in his life and had been a lot of things, but he had never been powerless. Never.

Deep under the streets of Rome, the catacombs once again became the shelter of society's disenfranchised. The old monk shivered in the alcove he now called home. After the rapture, he realized the error of his ways and gave his heart to Jesus. It was the best day of his life, but there had been consequences. The new pope had very little patience for clergy who refused to accept the new world religion. In short order, he had been defrocked, excommunicated, and turned out into the streets. There were others in his position, of course, but not as many as he would have hoped. The deception of alien gods and alien enemies was too strong. Most of the old guard had capitulated without a struggle.

"But then again, you always were cantankerous, Ignatius," a voice rang out through the tunnel.

"Who's there?" the nervous monk called into the blackness.

"Are you hungry? I think I've got a sandwich here somewhere."

The old monk squinted against the darkness toward the approaching figure, which was wearing a starched cassock.

"Vinnie?" he asked.

"So, you recognize me," Vinnie said as he sat beside his old enemy. "Since the rapture, I'm pretty young. I wasn't sure you'd know me."

Ignatius chuckled. "You're pretty memorable, Vinnie." His voice grew quieter. "I wasn't nice to you, Vinnie. I apologize for the way I treated you."

"Water under the bridge, Ignatius. We're all on the same team now." Vinnie reached into his pocket to produce a large sandwich of Italian meats on a fresh baguette. The smell of the fresh sandwich brought tears to Ignatius's eyes. He had been foraging in Dumpsters for the better part of three years. Vinnie handed the sandwich to him. Tears of joy flooded his eyes as he unwrapped its cellophane cover and dove into it savagely. They were silent for a while as Ignatius ate. The sandwich was the most delicious thing he had eaten in a long while. As much as he wanted to devour it, he already feared the moment it would be gone. He took one last bite to cherish, while wrapping the remainder of the sandwich and placing it like so much gold into his pocket.

"Vinnie," Ignatius finally said as tears filled his eyes, "I don't know how long it's been since I've had real food. I even long for the early days of my Dumpster diving. With less food these days, people are more careful. Garbage isn't what it used to be."

"I hear you, pal," Vinnie said with more compassion than Ignatius had ever heard from the man. "But you have to hear *me* now. Times are about to get much worse."

"All the horrors of the book of Revelation," Ignatius said with a knowing frown.

"Yeah," Vinnie said woefully, "and you have a part to play in the upcoming events. Nicely put, Ignatius, you'll need to trade in the Roman underground for subterranean Jerusalem."

"Easier said than done," Ignatius said defensively. "Your old pal Pope Peter has made me a pariah. I'm on the no-fly list. I don't even have the new travel documents required to leave Rome, let alone travel to Jerusalem."

"But Peter never planned on you traveling like Paul," Vinnie quipped.

"So, you're telling me to walk to Jerusalem?" Ignatius was at once repulsed and intrigued by the notion. The trek would be arduous. And despite all the love and unity talk of the new world government, the shadows still beckoned the dregs of society. The intriguing part was receiving a directive from heaven. How would it feel to actually be a part of God's plan, to have a divinely orchestrated purpose?

"You'll travel by night," Vinnie said somberly. "I can't promise you anything, but I get the distinct impression that the Lord will let me travel with you some of the time."

"I'm in, Vinnie, although I can't fathom what good I can do in Jerusalem. The two witnesses at the Wailing Wall are—"

"Witnesses in the truest biblical sense," Vinnie said sadly. "I always thought those guys would be great evangelists, but now I see they're largely witnesses for the prosecution, so to speak."

"What a sad time," Ignatius said woefully.

"But it's only for a short while. Life on the other side is great. For now, though, why don't you try to get some shut-eye? It will be dark soon, and we'll need to start your journey."

At the mere suggestion of it, Ignatius became extraordinarily tired. As his eyes became too heavy to hold open, he felt more than saw a flash of light. Then he heard Vinnie talking to someone.

"Do you think he'll be able to do it?" the voice asked.

"I don't know, Chris, but we have to give him the chance. If he succeeds, it will be the same for him as it was for us—it will be by God's grace." It was Father Chris. Ignatius managed to raise one eyelid and move his hand in a tiny gesture of recognition. He caught only the next bit of conversation before sleep overwhelmed him.

"True enough," Chris answered. "I just wish Will's fate lay in more capable hands."

TWENTY-FOUR

The sweet potato pie was ready to come out of the oven. Well, in all honesty, it had been ready since the beginning of the show. The oven was a prop. The important thing was that tubers were still growing. Leafy green vegetables were becoming very scarce, and grain reserves the world over were falling, but for now there was an abundance of tubers in America. Gloria pulled the cool pie out of the oven with oven mitts and deeply inhaled.

"Oh, I wish you all at home could smell this. I know what you're thinking," she said with a raised eyebrow. "I've thought it myself. If I eat, see, or smell another potato, sweet potato, or turnip again in my life, it will be too soon!

"But that's not the right attitude, and I chase it from my mind. The truth is, we're living in some tough times. And President Kurtoglu has made it clear that the effects of the Nemesis crossing will last for years."

She paused for a second to gather her thoughts. She had to be careful to preach the truth but to do it in a way that didn't elicit the scrutiny of the authorities. "You know, a lot of people think the Bible talked about this time. If you read those ancient words with the idea that they're describing the Nemesis events, well, they sure come to life. I would imagine I've read Revelation *eleven* times in the last few months."

She took a bite of the pie. The sweet potatoes used to make it were old and bore a slight mustiness that carried through to the finished pie. So much of their food these days had that old, just-about-to-go-over smell, taste, and texture. She smiled hard and swallowed hard. "Mmm. Anyway, as I was saying. If we are in the days prophesied of old, then we have to be on our guard not to be easily discouraged. We have to be thankful for every bit of normalcy we can find in these trying times.

"We've made more pies and we're going to plate them for the audience while we take a brief pause for a commercial message. When we come back, I have some exclusive footage for you. You don't want to miss it." She smiled broadly into the camera and prayed under her breath that the warm pies to be distributed to the audience tasted better than hers.

A makeup man came from the wings to give her a touch-up. She held up one finger and said, "Just a second, Riley." Reaching to a shelf under the pretend kitchen counter on the set, she pulled out a glass of ice water and drank deeply through a straw, undoubtedly smearing her lipstick. "Okay," she said to Riley as she sat on a stool.

The touch-up was fast. Gloria had to be conscious not to move her lips as she prayed earnestly for the strength to go through with the next segment. Her mention of the book of Revelation hadn't been off the cuff. She deliberately planted the seed before the commercial break. The mention of the book along with the number eleven would surely bring to mind the eleventh chapter of Revelation, the description of the two witnesses, for her truly Christian followers. It would pass right over the heads of the diehard Isa followers and, hopefully, of the censors.

The opportunity to do a live broadcast was nearly unheard of these days, but a series of glitches in network programming led to this rare chance. When she saw Michael's purloined video, she recognized God's hand in aligning the circumstances. This message had to be aired.

Riley finished and packed up his gear with just seconds to spare. The producer began the countdown to live broadcast, "Three, two, one." He pointed his index finger at Gloria.

She spoke in a voice that was soft but filled with urgency. "Ladies and gentlemen, we have come in possession of an amazing piece of footage from Jerusalem. It's a scoop from the Wailing Wall. Take a look."

The control room cut to the film. The footage was a bit shaky, but it clearly showed the two witnesses. They spoke in Hebrew. Michael translated through a sound modulator to disguise his voice. "These are the times of great deception. Do not be fooled. There is only one name by which men may be saved. It is only through the Lord Jesus Christ. Hear, Israel, and obey!"

The camera panned to the entrance of the plaza, where twenty of Isa's troops marched to within a few feet of the witnesses. At the command of their sergeant, the men all brought their assault rifles to their shoulders.

The sergeant read from a prepared script. "By the order of His Excellency, President Isa Kurtoglu, you have been found guilty of treason. Your divisive message threatens Earth's entry into a galactic federation. His Highness has issued countless cease-and-desist warnings, all of which you have ignored. You have thirty seconds to turn yourselves over to our custody. If you don't, my men will fire." To his men he yelled, "Aim."

One of the witnesses stared at the commander and then said, as translated by Michael, "It is we who should warn you. Put down your arms and turn your hearts to the Lord Jesus before it is too late. It is not God's will that any should perish."

The footage closed in on the commander. A small bead of sweat fell from his brow. He swallowed hard and said with a slight catch in his voice, "Fire!" The sound was deafening. Twenty automatic rifles fired multiple rounds. Smoke from the guns drifted across the view as the camera zoomed in on the witnesses. They stood stoic, not affected in the least by the bullets, which ricocheted with bright sparks off the Wailing Wall behind them.

The witnesses looked at their shooters with tenderness. Then one said sadly, "Fire." At once the men and their weapons burst into white-hot flames. In a matter of seconds they were reduced to piles of ash.

Looking steadily into the camera, the other witness said in deliberate English, "Woe to the inhabitants of Earth, for Satan is urgent to destroy because he knows his time is short."

When the video ended, Gloria's stunned audience remained dead silent. Gloria looked into the camera and said softly, "We'll be back after these brief messages."

Zack pointed the remote at the DVR in his office and snapped at the power button. He couldn't believe what he had just seen. Showing video of those ridiculous morons at the Wailing Wall! It was stupid even for Gloria.

He went to the large world globe dominating the area opposite his desk. Feeling under its wood base, he came upon the sensor that read his fingerprint and unlocked a hidden clasp. He pulled on the Northern Hemisphere, which opened to reveal several decanters of alcohol and fine-cut crystal glasses. He poured himself a glass of whiskey and downed it. He poured another before sealing the secret compartment.

What was he to do with her? She could easily ruin his ministry. He couldn't let that happen. He had taken action to protect the ministry from his parents, and he was willing to do the same with Gloria. But that wasn't likely to happen any time soon. He hurled the empty glass to the floor, shattering it. He paced like a caged tiger as he considered her threat to expose him. The evidence was damning. He would lose everything if this information came to light.

He grimaced at the thought of her haughty expression the day she explained that she had placed the information with someone with the instruction to make it public if she ever disappeared the way his parents had. "Someone!" he screamed to the empty room. Well, Zack didn't have to guess who that someone was now, did he? Michael—the ever-present pain in his butt. What he wouldn't do to see that man dead!

He rubbed fiercely at his forehead as if doing so could conjure an idea. There had to be a way to make Michael disappear. He wracked his brain. Nothing came, but something would … in time. Meanwhile, the airing of this video was sure to cause a stir with the powers that be.

There was a slight knock at the door. Zack's new secretary, younger and prettier than the last, opened the door a crack and said, "Zack, President Kurtoglu is on the line. I know you said to hold your calls, but I thought you'd want to take this one."

"You're right, darlin'," he drawled. He hadn't bedded this one yet, but it was only a matter of time.

He picked up the phone and bit his bottom lip. For years he had longed to have the attention of his alien son, but today he only feared it. He cleared his throat, pushed the button to engage the line, and spoke as cheerily as he could. "Isa, it's such a pleasure to hear from you."

"So, we're on a first-name basis now, are we, *Zack*?" Isa snapped. Zack winced.

"No … yes," Zack scrambled. "I mean … as potentate of the world, you are my leader, but I feel such a genetic kinship to you given our common origins. I … I guess what I'm saying, Excellency, is that I think of you as sort of a son."

"Then you are delusional," Isa said coldly. "Especially considering your wife's act of treason."

Zack winced. "You saw her program?"

"No, I called to wish you a nice day," Isa snapped.

"President Kurtoglu, let me explain. I had no idea that clip was going to air. And in all fairness to my wife, I think she was just trying to practice good journalism."

"If I had my way, she would be dead now," Isa said deliberately. "But to kill her immediately after she aired the video would make me look petty and weak. I have a crew working now to denounce the video as an obvious fraud.

"Your little wifey-poo is building quite a strong base of supporters who prefer the old-time religion, despite my desperate warnings about the ill-effects of divisive thought. She really is quite stupid."

"I've always thought so," Zack agreed. "But she's charming and has a way with people."

"Millions of them, judging by the ratings. My point is this, Zack. The more people who think as she does, the more vulnerable our planet is to the coming attack. I need to find these people and reeducate them. This is where you come in. I need you to forward to me her e-mail subscriber list, her customer list, and her donor list."

"Wait," Zack said defensively. "My ministry needs the money from her product sales and donors. Also, we are a bit of a glam couple. Our mailing lists aren't mutually exclusive, you know. You'll be cutting into my donor base as well."

"Let's just call it the price of higher ratings, Zack. Once Gloria's most ardent fans have been reeducated, your show will rank higher than hers. You want that, don't you?"

"Well, yes, but her show is profitable, and I've grown accustomed to a certain lifestyle."

"Once your wife has lost her fan base, she can easily be discredited in the media," Isa offered. "And of course there would be condolence money when your congregation learns of her treachery."

Zack pictured it all. He knew exactly how he would pout his face. He could hear the words he would say, feel the tears he would shed for the audience. Isa was right. It could be a veritable gold mine.

"If I may offer a suggestion," Zack said haltingly. An idea was forming, and it was stellar.

"I'm waiting," Isa said disdainfully.

"We've been trying without much success to get permission for Gloria to do one of her cooking shows at a FEMA camp—a show of compassion for the poor."

"Go on."

"If we got permission, two things would happen. First, the show itself would bring in more people who feel as she does. It would broaden your list of people prime for reeducation."

"I like what you're thinking," Isa said approvingly.

"We let the show air. Then, at a later date, once you have gotten full value from her subscriber list, we can discredit her by leaking to the press that she committed some sort of infraction while there. Maybe we could get secret footage of her praying in the name of Jesus at the camp."

"It's a start, Zack, but if we want to paint her as a subversive, we'll need a more heinous crime. I leave it up to you. Don't disappoint me."

"I won't," Zack assured a phone line that was already dead. Isa had hung up. Zack severed the connection from his end and immediately dialed another number.

"Jacob. Hi, it's Zack," he spoke into the phone. "I was wondering if you could handle a tech question for me. I would like to run a comparison of my donors, customers, and e-mail subscribers versus those for Gloria's show. I'm trying to isolate the people who are unique to Gloria's fan base." He listened as Jacob went into excruciating detail about how he would isolate the data.

"How long will it take? … Friday would be great! Thanks, Jacob. I really appreciate it."

A quick knock on his office door preceded Gloria's entrance. Suspiciously eying the broken glass on the floor, she spoke anxiously as she walked to his desk. "Zack, I don't know if you got the chance to see my show today, but I want to explain."

"I saw it," he said calmly. She struck a bewildered look, clearly not expecting his reaction. "Take a seat, darlin'."

"Oh, okay," she said in a soft voice. "Here's what I wanted to tell you, Zack. I received that video just as we were about to go on air. It's from an anonymous sender who said it was breaking news. I didn't have time to get the whole way through it before we went on air, but I saw enough to know it was a confrontation with those guys in Jerusalem. I wanted the scoop, and frankly I thought Isa's guards would win."

Zack didn't believe her for a moment. "I just got off the phone with Isa," he said severely.

Gloria covered her mouth and an unexpected gasp. Zack enjoyed the mounting fear in her eyes.

"How well do you know the source of that video?" he asked.

"Like I said, it was sent anonymously."

"Well, I guess that's why cooking shows shouldn't try to practice journalism," Zack said a bit more sternly. "Isa's people will release an analysis proving the footage to be a hoax. Looks like you were scammed, darlin'."

"I can't believe it was a hoax," she said resolutely.

"Well, it was!" Zack screamed, pounding his hand on his desk. "You can imagine Isa's reaction!" He lowered his voice a full register. "I barely managed to calm him. Let's just say he's willing to keep it in the family, just this once. In exchange he wants his old mom and pop to go easy on the politically incorrect stuff from now on."

She sighed. "So, I guess that means we won't be permitted to do a cooking show from one of the FEMA camps. Might as well kiss that idea good-bye," she said, hand to her forehead.

"On the contrary, Isa has offered to expedite it. He thinks it's important for people to see the aid he has given to the unfortunate."

"Why would he do that?"

"I don't know, Gloria," Zack said in an agitated tone. "Maybe because he's *not the Antichrist?* Do you see how this biblical paranoia colors your opinion of everything? We dodged the bullet on this one, darlin', but I don't know how many more times I'll be able to bring him to heel."

Gloria now assumed a more submissive nature. Zack couldn't tell if it was affected or real. "I'm touched and a little bit shocked you stood up for me, Zack. I know how much you think of Kurtoglu. Thank you."

He moved from his side of the desk, stood behind her, and rubbed her shoulders. "I love you, Gloria. We're a team. No couple has ever been through the things we've experienced together."

"I didn't think you still thought that way about me, Zack," she said with a sigh.

"I never stopped. I know that sometimes I get too caught up in the day-to-day and forget to say it. Let's be honest: I've gotten so caught up in the *year-to-year* that I've forgotten to say it. But that doesn't mean I don't feel it."

She reached to her shoulder to take his right hand. "Thanks for saying it now, Zack. I really needed to hear it, especially after I've been hoaxed on public television."

"Better to be thought of as someone who has been taken advantage of than some sort of insurrectionist." He bent to kiss her neck.

"Zack, as much as I love to be close to you, I have a meeting with the production crew in a few minutes, and now I've got to tell them the bad news that our scoop wasn't a scoop at all." She stood quickly and gave him a peck on the cheek as she made a beeline for the office door.

"Sweetheart," he called after her, "would you be kind enough to send my secretary in on your way out?"

"Sure," she muttered absentmindedly.

Within a few seconds, Zack's new secretary, Miranda, stood in front of his desk. He made eye contact and gazed for a few moments. She was lovely, and she looked so ... firm. He licked his lips slightly and said, "My wife has meetings. It looks like I'll be eating a TV dinner all alone at home if you won't agree to go out with me."

TWENTY-FIVE

Gloria introduced Michele to her audience. The show from the FEMA camp was going very smoothly. From the wings, Jimmy smiled at Michele. He could love her for the rest of his life. He knew she felt the same, but she didn't act on it because she believed they were in the tribulation. He had believed that too at first, but nearly three years had passed and the world was doing pretty well. He had to find a way to get her to take the next step.

He wasn't the only one who wanted this marriage. A woman had come out of the shadows claiming to be his birth mother. He hadn't believed her at first, feeling no connection to the burly woman who had presented herself. He had always imagined his mother to be a soft, sweet-smelling woman who made endless chocolate chip cookies and always wanted to hug him. He chuckled at the thought. Clearly he had been unrealistic, but Naomi DeRance? He couldn't believe it. Just this morning he had stood in front of the bathroom mirror, staring intently into his face. Truth be told, he could have gotten his heavy brow ridge and full eyebrows from her. He couldn't really tell.

Applause from the FEMA audience greeted Michele's announcement that her company would donate additional food to the FEMA system—taking them from very basic staples to a more diverse, flavorful diet.

The applause for Michele warmed Jimmy's heart. He had never met someone as altruistic and kind. At first he worried his feelings for her were a reaction to the despair of the times, but as the days passed, he realized he was desperately in love with the intelligent, witty, caring young woman. Feeling for the pen in his lapel pocket, he hoped his complicity in this operation would prove his undying devotion to her. It was no ordinary pen. It was actually a modified insulin pen containing a powerful narcotic. As the show wound to a close, Jimmy's job was to incapacitate a guard and steal his notepad device. Simple as that.

"What could go wrong?" he asked under his breath as his mind went through a seemingly endless list of scenarios wherein he was caught with the device. He watched the show carefully, keeping an eye on the hallway behind the stage. The guard made regular rounds. He should be back in the hallway within five minutes. They had planned a blistering music number—a sound cover just in case the guard didn't go down easily.

He stared intently at Michele from the wings as she chatted with Gloria in the interview. After what felt like an eternity, she glanced at him. He quickly raised five fingers—five minutes. Immediately, Michele reached out to touch Gloria's arm with all five fingers in what looked like a gesture of friendship to the audience.

He saw a shadow in the hallway. Had the guard come early? He pressed himself against the wall along the doorway and peered out into the hall. Zack? What was he doing here? Jimmy rushed past unused props back to the wings of the stage and stared intently at Michele. When she finally looked up, she looked past him, her eyes wide.

Jimmy turned to see Zack standing there with a large bouquet of flowers. He smiled and said hello, but Zack paid him no attention. He turned his gaze back to the set, where Michele was speaking in a desperate effort to give Gloria a heads-up. "Oh, Gloria, I just wish Zack could be here to see the fine work you're doing. I'm sure he would be so proud."

Gloria patted Michele's knee and said, "I'm sure he would be. He's very supportive of me, you know."

There was no doubt in Jimmy's mind that the message had been received. At Gloria's endorsement of her loving husband, Zack said, "That's my cue." He sauntered onto the set with his trademark too-broad smile.

"Oh my word!" Michele exclaimed as the audience applauded. "We were just talking about you." She rose to hug him. As the audience continued its applause, Gloria turned to greet her husband and fawn over the flowers he brought her.

After the applause subsided and the stagehands rushed a chair to the set for him, Zack asked as he took his seat, "What were y'all saying about me, Michele? Good things, I hope."

Michele smiled. Jimmy grinned with pride at how deftly she had handled the situation, but he wondered what to do with the guard in about a minute if there was no music cover. He felt for the pen in his pocket. He would have to wing it. He stepped into the hallway when he saw the guard's shadow.

"Excuse me," he said in a hushed voice, indicating toward the show. "Can you tell me where I can find the men's room?"

"It's just down the hall," the guard said softly, "but it's a restricted area. You can go to the one in the next hallway."

"Not without crossing in front of the stage," Jimmy said defensively. "I'll lose my job!"

The guard rolled his eyes. "Follow me. Don't leave my side."

Jimmy filed in alongside him, and they marched the few steps to the men's room at the end of the hallway. To Jimmy's great relief, the man followed him into the restroom.

Jimmy took a urinal, which was thankfully shielded from view by a divider. He quickly pulled the cap from the pen. Pretending to shake and zip, he cupped the exposed needle into the palm of his hand. In the meantime, the guard had decided to use the urinal next to him. As Jimmy walked behind the man, he plunged the microfine needle into the guard's neck and pushed the plunger. The guard never knew what hit him. He fell backward into Jimmy's waiting arms. It was then the music started.

"Good job, Michele," he said softly, grunting against the dead weight of the security guard. "If there had been a struggle, the music would have been timed just right."

Jimmy dragged the exposed unconscious man into one of the stalls. He took the man's notepad device, locked the stall, and crawled out under the door. Moving to the mirror, he untucked his shirt, shoved the notepad into the waistband of his pants, and redid his belt to hold it secure. He then billowed the shirt over his waist. He looked a bit unkempt, but nobody would even notice a stagehand looking a little rough at the end of a successful show.

He felt the buzzing of his cell phone and pulled it from the holster on his belt. Naomi. "I can't talk now," he barked in a harsh whisper.

"I need to know how it's going."

"The show is going well," he whispered.

"Have you told her I'm your mother?"

"I still don't know that you are," Jimmy said tersely. "I have to go."

"You got the birth certificate."

"Could have been Photoshopped. I can't deal with this right now."

"Fair enough," Naomi countered. "Just tell me Michele is safe and you guys are on target to get your plane back home."

"We're fine."

"Good. When you're married, I'll be the only relative who really gives a rat's butt about these businesses."

"So that's your angle," Jimmy said with disdain.

"No angle. But here are the facts: Kim's boys had every chance to learn and lead these businesses. They didn't want to. Michael isn't doing Michele any favors leaving her hanging out to dry the way he has. She needs me, the company needs me, and you need me."

"Or do you just need me to marry Michele so you can be … what … queen mum of the company?"

Her voice grew loud and shrill. "I'll be its savior, Jimmy. Someday, when all the madness is over, you and Michele will have kids who will thank me for what I'm doing."

The song ended. They were back from commercial break. If he didn't show up soon, Michele would think something had gone wrong.

"Can you hear how silent it is on my side?" Jimmy asked tersely. "It means the commercial break is over. I need to get back to my post."

"Fine. Go do your thing, honey." The word stuck in her throat a bit. Jimmy knew she didn't love him. "But remember, I wouldn't have needed to call you if you had checked in with me."

"I feel uncomfortable reporting Michele's whereabouts to you," Jimmy said fiercely.

"You'll be *more* uncomfortable if I give her the birth certificate and confess we had a plot to take the company from her."

"But it's not true!" he exclaimed in a whispered scream.

"You're right, it's not. But you've seen how little Michele trusts me. She'll believe it in a heartbeat, and then you'll be out on the street."

"You would be too," Jimmy barked and then winced at the echo of his voice in the men's room.

"My point exactly, Jimmy. Whether you like it or not, we're a team. You can't have Michele without me having the company. Do you understand me?"

"Y-yess," Jimmy hissed into the phone.

"Good," Naomi snapped and then abruptly hung up.

Jimmy reholstered his phone as the door opened. Zack stepped in and then jumped back a bit. Clearly he hadn't expected to see anyone.

"You're Michele's boyfriend, right?" he asked as he regained his composure.

"Yes. I'm Jimmy." He extended his hand with a smile. "Although today I'm just the visiting stagehand."

Zack shook his hand briefly. "In that case, you may want to get back to the stage. They're in the closing segment now. You'll be striking set in mere moments."

"Thanks, Mr. Jolean. I'll get there right now."

He ran from the restroom to the stage. His nervous heart pounded violently in his chest. That was a close call. If Zack had come in just a few minutes earlier, he would have seen Jimmy manhandling the guard's unconscious body. If he had come in seconds earlier, he could have heard the conversation with Naomi.

Michele caught his eyes the moment he made it to the wings. Clearly she had been nervously anticipating his return. He grinned and patted his stomach. She smiled broadly. Gloria thanked her for joining the show, and then the two hugged. The director yelled, "Cut!" and the show ended.

As planned, Jimmy ran to the set as it was being struck around Michele and Gloria.

"Michele," Jimmy said gravely for the benefit of those around them. "I have this message from corporate headquarters, sounds urgent." He showed her the home screen of his iPhone.

"Darn!" Michele exclaimed.

"Trouble?" Gloria asked.

"Tax auditor questions," Michele said, shaking her head. "Jimmy, call ahead to get the plane ready. I have to be back in Castello Pietro tonight."

"Oh, Michele," Gloria said in an exaggerated whine. "I had hoped we could visit tonight."

"Me too, Gloria. But it won't happen this trip." She hugged the older lady fiercely. Gloria whispered something in her ear, bringing tears to Michele's eyes. It was the first time today Jimmy had seen their nervousness. He admired both of them. Nerves of steel!

"Come on, Jimmy," Michele said sternly. "We have to go."

"Can someone get security to help them quickly to their car?" Gloria asked. The FEMA staff was all too willing to oblige.

While they had undergone rigorous security checks to get into the facility, their VIP exit was as simple as the facility director walking them to their car. Jimmy shook the man's hand. Michele hugged him and thanked him for the opportunity to help. He complimented her generosity as the limo driver opened the door for them. Jimmy didn't take a deep breath until they were safely on the family plane. Only after turning the notepad over to Michele did he relax, and then he did so only for a second before his mind tormented him with Naomi's threats.

Once Jimmy had left the men's room, Zack went straight to the mirror to check his hair and teeth. Looking closely, he had to admit he looked great. Oh, sure, he had aged a bit, but his trademark curls and bright smile hadn't faded. As he fussed with himself in the mirror, he caught a look at the bathroom stall behind him. For a moment he thought he saw a man lying on the floor. He turned around to check. It was. He called to the man. No answer. He moved to the stall and kicked at the man's shoe. No response.

"The opportunity to make the most of a fortuitous event," he said excitedly. His heart raced as he gingerly crawled under the stall. A security guard. He was warm. Zack felt for a pulse—not dead. He moved quickly to unlock the door and immediately exited the stall.

Brushing at his suit, he stood looking at the unconscious security guard as a stream of images flooded his mind. His breath quickened and his heart raced with adrenalin. All he had to do was squeeze the man's neck a little; the possible benefits were limitless. He could steal the man's phone and wallet, and use them to frame Gloria. In one scenario, he would threaten her as she had him with information about the deaths of his parents and secretary. And in the other scenario, he could turn her over to the authorities. He grinned as he anticipated her expression when she realized how miserably wrong her little FEMA camp adventure had gone.

He put his hands around the man's neck, closed his eyes, and squeezed.

TWENTY-SIX

I t was already hot in Jerusalem even though the sun had not yet risen. Michael was up early for prayer, as was his custom. Following that, he went to the local Starbucks for three lattes: one for him, and two for the prophets at the Wailing Wall. Despite the prophets' ancient origins, steaming hot lattes always brought smiles. The two men didn't always talk with Michael. Their agenda was heavenly—no passing the time or shooting the breeze for them. Today was different. It was the third anniversary of the rapture, and Michael hoped they would talk to him, help him to see how the prophecies would unfold. From Gabe's books, he had expected global upheaval for the entire seven years of the tribulation, but the world was getting its collective act together under Isa's reign. There were no longer wars or rumors of war, just the communist dream of workers united in a common effort to thwart an imminent threat.

He placed the coffees on the ground about fifteen feet away from Moses and Elijah. Nobody got closer than that after the dramatic demise of the soldiers Isa had sent to handle them. Michael was pretty sure they wouldn't hurt him, but he wasn't going to bet his life on it.

He stood smiling as they moved to their drinks. Usually, they took the cups, offered their appreciation, and returned to the wall. Not today. The one Michael had always thought of as Elijah spoke in that same mixture of languages known to Michael. Even though he had conversed with them in the past, Michael still had to think fast to catch what they said.

"You have many questions today, Michael," Elijah said. The desert breeze blew his wild gray hair onto his weathered face as he took a first drink of coffee.

"Yes," Michael said. He approached them gingerly.

"Come, friend," Moses beckoned with a smile. He took his first drink as well.

Michael moved to within a foot of them. They sat on the pavement. He did the same.

"The Lord's timing is not our own," Moses said as if he had read Michael's mind.

"Is the account recorded in the book of Revelation accurate?" Michael asked with a wince. "My brother's writings made it seem that everything would proceed sequentially at a steady pace. Frankly, I would have thought there would be much more devastation by now."

"You are looking for devastation?" Elijah asked with a decidedly Jewish-mother intonation.

Michael grinned. "No. It's just that I envisioned it differently."

"The judgments in Revelation have a nesting effect," Moses said deliberately.

"Yes," Michael said, "the seventh-seal judgment comprises the seven trumpet judgments, and the seven bowl judgments make up the seventh trumpet judgment."

"Correct," Elijah said. "And remember that the seal judgments are general, setting the stage for the more specific trumpet and bowl judgments. This is where wisdom is required."

Michael went over the judgments in his mind. The seal judgments described the coming of the Antichrist, global conflict, food shortages, widespread death, and persecution, followed by a great earthquake and the sky unwinding like a scroll. Clearly, Isa had come. The Dark Awakening was a global conflict in which untold millions had died. There were already food shortages, and persecution was becoming a reality. If these were "setting the stage," as Elijah said, then Michael could see them at work. The sixth one was a bit different.

"The sixth seal hasn't happened yet, but it will come very shortly," Moses said.

"An earthquake and the sky rolling back on itself like a scroll," Michael said softly. And then it hit him. It was more of a waking vision than a mental image. He felt the earth move under his feet, felt a horrific blast of heat, and looked to the sky to see its origin. There an orange and gold mushroom cloud filled the horizon. "The sixth seal is nuclear conflict?"

Moses nodded gravely. "In the very near future. Our time here is almost through," Moses affirmed. "My heart aches at the thought of the tumultuous times ahead."

"Well, I guess that answers my question. The events of Revelation are all true, and they proceed in a defined pattern, just not in a rhythm we infer."

"Correct," Elijah offered. "You must be careful to distinguish Daniel's seven-year Time of Jacob's Trouble from the Great Tribulation."

"Right," Michael said, thinking aloud. "Daniel's last week is seven years, but the Great Tribulation is only three and a half years—time, times, and half a time."

"You've passed through time and times of the first half of Daniel's week," Elijah observed.

"Which means we're about half a year away from the Great Tribulation," Michael said, completing the thought.

"We will not be here for the Great Tribulation," Moses warned. "When you see us depart, you will know the end is very near."

The end. Michael still had trouble envisioning it.

Elijah said firmly, "The devastation is an act of God put in motion from the beginning of time. The dark star. Have you noticed that the bowl judgments are a repetition of the trumpet judgments?"

"Yes," Michael answered, curious.

"When the dark-star system passes through the inner solar system, it will loop around the sun, crossing Earth's orbit on its way into the solar system and on its way out. Each incursion will bring about devastation—the trumpet judgments on the way in, the bowl judgments on the way out."

"And the period of prolonged darkness?" Michael asked.

"There will be a time during its incursion that Nibiru will block the rays of the sun."

"But Revelation also says the sun will get hotter."

"Indeed it will, with great magnetic disturbances on its surface."

Michael envisioned it, saying, "Coronal mass ejections. Only Nemesis/Nibiru could cause both the darkness and the excessive heat mentioned in Revelation."

Moses commented, "Did not Lord Yeshua say it would be a time of trial unlike anyone had ever seen on Earth?"

"Yes. Yes, He did," Michael replied somberly. His mind raced with horrible images of impending doom. Yet, Jesus had also said to look up when these things occur because redemption is nigh. Michael was having a hard time balancing his emotions. He knew that he, Michele, and Gloria would be fine if they died in the oncoming onslaught. Will was another story. If Will were taken before giving his life to Christ, he would suffer throughout eternity. But how could Michael get through to Will? Maybe Elijah and Moses could offer some insight.

Michael spoke hesitantly at first. "I dread the upcoming calamity. And I'm so afraid for my nephew. How can I get him to give his life to Jesus? Do you have any advice?"

"Sometimes the hardest thing is to watch someone make the wrong choices," a voice spoke from Michael's left. He turned to see Gabe sitting beside him with a sardonic grin.

"You're a sight for sore eyes." He leaned over to hug his brother. "Please tell me you're here to help with Will. It's driving me crazy how he backs away from giving his life to Jesus."

"Sounds familiar." Gabe grinned with a slow nod.

"So, this is how crazy I drove you?"

Gabe's chest heaved with a full laugh. "You were much worse."

"There is a plan for every one of us," Elijah said. "Whether he knows it or not, Will is in God's hands, and the Lord is not about to let him go."

"I can't tell you what a relief that is," Michael said with a sigh.

"He'll be fine," Gabe said. "And if there's a bit of anxiety on your part just to show you what a pain you were to me, well, I can't say I mind." Gabe chuckled jovially, teasing as he had when they were young.

"So, Will is my penance for keeping you in a constant state of worry for my salvation?"

"Let's just call it a happy coincidence." Gabe slapped Michael's knee and grinned broadly.

Michael looked to Elijah and said, "Would it be a sin for me to hit my resurrected brother?"

Elijah grinned and took a deep drink of his coffee. *Apparently he doesn't answer rhetorical questions,* Michael mused.

"No, he doesn't," Gabe answered Michael's thought. Michael offered a sheepish grin, realizing that the witnesses were likely to have read his mind as well.

"I'm just so happy to see you, Gabe. I wish you could visit more often."

"Well, that only happens when the Lord allows it. I doubt it will happen much in the future. The raptured saints were specifically removed from earth to avoid God's wrath. We won't be allowed to visit during the last three and a half years."

Michael's breath grew short with grief. His family had only visited a few times, but just knowing they *could* visit got Michael through his days.

Gabe put an arm around his shoulder. "I know it hurts, but trust me. From an eternal perspective, the time is very short before we'll all be together. You're going to have to hold onto that, Michael." Gabe kissed his brother's cheek lightly as he dissolved into thin air.

Moses placed a hand on Michael's shoulder as the younger man wiped at tears in his eyes. It was the first time either of the witnesses had touched him. Michael could feel the raw spiritual power pulsing through him.

"Nobody said it would be easy," Moses said in his odd, multilanguage patois. At the same time another voice said the same thing in English. Michael turned to see Chris speaking. Beside him Kim smiled the loving smile that had pulled Michael through so many rough times. They both knelt to the ground and hugged him fiercely.

"Everything will be glorious for you in a very short time, sweetheart," Kim said as Michael's tears flowed freely.

"Listen to your mom," Chris said softly. "You'll find peace in Jesus through all the horror."

"Ahem." Someone coughed from about ten feet away. "If you're done, Chris, I have an introduction to make."

As Chris and Kim ended the hug with Michael, Chris said, "We're ready, Vinnie."

"Good, because patience was never my long suit." Vinnie laughed. "Michael," he called in his Hoboken brogue.

"Hi, Father Vinnie." Michael grinned.

"Hi yourself, kid." Vinnie winked. "I want to introduce you to someone." Vinnie motioned to a desperate-looking figure by the Wailing Wall. He had the gaunt leathery features of someone who had lived a long time in the outdoors. His long gray hair flew wildly in the breeze. Around his shoulders was a blanket. He looked like an Old World hermit, but he carried a certain spiritual dignity.

"Kid, this is Father Ignatius," Vinnie said.

Ignatius bowed his head slightly and smiled. Michael did the same.

Vinnie continued. "He's living in the caves underneath the City of David. Could you get him some food every once in a while—maybe even be someone he can contact if he needs help?"

"Sure," Michael said, confused. "Whatever I can do to help ..."

"Good," Kim said. "Will's well-being depends on it."

"Will's?" Michael asked incredulously.

"At his encounter with Ignatius, he'll give his life to Jesus," Chris said with a smile.

"So Will's going to be okay. What a relief!"

After a few moments of silence, a thought came to Michael. He reached into his pocket to retrieve the old photo from Kim's safe. "While I have you here, can I ask how you all were at the same picnic in the early 1960s?" he asked. They vanished without a response.

"Michael!" someone screamed from the periphery of the square. Michael looked to see Will in his festooned Swiss Guard attire striding forcefully toward him. "You're late, and Lucky is furious. He sent me to find you, and this was my first guess as to where you would be."

Moses and Elijah stood. Moses stared fiercely at Will. The power of the stare knocked Will off his feet. Recalling their fiery response to Isa's military, Michael ran to his prostrate nephew. Elijah and Moses moved to their traditional positions in front of the wall, and Ignatius fled to the shadows.

Michael helped Will to his feet. He was groggy for a few seconds, but he righted himself and entered immediately again into his tirade.

"Jake, if I know you come here every morning, then Benny and Isa know it too. You're going to get us both killed."

"We'll be fine," Michael said dismissively, relying on the revelation that Will would eventually choose Christ.

Will nodded toward the witnesses and spoke in a low voice. "At some point, these two are going to run too far afoul of the government. I don't like the idea of you associating with them."

"Thanks, Dad," Michael said sarcastically.

"I'm not acting like your parent," Will said tersely. "I'm doing my job—protecting the family and keeping you safe."

Michael conceded the issue. "Okay. Do you have any idea what Benny's impromptu meeting is all about?"

"The prototype microchip passed its clinical tests. It looks good to go."

"Great!" Michael huffed. He felt his cell phone buzz.

He received a text from Michele: "We may be in some trouble stateside. Call when you get a chance."

Michael shook his head. Tough times were around the corner.

HALF A TIME

TWENTY-SEVEN

After finishing her call with Uncle Michael, Michele paced around her office as she waited to meet with the company's legal team. She ran her hand across the whitewashed French provincial desk that had once belonged to Mimi. Her company had just received a letter from the Justice Department ordering an audit of food allegedly sold on the black market.

"Black market!" she screamed to no one as she fell onto the broad royal blue and beige plaid of the sofa. The sofa had been so inviting when she and her brother Chris used to visit Mimi in her office. She wished she could just curl up on it without a care in the world, as she had done only a few short years before.

"These were charitable donations," she said to herself in reference to the vast quantities of food she had given to the poor. She read further; they also wanted to investigate if any of the food had been given to aid and abet insurgencies, which were now defined as any group not agreeing with Kurtoglu.

Her secretary buzzed to say the legal counsel team was assembled. She burst from her office and stomped to the conference room across the hallway.

"Thanks for coming so quickly," she said as she rushed to the head of the whitewashed table dominating the room. She took a look at the group. Stephen Wainwright, head partner of a very prestigious Atlanta firm, sat with his team of professionals—experts in government affairs and masters of the stifling amount of regulations passed since Isa had come to power.

Steve briefly introduced his team and made the point that he would

279

be responsible for coordinating their activities. Michele relaxed a little. She liked Steve and really needed to soak in some of his confidence.

"How bad is something like this?" Michele asked.

"It's never good to be the subject of a DOJ investigation," Steve said with a sigh. "But on the other hand, you'd be surprised how many investigations result in no charges or only small fines."

"That sounds promising," Michele said hopefully.

"It is, but there is still a stigma attached to being under investigation. You may find suppliers, distributors, and banks casting a wary eye at their business with you until the investigation is completed."

The door to the conference room burst open. Naomi flew to the nearest open seat, saying excitedly, "I came as soon as I heard. Sorry I'm late."

Michele offered a fake smile. *It's impossible to be late to a meeting to which you weren't invited.* She wanted to tell Naomi to mind her place, but there was no reason to alienate a powerful ally.

"We just got started, Naomi," Michele said graciously. "Let me catch you up. The DOJ is investigating us for the sale of food on the black market and supplying food to enemies of the state, thereby aiding and abetting them. Steve just told us these investigations often result in no charges or small fines, but our reputation may become a bit sullied."

"Excellent summary." Steve smiled. "The reputation risk, however, isn't only to your industrial relationships. An investigation by the DOJ will likely incite other agencies to take a harder look at you. Expect to hear from the IRS, the EPA, and OSHA."

"Ouch! What about financial institutions?" Michele asked warily.

"Generally your banks will be reluctant to term out any debt. They'll want to keep you in a short-term position until the investigation ends. In the old days that could have cost you a lot, but since Mr. Kurtoglu's announcement of Nemesis, the long-term markets have dried up."

"He's right," Naomi said glumly. "Even before this DOJ matter, the farthest out I could place debt was three years. Nobody is lending for the long term."

"That having been said," Steve continued, "expect your borrowing costs to go up. A significant contingency hangs over your heads. Your debt rating just took a beating. Trust me."

"Great!" Naomi exclaimed. She pulled down her glasses to look over them with a firm stare at Michele.

"Push the glasses back, Naomi. I'm in no mood," Michele said tersely. The older woman bristled as she returned her glasses to their place.

Steve continued. "I need to get my arms around the facts in order to determine how next to proceed. My DOJ contact said the government found pallets of your food products in hideouts of Christian militia groups. Have you been supplying them with food?"

Naomi nodded in silence.

Michele answered. "I've never dealt with a militia group because there aren't any. These were fathers, mothers, and children ostracized from society for their belief in Jesus."

"Let me put all my cards on the table," Steve said sternly. "I happen to think Isa Kurtoglu is a godsend to a forlorn world. He's our only hope, and all he asks is that we live in harmony. There is no place for religious separatism in the new world as far as I'm concerned. I'm still willing to represent you, but I'm not here to listen to your opinions. Understood?"

"Yes," Michele said briskly as Naomi grinned. Michele put her head in her hands for a few seconds. She needed to think. She would love to fire this guy on the spot, but she needed representation and he was the best. She looked into Steve's eyes. "I understand."

"Good," Steve said tersely. "I'll take it as a given you've committed the infractions listed. Is there anything about the fact pattern we can use to help your case? When the investigators see your records, I assume everything will come to light."

Michele's face softened as she saw a ray of hope. "They won't see anything in our records other than sales of food at a discount to a Vatican relief company."

"That's intriguing," Steve said, jotting down some notes. "So, you sold the products to a Vatican-controlled charitable organization ..."

"Sort of. The company sold the goods at a slight markup to a company I own that is registered in the Vatican. The DOJ won't have access to the products' destinations because all shipping happened through the Vatican agency."

"Did you ship through the US Postal Service?"

"No. With Vatican-owned eighteen-wheelers."

"So, from a US perspective, all the company did was sell at a slight markup to a Vatican-registered charitable organization."

"Correct."

"That ought to add a little wrinkle to their investigation," Steve said with a smile as he jotted down some notes.

"Yes," Michele continued. "I understand Vatican records were destroyed in great numbers during the Dark Awakening. Their focus is forward these days, with little regard to Vatican improprieties of the past. All of that is to say that the Vatican has precious little time for investigations into its actions."

"Convenient," Steve said with a broad grin and a roll of his eyes. "Let me ask you this: will we be able to rely on some political pressure from Pope Peter if the DOJ tries to gain access to Vatican records?"

Michele drew a deep breath. There was no speaking for what Benny might do. "Pope Peter is extremely busy, as you can imagine. My uncle Michael is his camerlengo. I doubt any document request would make it past him."

Steve grinned broadly. "Excellent fact pattern, Miss Martin. If you're going to fight the system, at least you covered your tracks—most ingeniously, I might add."

For the first time in the meeting, Michele relaxed in her chair. "Obviously I'll alert Uncle Michael to be on the lookout for anything from the DOJ."

"Of course you will!" Steve laughed. "Given the coming Nemesis event, we only need to stall for time. This wrinkle should put their investigation on hold for a few years."

Naomi slammed her hand to the conference table. "So we're supposed to live with the business and reputation disruptions for a few years? Seriously, Michele, wouldn't it be better for everyone if you just admitted to the wrongdoing and paid a fine?"

"It's not always that simple," Steve countered. "The penalties could also involve jail time for any of the company's officers found to be complicit."

"What if the company was only following Michele's orders?" Naomi asked, ignoring the hard stare from Michele.

"The 'I was just following orders' defense died at the Nuremburg trials," Steve said sternly. Michele thought he looked as annoyed as she was by Naomi's outburst.

Naomi softened her tone. "I see," she said in almost a whisper. "Well, given the gravity of the situation, I guess we'll have to play the Vatican card."

"Amazing how quickly she comes to heel," Steve whispered to Michele.

Michele nodded ever so slightly. "We are agreed that the DOJ will find nothing but shipments to a Vatican company, right?" she asked. The lawyers agreed, but Naomi remained silent. "Right, Naomi?"

"Yes. Of course, Michele," Naomi said remorsefully. "I didn't mean to look like I was throwing you under the bus. I was just trying to explore all avenues for the good of the company."

"For the good of the company," Michele repeated, "will you follow the game plan we just laid out?"

"Yes," Naomi said gravely.

It had never felt so good to be home. Michele went straight to the family area at the back of the mansion. To her surprise, she found Jimmy cooking dinner. The smell of homemade macaroni and cheese filled the air. He had been away finalizing the conversion of former orphanages to fake FEMA centers. She hadn't expected to see him until the weekend.

"You look like you've been through the mill," he said when he saw her.

She threw herself into a kitchen chair, tossing her briefcase onto the table. "The DOJ has initiated an investigation of our food company. They say they found our products at Christian militia hideouts." She rubbed at her temples to relieve the stress.

Jimmy came behind her and rubbed her shoulders. "That sounds pretty scary."

She moaned with pleasure, noting how she thrilled to his touch. She didn't know what she would have done these past few years without Jimmy's calming presence. "Well, the lawyers are on top of it. From the company's perspective, there is only a record of sales to Vatco, the dummy Vatican-registered company Uncle Michael and I set up to distribute the goods. The DOJ would have to petition the Vatican to see into Vatco's records. That should stall them for a while—and let's face it, we're three years into the tribulation. It should be pretty easy to stall legally throughout the remainder. Start to finish, corporate investigations can take years."

Jimmy bent to kiss her cheek. "Well, there you have it. It's not so bad."

Something in his voice caused her to turn to face him. He looked uncharacteristically nervous. "Michele," he said earnestly and softly as he looked deeply into her eyes, "I've been thinking about this for a long time. We love each other. I don't want to be without you in my life." He fell to one knee and pulled a diamond ring from his pocket. "We may not have much time together, but I want to spend it as man and wife."

She looked at the ring in disbelief. She had never even been on a real date in her life. True enough, Jimmy had been a constant source of comfort to her since the rapture, but marriage? She had put it out of her mind, focusing only on surviving to the end of the tribulation.

Jimmy looked crestfallen with her silence. "What are you thinking?" he asked softly.

"I ... I had pretty much locked away any thoughts of dating or marriage because of the times we face."

"Let's face them together, as man and wife."

"You mean 'woman and husband,'" she joked.

He held her hand. "Michele, don't brush this off with humor. I'm dying here while waiting for a response." He grinned awkwardly, tears in his eyes.

She was overwhelmed. Her mind was so geared to disaster that she hadn't left any room for happiness. Maybe she had been too short-sighted. Here before her was a man she had loved for years who was declaring his love for her. A smile broadened on her face as she looked past his long lashes to his hazel eyes. "Yes, I'll marry you!"

Jumping up from his knee, he pulled her from her chair and swept her into his strong arms. They kissed deeply. His mouth tasted sweet. For that moment she wanted nothing more than to spend the rest of her life with him.

She pulled away. "In the old days I would have wanted a large dream wedding. But now I want something small, just family and a few friends in the chapel."

"Whatever you want is fine with me," he said, not able to contain his grin.

"And I want to do it as soon as possible, while there's still some peace in the world."

"I'd do it right now!" Jimmy exclaimed.

"Well, we have to get Uncle Michael and Will back here, and I'd want Gloria to be my matron of honor."

Jimmy's dark brow furrowed. "If I were to choose anybody in my life to be my best man, it would be your dad. He was literally the best man I ever knew. Do you think Will would be my best man, kind of in honor of your dad?"

"I can't speak for Will, but I don't know of any reason he wouldn't. In fact, I think it would be a great way to make him feel even closer to the family."

Jimmy moved to the stove to plate the macaroni and cheese. "I'm so excited to be planning this! How soon do you think Michael could get here?"

"Well, there's always Uncle Benny to consider. He'll probably give Uncle Michael a rough time about leaving."

"So, let's invite your Uncle Benny too."

Michele grinned mischievously. "I'm sure Pope Pompous wouldn't be caught dead at my wedding, but inviting him isn't a bad idea. He can get his jollies by withholding his presence instead of withholding Uncle Michael's."

"Your uncle Benny is bossy and annoying, but do you think he's as bad as all that?"

"Worse. My parents shielded Chris and me from the truth when we were younger, but now that I've got the full story, it's easy for me to believe he's the False Prophet of Revelation."

"Do I really want to marry into this family?" Jimmy teased.

She laughed. "I'm not so sure. All the more reason to do this quickly, before you get cold feet."

"Not going to happen," he said as he placed the plates on the table.

Michele's phone buzzed. "If this is the office, they're just going to have to wait." Looking at her phone, she said, "Oops, it's the matron-of-honor-to-be. I can't wait to tell her the news!"

"Put her on speakerphone. We'll tell her together," Jimmy said gleefully.

"Hello, Gloria!" they chimed like bells.

"Uh. Hi. Is this Michele?" Gloria asked tentatively. For the first time, Michele noticed she was calling on the quantum-scrambled line. This was definitely a business call.

"Yes … and Jimmy," Michele answered soberly, in response to Gloria's tone of voice.

"Have you two seen the news?"

"No," Michele said with knit eyebrows. "What's going on?"

Jimmy moved to turn on the kitchen's television and stood dazed at the report. "Oh God! No!" he wailed.

"What's going on?" Michele asked, joining him at the television. The news was reporting that a security guard had been found dead in the restroom of the FEMA camp they had visited.

"A security guard was killed at the FEMA camp," Gloria said. "They found him in the men's room."

"Michele, Gloria," Jimmy yelled with a beet-red face. "That's the guy I drugged. Could I have killed him?"

"Not unless you strangled him," Gloria said sharply. "The man was found with ligature marks around his neck."

"I did nothing of the kind!" Jimmy exclaimed. "I gave him the sedative like we planned."

"Then I'm thinking our unscheduled guest was the culprit," Gloria said with disdain.

"Zack?" Jimmy asked in disbelief.

Michele took up the conversation. "Gloria, do you *really* think Zack is capable of murder?"

"Let's just say it wouldn't be his first," Gloria said dismally.

"Gloria, are you in danger?" Michele demanded. The thought of living with a murderer ran a chill up her spine.

"I have him over a barrel right now," Gloria said. "I have the evidence hidden in a safe place with instructions to go to the press if anything happens to me. Trust me, Zack may not love me, but he loves his fame and his half-baked ministry."

"Still," Jimmy said, "that doesn't sound too healthy. Can't you leave him?"

"For now, at least, I need to reach as many people as I can with my show, but the time will come when I have to bail out of this relationship."

Michele sighed. "I'm so sorry for you, Gloria. I almost hate to bring up the subject, but time is so short these days. Jimmy and I are getting married!"

"Oh, Michele, I'm so happy for you both!" Gloria squealed. "I really need some good news right now."

"I know!" Michele squealed along.

"Thanks," Jimmy said happily.

"I nearly gave him a heart attack earlier," Michele said with a laugh. "I wanted to say yes, but I said nothing. I hadn't allowed myself to think I could be happy."

"Don't do that to yourself," Gloria chided. "Even though times will get tough, it's a tremendous blessing to have a man like Jimmy to love. Let's thank God together."

After a short prayer of thanksgiving, Gloria agreed to assume the duties of matron of honor. When the call ended, Jimmy and Michele finished their dinner in the content satisfaction of the newly engaged.

As they cleaned up the table, the rhapsody of engagement left Jimmy's face. "I can't help but feel guilty about the security guard. With the sedative I gave him, he would have had no chance to defend himself against his attacker."

"You mean Zack."

Jimmy let out a long sigh and said, "Gloria's in an unhappy marriage. That might influence her thoughts on the matter. Face it; that camp is a glorified prison. For all we know, one of the inmates decided to take revenge on the guy."

She answered with a question. "Did I ever tell you Zack is friends with my uncle Benny?"

"Does that make him a murderer?"

"No, but birds of a feather and all."

Jimmy looked at her in astonishment. "Do you mean to tell me your uncle Benny is a murderer?"

"Well, it's not like I have proof or anything. But Uncle Michael suspects he tried to hire a couple of guys to kill him and my father while they were in college."

"What?" Jimmy screamed in disbelief.

Michele chuckled at his reaction—and the fact that something so horrible had become a sort of benign family lore. "Well, you should know what you're getting into," she teased.

"Then again, you're not Benny's blood relative, right?"

"No. He's Michael's uncle on his mother's side. Michael is my uncle on his dad's side."

"Speaking of Michael, it will soon be too late in Jerusalem to call him. Why don't you tell him the good news while I finish cleaning the kitchen."

"You are going to make me a good wife," she said with a wink and a smile. She pecked his cheek and left to call Michael.

Jimmy's cell phone rang. He grimaced as he looked at the caller ID. Snatching at the phone, he answered it. "I told you not to call me here," he said tersely.

"Nice way to treat your good old mom," Naomi said sternly. "Did you ask her?"

"Yes I did, but not because it's something on your agenda. I asked her because I love her and because her family is the only family I've ever known."

"I really couldn't care less about your motives. And your 'little boy lost' routine doesn't move me. Whether you know it or not, I'm doing this as much for you as I am for me."

"Tell me again. You have no plans to hurt Michele, right?"

"Hurt her? What do you take me for? I want to help her. I just want things at work to get uncomfortable enough that she'll prefer to be at home with her new husband. As a loving member of the family, I'll take the helm of this company before she destroys it completely."

TWENTY-EIGHT

Gloria watched the news coverage with her hand over her mouth. In her heart she knew that Zack had committed the murder. But why? What would he have to gain from it? She knew him well after all these years. He wasn't the type to kill for the thrill of it. The big motivator in Zack's life was and always had been greed.

The news story highlighted that the murder was discovered shortly after Gloria's live program from the facility. What a nightmare! She turned to her iPad to check online sources. She entered her own name in the search engine and went straight to the news tab. Skimming over the articles, she saw standard AP coverage of the murder—nothing different from what she had seen on the news broadcast. Then her eye fell upon a post of related items. After clicking on it, she read a brief article about government raids on Christian militia groups accused of planning subversive activity across America. All baloney, of course. These were just moms and pops whose world had been pulled out from under them by Isa's corrupt government.

A small sentence at the end of the article—a throwaway comment—caught her eye. Computers retrieved by the police revealed frequent log-ins to Gloria's website as a common denominator among those arrested. The article was quick to assert that she was not considered part of any militant plans. Zack separated their mailing lists. She was willing to bet that the arrested people were members of her mailing list but were not also on Zack's list. So he had found a way to beat her in the ratings after all.

She tossed the iPad to the coffee table in front of her. "Oh, Lord," she prayed, "I don't know how long I can live with this horrible man.

Please give me the strength to carry on, and the understanding to leave when the time is right." She cried at the thought of families taken from their homes to the camps. Little boys and girls born after the rapture would celebrate Christmas in a FEMA barracks. "Zack, how could you?" she called to the empty room.

"Don't look at it like you set them up for disaster," her father's voice spoke from her left.

"Dad's right, sweetheart. You didn't cause this; you prepared them for the inevitable." Her mother spoke from her right.

She turned to each of them. They came together and hugged. Her mother looked so beautiful and young, her hair glistening as if made of light. Then she turned to her dad, to that angelic face she had dreamt of so often as a little girl. He reached out and gently wiped a tear from her eye.

"Sweetheart," Fran said softly, "we're allowed this one last time to see you before the Lord's wrath is poured out on earth."

"We want to encourage you to be strong," Tom said with a grin uncharacteristic of the grim news he bore. "Look past the bad days to the Lord's return, pumpkin. Then we'll be together with Him forever."

"Dad's right, honey," Fran continued. "Don't take your eyes off the prize. And don't doubt yourself. It's a horror that these people have been taken to the camps, but your message awakened in them a love for Jesus. He'll be with them in a way they had never known. Hold onto that thought."

Gloria sat with her parents in silence, just feeling the healing touch that can only come from a mom and dad. She was mentally exhausted from the constant mind games with Zack. Gradually she fell asleep in their arms and didn't awaken until she heard Zack come home.

"Zack?" she called to him.

He didn't answer.

She rose from the couch and found him in the kitchen pouring a glass of lemonade.

"Zack, have you seen the news?"

"What news, darlin'?" he asked with an arrogant grin. He knew exactly what she was talking about. His cat-who-ate-the-canary grin confirmed her suspicions.

"You know what news," she said indignantly. "A FEMA guard was murdered. They found him after our broadcast there."

"You don't say," he commented before taking a long drink of the lemonade.

She ignored his arrogant reply.

"Why did you do it, Zack? And while we're at it, can you tell me why the government is rounding up Christians who just happen to be on my mailing list?"

He said with a smug grin, "Now that you mention it, that would explain your show's sudden drop in viewership. Your ratings took a nosedive over the last couple of days." He pulled out his cell phone to show her a downloaded line chart depicting the serious dip in her ratings.

"Zack!" she screamed. "I don't care about the ratings. I care about innocent people being carted off to a camp somewhere."

"Well, that's where we're different, Gloria. I *always* care about ratings. And you should too. My ratings have allowed you to live a life of splendor."

"Do you think I care about *any* of this, Zack?" she screamed as she waved her arms about the ridiculously ornate mansion.

"Well, maybe you'll care about this," he said, pulling from his breast pocket a cell phone in a plastic bag. He waved it in her face.

"What's that?" she asked, leery of his exuberance.

"The dead man's phone, and let me assure you that only your prints are on it. Same with his wallet. Can you imagine my ratings when I tearfully explain—" he screwed his face into a mask of torment and grief and spoke in the mock anguish he would use on his show—"I ... I found them in Gloria's purse. Being a loyal citizen, I had no choice but to turn them over to the authorities. Ladies and gentlemen, there's no easy way to say it. My lovely wife was radicalized by the Christian right." He wiped his face and drew a huge sigh. He frowned as if it would be nearly impossible for him to continue, and then he swallowed hard with resolve. "The love of my life has been seduced by the remnant clinging to their belief that God and guns will solve everything. Somehow they convinced the most loving, caring person I have ever met to commit a senseless murder in the furtherance of their cause."

Gloria stared at him with a deadpan expression, slowly applauding.

"What a wonderful performance, Zack. You mean to tell me you committed murder to get one up on me?" she asked with blistering disdain.

His face contorted in anger. "You don't know what you bit off when you threatened me with that flash drive. You can't beat me at my own game, missy!"

Her first instinct was to be afraid of him. She hated it when he went over the edge. But this time something was different. If he killed her, then fine. She'd be in heaven with the Lord. Like her father and mother said, there would be pain, but then the glory would come. "You pathetic little man!" she mocked. "You couldn't stand that I had the goods on you, so you committed murder to turn the tables. You're psychotic, Zack!"

He crossed his arms in front of his body. He said nothing and stared savagely at her, clearly trying to make her back down.

She got in his face. "At best you've only made us even, Zack. I can assure you of an explosive exposé of your lifetime of crimes before you even have the chance to give that performance."

He sneered. "For now. But as your audience slowly dwindles, your ability to command respect will diminish as well. I have no problem playing this game for a long-term win, Gloria."

She grew furious at that smug face. She wanted to reach out and choke him, but she quickly corrected herself. She had to maintain control, both because it was the right thing to do and because he was baiting her. She had no intention to give him what he wanted. She spoke calmly, as if finding a teachable moment with a child. "Zack, you hurt all those people to get back at me. And you not only put *me* on the chopping block. Michele's company is under a DOJ investigation for products found with those Christians. How could you do that?"

He laughed heartily. "Really? This day keeps getting better and better."

"You have nothing against that poor girl." She stood nose-to-nose with him.

"But I hated her father, Gloria. Hated him and his ridiculous brother! You'll never know how much you hurt me and our marriage by your fascination with Michael."

Her first reaction was to tell him what a crock that tale was, but she had learned a lot over the years. You can't hope to deal with an insane person sanely. Zack clearly wanted to shift blame for all their troubles onto Gloria. She could get out of this confrontation and buy some time if she followed his lead.

"Oh, Zack," she said softly, as if suddenly hurt and introspective. "There was never anything real with Michael, not even a dalliance. I was attracted to him, but I never, ever wanted to violate my vows to you. I love you, Zack. I always have."

He put his hands over his face and sighed. She could actually see him pushing his eyes to form tears! She wondered if he had ever really been honest with her. It didn't matter. What mattered was that she was now onto his schemes, and she had every intention to use them against him. She tenderly pulled his hands from his face and gently wiped at the tear he managed to press from his eye.

Looking deeply into his eyes, she said, "It's okay, Zack. It's always been okay with us. I never wanted to be anywhere but by your side."

"And you're not mad at me for turning over your mailing list?" he asked suspiciously.

Still looking into his eyes, she shook her head and said, "I'm concerned for those people, and I think Michele is a nice kid, but none of that means I'm not on your side. I take our wedding vows seriously." She held his hands in hers as she pondered how incredibly sincere she sounded. If he held true to character, he would soon be too taken with his skills of manipulation to be angry. All he would feel was pride.

"For the record," he said with a half smile, "I always want to be by your side as well, and I'm sorry that jealousy led me to some bad decisions. But I only did these things because I love you, darlin'."

"Oh, sweetheart," she fairly sang as she wrapped herself around him in a hug. Makeup sex shortly ensued. She felt dirty and whorish for pretending to enjoy intimacy with him, but it was the price she needed to pay to keep him calm for a while longer.

Lying in bed afterward, she said with a smile, "Michele is getting married. It will be a quick wedding, probably within the next couple of months. She's asked me to be her matron of honor. I'm sure you'll be invited as well."

Stroking her shoulder, he said, "I have so much work to do. We're already starting to rehearse for Riverside's Winterfest Holiday Spectacular."

"I guess it's only a few months away now," she said thoughtfully. "Time is just flying by," she lied.

"Yeah. It seems like just a couple of weeks ago we were cleaning up from last year's Holiday Spectacular."

She got out of bed, put on a robe, and checked her phone. There was a message from Michele. She went to her office and shut the door before returning the call.

"Michele, it's Gloria."

"Hi," she sang into the phone like a girl in love. "I talked with Uncle Michael. Plans are crazy in Jerusalem. Isa is demanding the temple be completed in time for Hanukkah. Not so much stress for the Jews. The Temple Institute has had plans for years, but there are daily disagreements with Muslims at the new Dome of the Rock, and Benny is adamant that the new St. Peter's Basilica be completed as well. Because Uncle Michael is so well versed in the different languages and cultures, he has been the one brokering peaceful coexistence. He sounds beat up."

"Poor thing. There are times when I feel like I have it bad with Zack, but your uncle Michael is in the thick of it, and under Benny's thumb to boot."

"Well, the good thing is that there's a lull in the schedule. All parties have agreed to stop construction to honor the Eid al-Fitr celebration at the end of Ramadan. It will be a perfect time for Uncle Michael and Will to get away. Do you think we can pull off a wedding in early December?"

"I don't know, sweetie. There's a lot to do."

"I've been going through some things here. Amazingly, I fit perfectly into Mom's wedding dress, and I found the candelabras used in Mom and Dad's wedding."

Gloria remembered the event well. The wedding was simple, elegant, and intimate. "That's great, Michele! It doesn't leave much planning. A tux for Jimmy and a lovely meal should round out the ceremony."

"True enough. And because I have Vatican citizenship and Uncle Michael will perform the wedding, the legalities can be handled by a stroke of his pen. The meal may be a bit tougher. I'm not as good as my grandmother at planning or executing a party, but I was thinking my matron of honor has lots of experience."

"Say no more. It will be my pleasure. I'll come out there the week before the wedding to make sure everything goes off without a hitch. Oh, honey, I know you really wish Mom and Mimi could be there for you, but I promise you, I'll do for you like you were my own daughter."

A stifled catch in Michele's throat told Gloria her offer had been warmly accepted. Gloria continued past the brief moment of silence. "What about colors? Thanks to the television shows, I have gowns in most colors."

"I was hoping to stay with blue and white, like my mom."

"I have the perfect dress." Gloria felt her spirits lifting. "With everything else that's going on, my heart is just singing with the opportunity to have something to celebrate!"

"Speaking of which," Michele ventured, "Uncle Benny was kind enough to decline the invitation. This is awkward, but I was wondering—"

Gloria cut her off. "Zack won't be attending."

Michele sighed with relief. "So it will be just you, Uncle Michael, and Will. It should be a very loving environment."

"Who is Jimmy's best man?"

"He chose Will, and I couldn't be happier."

"That's just lovely," Gloria said.

They chatted a bit longer.

Before closing, Michele said, "Oh, before I forget, Uncle Michael broke the coding in the guard's work pad. It wasn't easy. He could only find one of his original programmers. The others have all vanished."

"Vanishing isn't such a strange occurrence in the Kurtoglu regime," Gloria offered. "More to the point though, honey, given the recent publicity, do we dare use the hacked information?"

"The way I see it, we have no choice if we want to save Christians. Jimmy's already combing through the data to make sure our camps have the correct digital profile. Besides, the programmer already put our orphanage addresses into the FEMA database. As far as the government knows, we're live already."

"I understand we have to do it, but the risk profile just jumped tremendously thanks to Zack's actions. He has the guard's cell phone and wallet, and he has found a way to transfer my prints to them. He's threatening to turn them over to the authorities."

"Oh, that's terrible!" Michele shrieked.

"I think I convinced him of my love for him. In his mind, he put me back to subservience with the threat. At some point, though, I may have to go into hiding."

"If it comes to that, Gloria, Mimi built some secret places on the estate. Come here if the chips fall."

"Thanks, honey," Gloria said sadly.

Giacomo Stuarti walked down the quiet early-morning streets of Rome toward the Vatican. He was the last of the old guard of programmers at the Vatican's science facility. The new guys were okay, but he missed the fellows he had started with. All had been transferred to other locations.

Giacomo told himself it was normal, but he had never worked somewhere that transferred employees with no advance notice. One day his friends were there; the next they were gone, with no good-bye parties, no handshakes or good wishes, and no time to clean out their cubicles. Who was he kidding? There was something very strange about it all. If only he had clearer recollections of his work! He apparently did a good job, but for the life of him, he could never remember the projects he worked on. Neither could his friends. They had spoken of it often, figuring that some sort of trick wiped their memories each day when they left the facility—Vatican security and all. It didn't bother him much until his friends disappeared one by one. Whatever happened to them, Giacomo was pretty sure they hadn't been unceremoniously transferred as claimed.

Maybe the Lady and her people had abducted his friends. The world seemed to think she was a godsend, but Giacomo had a near-panic reaction every time he saw a photo of her, and photos of her were everywhere. Every corner had a billboard photo of Kurtoglu and the Lady with an exhortation: Prepare; Work Will Bring Freedom; Don't Give into Your Fears; Follow Us to a Glorious Future.

He was brought back to reality when a man in a black suit crowded him on the empty sidewalk. The man pulled a Taser from his pocket and fired. The man's face was the last thing Giacomo saw before losing consciousness.

TWENTY-NINE

The plane to the States was nothing short of luxurious. With the world's resources diverted to the impending threat, travel was dramatically restricted for rank-and-file citizens. The elite took no time to commandeer the unused aircraft and retrofit them into flying palaces. The plane Will rode now with Michael had been a 747 commercial jet redone to include two large bedrooms, a full dining room, an expansive galley, and a modified gym. It was, in a word, crazy, and it was just more fuel for Will's growing hatred toward Isa Kurtoglu. Will's position gave him incredible access to the real world behind the Kurtoglu myth. He presented himself as an altruistic hero with unique genetic qualifications to save the world. Behind the scenes, though, he was petty, demanding, spiteful, and, in Will's estimation, incapable of love.

"Will, it's dinner time," Michael called in a mock singsong voice from the dining room as the cabin steward came to get him. This particular aviation atrocity flew under the banner of the Vatican. Benny didn't believe in stewardesses, only stewards in tight-fitting clothes. Will followed the perfectly coifed Hollywood heartthrob wannabe to the dining room.

"What are you serving today?" Will asked as he took his seat.

"We'll start with a light lobster salad. For your entrée, I have chateaubriand and roasted root vegetables. Dessert will be Italian cream cake."

"Sounds ... luxurious," Will said with a grimace.

Michael laughed. "I know it's grossly exorbitant, Will, but it's one of the many things we have to deal with in the new world. I don't like that Benny and Isa have stolen from people all over the world either, but there's no other air travel available. I say we relax and enjoy it."

Will slouched in his seat and crossed his arms as the steward poured his wine, no doubt an outrageously expensive vintage. When the steward left the room, Will continued the discussion. "You're probably right, Jake. I just hate to be a part of it—and I wouldn't be if we had just allowed those bedouins to kill Lucky." He used the alias under which he had met Benny just in case the steward's ears were as big as his biceps.

Michael shook his head. "We've had this discussion before. This has all taken place already in the mind of God. He doesn't see past, present, or future. By virtue of the fact it was given as prophecy in the Bible, it has already happened. Whether you like it or not, Lucky is destined to a certain role. Neither of us can change it."

Silence ensued as the steward served the first course, lobster mango salad. Will tasted it. Delicious. When they were again alone, he spoke. "But, Jake, we have to fight it. We can't give in."

"We can't win against this regime, but we can refuse to give in to evil, Will. Our job is to survive this and help as many Christians as we can until the Lord returns."

Will wiped his hands across his face. There had to be more that could be done. The current conditions were political as well as spiritual. "There has to be a political game plan as well."

"Like what?" Michael demanded. "There are no elections. You can't vote him out of office. And have you taken a look around the world? People have bought into his lies. No one could get the critical mass to stage a successful insurrection."

Will sighed. Something could be done, but certainly not something he could discuss with Michael, or anybody for that matter.

Michael's tone softened. "Look, buddy, I understand your frustration. I understand your anger. But I also understand that the only way to deal with it is to give it over to Jesus."

"This can't be prayed away, Jake," Will said resolutely.

"Of course it can't. It's God's will."

"So many people are being hurt by this. If this is God's will, then maybe I don't want to be God's Will."

Michael dropped his fork in frustration. "We are fast approaching a time when there will be no middle ground, Will. At some point, you are going to have to choose Jesus or Isa as your savior. And you know as well as I do that Isa isn't the way to go!"

The steward brought the steak, giving Will the time to ponder Michael's words. True enough, he could never look to Isa as a savior. If it came down to a choice, he would follow Jesus. In fact, he believed full well that Jesus was the Messiah. He just didn't understand how to give his life to Him. Life had made Will fiercely independent at a very young age. He was fearless about most things. Most things. His singular overriding fear was of not being in control. For years, he and only he controlled his life. It was hard enough to get used to being part of a family. He didn't see how he could ever cede control of his mind and heart to anyone, even Jesus. That's why he hadn't made the commitment to Him, why he had never married, why he had never even entertained the notion of becoming a father.

The steward left. Michael tasted his steak before continuing, "The circumstances of your life have hardened your heart, Will. I see how difficult it is for you to trust people."

Will took a bite of his meat. It melted in his mouth, undoubtedly Wagyu. He followed it with a drink of wine. "I admit it. I'm pretty closed off. It takes a lot for me even to yield to our family."

"I know. I see it, and it makes me sad for you."

"If you ever pray for me, Uncle Michael, pray that I can overcome it."

"If? I pray for you all the time!"

Will smiled.

Michael continued, "I pray that He overcomes it. It will be the power of the Holy Spirit working in your heart that will soften it."

"Well, maybe you could pray extra hard for me this weekend," Will said with an awkward scowl. "There's something about Jimmy I don't trust."

"What are you saying?" Michael asked gravely.

"I have no facts to base it on. Just a feeling. I don't know what it is. One thing is for sure, I feel awkward being his best man."

Michael answered, accentuating his comment with a wave of his steak knife. Will mused that too much time in Italy had left him talking with his hands. "Don't read too much into that. It *should* feel odd that he chose you as his best man. You don't know each other very well."

"Exactly. It's like he doesn't have any friends, or like he is desperate to please Michele. Either way, it indicates something lacking in his character, if you ask my opinion."

Michael chuckled. "For the record, I didn't ask your opinion," he said with a half grin and the wave of another knife as he buttered his roll. "But maybe I can enlighten it a bit. Jimmy loved your father as his own. He told Michele he asked you to honor the memory of your dad. No character fault, just a loving gesture."

Will whistled softly. "Wow, I really misjudged that one!" He let out a sigh of relief. At least the oddness of being best man now made sense. But the underlying distrust of Jimmy hadn't abated.

"The question you have to ask yourself, buddy, is whether you have misjudged other situations as well. You tend to be suspicious of people who get too close."

"I don't feel suspicious of you or Michele," Will countered.

"Your father touched your heart in visions, making you more open to us."

"But I'm not all that fond of Lucky," Will continued with a sly grin.

"That just shows you have a head on your shoulders. Benny's been on pretty good behavior since Mom scared the hell out of him, but you never know when he'll turn on us. The last time I saw your father and Chris, they said they wouldn't be able to visit us much longer. Benny's fear will wane, and with it his kindness."

"When do you think that will be?" Will asked.

"Soon enough. We're coming on the midway point of the tribulation. Soon all hell could break loose."

"That sounds ominous. Do you expect anything in particular?"

"At some point, Isa will declare himself to be God. I think that's the reason behind the push to get everything finished on the Temple Mount."

Just the mention of the Temple Mount brought stress to Will as his mind ran through continuous security checklists for the opening ceremonies. "What a fiasco that's going to be! At least there'll be no guns. Isa's soldiers went door to door throughout Jerusalem searching for guns not turned in when the government outlawed them. When they found a gun, there was no time for explanations or excuses. Every member of the household was summarily executed and the home razed. There won't be a firearm in all of Jerusalem by the time the festivities begin."

Michael sighed at the carnage. "What about someone smuggling one in?" he asked.

"Access to the city will be tightly controlled. Every person will be thoroughly searched. Nobody will get near the Temple Mount without passing through tight security checks."

"Sounds like Isa reads the Bible," Michael muttered, almost to himself.

Will quizzed him. "What's going on in that mind of yours, Uncle Michael?"

"In Revelation, it implies that the Antichrist will die of a head wound. I always imagined it would be from a rifle—like the JFK assassination all over again."

Will left most of his apprehensions at the door to the family estate. He warmly hugged Michele, and Jimmy treated him like he was made of gold. Over lunch in the family kitchen, Jimmy told him of his desire to honor Will's father in his selection of best man. They spoke for a while about Gabe, and it seemed as if he came alive to Will in the stories Michele and Jimmy told. He had missed out on a lot. Gabe appeared to have been a great dad.

Throughout the conversation, Michael sat quietly with Gloria. To Will they looked tired and sad, as if the impending ugliness had already come upon them. Michael paid attention to every word said, though. Just as Will began to feel sad at never having known his father, Michael slapped his shoulder lightly and said, "He's so proud of you, Will. I know Gabe better than I know anyone. If he even had an inkling you were around, he would have found you at any cost."

As if she just realized he could feel that way, Michele added her assurances. "Uncle Michael's right. What's more, I can tell you that Chris and I would have loved a big brother."

"What about your mom?" Will asked tentatively, thinking of the many photos of Tina around the house.

Michael whistled through his teeth for a second as he thought about it.

"She would have been fine in the long run," Michele said. "And any hesitance would have had nothing to do with you. It's just that she tried to shield Chris and me from my father's rough past."

Gloria moved close to Will and kissed his cheek. "She would have fallen in love with you, Will. I never met anyone more motherly. I never met anyone more concerned about orphans."

"Not to mention the fact that you look so much like your father." Michael grinned. "Tina was a pushover for your kind of oafish good looks."

"Oafish?" Will couldn't contain a grin.

"Considering the Swiss Guard uniforms," Michele said devilishly, "I would have gone with the word *clownish*."

"Tough crowd." Will laughed. Picking up his dishes, he moved to the dishwasher and said, "Lucky didn't do us any favors giving us a scant two days for the wedding. It's already bedtime in Jerusalem, and we have a few hours until the ceremony. I'm going to shoot for a quick nap so I don't fall asleep during Uncle Michael's stirring sermon."

"Wish I could nap too," Michael said dejectedly, "but my 'stirring sermon' still has a few bugs I need to work out."

"Take a nap, Uncle Michael," Michele said with concern. "The important thing is that we're all here. I'll appreciate a blessing from you as much as any sermon you could deliver."

Will and Michael walked up the stairs to their rooms in tired silence. Will barely had time to hit his bed before falling into a deep sleep. An intense dream ensued.

In the dream, Will was on the Temple Mount, running security for the unveiling of the new complex. With the construction complete, the site was something to behold. In the center of the Temple Mount complex stood two tall bronze pillars in front of the new Jewish temple. The structure was recessed on the center of the Temple Mount, sharing a grand courtyard with the rebuilt Dome of the Rock Mosque to its left and the new Basilica of St. Peter II to its right.

Beautiful as the complex was, it bore no sense of spiritual grandeur. Will marveled at the lack of peace and the pervasive heaviness. Aware of his duties, he scanned the empty platform continually for any security threat. As Will watched, Benny appeared on a platform set up between the pillars for the dedication ceremony. His attire was more outlandish than usual. He looked at Will, who saluted in return, signaling that all was calm.

Benny smiled broadly and began his address. To Will's amazement, the courtyard was suddenly filled with people. He walked along the perimeter, scanning both the crowd in the courtyard and the crowd below, who were watching the ceremony on huge screens. Benny spent a long time introducing faith leaders from around the world, all of whom converged to this immense physical expression of the united religions of the world.

Will noticed a slight commotion at the opposite end of the courtyard, toward the steps of the basilica. At first, it was just a slight shuffling of the crowd, but then the movement was more strenuous and cries from that direction reached him. He pulled his bow from its harness on his back, grabbed some steel-tipped arrows from his quiver, and strode purposefully behind the podium toward the direction of the trouble. The few screams grew to a chorus as the priests and Christian leaders near the platform erupted in blood at the hands of a prehistoric beast. Looking much like one of the raptors from the *Jurassic Park* films, the lizard stormed through the Christian delegation killing anyone in its path as it headed toward Benny's podium.

Will looked at the horrible beast, realizing it wasn't a beast at all. Its eyes were extremely intelligent. When Will looked into them, he was drawn to the animal. As he stood with bow drawn, the beast's eyes beckoned to him. To the right of the beast, the Lady appeared. She called to him. "Don't be afraid, Will."

"Will!" Benny screamed. "Put that weapon down! What do you think you're doing?"

"Don't listen to him!" shouted another voice from the opposite direction. Will turned quickly to see the two witnesses approaching. He shifted position, his weapon still drawn. The beast and the Lady were to his right; Benny was in front of him; and the witnesses were to his left. He didn't know what to do. He called into the crowd, "Uncle Michael! Uncle Michael! What should I do?" Then a crippling awareness came over him: Michael wasn't there. He was gone. Will didn't know where.

He awoke with a start. For a few moments, he sat confused in that state between deep sleep and wakefulness. He looked at the family photos decorating his father's suite of rooms and did a little mental checklist as he came awake. He was in Georgia. Check. They had come for Michele's wedding. Check. He had fallen asleep. Check. There was someone pounding at his door. Check. Someone pounding at the door?

He ran from the bedroom and across the sitting room to answer the door. A freshly showered Michael greeted him.

"Why did you lock this door, Sleeping Beauty? You're going to be late."

"Force of habit, I guess."

"Are you okay? You seem a bit out of it," Michael said suspiciously.

"I'm … I'm fine. Too much on my mind. I had a dream I was at the opening ceremony of the Temple Mount." Will grinned awkwardly.

"I'd call that a nightmare," Michael quipped.

THIRTY

Michael took a few moments to enjoy the ambiance of the chapel. Soon everyone would be there for the wedding, but for the time being, it was his to enjoy. Even when his beliefs had been little more than pagan, he found the chapel to be a warm, inviting space. Now he understood it was the abiding presence of the Holy Spirit in the place that made it special.

And, of course, there were the memories. He closed his eyes, trying to feel the way he felt as a ten-year-old when he, his mother, and Gabe had presented the chapel to Chris as a Christmas gift. He and Gabe adopted Chris as a father figure that night. He smiled at a vivid recollection of his mother and Chris hugging him as they approached the drug rehab facility to visit Gabe. Michael sighed as he felt Chris's calm strength and smelled his mother's perfume. What he wouldn't do to know their quiet reassurance one more time.

"All in good time, Michael," he said to himself. "We're halfway to the finish line. But, then again, this last half is going to be hell."

He began to light the multitude of candles Michele and Jimmy had set around the church. Michele wanted to replicate the look of her mother's wedding. Michael smiled at the memory of that evening.

The door of the chapel opened. Through the dim light, Michael saw Gloria ushering in the chamber musicians. In short order the chapel was alive with the sounds of a string quartet warming up. Michael donned the priestly garments in the chapel's sacristy. He felt sure he could smell faint remnants of Chris's cologne on them. He filled cruets with water and wine, and took out a large, solitary communion wafer. After all, he was the sole Catholic in the room.

Even if he weren't, he would have been alone. Benny had suspended all Catholic sacraments, declaring them an impediment to the unification of world faith traditions. *Funny, when I was free to celebrate Mass, I was the last person to want to do it. Now that it has been taken from me, I miss it.*

As Michael placed the chalice on the altar, Jimmy and Will took their places. Will wore a gray suit and had pulled his hair straight off his face. He looked striking as his emerald eyes glistened above high cheekbones. Beside him was Jimmy, whose swarthy complexion played handsomely against the starched white high collar of his tux. Both men were in excellent shape, accentuated by shoulder pads in their suit jackets. "Ah, to be young again," Michael whispered with a smile.

"You clean up pretty nicely, Will," Michael said with a chuckle as he joined them. "Jimmy, are you nervous?"

"Nah," Jimmy said. "Michele's the one for me. Besides, even if she weren't, it would only be for three and a half years, right?" Jimmy chuckled. Will raised an eyebrow. Michael wasn't ready to say that Will was right about Jimmy, but he didn't like the young man's response.

"Be that as it may," Michael said sternly, "you have to go into this with every intention to spend the rest of your life with Michele. If you wouldn't be willing to grow old with Michele, let's just cancel this here and now. No harm, no foul."

Will opened his mouth to join in the discussion. Michael shut him down with a stern look.

Jimmy looked Michael in the eye and said with mortal seriousness, "It was a joke—probably not a very good one. Michael, I love Michele with my whole heart. I can't imagine living without her."

Michael stared at him with a softer expression, but it nonetheless remained stern. He thought to himself that the boy was lucky to be dealing with him rather than Gabe. "Don't ever hurt her, Jimmy. She's been through enough. We've all been through enough. We have to stick together."

"I'll never hurt her," Jimmy said resolutely.

"Good," Will said sternly. "Because if you do, I have an arrow with your name on it."

Fury overtook Michael. He grabbed Will briskly by the arm and pulled him roughly to the side. Red-faced, he spoke in a tight whisper.

"Will! You just threatened to *kill* a family member! Does that strike you as a bit odd?"

The younger man crumbled under Michael's rabid disapproval. Michael saw Will's years of heartache—never belonging, never really knowing love. He looked at the childlike, dejected face in front of him. "I love you, Will. Can you get that through your thick head?"

"I know," Will mumbled. "Ditto."

"Good. At least we agree on something. Can we also agree that we're not going to kill anyone in the family?"

"I wouldn't really hurt Jimmy. I could never do that to Michele," Will said with a self-loathing sigh.

"Good," Michael said with mild exasperation. "So can you put the high-testosterone talk on the shelf when we're trying to sort out family matters? And not just about Jimmy, but also when we're discussing Benny."

"Yeah, I guess. But I want to go on record. I'm not really related to Lucky, you know."

Michael glared at him for a second and then softened his gaze. With a sigh, he said, "We're going to end this the way Chris dealt with me. Give your uncle Michael a hug."

Will hugged him and held him close for several seconds. They had been friends since they met on the highway outside Atlanta. They had been coworkers in Vatican affairs. And through it all, Michael had tried to break down the younger man's walls—to get him to accept the love of a family. And finally, in the warm presence of this wonderful chapel, Michael knew the walls had been breached. At last, Will had come home. Michael wiped at his eyes.

Pulling out of the hug, Will asked, "What are you crying about?"

Michael smiled. "It's either your failure to use deodorant or a feeling that you finally understand you're a vital member of this family with nothing to prove."

"Well," Will said, smacking his uncle's shoulder, "I applied deodorant twice. So I'm guessing it's the latter. Thanks, Jake. For everything."

Will took his place next to Jimmy. Michael heard him apologize for the threatening remark and then welcome Jimmy to the family. He silently thanked the Lord as the musicians began to play the processional.

Michael gasped as Michele entered the chapel. She looked absolutely stunning in her mother's wedding dress. Her figure was flawless, and her face was fiercely beautiful with her perfect complexion, high cheekbones, and blonde hair pulled back in a loose bun. Had she really grown up so much? He thought about how deftly she handled the family business and maintained the secret lair underneath the chapel. *I guess I knew she had grown up, but seeing her now as a beautiful woman and not my little girl ...* He grinned broadly.

Michael wasn't the only one floored by her appearance; an expression of awe accompanied Will's stare. Michael's grin broadened to a full-on smile at the expectant groom's unexpected tears. Jimmy wiped at his eyes as he said over and over, "You're so beautiful." The music stopped as first Gloria, and then Michele, joined the men at the altar. Gloria smiled lovingly at Michael. He returned her gaze.

"Before we begin, let me just say you two look absolutely beautiful," Michael declared.

"I worked hard on this makeup, Uncle Michael. Don't make me cry until after we take photos," Michele teased.

"Okay. Okay." He grinned. "Since there was no rehearsal, let me give you a quick rundown. I'll be saying the nuptials as part of a Mass. Basically, I'll be recalling Jesus's Last Supper and Passion. Then I'll consecrate Communion for myself."

"Could we take Communion too?" Gloria asked.

"Before Pope Potty Mouth did away with the sacraments, it wouldn't have been allowed. Now nobody takes Communion."

"Is that a yes?" Michele asked.

Michael sighed. He knew it would break the tradition that used to be called canon law, but canon law was defunct in this new world. "Here's the thing, though. Communion in my tradition requires a belief that through the action of the Holy Spirit you are actually eating the body and blood of Christ. It's a spiritual leap of faith."

"I can make it," Gloria said with a smile. "It's been so long since I've been to a Communion service."

"I agree," Michele said strongly. "We've seen enough evidence to believe in miracles and the action of the Holy Spirit. I'm in."

"That would be a stretch for me, Jake," Will said softly.

"I don't think I'm ready for that either," Jimmy said somberly.

"Well, then, Communion for three," Michael nearly sang, unable to repress his happiness not to be taking Communion alone.

The service was very intimate as all the attendees gathered around the altar. Michael strongly felt the presence of the Holy Spirit, and it showed in his sermon to the young couple. He felt light as a feather as he finally understood what it meant to let the Holy Spirit speak through him. In the past, he used to prepare meticulously penned sermons. They were intelligent, articulate, and in the final analysis, intimidating to the listener. He realized now that those attempts had been more about glorifying himself than about glorifying the Lord.

There wasn't a dry eye in the house as he spoke of how the couple's commitment was a representation of Christ's commitment to those who follow Him. Michael wasn't the least oblique in describing the bad times to come. He emphasized that Michele and Jimmy would be a comfort to one another in this life. He challenged all present to meet the coming hardships head-on, not with fear or aggression, but with love. He spoke to the bride and groom but found himself on several occasions staring at Will to drive the point home.

Michael pronounced the couple man and wife. After their kiss, he asked them to bow their heads while he prayed over them. All bowed their heads and closed their eyes as Michael invited the Holy Spirit to touch every heart in the room. He opened his eyes a crack to see if the prayer was making any impact on Will. Nothing that he could see. Then he noticed movement behind Will. Opening his eyes fully, he looked out into the chapel to see Chris, Kim, Gabe, Tina, and young Chris, who was now a tall, handsome man.

"I think the Lord has allowed a special present for you, Michele. Open your eyes," he said in a hushed tone of awe. As she opened her eyes, Michael pointed to the pews behind her.

A combination gasp and scream erupted from Michele. The others opened their eyes as she ran down the aisle to her family. Michael watched in tears as they hugged and kissed the young bride. The others watched as well, until Gabe said, "We can't be here long. We won't be allowed to come back very soon. Doesn't anyone else want a hug?"

Everyone else ran down the aisle as well. Gabe had been right. The group didn't stay much beyond a hug, but it was wonderful. Michael was moved to tears when Gabe introduced Will to Tina and his younger brother Chris, who both welcomed him warmly to the family.

Gabe said softly as he wrapped Michael into a hug, "Thanks for taking care of the kids, Michael."

"The pleasure's mine, Brother," Michael said as first Tina, and then Kim and the others, joined in the hug.

And then they were gone. It was beautiful to be with the resurrected family members, but a lonely reality came crashing down on the remainder as they returned to the altar to finish the Mass.

Michael consecrated the host and broke it into three pieces. He ate one piece, following it with a drink of consecrated wine. As he took the golden plate with the other two pieces of the Communion host to the wedding party, the door at the back of the chapel creaked open. Michael jerked to attention, peering through the dimly lit room to see Naomi DeRance waddling down the aisle in a dress and what appeared to be a first attempt at makeup.

"Naomi," he said with an unsure tone.

"Am I too late for Communion?" she asked.

"Ah, normally I would say yes," Michael said, "but today is a day of many unusual things." Silently, he hoped he was seeing some kind of conversion for the woman who had become their biggest nemesis in the family business.

Michael looked intently at Michele, silently asking the bride if she had invited Naomi. Michele shook her head no. Turning around she asked abruptly, "Naomi, why are you here?"

"I wouldn't miss my son's wedding for the world!" Naomi exclaimed.

Michele turned immediately to Jimmy. He shook his head and rubbed at the tension in his eyebrows. "I was going to tell you after the honeymoon," he said weakly.

"Who keeps the identity of his mother a secret?" Michele demanded.

Jimmy's arms flailed. "It's not what you think! I just found out myself when Naomi faxed me copies of my birth certificate."

It was all a little too convenient for Michael. He hadn't felt this uncomfortable in a church since Benny hijacked his ordination. Both occurrences had the feeling of a coup. Just like at his ordination, there was nothing to do but finish the service. They could sort it out at the house.

He turned Michele gently toward him and offered her Communion, followed by a drink from his chalice. He repeated the gesture with Gloria, but he didn't offer any to Naomi. She didn't protest. Then he quickly pronounced the final blessing and cued the recessional from the string quartet.

When the music began, he bent forward to hug his niece. "Don't let this ruin your wedding day. We can deal with Naomi later."

She hugged him fiercely. "Thanks, Uncle Michael." She took her groom's hand, smiled lovingly at him, and proceeded down the aisle with him.

Before turning to go down the aisle, Will stared at Michael with a knowing look, as if to say, "I told you there was something not to like about Jimmy." Gloria rubbed Michael's arm briefly in a show of support before she and Will followed the bride and groom down the aisle.

Once they left, the string quartet packed up to take their show to the estate, where they would play through dinner. Michael was again alone in the chapel.

Michael's mind raced as he extinguished the candles. This couldn't be a good development. Clearly Naomi was after greater influence in the company—at the very least. Then again, what could it matter? Let the Queen of the Damned run the company the whole way to hell. Could he possibly care?

And yet, he knew there was more to the equation. The family businesses had massive food and energy reserves at their disposal. Combined with the false FEMA camps Jimmy had created from the old orphanages, they could save thousands of Christians from the impending slaughter. For that reason alone, they would have to fight to maintain control. It was undeniable now that their operations could be compromised. Had Jimmy told Naomi about the camps? Would he tell them truthfully if asked? After all, he kept his knowledge of his mother a secret from his bride-to-be. What else might they be conspiring to do?

An aching moan escaped Michael as he extinguished all but the dim altar candle. His head swam as he returned to the sacristy to purify the chalice and change out of his robes. Was it now too dangerous to proceed with their plans? Could they win Naomi over to their side, or at a minimum, could they bribe her with more power and money to keep their secrets? It was a mess, and they were only days away from the midpoint of the tribulation. Those fake camps would be needed desperately in no time.

He finished changing but didn't feel like going to the house right away. He knelt at the altar to pray for the strength, dedication, and power of the Spirit they would need to get through the upcoming trial. His prayer was fervent. His eyes were closed. Only a slight creaking of old wooden floorboards alerted him to the fact he was no longer alone.

He opened his eyes slowly, hoping it was Gabe, his mother, or Chris. Instead, he saw a shadowy figure in black pants and a black shirt. Powerfully built, he wore a black balaclava over his head. Michael stood quickly in a panic as the figure exposed a small gun in his right hand. He fired a dart at Michael. It hurt where it pierced his arm. Michael pulled the dart from his arm before falling to the floor.

Oh God, help my family was his last thought before everything went black.

THIRTY-ONE

Benny walked the perimeter of the Temple Mount with Isa. Long ago he realized his personality was easily as strong as the entity Isa had installed in him on that fateful day at the United Nations. By and large he was able to keep Nergal in the background with his own personality in the forefront, but sometimes it was a different story when Isa was around. Before the introduction of this ascended master, Benny would have fallen all over himself to gain the attention of the man-god by his side. The ascended master, however, walked with Isa as more of an equal, a trusted advisor. To be sure, this entity worshipped Isa, probably more than Benny did, but more from the standpoint of some shared ancient history than the groveling subservience in Benny's heart.

"So it looks as if we are ready to go," Isa said with a smile.

"I could use another two weeks to make sure things are perfect," Benny said.

"I told you before," Isa said with slight exasperation, "this has been planned for a long time. The date is set in stone. Speaking of which, when will the cameras be set in place?"

"Tomorrow. They'll be all over the platform, and we'll have aerial coverage from drones. All will feed into the studio control center in the basement of the basilica. Our production team is top-notch."

"Good. Since I have no bad side, I'll want to be seen from all angles."

Benny offered a weak smile. He was slightly annoyed by the remark, but the ascended master found it to be very amusing.

"There's one more thing," Isa said. "I want you to position cameras down below near the two hecklers at the wall."

"Why? They'll ruin the sentiment of the proceedings."

Isa laughed. "They'll be the first sacrifice before the new temple."

"We'll finally be rid of them?" Benny chuckled with glee at the prospect.

"Finally!" Isa grinned.

As they headed back to his suite of offices in the basilica, Benny fought for, and won, preeminence over the ascended master.

"Isa ..." he began cautiously.

"Ah, the truest form of Benny has come to the table," Isa said with a touch of sarcasm. "You know, I had hoped for a much more seamless integration of your personalities."

"I'm sure you did, Isa," Benny said a bit smugly. "When it's all said and done, I've had trust issues all my life. It's just not my nature to cast my lot so irretrievably with anyone or anything."

"I've long admired your resolute selfishness, Benny. To tell the truth, I would miss you if your personality had been totally subsumed into a merged entity."

"Thanks," Benny said submissively. "Isa, I'm troubled. Will called me yesterday from the United States. Michael has disappeared."

"I don't understand. What do you mean ... 'disappeared'?"

Isa's surprise worried Benny. He laid out the facts in short order. "He married my niece and her fiancé at the family chapel yesterday. He stayed behind to close up while the rest of the wedding group went to the estate. They expected him to join them in about fifteen minutes. After an hour, Will went to check on him. He was gone. There was a dart on the floor. Will suspects it contained an anesthetic because the Swiss guardsmen at the gate and guardhouse had all been similarly incapacitated."

Isa stopped in his tracks. "This is serious."

"It's not your doing then?" Benny asked carefully.

"No. Of course not! I made a promise to you, Benny. I said that I wouldn't hurt your family."

Benny felt instant relief that Michael hadn't run afoul of Isa, but he feared for his nephew's well-being. If Isa was actually being truthful and wasn't behind Michael's abduction, who was? "I'm afraid we're at a loss to know who did it. Surveillance cameras show only a very muscular man covered in black from head to toe. Not so much as a stray fingerprint on the darts, other than Michael's fingerprints on the one that took him down."

"This is a grievous offense!" Isa railed. "It is a direct assault on my authority. We must find him and bring him safely home. I can't let the world think we are vulnerable to subversive actions, most probably from the freaking Christian militia."

"The papacy has a very fine secret service. The head of that organization helped us when Michael was kidnapped years ago."

"I shot that man," Isa said defensively.

"Apparently he recovered," Benny said with a wince, hoping it wouldn't be interpreted as a comment on Isa's aim. Isa didn't like his employees to see him as anything less than perfect.

"Of course he did," Isa protested. "If I had meant to kill him, he would have died."

"Perhaps you spared him for such a time as this," Benny said with cloying saccharine praise.

"Have you spoken to him about finding Michael?"

"First I wanted to be sure that you hadn't removed Michael. I have an appointment with him this afternoon. Will should be here by then to take him through the evidence."

"Good. But more should be done. You must make an appeal to the press. Let them know we will not stand for such an act of treason. You must be harsh in your criticism of these religious fanatics," he ordered.

"I will do just that," Benny said in agreement.

"You may quote me as saying that I will bring excruciating pain to anyone who hurts Father Michael ... or *any* of my staff for that matter. Their end will be slow and unmercifully painful."

Benny gulped. He had always preferred surprise attacks—a little poison in some soup, a laced needle into an IV bag, tampering with brake lines, were his way of dealing with oppressive forces. He was leery of a frontal attack. "I may tone it down a bit so I can keep it within the ecclesiastical framework we have so carefully crafted."

"Do what you want, Benny, but things are about to change. Once I am presented to the world on the Temple Mount, I won't suffer even the slightest hint of rebellion against my reign. To do so would be to abandon the rest of the world's population to the horrors approaching earth. I take very seriously my calling to save the world from this coming crisis."

"I'm sure you do," Benny appeased. "And may I thank you for taking the time to care about my nephew when there is so much at stake. It shows the greatness of your character."

"Indeed," Isa said in a prickly manner. Benny wondered if he had laid the praise on a little too thick. "Whatever you do, don't allow your distraction over Michael's disappearance to compromise the fine work you're doing on the Temple Mount. You're in the home stretch on this project, Benny. Don't blow it." Isa turned on his heels and left Benny without further ceremony. Benny returned to his office, stopping short at Michael's desk.

Michael's desk. Maybe there was a clue to his whereabouts. Michael had always been secretive. No doubt he had his hands in something he didn't want Benny to see. Benny mused that this was actually one of Michael's most endearing traits in his opinion. More people should be so inscrutable.

There was a pile of unopened mail. Benny went through it to pick out any sensitive information before Will and the agent traipsed through it looking for a clue. Most of it was decidedly mundane: expenses, closures and auctions of church buildings, World Council of Churches pronouncements harmonizing aspects of various religions. In the long run, it looked like a pile of filing waiting to happen.

Then he opened a particularly important-looking letter from the United States attorney general. This could be interesting. He read the letter quickly. The United States had discovered evidence of malfeasance in the family business, transferring of company funds and assets to Vatican companies that then supplied Christian rebels. They were requesting permission to examine the records of Vatican companies that Michael and Michele had established.

"You've been very naughty, Michael," Benny chided. "If we ever find you, I'll have to take you to task for this." Then again, Benny wondered if Michael's absence wasn't a blessing in disguise. Michael would simply have denied the request in Benny's name. What if Benny took advantage of Michael's absence to cooperate with the United States authorities?

He sent a quick e-mail response promising his total cooperation and naming Naomi as his contact for business matters in the United States. He felt a momentary pang of conscience and looked around the room suspiciously, waiting for Kim to appear out of nowhere to bring him into line. It didn't happen. "Well, maybe you've finally moved on, Kim. I loved you, but it's not like Michele is our blood anyway. Besides, she really crossed a line this time."

No response. Well, good riddance then. Kim never stopped by to say hello. She only ever came to rain on his parade.

It wasn't long before Will came streaming into the office. He looked like hell. Clearly he hadn't slept. His eyes were beet red and glazed over. He had never looked more like his drug-addled father.

"Lucky," Will said with a catch in his voice. "I don't know what to do ..."

"Sit down, Will. I think we have it covered."

"What do you mean?"

"I spoke with Isa about it."

"Oh," Will said with a little too much disdain for Benny's taste.

"You may not know this, but the Vatican's secret service is among the best in the world."

"I've heard, Benny. I work security, remember?"

"Yes, but Swiss guard security forces are the poor ugly stepsisters of the Vatican's secret service. They rival the CIA, MI6, the Mossad, and the old KGB."

Will paced. "No time to brag here, Lucky. Will they help me find Michael?"

"They'll be tasked with finding Michael. *Your* work is my security, and *my* work is on the Temple Mount. Isa was very clear that I mustn't let Michael's misfortune compromise my work. And you mustn't either, Will. This event is too important."

"Michael's misfortune!" Will screamed as he got in Benny's face.

For a second, Benny was afraid of the young man. He reached out and grabbed him by the shoulders like he would a naughty child. He briefly thought about how well-formed those shoulders were, and then he shook his head slightly and got down to business. "I didn't mean any disrespect, Will. I'm distraught about this too, but I'm smart enough to put it in the best hands, and leave it to the finest minds, in the world."

Will stared at him for a second as his tired mind processed Benny's words. *Big shoulders, tiny brain!* Benny continued, "Isa wants me to go on air to demand Michael's release. He promises his personal retribution if Michael is harmed in any way. By the end of the day, we'll have the entire world looking for him. Leads will come in, and our agent has the best resources in the world to track them down. We'll find him, and we'll bring him home."

Will wiped furiously at the tears in his eyes as Benny moved in to hug him. Will didn't return the hug, but he didn't spurn it either. Benny's feelings at that moment were anything but familial. It was turning out to be an okay day after all.

Benny returned to Michael's desk long enough to order coffee service, and then he took a seat next to Will on the couch along the opposite wall. "How is the family taking it?"

"They're devastated. Jimmy and Michele canceled their honeymoon. Gloria has stayed on a couple of days to help. Even Naomi seemed to be distraught. By the way, Naomi interrupted the wedding to announce that she is Jimmy's long-lost birth mother." The tray of coffee arrived. Will added sugar and cream to his. Benny took his black. Benny's mind raced as he took a sip from the espresso cup. Had Naomi been working both sides? She really was a man after Benny's heart! A slight chuckle escaped his lips. He played it off as the coffee being too hot. *So Naomi thought she would take over the family business. I may have to teach her a thing or two about subterfuge.* This day really was going better than he thought.

"Let me guess," Benny said sourly. "Naomi thinks her newfound status as family will bring her control in our business."

"Jimmy seemed embarrassed. I didn't get the chance to talk to Jake about it, but he didn't look happy. Neither did Michele."

"I can imagine!" Benny exclaimed with Merv Griffin panache. "Michael would oppose any increase in her status at the company. You have to mention this to the agent. He'll be here in a few minutes. Don't you find it an odd coincidence that Naomi got through security to interrupt the wedding on the same afternoon security was breached for Michael's abduction?"

"I hadn't thought of that," Will said with a shake of his head. *Of course you hadn't.*

The door opened, and the agent barged in. He stopped short at seeing Benny. Clearly he had intended to announce his presence and then wait for a papal audience. "Holiness, I apologize for barging in. I assumed you would be in your office. And I am late."

"Not to worry," Benny said. "This is my grandnephew Will."

"I know all about him." The agent waved dismissively. "Is it he to whom I complain about the Swiss guardsman who relieved me of my firearm at the entrance to the city?"

"You have our imperious leader to thank for that," Will said, rising to shake the agent's hand. "President Kurtoglu has declared Jerusalem a no-gun zone. He won't even make an exception for our security teams."

"That must make your job all the harder," the agent said.

"Fortunately, I'm an expert shot with a crossbow, and I've trained a cadre of elite guards. We'll be able to keep the Temple Mount secure for the upcoming festivities," Will said confidently.

The agent turned abruptly from Will. "If I may get to the point, Holiness. I'm sure you didn't invite me here from Rome to discuss event security with your grandnephew."

"No," Benny said gravely. "I'm afraid Father Michael has been abducted ... again." Benny rolled his eyes and shook his head. "You did such a fine job retrieving him the last time. I wanted you on the case this time as well."

"Tell me the details. When and where was he last seen? Who saw him? Was there evidence of force used in the abduction?"

"It happened at Castello Pietro. Will was present at the time, which I hope isn't indicative of his ability to protect us in the upcoming celebration," Benny said, ignoring Will's hurt expression. "You're welcome to use this office. Will can brief you on everything. I went through Michael's desk but found nothing other than our normal correspondence. In the meantime, I have to get to our studios. President Kurtoglu has tasked me with placing a worldwide alert. By the end of the day, every eye on the planet will be looking for Michael."

The agent grimaced. "That could work to complicate matters. If you remember, I like to work alone, in the shadows."

"If *you* remember," Benny said smugly, "I'm the pope. You serve at my pleasure. Go find my nephew." He left the room as the agent's expression mirrored Will's disdain. Damn, it felt good to be pope!

The camera closed in on Benny's heavily made-up face. "Rest assured, President Kurtoglu and I will stop at nothing to restore Father Michael safely to us. And we will be even more resolute in our determination to wipe out the scourge of religious fanaticism responsible for such a heinous act. There will be justice, and it will be swift. Humanity, in order to save itself from the impending danger, must not relent in its eradication of all noninclusive religious remnants. We must act relentlessly and mercilessly as if our very survival depended on it—because in the final analysis, it does."

Zack turned off the television and took another long drink of whiskey. "To Gloria," he toasted. "I loved her once."

Naomi was happy to get home and away from the Martin estate. Timing was everything, and without Michael to support her, Michele would be weak in the boardroom.

She opened her e-mails to see that she had been copied on Benny's response to an attorney general request. She drew a bath, hoping that it would relax her so she could get to sleep. There would be a lot to do tomorrow.

The Russian president chuckled out loud at the pope's worldwide telecast. Such an incredible breach of security in the papal ranks meant that Isa and his government were more vulnerable and far weaker than he had imagined.

Someone had made it to the inner sanctum to kidnap the hapless papal assistant. If they'd had any idea where the man was, they would have pursued the kidnappers. An appeal to the entire world might as well have been a cry of uncle. It would be an inviolable breach of Vladimir's Soviet training if he wasted such an opportunity.

It was on!

Isa giggled slightly. He turned to the Lady and said, "The Russian took the bait."

THIRTY-TWO

Michele sat behind her grandmother's desk at the estate. Well, technically, Uncle Benny had made it his, but he rarely came to 'Castello Pietro' these days. Michele had long ago begun to think of it as her grandmother's again. She listened intently to Will's report over the speakerphone.

"I don't think we have any option but to trust this guy who only goes by "the agent." Up front, I have to tell you I don't like such cloak-and-dagger. This guy hides too much to be trustworthy. And it doesn't make me feel any better that Benny set up the meeting with him."

"Uncle Benny set it up?" she asked curiously.

"Apparently this is the same guy who found Jake when he was kidnapped years ago."

"I remember that time. It's when Dad was shot. For what it's worth, both Dad and Grandpa Chris spoke very highly of him. They thought he was excellent at his job, but ..." She paused to concentrate, to clarify a vague memory.

"But what?"

"It's a vague memory, Will, but I think I heard Dad and Grandpa Chris say that the guy died in Uncle Michael's rescue."

"Well, there you go," Will said. "Benny set up the meeting and lied to me about the man's identity."

"Like I said, it's a vague memory—certainly not enough to support those suspicions."

"Isa's a monster and Benny's his puppet," Will said bitterly. "I think the only mistake is to assume there is a depth to which they won't sink."

Michele chuckled slightly at his melodramatic phrasing. "Depth to which they won't sink?" she mocked.

Will said in a slightly lighter tone, "So, I have a penchant for the dramatic."

"I'm not saying you're wrong, but let's look at some facts. From what Uncle Michael told me, Mimi was the only person Uncle Benny seemed to love. Uncle Benny promised her to look after us when she appeared to him after the rapture. So far he's been good to his word."

"What then? The agent didn't die in Michael's first rescue?" Will asked.

"Like I said, it's a vague memory on my part. I shouldn't even have brought it up. The important things are that this guy is supposedly good at what he does and that he's going to look for Uncle Michael."

She could sense him stifling his suspicions to move the conversation forward. He conceded without much conviction, "I guess you're right. Hopefully Benny's plea to the world will turn up some good information. Besides, I'll join the search once we get past the Temple Mount opening."

"Do you think Benny will give you time off?"

"Between you and me, Michele, I only took the job to be close to Uncle Michael. Partly it was selfish because he was fatherly to me. Partly it was so I could protect him. Looks like I failed miserably at that. Without him I have no reason to hang out in Jerusalem with Benny. My time here is shortly coming to an end."

She felt a surge of hope and the recoil of fear. It would be great to have Will as part of the investigation. He wanted to find Uncle Michael as much as she did. Yet she worried that he would be putting himself in danger—especially if Isa and Benny turned out to be involved in Michael's disappearance. "Will, you have to be careful. Besides, you don't have any leads."

"Not exactly true."

"What are you talking about?"

"I gave the agent photos of the chapel, the dart, and other evidence."

"Yeah?"

"In a nutshell, I put a microscopic RFID tag on each piece of evidence. It was a stab in the dark. I figured he would find them right away. So far he hasn't. He'll lead me to Jake."

"Sounds awfully dangerous to me." Michele sighed.

Will laughed loudly. "More dangerous than daily interaction with Benny and Isa? No way!"

"I guess you've got a point. Just promise me you'll be careful, okay?"

"Okay. I could say the same to you. What's up with your testosterone-laden mother-in-law?"

She choked down a laugh. "She went home shortly after you left. Hopefully we're over the awkwardness. She approached Jimmy a while back with a birth certificate. It had him really confused. He was going to tell me after the wedding—and then she showed up. I kind of feel bad for him."

"So, you don't think he's in cahoots with her to take control of the family businesses?"

"No. I seriously think she's playing him. In fact, I'll have someone look into that birth certificate to see if it's even real. Jimmy has wanted a family so badly all his life, he just accepted it at face value."

Will sighed. Michele could tell he was less convinced of Jimmy's innocence than she was. "Good thinking. Be careful, though. Anyone who would go to those lengths to get some power may well be capable of much worse," he cautioned.

"I'll be okay. Right now I just want to concentrate on my honeymoon—"

"Which you failed to go on," Will said, finishing her sentence.

"We didn't go away, but there's still a need for us to settle in as a couple."

Will laughed. "Do you mean 'settle in' or 'set-tell iyyyn'?"

"Both. I had a conversation with Gloria after you left, explaining that I was thankful she stayed on in the wake of Uncle Michael's absence but that Jimmy and I needed time alone."

"You vixen!" Will teased.

"Hey," she teased in return. "I'm a married woman now, just doing my duty for God and country."

"Yeah. I feel the call of duty myself every once in a while, but I don't think I'll find my mate in this crazy world."

"I know what a blessing it is that I've found Jimmy. As for you, I'm guessing a ponytail and multicolored balloon pants aren't attracting your type."

"Basically they only attract your uncle Benny," Will said sourly.

Michele laughed. "He's no more my uncle than he is yours, dude. And to be fair, you showed up here with pretty flamboyant attire you chose long before you met Benny."

"It was for a stage act! And I had a girlfriend," Will protested.

"Oh, please, Will," Michele teased. "You shot at her with a cross-bow. She wasn't a girlfriend. She was a target."

He sighed. "The world just doesn't understand a Renaissance man. Can you hold on a minute? I have a text from the estate's guardhouse. Looks important."

As she waited for Will to make his phone call, Jimmy popped his head into the room. "Just a heads up. The front gate buzzed to say Naomi's here."

"Great," she said halfheartedly. Then she heard Will calling to her.

"Michele! Michele! Michele! Get out of there! Naomi has the feds with her and some Vatican pass from Benny. They're coming after you for the charity companies."

Michele pushed past Jimmy. He tried to stop her for a second, but she shoved him hard. What was Naomi doing? How did she get the Vatican's permission to bring federal officers? Benny! Without Michael to intercept any communication, Naomi could easily have gotten Benny's ear, or the other way around. Michele ran to the chapel faster than she had ever run. She had to get to the bunker and seal it from view before they could find it. If she could hide there, they would find nothing. All records of the dummy Vatican companies were housed there below the chapel.

For some reason, she had never shown Jimmy the bunker. Whenever she thought of showing it to him, something always came up to distract her. And to be totally honest, she loved having a place that was hers alone. Not knowing where he stood with Naomi's plan, she was thankful now that it had never come up.

She had supplemented the chapel door's lock with fingerprint-recognition software for an event like this—if she ever needed to run for cover. The system recognized her instantly. She entered the chapel, threw the door shut behind her, and locked it. Hopefully it would give her the time she needed to get into the bunker.

She heard Jimmy and Naomi talking to the officers as the chapel floor above her slid into place, obscuring the bunker from view. She went into the bunker's office and accessed the estate's surveillance software, which allowed her to follow the investigation.

On the monitor she saw Jimmy open the chapel. "See," he said to the group, "the chapel is empty. Search for yourselves." Agents ridiculously dressed in Kevlar and sporting assault rifles went through the chapel looking under benches, tearing through the sacristy, and laying bare the confessionals.

"Clear," the armed men repeated in succession to their commander. They left the chapel without closing the door. No doubt they were tossing the estate too.

As she followed their movements on the cameras, she dialed Will's cell phone.

"What's going on there?" he yelled as he answered the call.

"I'm safe in a hidden bunker. It's a place Mimi prepared when the world was worried about the Y2K event."

"So, they can't find you?" he asked impatiently.

"Impossible," she said. "They've already searched all around me and left. I'm sure I'm safe."

"Good."

"How did you know to warn me?" she asked.

"The guards texted me that Naomi was at the gate with federal officers. They thought it strange when the feds said not to alert you to their presence, so they texted me."

She looked at the monitors while Will spoke. The men were going from room to room in the house, dumping contents from drawers and closets, making a total mess.

"I can hook into the security cameras from here, Will. I see them tossing the house. They won't find any records on the charities, by the way. I always made sure they were locked away in this bunker."

"Good girl!" he exclaimed.

Then her eyes focused on one monitor. Jimmy was in the family room at the back of the estate with Naomi. His face blazed with anger. It looked like they were fighting. "Will, I'm going to try to get some sound from the monitor in the family room. Jimmy and Naomi are arguing, and I want to hear what they're saying."

"Put the phone close so I can hear it too," Will said.

"Okay, here goes."
The sound was low, but they could make out most of the words:

Jimmy: How could you do this to me?

Naomi: Do what? Secure for you one of the largest, most profitable corporations in the world? Well, at least it *was* until Michael and his namesake had their way with it.

Jimmy: Shut up! Shut your mouth! There's no way I can be related to someone so foul.

Naomi: Believe it or don't, Jimmy. But I'm your mother, and I'll be in full control of that company either with your blessing or without it if I reveal your little FEMA camp scam to the authorities.

Jimmy: Why are you doing this? Michele is the most wonderful person I've ever met. This marriage is the first bit of happiness in my miserable life, and you're trying to ruin it!

Naomi: Oh, please. I'll let you in on a little secret, Jimmy. Words of wisdom from Momma. Love fades faster than you could ever imagine right now. But wealth and power? They stay with you throughout your life and pass to succeeding generations.

Michele shed tears to know that Jimmy wasn't a party to Naomi's treachery.
"Jimmy sounds like he's not part of Naomi's plan," Will said. "Does he know about the bunker?"
"No," Michele said quietly. Although he sounded innocent in the conversation with Naomi, she wasn't sure she wanted him to know about her hiding place. The implications were mind-blowing. She didn't trust him. What a way to start a marriage!
"Are you going to tell him about it?" Will asked.
"No."

"Good girl. Just stay where you are and watch the monitors. I've arranged for some Vatican communication."

"How did you do that?"

"Let's just say I used Jake's computer and took Lucky's name in vain."

Michele laughed at his manner of expression. "You could get in some serious trouble, couldn't you?"

"I told you, Michele. As soon as I get through this upcoming spectacle, I'm out of here. And Benny's way too focused on looking pretty for this upcoming event to notice anything I do."

"Got you," Michele said seriously. "Wait. Something's happening. The *federales* look confused. One is on the phone. Let me turn up the volume."

"No need," Will said. "He's learning that the papal offices sent an urgent communiqué to the head of Homeland Security. Apparently a breach of security resulted in an unauthorized use of American forces on Vatican property. Homeland Security apologizes for the inconvenience."

"No way!" she yelled.

"Way. And there's another little surprise coming."

Michele watched as the officers stormed into the family room to handcuff Naomi. "Will, what did you do?" she asked incredulously.

"Nothing too horrible. The Vatican is concerned about the proximity in time of your mother-in-law's security breach to get to your wedding and the security breach of Jake's captors. I doubt they'll hold her, but if she knows anything about his abduction, they'll get it out of her."

"Ouch. I'll have to explain that to Jimmy."

"Don't let him know I had anything to do with Naomi's arrest. If he's as innocent as he sounded, he and I will have to work on becoming brothers-in-law."

"What should I do then?"

She heard him chuckle. "You really do need a big brother, don't you? What you should do is start your honeymoon, silly."

She chuckled as well. "There's so much going on with Uncle Michael, and now Naomi's plot. I'm not much in the mood."

"Naomi has been neutralized. There's nothing you can do for Uncle

Michael. I'm on top of it. If your marriage is worth anything, you need to learn to trust Jimmy. Times could get really tough, really soon. Take advantage of this respite."

The private jet landed on the once-bustling tarmac of Houston's George Bush Intercontinental Airport. Gloria wished she could say she was happy to be home. The truth was that she had relaxed more at Michael's family home than she ever could in her own. The farce of her marriage had weighed on her. Living a lie and worse, living in the clutches of her murderous husband, had taken its toll. She hadn't realized how stressful it was until she got to spend a few days in a loving environment.

"Oh, Lord, You can't come fast enough," she muttered. A tear formed in her eye. She quickly wiped it away and then pulled a mirror from her purse to make sure her mascara hadn't smudged. Her husband and keeper hated smudged makeup. She fluffed her hair where it had fallen out of shape during the flight.

The plane taxied to the hangar where Riverside Fellowship rented space. From the window she saw one of the ministry's limos waiting for her. "Well, here goes nothing," she said as she left the jet, descended the stairs, and walked toward the car.

Once she reached the tarmac, two police cars sped around the corner, their lights flashing and sirens blaring. She was startled at first, wondering what had happened. Before she could even process it, the policemen were on her. They cuffed her hands behind her back. In the days before Isa, they would have read her rights.

"What's going on?" she asked innocently, even as her mind raced through the probability that Zack had taken advantage of Michael's disappearance to get her out of the way. One question railed through her mind: *Was Zack also responsible for Michael's disappearance?* If he was, she knew Michael was dead. Tears flowed freely.

One of the policemen put his hand on her head as he moved her into the squad car. At that moment, the backseat window of the limo slid open. Her last look at freedom was Zack's grinning face. His new secretary sat beside him, wearing Gloria's jewelry.

THIRTY-THREE

I n a scant couple of days, Benny would speak to crowds from the new basilica. He could barely wait as he walked through Abraham's Courtyard, the name given to the cobblestoned space joining the edifices on the Temple Mount. He went through every detail of days full of ceremonies planned for the reopening of the Temple Mount. Islamic prayer would reopen the Dome of the Rock on Friday afternoon, although the service would be brief. There was very little joy in what remained of the Muslim community to be sharing this space. The most vociferous detractors had disappeared over the construction period, no doubt at Isa's hand. The imams who believed him to be Mahdi would be present, even though they remained confused at his accommodation of the Jews.

The big Jewish day, of course, would be Saturday. The newly trained priests couldn't wait to butcher their genetically engineered red heifer. Disgusting! Benny himself had to wonder why Isa would allow such barbarism.

Sunday was the day Benny couldn't wait for. He would finally preside over a sea of adoring subjects from the balcony of St. Peter's. True enough, it was a small replica of the old one, but the plumbing was new. Benny liked the pomp and circumstance that had come down to the previous basilica through the ages, but he wouldn't miss the drafty hallways, dark chambers, and old smell of the buildings in Rome. This structure reflected his sensibilities. It was an entirely new space for an entirely new religion. And Sunday just happened to be December 25—Winterfest, a time of family, friends, light displays, and presents. What better day for the dedication of the new-world basilica?

He patted the obelisk in the square shared by the three religions. For all practical purposes, he presided over all faiths represented on the Temple Mount, and more. He burst into a grin at the thought of it. For years, he had dreamed of becoming pope, but now the idea of merely being pope was repugnant. He had changed the very nature of the office.

He heard a commotion down below and checked his watch. Noon. Right on the dot. From noon to three each day, the two witnesses preached to anyone who would listen. It was always the same: Repent; only Jesus can save us. Those two morons couldn't face two thousand years of history that fairly screamed the contrary. They couldn't comprehend that in their midst was a verifiable hybrid being who exemplified all the traits attributed to the mythical Christ of the gospels. Benny's encyclicals pointed the way to a new theology showing the writings about Jesus to be a prophetic foreshadowing of Isa's arrival to save humankind—not from some mystical, unfathomable death from sin, but from the actual, verifiable threat of alien invasion.

He walked to the edge of the platform to stare down at the two. He could only imagine how they smelled after living outside all this time. He crinkled his nose. He had warned Isa that these two would put a damper on the upcoming celebrations. Isa assured him they wouldn't, but Benny didn't know what Isa would do about it after the bonfire they had made of his men.

"Ah, Benny. I knew I'd find you here."

Benny jumped with a start. Isa had the most annoying habit of showing up every time Benny doubted his abilities. "Isa. You're looking well today."

"Why shouldn't I, Holiness? Today is the day I get rid of a three-and-a-half-year headache."

"You mean these two?" Benny asked as he pointed to the Wailing Wall below.

"Yes, I do. Follow me." He strode off toward the newly built stairway to the Temple Mount. Guards closed it off, both at the top and at the bottom, a mere fifty yards from the fire-breathing duo. Benny didn't follow. He wasn't about to become a charcoal briquette now, when the Temple Mount celebration was only hours away.

"Benny!" Isa shouted before descending the stairs. Benny stood resolutely. *I don't have enhanced DNA. I think I'll stay here, thank you.* No sooner had he thought it than his legs began to move. The ascended master was moving him! He fought, willing his legs to be still, but with one halting step after another, the being moved him to Isa's side.

"You might as well give in, Benny," Isa said with a grin. "I'm perfectly capable of helping the ascended master take full control of your body, but I want you awake to see this."

"Fine," Benny said with too much of a snarl. Recoiling at a flash of anger in Isa's eyes, he lowered his own eyes and followed his master down the stairs like a faithful dog. The guards at the bottom of the staircase parted to allow them passage. Isa marched to within twenty feet of the witnesses.

The witnesses stood still as statues. Isa stared them down. Benny's panicked eyes moved constantly from Isa to the witnesses and back.

Finally one of them spoke. "So, your time has come, Evil One."

"My time certainly has come," Isa said sternly, "but I'm not the Evil One. The title belongs to such as you. You would have mankind cower in the wake of the coming invasion. I will free them! In me they will be able to reach their true potential."

"The same old lie," the other witness said with disgust.

Isa pulled a handgun from his suit pocket. "You have murdered my men who ordered you to leave these premises. Today, I'm taking control. Leave or die."

The witnesses stood steadfast, each with his head held high. The one whom people called Elijah spoke. "We choose not to leave. As it is written in the book of Revelation, we must die ..."

He didn't finish his sentence. Isa shot him squarely in the head. He did the same to the other in a fraction of a second. They crumbled in a heap in front of the wall.

Benny winced despite Nergal's desire to stand at attention. Feeling his own personality rise more fully to the surface, Benny called to the Swiss guardsmen at the bottom of the stairs, "Clean this up, will you?"

"No!" Isa yelled sternly to the guards. He turned around to face the cameras. "Ladies and gentlemen of Earth, my brothers and sisters, these men have sought to make you victims in a coming invasion. Their dogma and doctrine are from a time when humanity didn't have the will or the means to resist invasion. That is no longer who we are. Today we take our lives back. Today we disavow religious cults that divide us so another can conquer us. Today we proclaim boldly that we are of Earth and that we will stand united in protecting our home—united in brotherhood, united in arms, and most importantly united in spirit!

"It is my intent to leave these bodies at the wall through our Winterfest celebration. Let all who come to the Temple Mount dedication ceremonies see them. Let the Earth see the inevitable course of events for all who cling to division and strife! A new day has dawned. Seize it! Prepare for the fight of your lives! And above all, prepare to win your freedom from would-be alien oppressors. Cast off the ties that bind you to old philosophies of servitude. Adopt instead the courage, will, and pride to overcome!"

The crowd was deadly quiet, waiting for his next words. He didn't speak but turned his back to them and sprinted up the stairs. Benny followed closely behind. By the time they reached the top, the crowd had erupted in a spontaneous hymn: "We shall overcome …"

Benny felt relieved to be back on the Temple Mount, relieved to have full control of his body again, and overjoyed to be rid of the two naysayers at the wall. "That was amazing, Isa!"

"So, you're happy I made you come with me?"

"Yes." Benny couldn't suppress a smile. "It was totally exhilarating." He meant it. He couldn't remember when he had last done something so liberating.

"Stick close to me. I have a lot more fun planned for the next couple of days," Isa said with a broad smile. He clapped Benny's back and began to walk away. He strode a few feet and then turned around with a menacing grin. "Oh, Holiness, the next time you hesitate to follow my orders, you'll join those two Bible-thumpers."

Benny's legs grew weak. He fell to the cobblestones with a thud and a grunt as Isa continued to walk away. His legs felt numb. He phoned Will in a panic.

True to his calling, Will came to him in a hurry. "Lucky, what happened?" he asked as he knelt down to check Benny's health.

The numbness was already starting to dissipate. "My legs just went numb," Benny said.

"I'll get an ambulance," Will said gravely.

"No ambulance. Just help me up," Benny said dismissively.

"What if you had a stroke?" Will asked.

"It wasn't a stroke. Between you and me, I hesitated to go with Isa to confront those buffoons at the wall. The numbness is just his way of showing disapproval. I'll be fine."

"In whose eyes?" Will asked in exasperation. "You two committed murder for the world to see." Will stared at him angrily.

Benny had very little patience for that look. If he had Isa's abilities, young Will would find himself with a lot worse than numb legs. "Just help me up, Will. You're not here to judge me."

Will helped him to his feet, but Benny couldn't stand on his own. He fell all over the younger man like an old drunk as the two made their way back to his apartment.

Benny still felt a little weak-kneed when Isa demanded to see him. He asked Will to walk with him to Isa's quarters in the basilica. It's not that it was such a long walk; they lived on opposite sides of the rotunda. Nonetheless, Benny felt more comfortable to have Will nearby. His mind filled with thoughts of Isa's unceremonious termination of Luciano Begliali. As they walked in silence, Benny felt a slight twinge, a subtle ache, for Michael. For the first time since news of his disappearance, Benny felt the pain of separation. Will was a poor substitute, but somehow his presence made Benny feel better about Michael's absence.

Benny knocked on the door to Isa's apartment, all fifteen thousand square feet of it. The grandeur didn't impress Benny. He had supervised every detail of the basilica's construction, and Isa had been unrepentantly nitpicky. Not one thing in the space had been good enough for him the first time. From flooring to the ceiling to the windows, he changed his mind after installation. Inevitably he would demand things be redone, while insisting that the completion date was a hard-and-fast deadline. Well, it was done. And it was beautiful. Benny doubted whether his boss had noticed or cared how miserable he had made Benny's life during its construction.

Will moved to the side of the door to stand guard and await Benny's return. Benny rolled his eyes at the younger man as the door opened. A butler ushered Benny through the marble foyer to Isa's oversized office. The office contained only two colors: black and white. Benny had tried to explain that the room would really pop with the addition of an accent color or two, but Isa wouldn't hear him. White marble floors, white paneled walls, and a white sculpted ceiling contained a black monster of a desk and black leather furniture. Benny involuntarily rolled his eyes; clearly Isa's decorating sense had come from the alien side of his DNA. "Speaking of which," Benny muttered to himself, "smells like the Lady is here." His nose twitched at the garlicky, fetid odor.

"Benny, how are you feeling?" Isa called from behind his desk.

"Stronger," Benny answered politely. "And I think I learned my lesson."

"Excellent," Isa sang. "Well, since you're not going to ask, let me tell you that I feel wonderful today. So alive and full of power. I tell you, Benny, if I would have known killing those two could be so exhilarating, I would have done it ages ago."

Benny smiled. He had no answer for the comment. "Good day, my Lady. How nice to see you," he purred.

"Likewise," she said as white saliva fell from her mouth. Benny willed his face not to move in distaste. He wondered if dentures would help her keep that stuff inside her mouth.

"You wanted to see me, Isa?"

"Yes, Benny, I do. I want you to release the latest video you recorded—the one where you stand with leaders of different faiths and pronounce that there are many paths to God."

"Oh." Benny stammered. "I was planning to release it as part of the opening ceremonies."

"You can show it then too. But I need you to release it now with a statement that I endorse the free practice of all positive religions. It is only separatist and divisive religious fundamentalists that are dangerous to our survival. I know what I'm talking about, Benny. The Anu aliens will feed off of any human division."

"Humanity has to be united at any cost," the Lady concurred. "It's your only chance."

"I understand," Benny said drolly. More to the point, Isa wanted to quell any uneasiness in the world population over his actions earlier in the day.

"I don't think you do," Isa said as he slammed his hand on the desk.

Benny had no doubts that Isa knew his last thought. He made a mental note to stay focused.

Isa continued. "Where do we stand with the production of implants? They're a very important part of our plan."

"You wanted production to be complete by next week. We're on track to make it."

"And the estimated time to inoculate the population?"

"The bulk of humanity can be injected in about a month's time if we run clinics twenty-four hours a day, which we plan to do."

"Very good, Benny. You will announce the new technology at the end of the Temple Mount ceremonies. Tie its release to the Lady's dire warning of the dangers of divisive thinking and the elimination of the two terrorists at the Wailing Wall earlier today."

"Easily done, Isa, but we've hinted that this technology will do more than protect from future magnetic anomalies. We've hailed it as an inoculation, but we haven't yet told people what they are to be inoculated against."

The Lady quickly recited a list of diseases afflicting humankind, from allergies to zits. "Amazing!" Benny exclaimed. "Is it true?"

The Lady hissed. Isa frowned. "Yes, Benny, it's true," Isa growled.

"I wasn't doubting you," Benny said defensively. "It was just an expression of my inability to comprehend such a powerful drug."

"It's not a drug, Benny. It is a nanochip technology designed to alter DNA. With the aid of science, I will impart to humanity the genetics of my enhanced immune system."

"So, everyone will be genetically altered to be like you?" Benny asked.

"Just their immune systems." Isa grinned broadly. "Imagine it, Benny. With one single injection, I will alleviate untold suffering."

"At least until the Anu get here," Benny cautioned.

Isa jumped up from his desk and paced excitedly around his office. "No, Benny. This technology will save us from the Anu as well. First of all, only those who declare their loyalty to me will get to enjoy my DNA. It's only fair. Once they have received my immune system, they will, as a side effect, see things my way. They will be more united than ever—and that's the key to defeating the Anu. And as promised from the start, they will no longer feel the mental effects of Nibiru's magnetic field."

"No repeat of the Dark Awakening," Benny concurred.

"No," the Lady affirmed. "The Anu are comparatively few in number. They have only managed to terrorize the planet in the past when Earth's inhabitants fell prey to the magnetic disturbance. This time they will meet a united Earth with weapons to take them out of the sky."

"They won't know what hit them!" Isa laughed heartily.

Benny grinned as well.

"There is something else," Isa said with a sly grin.

"What?" Benny asked.

"Russian troops have joined with my brothers' allies in Turkey, as well as Iran and a few other Shia governments, to attack me. They're on the border of Israel right now."

"What?" Benny shrieked.

"Relax." Isa laughed. "It's all part of a bigger plan."

THIRTY-FOUR

W ill's skin fairly crawled as he waited for Benny to leave Isa's quarters. It had already felt like a long day. Fear and dread had kept him from a full night's sleep since Michael's disappearance. The anxiety steadily worsened as days passed with no sign of him, no news in the search. Michele's near miss with authorities hadn't helped his nerves. And then watching Isa kill the witnesses only to leave their dead bodies lying in the street—well, it was the final straw. He was about to lose it. He wiped wearily at his fatigued eyes as he stood guard. Then he checked his messages for the thousandth time that day. Nothing from the agent. The agent probably wasn't even working. Nobody else was. The Winterfest holiday picked up right where Christmas left off, with the entire world scrambling to buy gifts.

Suddenly sirens screamed all around him. He jumped to attention as his mind processed the sound. It was the old Israeli missile warning system. He had heard about it but had never experienced it because the Middle East was at peace under Isa's control. He didn't even know where the nearest bomb shelter was. He guessed that he was not alone. All kinds of transients had made it to the area with Isa and Benny, attending to the reigning duo's constant needs. He had no protocol for this. Should he knock to see if Benny was all right? Did he really care?

He didn't have much time to ponder the decision. The door opened, and Benny ushered him in. "Come with us, William."

He followed Benny down a hallway to an elevator. Before entering, he could smell the Lady's acrid presence. She gave him the willies—more so than even Isa. He steadied his nerves and followed Benny onto the elevator.

"Really, Benny?" Isa asked disgustedly.

"He's my nephew," Benny said defiantly. Will happily stepped off the elevator. The last place he wanted to be was in a confined space with Isa and the Lady. Benny grabbed his arm. The elevator door tried to close but bumped into their arms.

"Oh, for crying out loud!" Isa barked. "Benny, let go of him. Will, come on the elevator. This is a great day for us. You might as well be part of it."

Will didn't move as he tried to come up with a reason to stay above ground. Isa barked, "William!" Though not of his volition, Will's legs carried him into the elevator.

"Thank you," Will said, "It is a privilege to serve." His words, in no way reflecting his feelings, came without any conscious conjuring on his part. He had just felt Isa's evil power close up. Jake was right. Isa was far more than a power-crazed politician.

Isa clapped him on the back and smiled. "You are in for quite a show, William." Will was confused by the calming power emanating from Isa. He gazed back as Isa's eyes, exactly like Michael's, radiated an instant feeling of peace.

"I know what you're thinking." Isa chuckled. "Your uncle and I have a bit of a genetic link." He held his thumb and forefinger millimeters apart to imply only a slight connection.

"Frankly, I never saw it," Benny said dismissively.

The Lady seemed to be stuck between a laugh and a cough as the elevator plummeted beneath the Temple Mount. Finally it stopped, and the doors opened to a cavernous room filled with computer equipment and technicians. It reminded Will of old photos of mission control during America's moon launches, with row upon row of scientists hunched over their computers and facing a full-wall screen.

"These scientists are the best in the world," Isa explained. "They have been tracking a swarm of debris knocked loose from the asteroid belt by the gravity of the approaching dwarf sun. These bits of cosmic shrapnel have been headed to Earth for over two years."

"Where will they hit?" Will asked.

"Call up the Golan monitors," Isa demanded of a man at one of the consoles. Large screens filled a semicircle ahead of them. They came to life with images of rows upon rows of tanks and troops. Will looked closely. He identified a Russian flag for sure.

"Oh no. No, no, no," Benny chanted. "It looks like World War Three," he whined.

"Calm yourself, Holiness," Isa said with disdain. Answering Will's question, he said, "My father's sons and some like-minded rebels have formed a coalition with Russia to dismantle my caliphate. Their plans will come to a swift end."

As he spoke, bright points lighted the sky above the advancing troops.

"Right on schedule!" Isa sang out in praise to the scientists.

The points of light grew to flaming balls. Many of them fizzled out. Will reasoned them to be small rocks burned up in the atmosphere. Others that were much larger struck in the center of the Russian army. A distant percussive sound rumbled through the lair. On the screens, smoke cleared to reveal a large crater where once men and equipment had stood. Panicked troops went to war with those around them. Iranians killed Syrians. Syrians killed Russians. Turkish troops fired at anything that moved. More fiery rocks fell from the sky, decimating mile after mile of countryside. In mere moments, the vast army was no more. Will felt his legs grow weak. The devastation and carnage were too horrible to be believed. His mind fought the images of writhing bodies and mangled equipment as far as the eye could see.

"Come," Isa said happily to the Lady, Benny, and Will. It was all Will could do to contain himself. What kind of monster could take pleasure from such horror? The three followed Isa to an office at the side of the large room. Office walls facing the control room were made of two-way mirrors. The mirrored wall gave way to a full view of the control room and its screens from the confines of the office.

"So, our enemies just happened to be at the site the meteors hit?" Benny summed with childish glee.

"So to speak," Isa said with a grin as he regally sat behind the desk. "My 'brothers' thought they were acting against me, but in reality, they played into my hand."

"Well, if you ask me, Russia needed a bit of a lesson," Benny said sanctimoniously.

"Actually, I came in here to call Vladimir to gloat a bit. I thought you would want to hear."

Will stood aghast as Benny laughed heartily. "You bet I do!" He pushed past Will and took a seat opposite Isa's desk as Isa pushed the speed dial on his speakerphone.

"What do you want?" the gravelly voice of the Russian president asked.

"Unconditional surrender," Isa said sternly, "as well as your death as a traitor, of course."

"Not very likely," Vladimir answered drolly. "You don't really think I gave you control of all our nuclear weapons after your little appeal to the UN, do you?"

"I'm well aware of the ones you held back," Isa said with a slight chuckle. He called up a screen on his computer.

"Well, know this," Vladimir said sternly. "I will blow Jerusalem off the face of the map unless you promise me safe passage from Moscow to an undisclosed location."

Isa typed some commands into his computer. "Vladimir, do yourself a favor. Take a few moments to check your nukes. I think you'll find that the birds have flown the coop."

Vladimir spoke hastily to an aid in Russian. Isa summarized for the group. "He is now learning that the nuclear weapons he hoped to use against us have launched. His few remaining weapons are at this moment flying to Rome, Paris, London, New York, and Washington. Of course, the former NATO alliance held back some of its own nukes, which are now flying to points in Russia."

Will clutched at his head in horror. "No!" he screamed.

Isa stared at him sternly. Will wanted to scream again, but he had no control over his voice. He involuntarily took the chair next to Benny and sat silently. Isa hissed, "Sleep."

Will awoke in the small apartment he called home. It was no elaborate affair, just a bed, a desk, a small refrigerator, a hot plate, and a bathroom. His quarters in the basement of the basilica were in no manner like the elaborate apartments created for Benny and Isa. His head pounded. He tried to remember how he had gotten home. His last memories were of an underground bunker with Isa and ...

He jumped out of bed. He was fully dressed—a clear indication he hadn't gotten into bed of his own volition. Snatching the television remote, he turned on the news and looked on in stunned amazement at coverage of utter devastation. A Russian coalition of armies had tried to attack Isa in Jerusalem. The news reporters expressed continued awe that they were destroyed by a meteor shower. They showed clips of Isa expressing sadness at their foolishness and warning the world that he had worse at his disposal should any other government decide to part ways with him.

Will punched the wall. He hated Isa! The coverage changed to photos of fires and charred masses of steel and concrete. Will ran to the screen as he read the news crawl. He was looking at devastation in what used to be New York and Washington. There were now smoldering craters where once millions had lived and worked. Russia had managed to destroy these cities along with other Western capitals as part of its surprise attack. There was something niggling at Will's brain, a dim memory.

"Come on," he said to himself in an effort to resurrect the images at the back of his brain.

"Oh God!" he exclaimed as he remembered Isa ordering the destruction of those cities. Fury raged in him. Something had to be done about this evil man, this hybrid thing, or whatever he was. He held his head as if it might burst from pent-up rage.

The coverage moved to the Temple Mount with a preview of the day's activities—the dedication of the Jewish temple. "What?" Will screamed. He grabbed his phone. The date and time confirmed that he had been unconscious for more than a day. The news latched onto the Temple Mount activities as a symbol of peace in a world that had gone terribly wrong. The reporter expressed hope that the day's Jewish dedication would go off without a hitch as the coverage moved to the previous day's Islamic celebration. As a welcoming gesture to all religions, Benny had planned to release doves from the basilica at the end of each ceremony. Yesterday's release was met with a barrage of hawks that tore the doves from the sky, leaving little more than blood, feathers, and bird poop in their wake.

The coverage went to a commercial break. Benny's new video played. He spoke of all religions leading to the same end: love. Representatives of all faiths looked into the camera and said, one by one, "I believe in love," the new mantra of the worldwide religion. Will checked his phone again. He had an hour to get on-site for the Jewish ceremony. Then he noticed a text from Michele: "Okay here. U?" She had sent it yesterday. She must be worried out of her mind. He texted back: "Okay here. Very busy. Luv U."

He showered quickly and dressed in a fresh uniform. He checked his quiver, making sure he had his finest arrows. Then he double-checked the tension on his crossbow, tuning it to perfection as the news report continued its coverage. He looked up just in time to see a news crawl: "Wife of television preacher Zack Jolean jailed in suspicion of the murder of a FEMA camp guard. Reverend Jolean found the dead man's wallet and cell phone hidden among his wife's belongings and notified the police."

His head raced. Michael gone. Attempted arrest of Michele. Gloria in custody. This war was personal, and his response would be as well.

He resumed command of his squad and thanked them for their diligent work in his absence. He checked the perimeter of the courtyard and signaled to the guards below to allow the invited attendees to ascend the stairs to Abraham's Courtyard.

Jewish priests scampered around in the bright morning sun as their sacrificial red heifer roasted on an altar outside the temple. The sacrifice must have been gruesome to witness, but the aftereffect was the smell of a good old-fashioned Southern barbeque. Will marched to the courtyard in front of the basilica, where Benny waited with an entourage to march to the podium set up between the two pillars in front of the mammoth temple. He stopped in front of the pope and saluted.

"Glad to see you're feeling better, Will. You took one heck of a tumble," Benny said with the kind of papal concern he reserved for the cameras, which, of course, were whizzing as reporters captured every moment for posterity. Drones flew overhead to make sure the events were filmed from every angle.

Will played along with the pretend pontiff. "Thank you, sir," he said in the sharp staccato of a soldier on duty. He saluted again and continued his rounds as he ticked off in his mind the agenda for the day. Following the morning speeches where rabbis thanked the new government for fulfilling a two-thousand-year dream to rebuild the temple, the high priest would enter the holy of holies to inaugurate the structure. All the while a large chorus planned to sing songs supposedly recovered from the time of King David as Isa's procession entered the courtyard. After the high priest exited, he would bring God's blessing to Benny and Isa.

The sunlight was brilliant, and the weather was surprisingly hot for a December day. Winds from the desert drove a constant hum in the microphones as first Benny and then the rabbis complimented each other and blessed Isa for making the reclaimed Temple Mount such a miraculous symbol of peace. Each expressed anguish at the fate of the Western world following the Russian attack, and hope that the Temple Mount would be a beacon of unity for all humanity. "All that remains of humanity," Will said to himself. He scanned the area outside the temple for an alcove, one that would give him the view he needed without being visible to the cameras. It took a while to catalog the revolving orbits of the various drones, but he was convinced he had found a spot in an alcove just behind the large brass pool in the front of the temple. Its water was tainted pink with the blood of the sacrifices. Protecting the sensibilities of the viewers, the televised celebration avoided the sacrificial aspects of the ceremony. All the better for Will.

He ducked inside the alcove as the high priest passed him to enter the holy of holies, little bells in the hem of his garment announcing his passage. Nobody but the high priest was allowed to see the holy of holies. Cameramen were banned from the doorway. The only coverage would be long shots from the podium and from the drones. The choir ramped up their mournful chants as the high priest passed.

While the high priest was inside, the other priests outside the temple prayed in Hebrew with rapid, synchronized bowing motions. At the basilica side of the courtyard, the crowd began to cheer as Isa moved toward the podium in Benny's pope-mobile. The Lady followed behind in a similar vehicle, but all eyes followed the charismatic Kurtoglu. The little elevated platform inched through the crowd as Isa beamed smiles in all directions. He certainly looked the part of benevolent ruler—handsome, brilliant, and kind. Will knew better than to be taken in by the charm. Isa's entourage slowly made its way to the podium as the choir unexpectedly broke into Handel's Hallelujah Chorus. The Christian overtones of the tune caused the Jewish priests to lose their rhythm for a second, but they soon resumed their chanting.

Will took two arrows from his quiver, put one in his bow, and aimed. He followed Kurtoglu's movements. As Isa stepped out of the pope-mobile, Will fired. His aim was true. Isa fell backward as the arrow hit him in the chest. The other arrow followed, hitting his temple as he fell.

"Will," someone called from the shadows at the side of the temple.

Will looked to see his father and a priest standing beside an old monk. Gabe motioned for him to come to them.

As Will reached their position, Gabe took Will's bow and handed it to the old monk. The priest said, "You're on, Ignatius."

"Right, Vinnie," the man said. He ran into the crowd with Will's bow, screaming that Isa was none other than the Antichrist. Swiss guardsmen trained their bows on him, taking him down before he made it to the podium. Will's eyes flooded with tears. He was overwhelmed at the old monk's sacrifice—he had given his life to take Will's punishment. Will started after him, but Gabe held him back.

"I have to put you to sleep so that it looks like Ignatius incapacitated you. Give your heart to Jesus, Son. He already gave His life for you," Gabe said as Will's legs grew too weak to support his body.

"Dad, I need to find uncle Michael," he murmured.

"You need to give your heart to Jesus. When you wake up, go to Petra." Gabe and Vinnie disappeared. In a vision, Will saw Jesus reaching out to him. His warm smile invited Will. The wounds in His wrists drove home His incredible love. Will wanted nothing more than to be with Him.

"Forgive me, Jesus," Will cried out in his mind. His sedated body produced little more than a mumble. "Come into my heart, Lord."

THIRTY-FIVE

The shocked high priest protested as the Swiss guardsmen physically removed him from the holy of holies, seating the bleeding semiconscious Kurtoglu on the mercy seat atop the replicated Ark of the Covenant. Benny cried softly as the guards left him with Isa and the Lady in the small room. The light of a single candelabrum bounced in intricate patterns off the gold-covered walls.

Isa's breaths were heavy and uneven, each carrying with it a spasm of pain. Blood poured from the wound in his chest and the marred left side of his head, slowly covering the mercy seat.

Benny didn't see how he could survive these wounds, unless the Lady could help him. "Can't you do something for him?" he moaned to the alien creature.

The Lady stared at him for a moment, considering her answer.

"You heard him," Isa added in a barked whisper.

"I heard both of you," the Lady said with a smug grin. "I was just relishing the moment when you realize I'm in control. I'll let you two in on a little secret: I always have been."

In a burst of anger, Isa rallied. He grabbed the Lady's throat with one hand and squeezed her scrawny neck until her slit of a mouth formed an *o*. "I hate you! I always have!" Isa exclaimed in a hoarse voice, his breath airy. Benny was paralyzed with fear. He didn't want to take part in this fight. Either winner was likely to exact revenge on the poor sap who backed the wrong side.

"Good," the Lady purred. "Good. This is exactly the emotion I want you to feel." The Lady's body began to glow.

Benny hoped this was a show of compassion from her. His hopes

345

survived only a brief moment. The light form that once was the Lady changed shape. It grew to a massive size. Benny would have guessed seven to eight feet tall, with shoulders as wide, crowding the small space of the holy of holies. Then the light diminished to reveal a dark winged creature, its raven hair pulled straight back from a chiseled face that must have once been very handsome, its dark-feathered wings fluttering as if exalting in their newfound freedom. The creature's eyes were deep blue, a nearly perfect offset to the pale blue hue of his skin. A pointed nose, and a mouth that was a bit too large, completed the face. Benny looked aghast. The creature looked like a ruined piece of art, something that had started out as beautiful in the artist's mind only to be disfigured in a drunken fit of rage. Benny found it to be simultaneously attractive and abhorrent.

"Father!" Isa exclaimed weakly as the creature's taloned hand grasped his.

"F-f-father?" Benny muttered.

"Silence!" the creature barked. "Kneel before your lord Lucifer!"

Benny fell to his knees. He was awestruck. He had never seriously entertained the existence of such a being. He tried to speak but could not.

The creature returned his gaze to Isa. "This may hurt a bit," he said with a malicious grin. Then using the talon-like fingers of his right hand, he pressed on Isa's wounded head. As he increased the pressure, driving his claws deeper into Isa's face, the man shrieked in pain. It was then that Benny found his voice as well. He screamed incessantly, his voice joining Isa's in endless echoes off the gold-clad walls of the strange chamber. Underneath it all was a garish satanic chuckle.

Benny couldn't judge how long they remained like that. It felt like an eternity, but he guessed it had actually been less than a minute. Then the figure was gone. Benny went to Isa's side in the eerie silence. The man was slumped over in the mercy seat. Benny touched his hand—stone-cold. No doubt about it in Benny's mind: Isa was dead. He slipped a bit as he turned away. Looking down, he saw a blob of pus-like goo where the Lady had stood. Benny guessed the goo was little more than a cast-off shell no longer needed by Lucifer.

He went into the courtyard, where an emergency response team waited. He motioned for them to fetch the body. Around him the

Jewish priests lay prostate, all crying at the pollution of their new temple. The high priest wailed incessant Hebrew prayers and ripped at his priestly attire, pulling off strips of it with each attempt. *What fools! We've lost the greatest human to grace this Earth, and these guys are wailing about their temple.* Benny pondered that the world had lost its last best chance to survive the coming disaster. Looking at these desperate, pathetic men, he despairingly thought the impending doom was a fate well deserved.

A paramedic tapped him on the shoulder. Benny turned to see the man in tears, shaking his head somberly. Isa was dead, just as Benny had suspected. He told the paramedics to use their ambulance to take the body to the basilica. There he laid society's would-be savior to rest on the main altar, beneath the expanse of the rotunda. Jewel-toned rays glistened from the rotunda's stained glass windows, bathing Isa's body in ethereal light.

He paused for a moment to take in the sight before motioning to the security team to let him out. The roar of the press greeted him as he announced the death of the world's first president. For a second his grief was suspended as he saw the pain and despair on the faces in the crowd. These people needed a leader. With a slight chuckle, he squared his shoulders and decided it might as well be him.

EPILOGUE

The drugs finally had worn off enough for Michael to make a rational appraisal of his surroundings. His hands were bound in front of him. He was naked and surrounded by total darkness. He tried to stretch out his legs but couldn't. He tried to sit up, but his head hit the roof of his container.

His mind raced to his past when he had financed mind-control techniques for a group of programmers. This was the same group whose members had disappeared one by one over the past three years. Now he was in a sensory-deprivation chamber himself. He had to stay mentally strong. He prayed for strength and for an end to this torment as jets nearly flooded the chamber with ice-cold water. He raised his head to an air bubble at the top of the chamber. It was then that he smelled the noxious gas. He lost his battle to stay conscious as the water drained.

Miles away, in a lofty chamber, a body bathed in muted light smiled—softly at first, and then broadly. Soon the entire basilica rang with his laughter.

AUTHOR'S NOTE— THE DARK AWAKENING

The beginning part of this novel details a fictional event known as the Dark Awakening. As is often the case, the underlying truth is more unbelievable than the fiction. There is documented evidence of the creation of multiple personalities through the horrific process known as satanic ritual abuse.

Russ Dizdar, a particularly courageous man of God, is involved with deliverance ministry. He has come face-to-face with multiple personalities forced on unfortunate souls through torture. Invariably, in his efforts to deliver these tortured souls, he has learned of their hidden agenda. The multiples look forward to what they call "the Black Awakening," a time when they will be ordered to bring about worldwide destruction. If Russ's findings are correct, then the biggest weapon of mass destruction may be hiding in our communities today.

If any reader is interested in this topic, I invite him or her to purchase Russ's book *The Black Awakening*. It is not an easy read, and it is not for the faint of heart, but it offers a real-world insight into the fiction of this novel. *The Black Awakening* is published by Preemption Books and Products and is available on Amazon.com.

SELECTED BIBLIOGRAPHY

I. Books

Anderson, R. *The Coming Prince*. Three Rivers, Hertfordshire: Diggory Press Ltd., 2008.

Berliner, D., with Marie Galbrath and Antonio Huneeus. *UFO Briefing Document*. New York: Dell Publishing, 1995.

Colman, J. *The Conspirators' Hierarchy: The Committee of 300*. 4th ed. Las Vegas: World Intelligence Review, 1997.

Dizdar, R. *The Black Awakening: Rise of the Satanic Super Soldiers and the Coming Chaos*. Canton, OH: Preemption Books and Products, 2009.

Dolan, R., and Bryce Zabel. *A.D.: After Disclosure—The People's Guide to Life After Contact*. Rochester, NY: Keyhole Publishing Company, 2010.

Dolan, R. M. *UFOs and the National Security State: Chronology of a Cover-Up, 1941–1973*. Charlottesville, VA: Hampton Roads Publishing Company, Inc., 2000.

———. *UFOs and the National Security State: The Cover-Up Exposed*. Rochester, NY: Keyhole Publishing Company, 2009.

Estulin, D. *The True Story of the Bilderberg Group*. Walterville, OR: TrineDay, LLC, 2007.

Flynn, D. *Temple at the Center of Time: Newton's Bible Codex Deciphered and the Year 2012*. Crane, OR: Official Disclosure, 2008.

Foden, G. *The Last King of Scotland*. New York: Vintage Books, 1998.

Fowler, R. E. *The Andreasson Affair: The Documented Investigation of a Woman's Abduction Aboard a UFO*. Newberg, OR: Wild Flower Press, 1979.

_____. *The Andreasson Affair, Phase Two*. Newberg, OR: Wild Flower Press, 1982.

Grant, J. R. *The Signature of God: Astonishing Bible Codes*. Colorado Springs: Waterbrook Press, 2002.

Griffin, G. E. *The Creature from Jekyll Island: A Second Look at the Federal Reserve*. Appleton, WI: American Opinion Publishing, 1994.

Hamilton, W. F., III *Project Aquarius: The Story of an Aquarian Scientist*. Bloomington, IN: AuthorHouse, 2005.

Hitchcock, M. *The Complete Book of Bible Prophecy*. Wheaton, IL: Tyndale House Publishers, Inc., 1999.

Hogue, J. *The Last Pope: The Prophecies of St. Malachy for the New Millennium*. Boston: Element Books Limited, 2000.

Horn, T. *Apollyon Rising 2012: The Lost Symbol Found and the Final Mystery of the Great Seal Revealed*. Crane, MO: Defender, 2009.

Nephilim Stargates: The Year 2012 and the Return of the Watchers. Crane, MO: Anomalos Publishing, 2007.

_____. *Zenith 2016*. Crane, MO: Defender, 2013.

Horn, T., and Nita Horn. *Forbidden Gates: The Dawn of Techno-Dimensional Spiritual Warfare*. Crane, MO: Defender, 2010.

Horn, T., and Cris Putnam. *Petrus Romanus*. Crane, MO: Defender, 2012.

Horton, M., ed. *The Agony of Deceit: What Some TV Preachers Are Really Teaching.* Chicago: Moody Press, 1990.

Hunt, D., and T. A. McMahon. *America, the Sorcerer's New Apprentice: The Rise of New Age Shamanism.* Eugene, OR: Harvest House, 1988.

Imbrogno, P. J. *Interdimensional Universe: The New Science of UFOs, Paranormal Phenomena, and Otherdimensional Beings.* Woodbury, MN: Llewellyn Publications, 2008.

_____. *Ultraterrestrial Contact: A Paranormal Investigator's Explorations into the Hidden Abduction Epidemic.* Woodbury, MN: Llewellyn Publications, 2010.

Jeremiah, D., with C. C. Carlson. *The Handwriting on the Wall: Secrets from the Prophecies of Daniel.* Nashville: W Publishing Group, 1992.

Knight, C., and Alan Butler. *Before the Pyramids: Cracking Archeology's Greatest Mystery.* London: Watkins Publishing, 2009.

Krieger, D., Dene McGriff, and S. Douglas Woodward. *The Final Babylon: America and the Coming of Antichrist.* Oklahoma City: Faith Happens, 2013.

Lindsey, H. *The Late Great Planet Earth.* Grand Rapids, MI: Zondervan, 1970.

_____. *There's a New World Coming: An In-Depth Analysis of the Book of Revelation.* Eugene, OR: Harvest House, 1973.

Marrs, J. *Alien Agenda.* New York: HarperCollins Publishers, 2008.

_____. *The Rise of the Fourth Reich.* New York: HarperCollins Publishers, 2008.

_____. *Rule by Secrecy.* New York: HarperCollins Publishers, 2000.

Martin, M. *Windswept House.* New York: Doubleday, 1996.

Milor, J. W. *Aliens and the Antichrist: Unveiling the End Times Deception.* Lincoln, NE: iUniverse, 2006.

Missler, C., Dr. *Prophecy 20/20: Profiling the Future through the Lens of Scripture*. Nashville: Thomas Nelson, Inc., 2006.

_____. *Cosmic Codes: Hidden Messages from the Edge of Eternity*. Coeur d'Alene, ID: Koinonia House, 1999.

Picknett, L., and Clive Prince. *The Stargate Conspiracy: The Truth About Extraterrestrial Life and the Mysteries of Ancient Egypt*. New York: Berkley Books, 1999.

Putnam, C., and Tom Horn. *Exo-Vaticana*. Crane, MO: Defender, 2013.

Redfern, N. *Final Events and the Secret Government Group on Demonic UFOs and the Afterlife*. San Antonio, TX: Anomalist Books, 2010.

_____. *The NASA Conspiracies*. Pompton Plains, NJ: New Page Books, 2011.

Rice, A. *The Teeth May Smile, but the Heart Does Not Forget: Murder and Memory in Uganda*. New York: Metropolitan Books, 2009.

Richardson, J. *The Islamic Antichrist: The Shocking Truth About the Real Nature of the Beast*. Los Angeles: WND Books, 2006.

_____. *Mideast Beast: The Scriptural Case for an Islamic Antichrist*. Washington, DC: WND Books, 2012.

Romanek, S. *Messages: The World's Most Documented Extraterrestrial Contact Story*. Woodberry, MN: Llewellyn Publications, 2009.

Rothkopf, D. *Superclass: The Global Power Elite and the World They Are Making*. New York: Farrar, Straus, and Giroux, 2008.

Sherman, D. *Above Black: Project Preserve Destiny—A True Story*. Kearney, NE: Order Department, LLC, 2008.

Sherman, E. R., with Nathan Jacobi, PhD, and Dave Swaney. *Bible Code Bombshell: Compelling Scientific Evidence That God Authored the Bible*. Green Forest, AR: New Leaf Press, 2005.

Shoebat, W., with Joel Richardson. *God's War on Terror: Islam, Prophecy, and the Bible*. New York: Top Executive Media, 2010.

Shriner, S. *Bible Codes Revealed the Coming UFO Invasion.* New York: iUniverse, 2005.

Smith, W. B. *Deceived on Purpose: The New Age Implications of the Purpose-Driven Church.* Magalia, CA: Mountain Stream Press, 2004.

Strieber, W. *Breakthrough: The Next Step.* New York: Harper Paperbacks, 1996.

_____. *Communion: A True Story.* New York: Harper, 1988.

_____. *Confirmation.* New York: St. Martin's Press, 1998.

_____. *Transformation.* New York: Avon, 1998.

Vallee, J. *Messengers of Deception: UFO Contacts and Cults.* Brisbane, Australia: Daily Grail Publishing, 1979.

Ventura, J., with Dick Russell. *63 Documents the Government Doesn't Want You to Read.* New York: Skyhorse Publishing, 2011.

Yallop, D. *In God's Name: An Investigation into the Murder of Pope John Paul I.* New York: Basic Books, 2007.

II. Other

Various Internet interviews with Gil Broussard, who has stunning analyses of the Nibiru topic.